Hidden In Plain Sight

The Wolf Within Series

Amy Lee Burgess

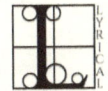

LYRICAL PRESS
Kensington Publishing Corp.
www.kensingtonbooks.com

Lyrical Press books are published by
Kensington Publishing Corp. 119 West 40th Street New York, NY 10018

Copyright © 2012 by Amy Lee Burgess

All Kensington titles, imprints, and distributed lines are available at special quantity discounts for bulk purchases for sales promotion, premiums, fund-raising, and educational or institutional use.

Special book excerpts or customized printings can also be created to fit specific needs. For details, write or phone the office of the Kensington Special Sales Manager:
Kensington Publishing Corp.
119 West 40th Street
New York, NY 10018
Attn. Special Sales Department. Phone: 1-800-221-2647.

Kensington and the K logo Reg. U.S. Pat. & TM Off.
Lyrical Press and the L logo are trademarks of Kensington Publishing Corp.

First Electronic Edition: July 2012
eISBN-13: 978-1-61650-370-3
eISBN-10: 1-61650-370-X

First Print Edition: July 2012
ISBN-13: 978-1-61650-855-5
ISBN-10: 1-61650-855-8

Printed in the United States of America

As Stanzie discovers her wolf, she learns being herself is more danger-

ous than ever.

Where is Bethany Dillon? The seventeen year-old girl is missing from the Maplefair pack and Constance Newcastle--Stanzie--and Liam Murphy must find her. Fast. A serial killer still has not been caught. Bethany could have run away, or killed herself. But no one in her pack seems to know the truth. Or, they're just not telling.

Constanceís knack for uncovering secrets leads her into peril, and to save Bethany, she must break every rule. She risks losing everything, including Liam...and her life.

Books by Amy Lee Burgess

The Wiolf Within Series
Beneath the Skin, Book One
Scratch the Surface, Book Two
Hidden In Plain Sight, Book Three
Inside Out, Book Four
About Face, Book Five
Across the Line, Book Six

Published by Kensington Publishing Corporation

For Chris Wilbanks, who has faithfully read all my novels, even the ones I never finished. You've been a steady friend and inspiration in my life, for which I'll always be grateful.

Acknowledgements

As always, thanks to Nerine Dorman for patiently showing me how to be a better writer and for suffering through all the rough drafts of this particular novel. Every author ought to be as lucky as I am to have an editor like you. Thank you, everyone at Lyrical Press for giving me the opportunity to share Stanzie and Murphy with such a wide audience. Also, eternal gratitude to my beta readers, Kim and Portia, who never fail to give me constructive feedback. You guys rock!

Chapter 1

I follow Friend in the woods. Trees can be woods. Trees can be oak. Can be willow. I like willow trees. They pretty. Both words for the same thing. My head is so big with words. But many words left to find. When will I? Friend wants to run and play but there are words I do not have. Friend run fast, I run fast. I scared to be just me in the woods. I scared I need word I not find yet. I scared. I wish I had word for why but that one hides. All words hide. I find. Dig up from inside my head, from ground, from sky. Words hide but I find. I find them all. Then I not scared no more.

* * * *

The day after shifting into wolf form could be rough. It depended on how much water we drank before we shifted and if we were stupid enough to drink alcohol.

Murphy and I hadn't planned to shift, it had happened organically after a bottle of white wine and two hours of intense sex. Vaughn had gone out drinking at the pubs on Beacon Street and we'd had the condo to ourselves for a change.

It had been Murphy's idea to shift. The wine had been my idea. Sex had been a mutual decision.

It was April and spring had definitely sprung in Boston.

The three of us sprawled on a wooden bench beneath a willow tree on Boston Common. The branches dipped into a small pond where four ducks quacked indignantly to cover up their innate fear of us. We were Pack and they knew it, although in human form we wouldn't touch them. Wolf form? Yeah, they would be smart to avoid us.

Vaughn had his long legs stretched straight out in front of him as he consumed a foot-long hotdog smothered in chili. The smell of it nauseated me, and I tried to breathe through my mouth to dilute the scent.

On my other side Murphy watched joggers run past. One girl was seasonally optimistic in a pair of bright red shorts with white piping. Her legs looked cold to me but Murphy obviously found them attractive. He tracked her with his dark eyes but then I noticed him grin because he was aware I watched him do it. I swore that man loved to fuck with me.

I stretched my legs out and ignored him. They ached like a bitch. I sucked water from a huge plastic bottle but it was too little too late. A limping retreat back to the condo seemed more and more likely.

Vaughn ignored the jogger. He ignored all the Others—regular humans. He semi-ignored us too, but only because he was so engrossed in his damn chili dog.

"That's disgusting." I was unable to keep silent anymore. "How can you eat that, Vaughn? It smells awful."

"But it tastes great," he said around a mouthful.

Murphy chuckled and I wanted to elbow him in the ribs but I was too sore.

The three of us idled in the spring sunshine, happy despite all the bullshit that had taken place three months previously when Vaughn's bond mates had died.

Callie had shot herself in the head when it had become clear she would be exposed as a conspirator in the underground movement within the Great Pack that attempted to scare us all back to the old ways. She'd murdered their bond mate, Peter, with a fatal dose of narcotics that he'd thought had been pain medicine for a migraine. She hadn't wanted him to know she'd helped murder my bond mates, Grey and Elena, in a rigged car crash nearly three years ago.

Vaughn had been left behind. He and I had both watched Callie kill herself and still had nightmares about it. After their funeral, Vaughn had come to stay with me and Murphy in Boston. He'd left Riverglow, but he wasn't in exile. As soon as he found a bond mate he could rejoin a pack, but it had been barely three months and a new bond mate was probably the furthest thing from his mind.

Murphy and I belonged to Mac Tire, the largest pack in Great Britain. Technically, we were supposed to live in Dublin, but our Alphas, Padraic O'Reilly and Fiona Carmichael, had given us leave to stay in Boston while Murphy and I worked on my wolf.

My wolf was not as evolved as others. I'd kept her deliberately childlike and free, but now I sought for her to catch up with everyone else. It had proven to be a long and difficult process. Paddy and Fee had nearly lost patience with us, and now we had Vaughn as another excuse to avoid going to Dublin. I was in no rush to see him leave, although I wished his suffering would ease. I hated to see him grief-stricken and in pain.

I heard him sometimes through the bedroom wall. Heard him jerk awake with a strangled scream. Heard him swear. Sometimes he punched the wall. Sometimes he cried. The nights where he cried I got out of bed and went to him and he clung to me like a child.

He hadn't cried in nearly three weeks, and I hoped the worst was over.

Vaughn wadded up the remains of his chili dog and tossed it and a bunch of paper napkins into a nearby trash can.

I reached up to touch the soft leaves above my tilted face. I was worried about my wolf. Since Vaughn had come to stay with us, Murphy and I rarely found the opportunity to have sex, let alone shift. Last night my wolf had been stubbornly reluctant to come out. For the first time since we'd started to shift together, Murphy had finished his transformation before me. Then my wolf had spent the entire time on a search for words for different types of trees. No playing. No fun.

The willow leaves were soft as they brushed my face. "My wolf knows willow tree. She knows oak and birch and maple too."

Murphy gave me a look that on anyone else's face I would have called infatuated, but since it was Murphy who looked at me, I didn't know what precisely to call it.

Maybe the infatuation was for my wolf. That made more sense anyway.

I glanced at my watch. "It's nearly two o'clock. Kathy said she'd get to our place around two thirty, so we'd better start getting back."

Tortured resignation stole over Vaughn's face. "Oh, Jesus, I forgot she was coming."

"How can you forget lemon squares?" Murphy demanded, in shock. "Or brownies. Or those goddamn delicious cookies with the stupid name?"

Amy Lee Burgess

"Snickerdoodles," I supplied. Murphy snorted the way he always did when someone said *snickerdoodles*. He thought the word was funny, but what was really hilarious was the way he snorted laughter every single time he heard it. And the way he wolfed them down almost without chewing.

"That woman is weird. Always smiling. Does anyone ever have anything that good going on that they'd smile like that almost every single second?" Vaughn said *smile* the way most people would say *cockroach*.

"She brings baked goods. She can come in clown face with a rubber nose that squeaks for all I care as long as I get something good to eat." Murphy seemed transported at the thought of all the possibilities.

"That's not all she brings," I remarked and Vaughn shuddered.

"Oh, hell, she's not bringing Whatshername again, is she? Mona? Monica?"

"After the way you treated her, not likely. Your rudeness knew no bounds, Vaughn," I scolded.

Vaughn extended his middle finger in my direction. "Why does that woman want to set me up? I am not interested in bonding with anybody who's in the same pack as her. I'd have to see her smiling all the goddamn time if I joined her pack."

"Get used to it, mate," advised Murphy. "For three years people kept trying to set me up before I finally got cornered by Stanzie."

"Asshole, I did not corner you," I mumbled under my breath as Vaughn burst into reluctant laughter.

"Sure you did," Murphy teased. "There I was, Vaughn, minding my own damn business at the first night banquet at the Great Gathering, and who comes waltzing over to my table on the arm of Councilor Allerton but the woman sitting between us today. And Allerton, wasn't he the last one in a long line of busybodies who relentlessly tried to pair me up with somebody? And her in this red dress looking so beautiful I couldn't even swallow my wine."

"You knew then you wanted to bond with her?" Vaughn didn't know the story. He wasn't aware of the conspiracy within the Great Pack. He thought Callie had done what she had solely to recapture Alpha status within Riverglow so she could have a baby. There was no reason for him to know about the conspiracy, and I wasn't about to add to his already heavy burden of grief and betrayal.

"Hell no, I ran the other way." Murphy grinned broadly, and when I stuck my tongue out at him, he winked.

"You were obnoxious."

"Didn't I know I was destined to bond with the woman the first time I saw her?" Murphy let his Irish accent show more than usual and I tried not to grimace because he was so full of shit. He put on a show for Vaughn but it hurt my feelings because I secretly wanted him to be telling the truth. Somewhere along the line over the past six months with this man, I'd fallen in love. His heart, however, still firmly belonged to his dead bond mate, Sorcha. It didn't mean he wasn't fond of me, devoted even, but of course I wanted more.

"You're so full of Irish blarney, Murphy."

The skin around Murphy's eyes crinkled when he smiled at me. "You don't believe me?"

"Not one word."

He gave me that damn infatuated look again which about drove me mad. "You should, because I'm telling you the truth."

Our gazes locked and I felt a strange clutch at my heart. "We'd better go if we want to be back before Kathy gets there."

My muscles gave a protesting twinge as I rose. I gulped down water in the hope it would do me some good.

Murphy, damn him, did not seem sore at all, even though he'd drunk as much wine as I had. Of course he was taller and heavier than me, but it still did not seem in the least bit fair.

* * * *

Our cheery yellow, two-family condo was in the Brighton neighborhood of Boston. Ours was the upstairs unit.

Kathy Manning stood by the front steps and we saw her when we rounded the corner of our street.

Although she was at least fifty years old, because she was Pack she didn't appear to be much past twenty-five, thirty tops.

Dressed in a pair of cream tailored pants and blazer with a turquoise blue shell top beneath it, she fiddled in her oversize brown leather Coach bag. Her shoes were plain caramel Gucci flats with cute little leather bows on the toe. A gold tennis bracelet gleamed from one wrist, and her bond pendant hung from a fine link gold chain that encircled her throat. A Macy's shopping bag rested at her feet, which made Murphy's eyes gleam. He obviously hoped the bag contained something edible and sweet.

She was aware of us the moment we turned the corner even though we were still more than half a block away. Aside from a slight stiffening of her body, she ignored us and continued to poke around in her bag.

As we approached, she stopped rummaging in her bag and straightened. She gave us all one of her bright smiles and I was reminded of an elf. Barely topping five feet, she had short, pixie-cut brown hair and slanted gray-blue eyes. Her makeup was minimal yet effective.

"Hello, Vaughn." She singled him out, much to his dismay.

"Councilor Manning."

"Vaughn, dear, what can you tell me about Maplefair? There's a situation brewing there and unfortunately Vermont's Regional Councilor has just moved up to the Great Council and somehow I've been asked to handle things. It's rather awkward for me at the moment because I don't have an Advisor since mine was voted Alpha of our pack last month."

She flashed a smile at me and Murphy because we were Advisors to Councilor Jason Allerton. He served on the Great Council which oversaw the entire Pack and also the Regional Councils across the world. She was also Allerton's mistress and had, for some reason, decided to watch over the three of us.

"Why ask me about Maplefair? I haven't belonged to that pack in twenty years." Vaughn's tone was suspicious and Murphy gave him an interested look.

"Well, you were quite close with the pack's Alpha female at the last Regional, weren't you? I thought you might still be in contact." Kathy's smile was bright and innocent.

Dull spots of color burned Vaughn's cheeks. "It was two Regionals ago, actually, and all we did was hunt together. We're not exactly best buds, Councilor."

"Call me Kathy," she invited with a coquettish toss of her head. Vaughn gritted his teeth.

"You initiated her wolf years ago, didn't you?"

"Oh, for Christ's sake. What is this? So I initiated her wolf and I went on a Great Hunt with her fifteen years after that. What are you trying to say? I don't stay in touch with her. I don't stay in touch with anyone in Maplefair." Vaughn's fists clenched and Murphy took a step closer to him, disturbed by the tension. Whether he meant to protect Kathy or form a united front against her I wasn't sure.

I tried not to gape. Vaughn had hunted with Jossie Wilbanks? Since when? After he'd initiated her wolf, Jossie had thrown herself at him, intent on persuading him to sever ties with Peter and Callie so he could bond with her. He'd wanted no part of that.

Jossie and I had been good friends when we were teens, but things had gotten weird between us after the initiation of her wolf. She'd been determined to bond with Vaughn, and I'd been mortified at the brazen things she'd done when it was clear he wasn't interested.

Then I'd met Grey. We'd joined Riverglow and Vaughn became my pack mate. Jossie had tried to use my access to Vaughn to her advantage and I'd been caught in the middle.

We'd had a huge fight when I'd bluntly told her it was never going to happen between her and Vaughn. A year later she'd announced her intentions to bond with Nate Carver, who was a fifth-generation member of Maplefair, Vaughn's birth pack.

When I'd accused her of bonding with Nate only because he was Maplefair, we'd had another huge falling out and she hadn't spoken to me for a long time.

Out of the blue one year, she'd sent me a Christmas card and we'd patched things up as best we could—mostly through the mail.

Through it all Vaughn had refused to have anything to do with her.

Yet he'd hunted with her? Slept with her at a Regional and shifted with her? That was quite a reversal, and he was defensive as hell about it.

My mind boggled.

Kathy picked up the Macy's bag and handed it to Murphy. When we went inside, Vaughn trailed behind us.

Murphy made coffee while I set out a plate of the baked goods Kathy had brought us.

"Snickerdoodles," I called over to Murphy, who threw me a delighted grin over his shoulder as he juggled the good cups and saucers. Normally we used mugs, but we knew better when Kathy Manning visited.

Vaughn slouched in the chair farthest from Kathy's. After we'd all consumed cookies and coffee, Kathy set down her cup and looked between us all.

"Stanzie, I'd like you and Liam to pay a visit to Maplefair. The situation I mentioned needs resolution and it's time the Council stepped in."

"The Regional Council can't resolve it?" I was confused.

"As I said, the New England Regional Council is in a bit of a flux state at the moment. There are some gaps that need to be filled in the ranks.

"One Council member has recently resigned due to age. Another was tapped to serve on the Great Council. Their Advisors no longer serve obviously. Because of this situation in the Regional Council and because I'm currently between Advisors, Councilor Allerton has offered me your assistance. You'll report to me and if necessary the Great Council will be brought in. I'm hoping it won't be. I'm hoping Bethany will come back or least be found, but that remains to be seen I suppose."

"Who's Bethany?" I sat up straight in my chair.

"Bethany Dillon. She's seventeen, and she's been missing since Thursday."

"She ran away?" Murphy leaned forward. He'd been blissed out on a sugar high, but now the conversation had drawn him in. "Is she fighting with her parents?"

Kathy sighed and picked up her coffee cup but didn't drink from it. "They say not. They say she's been withdrawn and moody lately but they put that down to the fact she hasn't been allowed to see her boyfriend. He's in the pack too. He's nineteen. In view of what happened at the Regional Gathering, they've been kept apart as much as possible."

I bit my lip. "What happened at the Regional?"

"Oh, what normally happens. A group of teenagers got together and shifted during the Great Hunt the way they sometimes do no matter how you guard against it. It happened that way to you didn't it, Stanzie? You shifted at a Great Gathering when you were a teenager, right?"

I flushed with remembered embarrassment.

"Bethany and Cody say they are in love and want to bond, but they'll have to wait until they reach majority," Kathy said.

"So why keep them apart until then? What difference does it make? Now that they've shifted, why not let them be together?" I knew I was advocating pack heresy. Pack generally shifted the first time between seventeen and twenty, but we were supposed to be initiated by an experienced member of the pack in order to develop our wolves. Shifting for fun with lovers came later.

Kathy gave me a measured look from beneath half lowered lashes. Once again she resembled an elf—enigmatic, all knowing and nearly impossible to relate to.

"It makes a big difference to their wolves, dear. No one is telling them they can't see each other—they aren't supposed to shift together. The boy, Cody, is willing to work with an experienced partner, but Bethany is being stubborn."

This conversion veered way too close to my own experience and I fervently wished we could talk about something else, but of course we couldn't.

"Well, he didn't disappear too, did he? They didn't run away together?" Murphy asked.

"No," answered Kathy with an elegant lift of her shoulders.

I took a deep breath. "Are you sure Bethany wasn't pregnant?"

Kathy gave another graceful shrug. "Her mother said she got her period after the Regional."

"I don't see why she would run away without him," I insisted.

Kathy nodded. "I know. This is a troubling situation. That's why the Council wants to look into it."

Then, with a devastating directness that took my breath away, she said, "You know it's no shame to admit you got pregnant at that Great Gathering, Stanzie."

"What the hell are you talking about?" My mouth hung open and I closed it with a snap. "We're talking about Bethany. You said she wasn't pregnant. Why are we talking about me? What does that have to do with anything?"

"I was just trying to piece together why you are so afraid to have a baby," Kathy mused. "I just wondered if having to have a discreet abortion after sneaking out and shifting with another teenager has created this silly fear of yours."

Murphy's face darkened at the word *silly* but he didn't say anything. Probably because I was so betrayed and pissed off I didn't give him a chance.

"Kathy, you're wrong. I did not get pregnant after I shifted. Besides, the grandmothers gave us all something horrible-tasting to drink after we shifted back. All the girls. My father was right there to force me to drink it. They said it would most likely prevent conception and I had to drink that shit for a whole week. Paul made me drink it for two just in case." My mouth twisted at the remembered vile taste. "Didn't they make Bethany do the same damn thing? I thought it was de rigueur in cases like that."

"Yes, I believe they did. Also, as I said, her mother has reported she did get her period after that. No one is saying she got pregnant at the Regional. She's either run away or maybe she's hiding in plain sight somewhere within her pack. She may have had an accident or killed herself in a lonely field. She may have taken a bus to New York or even here to Boston. There's a lot of things that may have happened and for her sake I hope we find the truth."

She and Murphy both continued to stare at me. I felt flushed and guilty even though I had no reason to be ashamed. Vaughn stared at me and I was sure he wondered whether I'd told the truth.

"Honestly, I didn't get pregnant. I've never been pregnant."

"Your fear of having a baby, Stanzie, has to come from somewhere." Kathy's voice was warm and soothing as butterscotch but I wasn't lulled by the false sweetness.

It was truly amazing how this woman took every opportunity to wave my fears in front of my face as if we stood in a bullring and I had hooves and a fucking tail while she sported a toreador's outfit and a red cape.

We were supposed to be concentrating on the missing girl, not some phantom pregnancy in my past. Vaughn opened his mouth as if to argue, but closed it again. I knew damn well what he thought because we'd been pack mates for a decade and he knew how I felt about babies. Yet I could tell by his expression he still wondered if I'd gotten pregnant the first time I shifted. So did Murphy. Goddamn Kathy Manning. Goddamn her.

"You're a Regional Councilor. You should know all the nasty secrets of the New England area packs. I don't have a nasty secret about being pregnant, Kathy."

"Your birth pack is extremely reticent and close-minded. There's hasn't been a member on either Council or even an Advisor from Mayflower for years." That fact seemed to puzzle, even exasperate her. "These cases are supposed to be brought before the Regional Council. At the very least we're supposed to be notified."

"Well, Maplefair notified you," I tried to bring the focus back to Bethany.

"Yes, Jocelyn and Nate brought it to our attention right away." Kathy nodded. "You and Liam will be staying at their house in Easton. They're restoring the most adorable rambling old farmhouse and are expecting you tomorrow afternoon."

Murphy shifted in his seat, a look of protest spread across his face.

"We haven't said we'd do this yet," he objected softly.

"Councilor Allerton offered me your services, remember?" Kathy swept on as if Murphy hadn't spoken and he rolled his eyes. "Jason's attending to some personal business at the moment, but you can call him and confirm that if you doubt my word."

Murphy grumbled something under his breath, which Kathy ignored with her usual serenity.

"Hopefully, this situation won't take long to resolve and you can return here. Although I would think Dublin might be nice this time of year. Isn't that so, Liam?" She turned her gaze in Murphy's direction.

He blew out his breath gustily. "We're well aware of our pack obligations, Councilor Manning, thank you just the same for the reminder."

"I know *you* are, Liam." Kathy's voice oozed sympathy and I could almost hear his teeth grind. I kept my gaze fixed on my coffee cup.

After she dabbed her mouth with her napkin, Kathy rose gracefully to her feet. Murphy was on his half a second later. I didn't bother to get up. My head was full of memories of the past.

* * * *

"Oh, god, Rudi." I am scared because my body feels weird. Something is wrong. My face burns, my skin itches. A strange pressure builds inside me and it needs to be released. Now.

Rudi's face in the moonlight is unearthly and beautiful. He is so perfectly gorgeous—everything Wes Hanover is not. But I can't concentrate on Rudi's face or Wes Hanover's either. Pain, shocking and bright, stabs me.

I can hear the others in the cane field. One of them howls. It is not a human sound, but that thing within me howls back, ripping me to shreds in the process.

"Rudi," I cry, aware that he is on all fours and his back is arched like Halloween cat's, but his face is not feline. It is lupine. It is...wolf.

* * * *

Vaughn's chair scraped against the laminate floor and tore me away from the memory. I watched him walk out of the kitchen as Murphy's footsteps sounded on the stairs. I shoved my own chair back and retreated into the living room.

* * * *

Murphy found me and sat next to me on the sofa. He took one look at my face and knew something was wrong.

"You thinking about Rudi?" He was so damn perceptive. Too damn perceptive sometimes.

I nodded and he put an arm around my shoulders.

"I'm sorry, honey."

The last time I'd seen Rudi Grunwald, his eyes had been empty. Dead. Just like him. Murdered by a Paris grandmother—another casualty of the conspiracy. All because he worked in the world of the Others and had made name for himself in technological circles. He drew attention to himself instead of existing in the shadows where the Pack had lived for millennia.

"I'm so happy with you, but I wish he weren't dead." If he hadn't died at the Great Gathering, I would be in Germany now with Rudi's pack. We'd be bonded. I couldn't imagine life without Murphy, but it wasn't fair Rudi was dead.

Murphy played with ends of my hair. I'd put it back in a messy bun, but some of it had escaped. I thought of us the night before, of him above me in the bed, how he'd felt inside me, his expression as he'd concentrated and tried to hold himself back so I could come first. Love rushed through my veins and I smiled at him.

He gave me another infatuated look and my smile faltered.

"Why do you look at me like that?" I couldn't help ask.

Wistfulness replaced infatuation. "You don't like it?"

"I don't understand it." He loved Sorcha even though she was dead. Why did he look at me the way he did? I was his bond mate and he was devoted to me, but what he felt for me couldn't touch what he'd felt for her. Already I suspected my love for him went even deeper than what I'd felt for Grey. Which confused and terrified the hell out of me because I'd loved Grey so much and when I'd lost him, my whole world had crumbled. I didn't ever want to feel like that again. I didn't ever want to be so vulnerable, so wrapped up in another person that I exposed myself to potential devastation. But I had the sinking suspicion it was way too late.

"It's simple really." Murphy took a deep breath and for a moment I swore I saw fear in his dark eyes, but then he smiled at me. "Stanzie, I—"

Vaughn's bedroom door slammed. Murphy and I both jerked and the moment between us shattered.

Vaughn stalked into the living room. He saw something on our faces and drew up short, his smile nervous.

"Sorry. I didn't mean to interrupt. I just wanted to tell you that I'm coming with you to Vermont tomorrow."

Murphy regarded him silently for a moment. "You know the girl? Bethany?"

Vaughn grimaced. "She's seventeen and I left the pack twenty years ago. Does it seem likely that I know her?"

"Precisely my point, Vaughn."

"I knew her mother. Gina Dillon. She's about ten years older than me and she initiated my wolf. Is that a good enough reason maybe?"

Murphy sighed. "Sorry. I didn't know that."

Vaughn shrugged.

"We're staying with Jossie and Nate," I reminded him. "You gonna be all right with that?"

"Sure, why not?" The challenge in Vaughn's eyes was unmistakable. "Jossie's the one that spent years chasing me, not the other way around, remember?"

"I remember," I agreed. "I also remember you did a lot of running away."

"Oh, fuck you." His mouth tightened. "It was fifteen fucking years ago, Stanz. She's been happily bonded with Nate for over a decade. Stop living in the past."

"Whose idea was hunting together at the Regional?" I wondered.

"What is this third degree bullshit? Is it because I'm not a goddamn Advisor? I'll keep out of your way, I swear. Why do you have to be like this?"

"I'm just amazed that after running away from her as fast you could fifteen years ago, you went and slept with her at a Regional. It doesn't make any sense."

"You weren't there. Why is it a crime if two people decide to let bygones be bygones? And it's not like we fell into bed together. It was a hunt. There's a little bit of a difference. It was a chance to—I don't know—put it all behind us. She's not eighteen years old anymore. She's the Alpha of Maplefair. She's long since gotten over me."

We glared at each other. Neither one of us would look away.

"Are you two actually fighting?" Murphy sounded a little incredulous.

"No!" Vaughn broke eye contact and flushed. "Stanz? We're not fighting, are we?"

He sounded so forlorn I was ashamed of myself.

"No, I'm sorry. I'm confused. I missed a lot the past couple of years, I guess. It's none of my business anyway. I'm defensive because I'm used to being dragged into the middle of it with you two. She never really forgave me for being on your side."

"You weren't on my side, you were my pack mate. You had my back." Vaughn came to the sofa, dropped to his knees and buried his face in my lap. I stroked his long, dark hair.

"You always have my back, don't you?" His voice was muffled and contrite.

"Always," I vowed. Murphy put his arm around me and I let my head drop to his shoulder. Vaughn shifted so he sat on the floor, against our legs. We rested together companionably, so comfortable conversation was irrelevant.

Chapter 2

The small, light green leaves adorning the maple trees on either side of the winding country road danced in the spring breeze.

I watched them from the car window, mesmerized by their peaceful beauty. Vaughn sprawled out across the backseat, his nose buried in a book.

Murphy drove the car, but I knew he enjoyed the spring scenery every bit as much as I did.

"We're nearly there." He aimed a smile in my direction.

Easton, Vermont was about halfway between Stowe and Waterbury, perched on the edge of the Little River State Park. The park was Maplefair territory. One other pack, Snowmoon, resided in Vermont—the state was rich in parks and forested land—but Little River was Maplefair's. They didn't go to the state park Snowmoon favored and Snowmoon didn't come to theirs. It wasn't forbidden, just ill-mannered. Packs were territorial and one of the duties of the Regional Council was to sort out various territory complaints and challenges as they arose.

"I haven't seen Jossie in ages." I spoke my thoughts aloud to include him, but Murphy had never met anyone in Maplefair and had only the slightest idea who I was talking about.

"Yeah, it's a terrible long way between here and Boston," he remarked and distracted me from the spring wind. His smirk was sarcastic. He was angry at Jossie for not coming to see me during the past two years I'd been living in Boston.

"Murphy, I took myself away from the Pack," I reminded him.

"Yeah, I know that, but that doesn't preclude people taking some time out of their lives to say hello once in a goddamn while."

Vaughn, the coward, was acutely aware of every word we spoke. I could tell he was listening because he didn't turn the pages though he hadn't looked up from his book.

"I barely spoke to her when I was in Riverglow." I was defensive even if a small part of me wanted to agree with him. "I told you we had that falling out. After that first Christmas card, we still didn't really see each other much. Maybe the occasional phone call. We'd see each other at Regionals if we went. We didn't always go."

There were a few reasons, but the primary one was because of my wolf. It had been unspoken but true. My wolf had never been one to follow the leader and before I'd started to bow out of them, Great Hunts at Gatherings had probably been logistical nightmares for Grey, Elena and Vaughn.

Beside me Murphy made a disparaging noise in his throat and, for a moment, I thought he might lower his window all the way and spit, but he didn't. He kept driving.

"You're going to be nice to Jossie, right? She is Alpha," I lectured him and he gave me an indignant look.

"I'm always nice," he protested then he laughed. "I'm always civil. At least at first."

I sucked in a deep, heady lungful of air and saw the dented red mailbox we'd been looking for at the end of a long dirt driveway.

Murphy turned in and the Prelude bounced along the rutted length of it for at least a quarter mile until the trees cleared. We saw a large, rather ramshackle farmhouse—two stories with an additional wing built on, as well as a lovely wraparound screened porch. Through the screens I saw lots of bright white wooden rocking chairs and a small glider.

The barn had been converted into a garage but only one bay was open, and that one was filled with sawhorses and tools rather than a car.

A dusty black Ford Explorer was parked in front of the closed bay, a baby stroller positioned by the porch steps.

Murphy parked behind the Explorer and we got out. As he and Vaughn went to the trunk to get our luggage, I moved closer to the porch, drawn by the stroller. Kathy hadn't mentioned that Jossie and Nate had a baby. It was possible—they were Alphas.

Bright yellow daffodils waved in the breeze from a small flower garden in front of the porch. Clothes flapped on a line erected near the additional wing. Baby things hung next to adult-sized garments.

I was about six feet from the porch steps when I heard the growl.

Murphy and Vaughn heard it too and, from the corner of my eye, I saw them turn.

"Stanzie, get inside the porch." Murphy's voice was urgent but soft. The fact he didn't yell sent alarm bells jangling down my spine. He had a better view of the woods behind the house and barn than I did. My view was blocked by the addition.

Before I could get to the porch steps, a dark gray wolf materialized from around the corner of the farmhouse, hackles raised, lips wrinkled back from sharp teeth.

It was the biggest wolf I'd ever seen.

I looked at him and ignored Murphy's frantic pleas for me to get inside the porch.

"I think it's Nate," I told him. "It's somebody Pack definitely."

"I figured that out myself. Please get inside the porch, Constance."

When Murphy called me Constance, he was either scared or mad. I knew I shouldn't ignore him, but felt compelled to point out the facts.

"He's Pack and so are we. He won't hurt us. It's against Pack law."

Everyone knew we weren't allowed wolf-on-human violence. Even my poor wolf before she'd started to evolve had known it was wrong to bite—even wolf to wolf. Not that she hadn't bitten Murphy's wolf anyway.

Wolf-on-wolf violence was only punishable if severe injury or death resulted. There was a certain leeway allowed if the odds were balanced.

There was no leeway involved in wolf-on-human violence. If Nate bit me, there'd be an investigation at least by the Regional Council and more than likely the Great Council would send an Advisor too.

Because of our laws and the strong indoctrination we all underwent as both wolves and humans, I thought I was safe even though he shouldn't have growled, not after he picked up my scent and realized I was Pack.

The big wolf continued to growl. In fact, each time we spoke, his volume got a little louder. He kept his tawny-gold eyes fixed menacingly on me.

"I'm Pack," I told him, uncertain of how much he understood. My wolf would probably have heard just so much gibberish because she was used to *thinking* in words, not *hearing* them. Murphy's wolf might have understood spoken words. I'd never thought to ask him.

"Stanzie, please, I'm begging you." Murphy was only a few yards away but it might as well have been a continent because there was nothing he could do if the wolf attacked me except watch. Vaughn's face was white with dread.

For the first time I felt fear, and didn't like it. We didn't fear our own kind. At least I never had until the conspiracy had been unmasked. Just because we were near strangers didn't mean Nate should go all territorial.

I took a small step for the porch stairs and calculated how close I would need to get before I could make a break for it and which way the door worked. If I guessed wrong whether the goddamn door opened inward or outward, I was fucked. Who the hell was I kidding? I was probably fucked no matter what I did. Wolves were way faster than people. By the time I made the stairs, he could leap across the space between us and knock me down with ease.

"I don't think I can make it, Murphy. I'm afraid if I run he'll attack me."

"Shit," was Murphy's less-than-helpful response. "I'm gonna slam the trunk down. When he reacts to the noise, get the hell inside."

"What about you?" I started to say but the trunk slammed and Murphy yelled something in Irish. The wolf didn't take his eyes off me.

Unfortunately by the time I processed that, I'd already sprinted three of the six feet between where I'd stood and the porch steps.

About a half second before he brought me down, I sensed his leap and tried to cover my head with my arms, but it was no use.

Murphy screamed my name. So did Vaughn. I tensed and waited for the agony as the wolf's teeth tore into the soft parts of my arms, but all I felt was hot breath on the back of my neck. And then a slobbery tongue in my ear.

"Oh, fuck me," I muttered into the dirt beneath my mouth as I tried not to choke on it.

The wolf continued to lick me until I rolled over, then he swiped my face. I gave him my throat because he was an Alpha male and he took it in his jaws, but did not break the skin.

This was how it was supposed to go. A little unorthodox since I was still in human form, but this was acceptable Pack behavior. He asserted his dominance and I acknowledged his leadership.

"I told you." I used the male wolf's broad shoulders to brace myself as I got to my feet. His fur was thick and soft and he smelled like he'd been rolling in leaves. Twigs and leaf bits stuck in his fur and I began to brush them out with my fingers.

Murphy and Vaughn rushed over to us. Murphy looked ready to explode and Vaughn wasn't far behind.

"This is bullshit," declared Murphy as the wolf wagged his tail at us all. His tongue lolled out of the side of his half-open mouth. By wolf standards he was smiling. He made a chuffing sound, almost like a sneeze—the lupine equivalent of a laugh.

"Now you're making fun of us. Bad wolf," I lectured, but I couldn't help my smile. I patted his head and he gave a happy yip before he trotted off toward the clothesline.

"I'm glad one of us is amused because I'm about ready to kick his ass." Murphy's dark eyes glinted dangerously. Vaughn did not look remotely amused.

The screen door banged open and we swung around to confront a petite woman with long chestnut hair and huge brown eyes. She wore a green-and-white floral print sundress and her feet were bare. A small black wolf's head was tattooed on her left shin. I'd been with her when she'd gotten it at a Regional Gathering when she was sixteen and I was fifteen. She'd dared me to get one too but I was too chickenshit my father would find out and kill me.

A baby who looked about a year old balanced on her right hip. She clutched at her mother's arm with one chubby hand. The other was curled around a small stuffed bunny.

The woman's gaze traveled over all of us and registered several emotions from happiness to wariness. When she fully focused on Vaughn, her face froze.

"Hey, Jossie." He raised a hand in greeting.

Jossie Wilbanks bit her lip and, for a moment, I didn't think she would reply. Just as she opened her mouth, Nate Carver walked from behind the clothesline where he'd shifted back into human form.

"Sorry about that, we didn't expect you until later this afternoon." He'd dressed in a pair of jeans and a blue t-shirt that smelled of the fresh spring breeze.

I'd forgotten what a giant of a man Nate was—at least six six, probably taller.

His light blond hair was buzz cut close to his scalp. Brown eyes fringed with thick lashes were his best feature. He was not handsome, but he had something that attracted people to him. He was open and friendly, charismatic, with a sense of humor. He'd shown that to us in wolf form.

"He was looking for Bethany." Jossie rushed into speech. "In fact, the whole pack is going to shift tomorrow and scour these woods if that's all right with you?"

I was a little surprised she asked our permission, but then I remembered we were Advisors to the Great Council and, even though we were not Alphas, we had power. It was an interesting thought.

"I think that's a good idea." Murphy's eyes were appreciative as he gazed at her. Pack men were drawn to Alpha females with babies. Somehow the sight of a nursing mother made them both protective and aroused. She smiled at him, but held the baby like a shield between her and the world.

"Stanzie, it is so good to see you!" Jossie turned her gaze to me and the spring breeze carried a hint of her scent to me. Lavender soap and the faint tang of citrus shampoo. No perfume.

"Have you really been in Boston for the past two years? Is what I'm hearing from Councilor Manning true?"

I nodded.

"Why didn't you let anybody know you were so close? After I found out Riverglow cast you out I called your parents to see if they had any contact information and they said they didn't. I know you were exiled, but only by Riverglow. The Councils cleared you. Why didn't you want your friends around you? I would have gone crazy alone if I'd been you."

I didn't answer because I had no answer.

Jossie, astute at reading expressions, frowned, and her eyebrows slanted together ominously. "They lied, didn't they? They knew all along where you were."

Her words hung there in the space between us.

"We don't really talk much anymore, Joss," I whispered. I thought of the monthly calls I'd made when I had been exiled. The messages I'd left they'd never returned. Then there were the three messages I'd left in the past three months since Murphy, Vaughn and I had taken up residence in Boston. None of those calls had been returned either.

"Nobody falls faster or harder in a pack than the child of a founding family." Nate was the one to break the uncomfortable silence. "You're what, fourteenth generation?

"Fifteenth," I said.

"And you threw it all away to join Riverglow?" Nate gave a low whistle. Vaughn's mouth got small but he didn't say anything. Riverglow wasn't his pack anymore.

"I'm fourth generation. Doesn't mean shit to most packs, but I still get the pressure to keep the pack going. You're Mac Tire now, right?" Nate was relentless. "If that doesn't impress your family, nothing will. This your bond mate?"

I introduced them. Murphy's hello was not very warm but Nate didn't seem to notice.

"Mac Tire your birth pack?"

Murphy allowed as it was.

"So what generation are you?"

After a moment's thought, Murphy said, "Thirty-one."

Nate burst into laughter. "Well, that makes me and Stanzie look just plain silly, doesn't it? Thirty-one. Jesus. You descended from a founding family?"

"No way." It was Murphy's turn to laugh and not very politely. "The founding families left are on the fiftieth generation at least."

That put the pack's inception more than twelve hundred years ago.

"We don't have packs anywhere near that old here in the States," said Nate after a moment's respectful silence as he absorbed the history.

I was flabbergasted myself. I'd known Mac Tire was old and I'd known it was Murphy's birth pack, but I'd never known it was that old, nor did I realize that Murphy's family had been in the pack for centuries.

"Mayflower's the second-oldest in the country, Stanzie?" Nate looked to me for confirmation.

"Third," I said. "The Jamestown pack is older by a couple decades and then there's Spiritwolf."

"Now there's a pack that's old. You'd think there'd be more Native American packs, wouldn't you, but there's not."

"Because our ancestors came from Europe and did to their packs what the Other Europeans did the Native American tribes. Conquer and divide. Take their territory." Vaughn's tone was derisive.

"Hey, if you can't protect your land, you don't deserve to have it." Nate walked to the porch steps. "Get your luggage and come on in. Joss, looks like we need two spare rooms made up instead of the one. Unless you three are a triad now?"

He turned back to look at us appraisingly.

Vaughn flushed. "Nah, we're not a triad." For some reason he wouldn't look at any of us, especially Jossie.

* * * *

Dusk settled around the eaves of the old farmhouse a little bit at a time. Incremental shadows crept across the dirt drive and the flagstone path that led to the porch where we all sat with glasses of wine.

Jossie rocked her daughter in one of the wooden rocking chairs while I snapped the ends off a bowl of green beans that had been grown in the back garden last summer and frozen until just today.

Murphy and I sat on the glider and, while I snapped beans, he gently propelled us back and forth, careful not to jar the bowl in my lap.

We'd unpacked our things in an upstairs bedroom with strange angles and wallpaper older than both of us put together.

Vaughn's room was across the hall—full of even more eaves and angles but his walls were painted a soothing moss green.

Jossie, Nate and Heather slept in the addition on the ground floor.

They'd slowly remodeled the farmhouse since they'd moved into it after they'd bonded ten years ago.

"This is nice, Jossie," I said as the dusky shadows crept closer and a whippoorwill began a plaintive song from the pine tree near the barn. "A lot different from Boston."

Jossie smiled. Her daughter, Heather, rested in her lap and faced the front of the porch. The glider sat to the side so Heather had to crane her neck to keep me and Murphy under her wary gaze.

I snapped a green bean in half and gave her a little smile, which made her eyebrows lower suspiciously.

Murphy was getting a real kick out of the baby's attitude. He blatantly flirted with her, but she was having absolutely none of it, which secretly tickled me. Here, at last, was one female who wouldn't succumb to his Irish charm.

Vaughn stretched his legs out in front of him as he slouched in his rocking chair, wine glass perched on the wide arm rest near his hand. He hadn't said anything since we'd gathered on the porch, just looked out the screen at the gathering darkness. I wondered what he was thinking about. Callie? Peter? Jossie? A combination of everything? Or maybe nothing at all.

Nate bustled back and forth from the porch to the kitchen to fetch more wine, a plate of cheese and crackers, and put on a jazz CD then adjusted the volume so it didn't interfere with the desultory conversation. He couldn't keep still and brimmed over with vitality and energy.

Jossie had always been energetic, but Nate took it to all new heights. How she managed not to go crazy with his frenetic movements was beyond me. He never sat still for more than three minutes before he jumped up to get something or to start another project.

"Want some beer, Liam?" Nate offered right on schedule. He'd sat for two and a half minutes. I'd timed him. "I brew it myself. Got a little home brewery in the basement. I'm sure it won't compare to what you're used to in Ireland, but it's pretty good, if I do say so myself."

Murphy's wine glass was still half-full, but he agreed to try the beer because he was a nice guy and Nate had a puppy dog look of expectancy.

Nate leaped to his feet and, in his excitement, nearly forgot to duck his head on the way in the front door. Luckily he remembered at the last second and avoided a possible concussion.

"God, he's tall," I shook my head. "Does he ever sit still, Jossie?"

Murphy smothered a laugh and gave me a gentle nudge in the ribs with his elbow. Sure I was being rude, but Jossie and I went way back. The bad blood between us seemed distant and meaningless on this twilit porch. It was almost like old times when we'd been teenagers together.

"No," said Jossie with a martyred sigh. "He's constantly in motion." For some reason she blushed and was quiet for a small beat of time that intrigued me. "One project after the other. That's why I'm thankful for this old farmhouse. You should have seen it when we moved in. The roof leaked in twenty different places, some of the floorboards were rotten and the plumbing was practically nonexistent. He did it all himself mostly. What he didn't know how to do, he taught himself. I thought he was crazy when he wanted to live in this place just because it was on the same road as most of the Pack's houses and near his great-grandmother, but now I'm grateful."

"He's done a brilliant job," Murphy said. "I like to do a bit of renovating myself, but my meager talents mostly run to the cosmetic side. Painting, putting in new cabinetry and fixtures, that sort of thing. Plumbing and roofing are way out of my range."

"You could learn." Nate reappeared with a pitcher of beer and five glasses. Apparently we were all going to drink beer. "It's not that hard."

Murphy grinned and watched him pour a frothing glass of dark beer. I stared at it doubtfully.

"I filtered it three times. There shouldn't be any bits floating in it." Nate laughed at my expression.

I grimaced at the thought of bits. It wasn't that. It was just the fact that he'd made it. I was leery of someone Pack who made things to eat and drink that I hadn't watched them prepare. Kathy Manning was an exception, but I'd spent time with her and watched her cook. The prickling of unease made me realize how paranoid I had become since I'd uncovered the plot buried within our Pack.

Nate held the first glass out to Vaughn. At first I didn't think Vaughn was going to take it, but after he and Nate exchanged a look that excluded the rest of us, he accepted the glass. Jossie kept her head down and rocked the baby, but I could see the nervous flutter of the pulse beat in her throat.

Nate filled a second glass and gave it to Murphy.

Murphy had no qualms. He gulped down a mouthful without blinking. When he didn't immediately expire, and a pleased smile spread across his face, I accepted a glass, aware of Nate's genial amusement. He didn't know about the conspiracy, so he was still convinced I was worried about floating bits of hops.

The beer was dark and nutty, not bitter precisely, but not what I was used to tasting when I thought of the word *beer*. Nate still smiled, but now he was also a bit defensive.

I took another sip and then another. I didn't like it as much as Murphy obviously did, but it was a taste I could get used to. Eventually.

Vaughn sucked his down too. Beer was like mother's milk to that guy. He always had a least three different kinds in the refrigerator. He set aside his nearly full wine glass and embraced the beer with gusto.

Nate watched all our reactions and seemed satisfied. Two seconds after he refilled both Murphy's and Vaughn's glasses, he sneaked an inevitable look at his watch.

"Have I got time, babe, to go visit Grandmother Emma?"

Jossie gave him a smile that made her look almost like the teenage girl I'd once been great friends with.

"Be back here for six. Dinner will be on the table. We've got to discuss things, Nate."

"I know, but Emma's lonely. Plus I think there might be a storm tonight and I've got to make sure all her windows are closed." Nate waved at us all as he leaped down the porch steps. I heard the garage door trundle up and he reappeared on a motorcycle, his blue helmet flashed in the last of the dying sun—then he was gone up the dirt drive back to the road.

"Emma is his great-grandmother by blood, not just a grandmother in the pack," Jossie explained. "She and her bond mate founded this pack. About twenty years ago, there was a terrible family feud and to this day the only blood family member Emma will talk to is Nate. One of the reasons we took over the farmhouse is because she's only two miles up the road in the closest house to ours. Most of the pack lives on this road, but farther down in the opposite direction."

Vaughn's fingers tightened around his beer glass as he became very still.

Jossie shot him a confused look and burst into speech as if to cover up for a faux pas. "All this area was a farm once. This is the actual farmhouse. Everything else is newly built within the last hundred years or so. After founding Maplefair, Nate's great-grandparents worked on the farm. When the farmer died, he left them the land Grandmother Emma's house is built on plus a few other parcels. The rest of the pack lives on those lots. We build as we need to. He's a good guy, my bond mate."

She spoke almost as if she thought we believed otherwise and I frowned.

"Makes a hell of a beer," Vaughn raised his glass in appreciation, but somehow the accolade fell short.

"Hear, hear," seconded Murphy and they both downed half the contents of their glasses.

I took another tentative sip and tried not to shudder. Eventually seemed a long time away.

* * * *

After dinner we gathered back on the front porch by common consent. More beer was poured, but Jossie took discreet pity on me and implored me to help her drink a bottle of wine. As she was breastfeeding, she could only have one glass and she didn't want to waste it.

Heather nursed while Jossie rocked, her head back so she could stare up at the ceiling fan, which was festooned with a cobweb that seemed to mesmerize her.

Murphy and I had the glider again and we sat thigh to thigh. Once in a while he'd look at me with that infatuated expression and, every time he did, I felt strange and giddy inside.

Vaughn slouched in his rocker, head tilted while perhaps he listened to the chorus of crickets outside in the shrubbery. We sat in near darkness save for several votive candles in stained glass containers hung from nails along the porch wall. The only electric light came from two spotlights on the barn, trained down on the cars parked in front.

"How long has Bethany been missing?" Murphy asked out of the comfortable, candlelit darkness. Everyone sat up a little straighter as the peaceful lassitude of the porch seeped away and frustration and mounting anxiety began to replace it.

Jossie stopped rocking. "Her mother said she saw her sleeping in bed on Wednesday night. She and her bond mate had a romantic dinner date planned for Thursday night, staying overnight at a hotel. They do that once or month or so. Bethany's door was still shut Thursday morning when Gina and Ron had to leave for work, and Gina said Ron pounded on the door and told Bethany she'd better get her butt to school, but Bethany didn't answer and he didn't push it. They're pretty sure she was there, though.

"Gina texted Bethany on her lunch hour to remind Bethany she and Ron were not going to be home that night. Bethany texted back that she remembered and to have a good time. Gina and Ron went to work on Friday straight from the hotel and got a phone call about eleven that morning from Nancy, the woman who home schools all the pack children. She has a son two years older than Bethany, the two are pretty close. Boyfriend and girlfriend."

"Councilor Manning told us how Cody and Bethany have been kept apart since they shifted together at the Regional," I said. Both Jossie and Nate looked dismayed.

"No matter how many times you tell them, you can't get some teenagers to understand about shifting together." Jossie shook her head. She looked at my guilty expression and belatedly seemed to remember I had once been one of those teenagers. She flashed me an embarrassed grin and I smiled in response, and waited for her to go on and tell us everything.

"Nancy called because Bethany hadn't shown up for class Thursday or Friday. She'd gotten a text from Bethany saying she was sick. She hadn't thought anything of it until Cody told her that he hadn't heard from Bethany since Thursday morning and he was worried. They were only supposed to be in supervised contact, but of course they got around that.

"Cody told her he'd driven past Bethany's house on Thursday night but hadn't been able to get anyone to answer the door. He'd held back on telling anyone because they weren't supposed to be in contact, but he finally broke down and begged his mother to call Gina and Ron.

"Gina ran home from work. Bethany's room was empty. The bed was unmade. Her pajamas from Wednesday were on the floor. It looked to them like Bethany had run away while they'd been at the hotel. But if she didn't go to Cody, where?

"They came to us to ask us if we'd seen Bethany. We called the Regional Council after we made sure no one in our pack had seen her. By then it was Friday night. Councilor Manning called me back to tell me to keep her apprised of what was going on meanwhile to look for Bethany at bus stations and local motels and malls, which we've been doing. Nothing. Tomorrow we're going to have a hunt and search the woods where we all usually shift because maybe..." Jossie's voice faltered. Bethany knew the woods much too well to be lost. Perhaps she was hurt and couldn't move, but that didn't seem likely. But then neither did suicide.

"We'll find her if she's out there," Murphy vowed after a moment of sympathetic silence.

"I don't understand why she did this. She wouldn't have left without telling Cody anything. Those two want to bond together when they're old enough. That's only three years from now. Not so long to wait. I don't see why she would run away. There's no reason for it." Jossie bowed her head. Heather stopped nursing to stare. She reached out a chubby hand and patted her mother's cheek as if to reassure her.

Jossie took Heather's little hand in her own and brought it to her mouth to plant a kiss on her daughter's palm. For the first time I saw the baby smile. When she did, she looked just like Jossie.

"Don't give up hope, Jossie," I whispered, sick to my stomach at the thought we might find Bethany's dead body and have to bear witness to the death of all her dreams.

* * * *

The rain struck the windowpanes of the farmhouse bedroom in angry little spats. Lightning crackled in the sky around the barn. The air seemed to sizzle. I held the curtains back with one hand, the palm of my other pressed flat to the cool glass.

More than anything I wanted to shift and run the way my wolf used to. Only I knew she wouldn't run if I shifted, she'd try to find the words for rain and lightning, and stand there in the wet darkness, fur soaked, as she tried to figure things out. Running and playing would be the last things on her mind.

I'd watched the storm for maybe fifteen minutes before Murphy stirred in the bed behind me and realized I wasn't there anymore.

"Stanzie?" He whispered my name, and struggled to see me in the darkness. Lightning flashed and he saw me by the window. "What's the matter, honey? Bad dream?"

"Yeah," I admitted and watched the rain pound down on our Prelude parked in the yard below.

"About Callie?" He probed, but gently. His voice was soothing and encouraging. I hadn't discussed Callie's suicide with him. I'd avoided the topic altogether with him and he'd waited patiently for me to bring it up for three months now. Every once in a while he opened the door a little to get the discussion going, but I closed it. Every single time.

"No," I told him.

"You want to talk about it?"

"Murphy?" I took a deep breath and held it for a moment before I released it. "Do I make my parents sound like monsters?"

"They do a good job of that all on their own. They don't need your help," he declared and I bit my lip.

"All you know about them is from me."

"And from Vaughn and Jocelyn and from them themselves. Three months, Stanzie, we've been living in Boston, and them only a few miles down the road. Not a phone call, not a fucking postcard, not as much as a single acknowledgment that you're around."

"I was fifteenth generation. You don't leave your birth pack when you're fifteenth generation. At least not in New England you don't." I don't know why I defended them but I did.

"You did." He sounded proud of me. Because he didn't understand.

"Come back to bed." Murphy patted the empty space beside him on the mattress. "We're going to shift in the morning and we need to be well rested for that."

"It's raining," I protested. "All the scents will be washed away."

"Not if she's still out there somewhere. We may not be able to pick up a trail, but if we spread out across the woods, we could still find her."

I didn't answer or move.

"We have to do something, Stanzie. Her parents have looked two towns over, checking all the motels, bus stops and train stations and they haven't had any luck. She hasn't bought an airline ticket in her name. She didn't bring clothes. All she has is what she was wearing and her purse, which had maybe ten dollars in it. She's got to be out there somewhere, maybe hurt and..."

"Maybe she's dead. Killed herself." My voice was too shrill. Murphy pushed back the covers and got out of bed to come to me. As soon as he was close enough, I threw myself in his arms, which surprised us both, but he hugged me back after only one missed beat. When he felt me shaking, his embrace got even tighter.

"Murphy, I don't want to shift. I'm afraid to shift in front of a whole pack of people. Especially if it's raining. My wolf doesn't know the word for rain. It's never rained since we've started shifting together and she doesn't know the word. All she's going to do is sit there and let it pound down onto her until she knows the word for it." I buried my face in his neck. I didn't know if he could even understand me because my voice was muffled and choked with fearful sobs.

"So she sits there for a few minutes and thinks of the word. Then she can move on." Murphy combed my hair with his fingers and, despite my agitation, I was soothed a little.

"She won't know what to do." I shook my head in denial. Memories of Regional Gatherings in the past pecked at me. Derisive comments about my wolf. The condescending laughter. Worse, the looks of pity.

Murphy kissed the top of my head. "I'll tell you what to do and you'll tell her. The same as it's been since we started shifting together, Stanzie. All that's going to happen is we're going to gather in whatever place they use and we'll all shift together. We'll..."

"Will it be like a Great Hunt? Will we all have sex first? In the same room?" I interrupted because I wanted to know every detail.

"Yes," he told me. "You know that's part of the Great Hunt, the group sex part. It bonds us all through scent and pheromones. You and I will be together the whole time, I won't leave you. After we're shifted, we'll familiarize ourselves with her scent. There'll be some of her clothes, probably the sheets from her bed, things with her scent on it. The Alphas will lead, we'll cover the woods and if she's there, we'll find her."

"Someone has to watch the baby. I can do that," I said and he sighed in my ear.

"You represent the Great Council. How are you going to do that staying here and watching the Alphas' baby? One of the teenagers in the pack will watch the children."

I hated the Great Council for a moment, resented being a fucking Advisor and despised having to be in the spotlight. I loathed the idea that if I didn't shift, I would make Councilor Allerton look bad because I was damned if I would do that. Not after everything he'd done for me.

"Is Vaughn going to shift?" I asked. Murphy kissed my ear lightly.

"I think he's planning on it. He can be with us if you want him to. After we shift and before if you like. He knows your wolf. Your wolf knows him. Would that make it better?"

He meant a threesome with Vaughn. He would do that for me. By Pack standards that wasn't a big deal, it was done a lot. But by Murphy standards that offered something he probably didn't really want to do.

"Maybe after we shift," I said and he kissed my ear again, this time gratefully.

Chapter 3

I had been wrong about my assumption the barn had been converted into a garage. It was, in reality, part workshop, part meeting place for the pack.

Meeting place as in a staging area for a hunt.

Former stalls had been turned into rendezvous areas for couples or threesomes, complete with soft mattresses covered in bright sheets, throw pillows, ambient lighting and even convenient built-in holders for water bottles.

Comfortable sofas ranged around the open part of the space. A bar too. When Murphy and I walked in, it was manned by a grandmother and grandfather, obviously a bonded duo, who passed out water bottles. They looked grim. Everyone did. Grim and confused. Normally, hunts were wonderful things. A time to frolic and have fun—to release the wolf within.

Today we had a somber purpose and no one was quite sure how to behave.

The moment I saw the grandmother as she passed out water bottles I thought of the Great Hunt at the Gathering in Paris. Rudi's imploring eyes as he'd begged me to save him just before he died.

I was wildly uncomfortable with the idea of shifting with strangers and now I had to take a bottle of water from a grandmother? My throat closed over in the first stages of panic.

Murphy understood at once and turned toward me, but Nate swooped upon us both the minute we cleared the door.

"Can I speak with you a moment, Advisor?" Nate used Murphy's title so it was official business.

Before Murphy could ask him to wait a moment, I said. "I'll go get us some water, Murphy." I forced myself to walk away from him.

At some point, in some small way, I had to stop being so scared of everything. These people were not going to poison me. I was here to help them. Not everyone in the Pack was involved in the conspiracy. If I couldn't take a bottle of water from a grandmother here, where could I?

Murphy's gaze burned into my back as he watched me go, but he didn't come after me. He knew what I was trying to do, but I also knew he wondered whether I could. He wasn't the only one.

"Good morning." I tried to muster a smile for the grandmother behind the bar. Her salt-and-pepper hair was drawn up into a bun. Her eyes were a startling green. The grandfather beside her had blue eyes and gray hair—what was left of it anyway.

"Good morning, Advisor." Her smile was sad and subdued, and I wondered if she had a blood tie to the missing girl. She held out a bottle of cold water and my heart thudded sickly.

Take it, Constance, take it, I ordered myself sternly, but my hand didn't move.

"Good morning, Grandmother Danielle." Vaughn appeared at my side and his shoulder brushed mine. "Good morning, Grandfather Joe."

"Vaughn!" They both looked a little unnerved at the sight of him. Vaughn's eyes widened. "We've changed a little since we last saw you, son." Grandfather Joe's voice was gruff.

Vaughn had been gone from Maplefair for nearly twenty years. Apparently, this duo had crossed from middle to old age in the time span Vaughn had been away.

Pack aged slowly, but we did age. The line between middle and old age was not very subtle. It all happened within a two- or three-year time span. One year a person could look forty-five, the next sixty. Age seemed to catch up with a vengeance after being held at bay for so very long.

"Grandmother Danielle still has the prettiest eyes in Maplefair," said Vaughn, as he recovered himself.

Vaughn, Peter and Callie had left Maplefair, with Jonathan, Nora and Grandfather Tobias in order to form Riverglow. Even after more than a decade, Vaughn had never told me the whole story of their departure. This grandmother and grandfather obviously knew the tale, but of course they wouldn't discuss it in front of me.

Secrets. All packs had them.

Grandmother Danielle giggled—a sound that more befitted a sixteen-year-old—but it broke the tension and made us all smile. Somehow I had a water bottle in my hand. I didn't even remember when I took it.

Vaughn wrapped a friendly arm around my shoulder and steered me away from the bar. He had a bottle of water too, clutched in his free hand.

This morning he looked boyishly attractive and his brown eyes appreciated everything about a woman.

It was in the air despite the reason for the hunt. Sex. I could smell desire and lust, and heightened sexual excitement. It tugged at me despite my fear of shifting.

It pulled at Vaughn too from the way he looked at me. For a moment I thought he might kiss me, but he opened his water bottle instead and took a long swig. I did the same.

Neither of us died, so I took another swallow.

"I just wanted to tell you that after I shift, I'll come and be with you and Liam." Vaughn's gaze traveled up and down my body suggestively, although he tried hard not to look at me that way. Lust warred with reluctant better judgment.

"You don't think my wolf's changed all that much, do you?" I took another swallow of water and watched him flounder. I couldn't blame him for not understanding how my wolf had evolved. He would remember the wolf from Riverglow—the one he'd had to protect and rush after.

"It's okay." I took pity on him. "I'm not really sure what my wolf will do, Vaughn. I just know she won't run and play like she used to do. She won't do that. She wants names for things. I'm not sure if she'll follow the pack or if she'll get distracted and want to find the name for something."

I looked away from the empathy in his eyes because I couldn't bear it. "I really don't want to shift, but I guess I have to because I'm an Advisor."

"I won't leave you." His fingers trailed lightly down my cheek and I looked into his familiar face. His touch made me shiver, but mostly I felt shame.

"I was so selfish, wasn't I? Refusing to work with my wolf. Making you, Grey and Elena my goddamn prisoners. I'm sorry, Vaughn."

"No need, Stanz." My name was a caress.

I hugged him then and felt his arms close around me tightly.

"It'll be all right," he whispered into my ear, as he rocked me.

People paired off and went into the tricked-out stalls. A woman moaned. Another laughed seductively.

I squeezed my eyes shut and let Vaughn hold me as a multitude of feelings tripped through my bloodstream, turned my knees rubbery and my thoughts carnal.

"Come on, you two." Murphy somehow had his arms around us both. "Let's be together, all three of us."

"Are you sure?" Vaughn's voice rumbled against my chest. My face was pressed into his shoulder.

"Positive," replied Murphy.

The conversation turned surreal and I was left floating between the spaces the words made after they were spoken.

No one asked me if I wanted to be with them both, but it was all right. I wanted what they did.

Impressions of bright pillows and sheets of varying shades of red, primal like blood, flashed in and out as Vaughn's mouth moved against mine—one hot kiss after another until I thought I would drown.

Murphy watched, his face alight. Each time I caught his eyes for reassurance or because I wanted to know he was there, he smiled at me, but he let Vaughn be alone with me.

As Vaughn tangled his tongue with mine, he feverishly removed my light cotton dress. His emotions crashed into me in a shimmering cascade—lust, love, longing, grief. A search for something elusive I didn't know if he could find within me.

We both were swept away by the power of the pack-wide orgy going on around us. Scent and sound combined into a mounting urgency that could be assuaged only by flesh against flesh.

Each time I opened my eyes under Vaughn's demanding passion, I saw Murphy. Once I reached my hand out to him and he took it and squeezed my fingers in a gesture of complete understanding and trust. I loved him so much it hurt.

"I'm so glad it's you," Vaughn murmured in my ear as we moved together upon the dark red sheets, my legs wrapped around his waist, ankles locked at the small of his back. My heels slid in his sweat, so I squeezed my legs tightly against his sides. He tangled his fingers in my hair then trailed them down the side of my face to brush my mouth. I bit his thumb and he nipped my earlobe. "This is my first time since...it... happened. I didn't want to be with a stranger. Oh, Stanzie, I want to do something good with my life. I want a second chance to do something good."

"You will," I whispered, and found his mouth with mine. We kissed greedily and he reached a hand between my thighs. I arched into his exploring fingers and hissed when he found my sensitive spot and rubbed.

Vaughn and I had been lovers when I'd been a member of Riverglow, but there was something new about his lovemaking today. An urgency, a sense of searching for something just out of reach that opened him up to me emotionally more than he'd ever allowed before. It was as if I saw and felt Vaughn for the first time and yet still I knew him.

"I want to be like you." His breath in my ear sent dizzying tingles down my spine. I shuddered against him so close to the edge I could taste it. "Do you think I can be?"

"Vaughn," I cried, helpless under the onslaught of the violent orgasm that barreled through my body. I took him with me and we both added our essence to the growing pack-wide energy, which electrified the entire barn. The rafters almost shook beneath the psychic onslaught of it. I imagined I could hear them screaming along with half the people in the room. A mass orgasm spread from one couple to the other in a blurry frenzy. Vaughn and I had started it, but the rest were quick to follow.

I closed my eyes and when I opened them Murphy was there with me, his face close to mine. He whispered to me in Irish as he slid deliciously inside me and although I'd thought I was spent, my pulse quickened and my body reacted to his like iron filings to a magnet. He was so hot inside me it nearly burned. When he bit my neck, I went crazy beneath him—a second incredible orgasm turned me inside out. I took Murphy with me just as I had taken Vaughn and everyone else who were still together.

I could feel them —all their ecstasy, love and loyalty. We were united by essence and something uniquely Pack. It would last throughout the time we were shifted and bond us into a hunting pack.

* * * *

Hand in hand, Murphy and I, with Vaughn, walked outside to the side yard. The storm last night had been intense but of short duration. Now the sun shone and the grass was only slightly damp.

A plastic tarp had been spread out near the edge of the woods. Heaped upon it were some of Bethany's things—the sheets from her bed, clothes from her hamper, a pink terrycloth bathrobe. A small stuffed rabbit with worn white fur and one crooked ear was heartbreaking to look at so I averted my eyes.

People gathered in a loose semicircle around her things—still in human form. Everyone was unselfconsciously nude.

We made our way to the circle. I stood next to Jossie. Her chestnut hair was unbound and fell to her waist. It still retained a light wave from being braided. Faint stretch marks made silvery pale lines across her otherwise tight stomach. Her breasts were full and I could smell her milk even though I knew she'd nursed Heather just before she'd come out to the barn.

My senses were sharpened to a fine point. For the first time in months, my wolf clamored for release within me. I held tightly to Murphy's hand as the pack exchanged glances. Everyone's eyes shone silver or amber— wolves' eyes. It was a side effect from sex and didn't last longer than half an hour or so. Murphy's eyes were amber gold and they glowed. Vaughn's were a darker shade of molten ocher. So were Jossie's. I knew from the mirror that my eyes turned silver blue. Not a word was spoken— we didn't need to speak. We couldn't precisely read each others' thoughts, but we somehow knew what we were going to do.

Shift, get Bethany's scent from her belongings, and hunt. Simple.

Simple, that is, for everyone else's wolves. I wasn't sure so about mine.

Something instinctual kicked in causing most of us to drop to the ground in unison.

My back bowed as my body contorted into near impossible positions. The younger members of the pack whimpered, unused to the searing, yet thankfully fleeting, pain. For them it took longer to shift. They didn't want to give up control.

The more we fought our wolves, the longer and harder the transition.

For me, after the first few times, shifting had become a snap. I'd learned to let go and give my wolf complete control. Before Murphy and the evolution of my wolf, shifting had been so swift, I'd been up and running while the rest of my pack had still writhed on the ground.

Today with Maplefair, I still attained wolf form faster than all the others, but it wasn't a blink of an eye anymore. I didn't give my wolf full control the way I used to and she resented it.

Usually it was our human form that fought against the shift—with me it was now the opposite. My wolf fought me.

All around us the air crackled with the psychic intensity as twenty people shifted at the same time. My last coherent thought as human was a plea to my wolf to please, please follow everyone else.

* * * *

So many Thems. So many I have no names for them. Scared. Friend here. Good Them here too. Me...I...I not see Good Them for long, long time. Me love Good Them. Me remember Good Them from Before Time with Him and Her. Good Them pushes me with nose. I do something? Thems smell things. Me smell too. Me...I...I smell Pack. Girl. Not know Girl. Oh, oh! What is name for this smell? I know. I know. I find the word. I find it! Little. Little one inside. What is name? I need to find! Find the word! It hides! Find the word! No, Friend, no Good Them, no play with me now. Thems gone, you go too. Me find word! Little...little one inside. ...ooo me so mad! Where is word! Where is word?"

* * * *

By the time the last of the Maplefair pack had shifted back and Bethany's things had been gathered up, the rain had returned. It drummed on the roof of the barn where we all assembled to discuss the hunt.

Grandmother Danielle and Grandfather Joe passed out water to the thirsty pack. Murphy, Vaughn and I had been the first to shift back and return to the barn. I nearly floated I'd consumed so much damn water. We were first back because we'd never left the clearing or the pitiful pile of Bethany's belongings. My wolf had been determined to find the word for the one particular scent she'd smelled on Bethany's light blue panties.

Neither Murphy nor Vaughn had said a word to me about my wolf's failure to follow the others and join in the hunt. Not one word about her obsession with Bethany's panties. I hadn't said anything either. I was disgraced, but I was also on fire with the knowledge of what I'd learned about Bethany through my wolf. The two things warred within me and bounced me back and forth between humiliation and restless excitement.

They stayed close to me, followed when I paced the confines of the barn. The only time they weren't at my side was when we had to relieve ourselves. They drank a lot of water too so they would avoid the muscle cramps and body aches shifting could cause without proper hydration.

When the last of the stragglers had come in and everyone was dressed and had water, we pulled folding chairs into a circle and sat. Murphy and I took chairs to the left of Jossie. She sat next to Nate. Everyone looked to them as the Alpha pair of the pack.

People were despondent. They hadn't found a trace of Bethany. The scent of despair filled the air and added to my already nearly unbearable tension. It was hard to remain still in my chair but I managed it.

Vaughn sat on my other side, so I was buffered between him and Murphy, but I still felt the burning weight of the Maplefair pack's judgment of me. Everyone had seen that my wolf had been obsessed with the smell of Bethany's panties. They'd waited for her to follow them. Nate's wolf had even tried to force me, but my wolf hadn't budged from a seated position, head cocked as she frantically searched within herself for the damn word that had proved so elusive.

Murphy's wolf could sometimes cajole her into playing, but only if she found the word for which she was searching and today she had not found the word.

"Well, that was a complete fiasco." Nate broke the subdued silence. Murmurs of agreement rose from the people crowded around in the circle.

"I think it's the work of the Stowe Strangler," declared a woman who looked to be in her late thirties—which meant by Pack standards she was over seventy. She glared around the room and dared anyone to disagree with her.

"Damn it, Marlene," exclaimed the man beside her, probably her bond mate. I gave a sudden jolt of recognition. These were Peter's parents— Vaughn's adoptive parents. Vaughn's parents and twin sister had been killed in a car crash when he'd been twelve. Peter had been the pack's closest child in age to him and they'd been best friends. Peter's parents had taken Vaughn in and raised him as their own.

Today, Marlene and Dave had made no move to talk to Vaughn that I'd seen and even now they'd taken seats as far away from him as possible.

In all the years I'd known Vaughn and Peter, they'd never talked much about Maplefair or their lives before Riverglow. A secret lurked beneath the surface, but they'd never let me in on it.

When Vaughn had arrived on the accident scene after I'd crashed the Mustang and Grey and Elena had been killed, he'd raced straight to Elena in the backseat. When he'd realized her neck had snapped and she was dead, he'd thrown back his head and screamed.

On the way down the ravine to the car, he'd kept crying out, "Not like this! Not like this!"

He'd been in love with Elena.

This particular memory was burned into my psyche and after I'd been exiled from Riverglow I'd tortured myself with it many times. It was only after countless repetitions that I recalled Vaughn's parents and sister had died in a car crash too. It took me so long to remember it because he never talked about it. His past was a big taboo.

I wondered again why he'd come here to Maplefair where his present was sure to collide with his past. Had it been so damn long it didn't matter anymore?

Even Nate, who was very forthright, hadn't said anything. He'd given Vaughn a few speculative looks, but he'd kept quiet, and so had Jossie. As a relative newcomer to the pack, she might not know everything.

Marlene's face became obstinate while Dave's flushed with mortified anger. "There's no need to go spreading rumors like that one around."

He chanced a look at Bethany's parents, Gina and Ron, who had gone very pale. Gina, a tall, voluptuous blonde, clutched at the arm of her bond mate. He was tall as well, with penetrating blue eyes and thin lips, which gave his face a perpetual look of cruelty. However, the way he patted Gina's hand made me think his looks were not representative of the real man.

"Who in the hell is the Stowe Strangler?" Murphy demanded.

Marlene shot a defiant look at her bond mate. "Bethany's not the only girl to go missing around these parts, Advisor!"

"The only Pack girl. The missing girls were all teenage runaways, prostitutes for God's sake. Bethany does not fit that profile. And only one body has ever been found. Even the police aren't convinced the cases are connected. Spreading this rumor is irresponsible, Marlene!" Dave lectured. "Advisor, don't pay attention to her. She sees conspiracy around every corner, I swear. Stowe Strangler! That's a name from the newspapers. The police keep saying they have no evidence there's a serial killer at large." He shot his bond mate another hard look and pursed his mouth.

"Are we taking this seriously?" Murphy turned to Nate and Jossie. She kept her head down, fingers locked together in her lap.

Nate shook his head decisively. "I don't think we need to consider it. Dave's right—the girls that have gone missing have all been drug addicts and prostitutes. Definitely underprivileged young ladies. Bethany's not any of those things. Yes, there have been five or six missing girls over the past several years, but only one body was ever found—in Stowe, which is fifteen miles away from here, but it might as well be a hundred. No one in Maplefair goes to Stowe. That's too close to Snowmoon's territory. We stay here near the state park and in town. Bethany certainly wouldn't have walked that far and she doesn't have a car. Her bike is still in the shed, right, Ron?"

Bethany's father nodded.

Murphy thought about it for a moment. "Let's move along. Nobody found anything or noticed anything in particular?"

"Well, I noticed—" I began only to be cut off by Gary Planchett. He was around my age and I'd known him since my first Regional, but in all that time we'd never exchanged more than a few words. He had a bully's reputation and our personalities did not mesh well. He'd had a thing for Elena a few years back and she'd shot him down scornfully. That hadn't done anything to endear me to him because I'd been Elena's bond mate.

"How could *you* have noticed anything?" Gary aimed a derisive smirk in my direction. "You wolf just sat there and didn't do shit. Your wolf's a joke, Stanzie, we all know that. Known it for years. Had to have babysitters for every hunt at Regionals because you didn't have the slightest clue. How you ever got to be an Advisor is a mystery. Must be who you're sleeping with because it can't be on your own merits. You didn't even last in a pack of misfits for Christ's sake. So don't waste our time telling us you noticed something, because you didn't notice shit."

An awful ringing silence descended. Even the rain as it drummed against the roof seemed sucked into a vacuum.

Both Murphy and Vaughn gathered themselves to go after Gary, but I spoke first to forestall the violence that simmered in the air.

"Finished?" I met Gary's gaze and made sure not to blink or look away. "Anything more you'd like to add?"

Although he had a jeering grin, he kept silent.

"Good because we're here to talk about Bethany, not me. Nobody here is in a position to do anything about my Advisor status so there's no point discussing that. If you'd like, I can put you in contact with Councilor Allerton and I'm sure he'd be fascinated to hear what you think the proper criteria for Advisors would be.

"It's very true my wolf didn't participate in the hunt the way everyone else did, but she was participating in her own way. She was trying to find a word to describe something she smelled. Her vocabulary and sophistication can, I'm sure, in no way compare with your wolf's, Gary, but she's coming along.

"The thing is while my wolf may not have known what to call the smell, I do. Bethany is pregnant. We were told she wasn't pregnant but actually, she is. Is this a surprise just to me? Is this common knowledge or have people been covering up for her? Or maybe she's been hiding it. Why don't we discuss that? You want to start, Gary? I'd love to hear more of your thoughts, especially if they actually have anything to do with what we're here for."

"No shit," muttered Vaughn under his breath, as he shot a deadly look at Gary. Beside me, Murphy struggled with his temper. I also suspected he was trying not to laugh.

Gary's face flushed, especially because while no one but Vaughn said anything aloud, it was clear the pack stood behind me, not Gary.

This fact surprised the hell out of me. While I'd spoken to Gary, my focus and world had narrowed down just to him and me. When I'd stopped talking, I remembered there was a whole barn full of people who'd listened to every word. And apparently agreed with me.

"Advisor Newcastle, we apologize for our pack's lack of respect." Nate also shot Gary a dark look. He emphasized my title—the first time I'd ever been addressed so formally. I'd never thought of myself as Advisor

Newcastle before, but that was my title and people were supposed to call me that when I acted in official capacity and at public functions such as this one.

"She wasn't pregnant!" A cry of protest burst from Bethany's father, Ron. "Was she, Gina? How could she get pregnant? She was kept away from Cody! We were always there when they saw each other!"

Belatedly, Ron realized that Cody was in the room and leaped to his feet, while his chair clattered across the floor behind him. Fists bunched, he stalked toward Cody, who jumped up from his chair.

"I smelled it too, Ron," Gina admitted, her face tortured. "She is pregnant somehow. She must have gone behind our backs to see him. But why didn't she tell me about this?"

"'Cause she was ashamed!" Cody's chest heaved with near tears. He was a tall, lanky boy with thin wrists and a face more boyish than handsome. In a few years he'd be more masculine looking, but now he was too youthful and eerily perfect. "'Cause she was afraid if you found out we'd never get to see each other. She was scared you'd take away even the times we can see each other when somebody else is there too, watching us like we're little kids or something. In a year I'll be old enough to bond. I'm not a little kid and neither is she, but that's how you treat us."

"She's seventeen, you little bastard," Ron said with a snarl, and started after him again. A man who resembled Cody got to his feet and stepped between the two.

"Let's not have a fight yet, Ron. Maybe Cody knows where Bethany is. Maybe she's hiding because she's scared to tell. Is that what's happening, son?" The man turned to Cody with a stern expression.

No." Cody's chest hitched. "I wouldn't let things go so far if I knew where she was. I keep telling you I don't know where she is and I'm scared, Ted!"

Cody's father frowned. "But you know more about this, Cody, don't you? You need to tell us."

We all waited because it was clear Cody knew something. It was also very apparent he did not want to tell us. The pressure built up, all of it directed at him and the sheer force of wills of the entire pack aimed at him must have been intense. He had no chance against it and broke a moment later.

"She said she was going to get an abortion. So no one would ever know. I wanted to go with her but she said she wanted to do it alone. I tried to talk her out of it, tried to get her to come and tell you and Nancy if she couldn't face her own parents, but she said no. She was going to do it Thursday when Gina and Ron were at the hotel. She texted me Wednesday night saying she'd call me when she got back on Thursday. But she never called. I went over there around three in the morning and she didn't answer the door. I went back on Friday like I told you. Nothing. She's vanished, Ted. I don't know where she went or what happened." He staggered a little beneath the psychic onslaught and caught himself up with effort.

"Abortion?" Jossie lifted her head to stare at Cody. She was furious and the boy quailed at the sight of her anger. "You mean she went to some back-alley abortionist? She couldn't have gone to a reputable place like Planned Parenthood. She had no ID, no driver's license or anything. They wouldn't have taken her. She would have had to have found a place that took cash, no questions asked. Those places are filthy, Cody. And dangerous. She might have destroyed any chance she ever had of having a baby. How could you have let her do something like that? If you want to bond with somebody, you have to be responsible. What kind of a man lets his girlfriend walk alone into a filthy hellhole like that?

"You two were kept apart for a reason and this is one of them. You're not ready for a real relationship. You only had to wait three years. No one was keeping you apart so you never saw each other. We asked that you not be alone together. But you went behind our backs and saw each other anyway, despite our counsel, despite our expectations. That is not Pack behavior. Is it?"

"Nnno, ma'am." Cody trembled as he answered her. Tears swam in his eyes. Even though he'd behaved badly, my heart went out to him. I'd been young and impetuous once and I knew what it was to have adult disapproval weighing down on top of me until I felt like I couldn't breathe, couldn't blink, couldn't do a goddamn thing without someone getting pissed off about it. Being a teenager was hell.

"We need to find all the abortion clinics nearby." Murphy looked as if he might be sick. I could smell his anger too, but I wasn't sure if he was mad at Cody or Jossie or maybe the whole damn pack.

"And what?" Gina sobbed. "Get them to admit they murdered my baby? Because she has to be dead. That's the only reason why she wouldn't have come back. They're not going to admit to anything! They'll say they never saw her. They butchered her. My baby!" She burst into ugly tears and I was glad to see Ron went back to hold her.

"No." Cody's face was so white I thought he might faint. He shook his head slowly and stumbled as he tried to get to Gina to reason with her. "She can't be dead. She's just...hiding. Isn't she? Ted?" He turned for help from his father who looked grim. It was that very grimness that undid his son.

Cody's sobs half strangled him and, as he ran blindly for the door, he almost knocked his father over.

Murphy pressed the knuckles of one hand against his forehead and grimaced as if his head hurt. "Gina's right. They're not going to admit to anything. We need to check the morgues too."

A wail burst from Gina, and Ron led her out of the barn. He was trying not to cry but I didn't think he'd hold out much longer.

Although Nate did not officially end the gathering, people began to leave. Before they left, most of them folded up their chairs and propped them against the wall. No one said a word.

With a slight squeeze to my shoulder, Murphy got to his feet and followed Nate and Jossie when they left the barn.

Vaughn bolted for the bar and, despite the fact he'd just shifted and should avoid alcohol for at least twenty-four hours, found a bottle of Jack Daniels and poured himself a stiff shot.

I folded my chair, placed it carefully against the barn wall and walked out into the light spring rain.

* * * *

By the time Murphy caught up to me I was soaked. My dress was plastered to my thighs. My hair hung in damp strings around my cheeks. I walked steadily around a small apple orchard. Apple branches, thick and stunted, twisted up toward the rain as if to beg for release. A drift of white blossoms littered the ground. I was barefoot and the petals were soft against my toes and soles.

Maplefair operated a small year-round produce stand. Mostly the pack grew corn, tomatoes, strawberries and apples. This orchard was one of theirs. In the fall they'd handpick the apples, sell some in bushel bags and bring others to a cider mill to be made into cider. The last time I'd seen Jossie had been the autumn before Grey and Elena had died. The three of us had taken a foliage tour to see the eye-popping beauty of the turning leaves. We'd driven through Easton on our way to Burlington and Lake Champlain and had stopped to buy cider and apples. Jossie had been minding the stand that afternoon and, while it had been tense for a moment, Jossie and I had hugged before we'd parted and I'd planned to keep in better touch but somehow never had.

Today the white blossoms gave promise of the apple harvest to come. I doubted I'd taste any of the fruit. By fall I should be in Dublin.

As if the thought of Dublin had summoned him, Murphy fell into step beside me, and waited for me to talk first as he usually did. I looked down at my bare feet and saw that the knuckles of his right hand were raw and bloody.

"What happened to your hand?"

He gave me a slanted smile through the raindrops. "Well, I thought I would give that little bastard with the big damn mouth something real to complain about to Allerton if he wanted to talk about how to choose Advisors."

"Murphy." I heaved a tired sigh and brushed some wet hair out of my eyes. "You know Allerton doesn't want you going around punching people. Remember last time."

"You make it sound like all I do is haul off and hit people." Murphy snorted. "I'm Irish, woman, I've got a temper and that little shite had it coming."

I didn't say anything.

"You mad at me, Stanzie?"

"For hitting Gary?"

"No, for convincing you to shift when you didn't want to."

The words hung there between us, wet and heavy with the rain so that I could almost see their shapes, their individual letters. My wolf's reaction to all the things he'd tried to teach her spelled the same inevitable thing in the end. She was not the same as everyone else's.

"No, Murphy. I'm not mad. I told you what would happen, you said that was all right, and everything I told you would happen did. You said you'd stay with me and you did. Why would I be mad?"

"Well, you're something," he said. "You're out here wandering in the rain for one thing. You've got that look on your face I don't like for another."

"What look?"

"The look as if somebody kicked you in the stomach and you don't want anyone to know how much it hurts."

I looked down at the mud and apple blossoms again. Something struggled inside of me, something dark and desperate I did not want to acknowledge but was powerless to hold back.

"I really thought until today that she might have a chance at being normal, don't you see?" I tried to explain myself to him, but I knew by the confusion that spread across his face he didn't understand. "My wolf, Murphy, is never going to catch up. I failed to take into consideration the fact that while I might be evolving my wolf, everybody else was too and most of them have years and years on me. Why, I'll bet that grandmothers and grandfathers can barely tell the difference between themselves as human and themselves as wolves. Maybe that's why they don't shift all that often. What's the point except you can run on four legs and old wolves aren't that fast. Isn't that true, Murphy? That your wolf is still evolving? That every year you get one step closer to yourself in wolf form?"

A pulse beat thickly in his throat. "Maybe. But that doesn't mean..."

I held up a hand and he stopped talking. Soft spring rain dripped through the cracks of my fingers and down my bare arm.

"My wolf wants the names for everything. Everything, Murphy, and she won't move on until she has the names. Only she's never going to get them all. There are so many goddamn things in the world with names that she will never know, not if she shifted twenty times a day for the next hundred years. All she's ever going to do is discover things she doesn't know the names for and then sit there until she finds them. Not only is she never going to catch up, she'll never be halfway normal. She never has been."

There. It was out. I'd said it. Not normal.

"Stanzie," said Murphy, helpless against my onslaught of logical insight. "Don't do this to yourself, please."

"People have been calling my wolf a joke for years. I didn't even hear it half the time. I tried not to let it matter because I thought I was the lucky one. I thought they missed it all—the beauty and the fun and the sheer weightlessness of not having to think about anything, of not having to be anything but a creature alive and full of joy. She was blissfully asleep and I let her be that way. But then I woke her up and now she's a broken, defective thing and there's no joy in shifting anymore. She doesn't feel alive and connected anymore. She feels trapped and disconnected, shut out from all the names of things. She thinks if she finds the names, she'll be safe again and full of joy. But she won't ever find all the names."

Murphy bowed his head and the rain ran in rivulets down his cheeks in a parody of tears. "I did this to you. Me and my vain confidence that I could show you something better, something different."

"You didn't do it," I said gently. "I did it. I agreed to it. I knew what I was doing and knew it would change everything. I thought it was time to grow up."

"You did it to please me. You wanted to please me. I know you did. You're always wanting to please me as if just the fact you're alive and with me isn't enough. You're always trying so hard, Stanzie. And your wolf's the same damn way. It's not good enough to learn words as they come, one or two at a time, no, yours has got to know them all before she can go to the next step. As if anyone could know everything. They can't. They don't. Your wolf's not defective, Stanzie, she's stubborn. She's become self aware, don't you see that? She'll come around, you watch. Just let her get her feet underneath her. If she wants more words, let her find them. We have time. It's not a race."

"I feel so out of my league with you." I stumbled over a tree root and he caught my arm and saved me from a fall. I turned toward him, shivered in the rain and took hold of both his arms. "I am trying to run with you and with Councilor Manning and Councilor Allerton, and I can't keep up. What the hell am I doing? I'm trying to be somebody I'm not. Christ, I couldn't even keep my place in a pack of misfits with the lowest status in all of New England. And half the reason the damn pack was so low in status was because of me—because of my wolf. Now you've got me

running with Mac Tire and the Councils, and I can't do it! I can't do it!"
I shook him as if that would make him see my point but he just stared at
me.

"Your wolf is evolving. I'm proud of you for what your wolf did today,
believe it or not."

"Proud of me?" I couldn't take it in. "But I disgraced us. I was the
Council's representative and I disgraced us."

"Why? Because your wolf sat in the yard and tried to find the word
pregnant? Look what you did with it? You turned the tide and the truth
came out. You handled that little shite like a true leader. You put him in his
place without even trying. You've got to stop doubting yourself."

He looked over my shoulder and stiffened a little, my first indication
that someone approached. I heard squelching footsteps in the mud and
turned to see Vaughn huddled up against the rain in his leather jacket,
hands shoved into pockets.

"Christ, what filthy weather," he remarked to me and Murphy as he
drew close.

I wanted to ask him why he was out in it then, but Murphy spoke first.
"I'm glad you're here, mate. I'm at my wits' end with this woman. Can
you say something to make her see reason?"

Vaughn looked straight at me and said, "Gary Planchett is a giant
asshole."

I laughed, I couldn't help myself. Murphy and Vaughn did too.

At some point my laughter began to ease the terrible pressure that had
built up inside my chest ever since I'd shifted back.

"Oh, by the way, that little rat bastard's got a black eye to go with his
fat lip." Vaughn took one hand out of his pocket and displayed his bruised
knuckles.

Murphy grinned and wrapped an arm around my shoulders. We started
back to the farmhouse, the rain cold on our faces.

* * * *

Murphy and I remained on the porch while Vaughn ran inside to get
towels. Murphy held me against him, clothes clammy, and we shivered
together until Vaughn returned with Jossie. They both had towels. Heather
bounced against Jossie's hip, her face drawn with suspicion as usual.

"Oh, Stanzie, here quickly, dry off!" Jossie handed me a towel and I rubbed it through my wet, stringy hair while Murphy did the same beside me. "I'll run you a bath."

"No, I just want to sit here for a while." I collapsed into one of the rocking chairs, and my dress stuck to my body like a second skin. As the rain penetrated, it had become see-through and I wore nothing beneath. I didn't care. I began to rock as I toweled my hair. So much had happened to me today. So much had battered at me. I felt like a toy being shaken around, chomped down hard in the jaws of a very big, very excited dog.

Murphy and Vaughn disappeared inside to bathe and change.

Jossie sat in the rocker next to mine and began to nurse Heather as she watched me, her face furrowed with worry.

"Nate's gone with some of the others to draw up a list of abortion clinics and make a few calls." For some reason Jossie didn't like the silence, so she filled it with words. I barely listened. Instead I concentrated on the squeak of the rocking chairs, the steady rhythm of the rain against the roof and the faint sucking sounds as Heather nursed. "I've got water boiling on the stove. I'm making spaghetti tonight. Do you like spaghetti?"

An answer was required—I realized this belatedly—and I stopped toweling my hair and feeling sorry for myself so I could look at her. She was almost in tears. I wiped rain from my face. "Spaghetti's fine."

"Would you watch Heather for me while I put the pasta and sauce on?" Jossie buttoned up her blouse and held Heather out to me. A gesture of trust and friendship.

"I'm soaking wet," I protested as Heather let out a prodigious burp that made Jossie smile. I laughed a little too and put a towel across my lap and another over my chest and shoulders so the baby wouldn't get as soaked as me.

"There's a book on the table. You can read it to her. She likes to listen to stories before she falls asleep. It'll be her bed time soon."

Heather was bundled in a pink sleeper with yellow capering ducks and blue cavorting bunnies. As I took her warm weight into my arms I could smell the baby shampoo in her hair.

She stiffened a little and I thought she might cry, but instead she settled into the crook of my arm and looked up at my face. Her expression was solemn and wary. When Jossie went inside, her brown eyes followed her mother's form and her small mouth screwed up as she prepared to scream in protest. For an instant I was reminded of the way Vaughn's mouth had looked as he'd struggled against tears after nightmares of Callie and Peter. People were so vulnerable when they cried.

"Don't cry." I bounced her a little against my body. Her head craned as she sought out my eyes with hers and we regarded each other for a moment.

"Want to hear a story?" I picked up the book on the table and began to read *The Little Prince* aloud to her.

At the sound of my voice she relaxed and a soft little smile tugged at the corners of her mouth. Apparently she approved.

As I continued to read, her eyelids drooped. She fought against sleep and once she managed to open her eyes as wide as they could go. Her little hand reached up and she touched my cheek as if to tell me she liked me or maybe that she liked the story.

I choked up for a moment, convinced I was going to be undone by the touch of a baby girl's hand but I managed to keep reading somehow. Her eyelids lowered again and, this time, stayed closed. A small sigh escaped her as she shifted in my arms. Her head dropped to the side as she surrendered to sleep.

I shut the book and as I set it aside on the table, I noticed Murphy stood in the doorway. He'd listened to me read.

"Can I hold her?" He stepped down onto the porch, his expression wistful. Careful not to wake her, I held her out and he took her gently into his arms. "Why don't you go take a bath, Stanzie?"

As I stood, he sat on the glider and began to rock it back and forth.

I went inside, and instead of a bath, I took a hot shower. As I lifted my face into the rushing water, I tried to erase the look on Murphy's face as he'd held the baby. It was impossible. As impossible as it would be for me to ever give him one.

* * * *

Nate was the last one to the dinner table, but I only beat him there by five minutes. Just enough time to put cheese on my spaghetti, pour myself red wine and take the first bite.

His face was somber. Instead of wine, he got himself a beer and slumped heavily in the chair next to Jossie's. We ate at the kitchen table, which was by a bay window that overlooked the back garden and the apple orchard beyond it. Both were shrouded in darkness and rain.

Nate's Adam's apple bobbed as he drank the beer in one long, unending swallow. I handed Murphy the bowl of grated cheese and he took it, but he watched Nate more than the dish.

Vaughn sat at the end of the table and broke off a piece of garlic bread from the loaf in the basket. He didn't seem to taste it, but he chewed and swallowed methodically.

"Nothing yet," Nate reported. He got up for another bottle of beer, and when he opened the refrigerator, bottles clinked together on the shelves in the door. Light spilled out onto the red tiled floor and his brown work boots. The toes were scuffed and streaked with fresh mud and bits of sawdust.

After he opened the bottle, he returned to the table as Jossie filled his plate with steaming spaghetti. For a moment the pasta looked like twisting entrails and I lost my appetite. I concentrated on my wine instead.

"Tomorrow we'll take a ride out to some of these places." Nate collapsed back into his chair and once again I noticed how tall he was, even slouched. "What a goddamn mess."

"What are you going to do about Cody?" I asked. Nate stared at me, a forkful of spaghetti halfway to his mouth. Vaughn drew back the hand he'd reached out for the bread on his plate. Murphy continued to eat, but his eyes were alert and wary.

Jossie set her wine glass down. Color burned in her pale cheeks and gave her the look of a convalescing fever patient just before a brutal relapse. "I don't want him in this pack."

"Exile?" Vaughn pushed the bread to the edge of his plate and sat back. Like me, he seemed to have lost his appetite.

"Yes." Jossie gulped at her wine then poured more, as her hand shook with what I assumed was rage. She wouldn't look directly at Vaughn. She hadn't the entire time we'd been there.

"The Pack isn't in the habit of tossing children out into the street like garbage, Jocelyn." Murphy's voice was cool, but his eyes were hot.

"He's nineteen. Hardly a child, Liam."

"He won't be of age until twenty. That's Pack law. Until then he's technically a child. You can't throw him out."

"You don't want to wait until we find Bethany, Joss?" Nate struggled to sound reasonable and not argumentative, but I could tell he was upset.

"We aren't going to find Bethany. If we do find her, she'll be dead."

"And that won't be punishment enough for the lad?" Murphy asked. "It's not as if he killed her himself, Jossie."

"He might as well have!" Jossie yelled. She pressed her lips together tightly and when she had control again she said, "He had the responsibility to speak up if he couldn't stop her. He had the responsibility not to get her pregnant in the first place. Did he ever listen even one time to the lectures about birth control? About how only Alphas are allowed to have children in a pack? He was old enough to get her pregnant. He was old enough to prevent it. He has to pay."

"That's going to make it better?" Murphy set his fork down and stared at her across the expanse of the table. Outside the rain beat on the rooftop and lashed against the windowpanes. A ghostly blur of apple trees faded in and out as the moon was obscured by the fast-moving storm clouds. '

"Liam, this isn't your pack!"

"I know that, but as an Advisor, I think I have an obligation to speak."

"On his behalf? The Council speaks on the behalf of people who screw up? Who betray us and go against our laws?" Jossie gulped more wine and tears glistened in her eyes.

"I don't speak for the Council." Murphy was frustrated, but kept his voice even. "I'm speaking as an Advisor to the Council and as a former Alpha who has faced a few issues like this. I'm trying to help you, believe it or not."

Jossie snorted and splashed more wine into her glass. Vaughn rubbed the skin between his eyes as if his head hurt.

"What kind of an Alpha were you if you would defend someone like Cody?"

"A compassionate one, I hope," said Murphy.

"What would you do, Stanzie? You brought this up. Tell me what you'd do." Jossie turned to me, her eyes accusatory.

"I'm not a big fan of exile, Jossie." I pushed my wine glass away and met her gaze.

For a moment I debated whether to continue and tell her what I thought. Oh, to hell with it. "I'd send him to college. You want him away from the pack, you want him to pay, send him to college so he can learn a profession, something that would benefit the pack. He can pay you back that way. Let him be a doctor or learn agricultural management. I'll bet your little orchards and corn fields don't pull in much, but maybe if someone in the pack had some real business management skills, you'd stop losing your land bit by bit every year, and maybe even expand."

"Oh, yeah, right. That's what we should do. Send the little bastard to college. Reward him for killing Bethany. Only the smartest and the most deserving of us go to college, Stanzie. You know what hoops we have to jump through to get someone Pack into college—especially if they've been homeschooled and haven't gone through a curriculum accredited by the Others. Besides, every spare penny I have goes back into this farmhouse and the little orchards and cornfields you refer to so disdainfully. I didn't get to go to college. Neither did Nate and he's fourth generation of the founding duo of this pack. Why should Cody go? Are you going pay for him?"

"If this were my pack, yes, I would," I said. "If you're asking for a donation, sure, I'll give you one."

"No, you won't. I'm not taking charity from you or anyone," Jossie yelled. "What is it with you? I'm not doing anything wrong here! What's the matter? Aren't the old ways good enough for you anymore?"

My heart gave a violent leap as I tried not to give away how much her words had jolted me.

"You're not quite a grandmother yet, Jossie," I remarked. Underneath the table Murphy put one hand on my thigh and squeezed a gentle warning. We both watched her reaction and Nate's. Could they possibly be a part of the conspiracy? Her alone? I didn't want to think about my friend being a part of it but sometimes people changed or weren't who I'd thought they were.

Jossie bit her lip and the guilt that spread across her face didn't seem to have anything to do with the conspiracy. "I'm sorry I'm yelling at you. I'm just...I'm so upset." She reached out for her wine glass, found it empty and looked ready to burst into tears. "I know some members of our pack have behaved despicably toward you and here I am doing the same thing. You're an Advisor and I'm treating you with no respect. I'm sorry."

"Joss, we're friends. You can yell at your friends sometimes, it's okay." I reached across the table to put my hand on hers and she gulped back tears.

"College isn't a bad idea." Nate twirled some spaghetti around the tines of his fork and chewed thoughtfully for a moment.

"I doubt the boy has the grades or the potential for med school, but that's not a bad idea about business management, Stanzie. Speaking of grandmothers, there's a couple that will kick and scream about that kind of major, but it's time our pack embraced the century we actually live in. It's a pity. Bethany was the brains of that duo. She could have been a doctor."

"Why do you talk like she's dead? Like it's a done deal?" Vaughn demanded. "Maybe she's in a hospital somewhere or even a motel, just trying to recuperate."

I wondered how she could have gotten to any of these places on foot. She hadn't taken her bike, and she didn't have a driver's license. Could she have hitchhiked? What kind of a person hitchhiked to an abortion clinic? That made no sense. Had Cody driven her and lied about it? Was he lying still about not knowing what really had happened?

"What are the chances of finding her alive after all this time?" Nate wiped his mouth with a napkin and assumed a mournful expression I found somewhat lacking, as if he had to try too hard to look that way. I thought he might be more intrigued with the idea of sending Cody to college. His mind was so quick—it leaped from one thought to the next just the same way he could not sit still for longer than three minutes. As if on cue, he shoved back his chair and rose to his feet.

"I'll get us some more beer from down cellar." He moved for the cellar door, which was just beyond the sink.

"If Bethany was so smart, why the hell would she go to some fucking shady clinic instead of a grandmother? Grandmothers can keep their damn mouths shut," muttered Vaughn. Exactly what I'd been thinking myself.

"If she'd gone to a grandmother in Maplefair, that grandmother would have spoken up. She wouldn't have let us flounder around like this," Jossie protested. "There's keeping your mouth shut to do someone a favor and then there's taking it to an absurdity."

Their eyes met and they stared at each other, as if trapped, neither one able to be the first to look away.

When Nate kicked open the cellar door, hands full of beer bottles, Jossie and Vaughn both jerked and tore their gazes away from each other as if caught in a guilty act.

Nate's grin did not falter, but I'm pretty sure he noticed.

Packs could be such festering pits of buried secrets.

* * * *

The continuous tap of the rain on the tin roof of the farmhouse should have been a soothing sound, but instead it added to a growing list of reasons why I couldn't fall asleep. I tossed and turned that night and thought about Bethany—a girl I'd never met.

Not much made sense about her story. To sneak around behind her parents' backs to be with her boyfriend was believable, but how she handled her pregnancy wasn't. Why hadn't she allowed Cody to drive her? She, like most of the pack, lived within a five-mile stretch of country road far away from the highway and even farther from any town big enough to have a seedy abortion clinic. How the hell had she gotten there?

I kept coming back to hitchhiking. Dangerous. Had we been too hasty to dismiss the idea of the Stowe Strangler—that amorphous entity that might or might not exist? Girls who hitched frequently got into bad trouble. Killing trouble. But where was her body then? Had she really vanished without a trace? Just after the grandfather clock in the downstairs foyer struck midnight, Murphy got tired of my constant thrashing around in the bed. He rolled over and pinned me to the mattress with his weight.

"Can't sleep?" I had to estimate where his mouth was from the sound of his voice. The darkness around us was intense because the blinds were drawn across the windows and no light from the barn seeped through the cracks. "I think I can help you out with that dilemma." Though I could not see his mouth, I could feel his erection hard against me.

"Murphy," I remonstrated, but then he figured out where my mouth was and kissed me. I ran my fingers through his hair and felt him push my nightgown up with one hand so he could explore my body. The moment I spread my legs, he was inside me—so hot and hard my breath caught in my throat. I murmured his name again and marveled about how damn good he felt.

I tried to be as quiet as I could so as not to wake Vaughn across the hall. We rolled so I was on top. I gripped the iron rails of the headboard and leaned down to kiss him, my hair a curtain around our faces.

"Stanzie," he whispered and I moved faster, harder. He raked his nails down my back as I shuddered. I wanted to tell him I loved him, but I caught the words back. Someday I would tell him, but not now. Tonight was for silent connection.

The orgasm caught me by surprise—I'd been so wrapped up in Murphy's pleasure I hadn't realized how close I was. As he felt my body convulse, he grabbed my hips so he could grind hard into me, then he came too. We held each other in the darkness and all my previous frustrated thoughts slipped away as little by little I lost the battle against sleep.

Chapter 4

The next morning at breakfast, we all decided on a plan of action for the day. Murphy and Vaughn took the abortion clinics and motels in towns and cities between Easton and the Lake Champlain area, while Nate worked his way back to the New Hampshire border in the other direction.

My job was to call local hospitals and morgues to ask whether a girl fitting Bethany's description had been brought in over the past four days. The list was not very extensive.

Jossie was command central with instructions to call everyone in if Bethany was found.

I took my cellphone out onto the porch to make my calls. Jossie kept hers in a pocket as she hung out laundry and weeded the gardens, while Heather amused herself in her playpen, which was set up in the grass near the clothesline.

It was a beautiful day. All the rain had cleared up overnight and the sound of the birds competed with the voices on the other end of my phone as I fruitlessly searched for Bethany.

The entire time things nagged at me. Murphy, Vaughn and Nate were driving all the way to Lake Champlain and New Hampshire—fifty miles at least in either direction—and Bethany hadn't had a car or even a bike. I'd brought that up at breakfast but they seemed to believe she'd hitched. When I'd pointed out hitchhiking was dangerous and that maybe the Stowe Strangler did figure into the picture, Jossie had gotten so upset she'd rushed from the table and slammed outside onto the front porch.

Nate had flung me an impatient glance before he followed.

"What the hell?" I'd defended myself to Murphy and Vaughn, who both looked sick. "It doesn't make sense. None of this makes any sense. What are we supposed to do? Pretend the Stowe Strangler doesn't exist?"

"Maybe he doesn't, Stanzie," Vaughn had pointed out. "Only one body's been found. The other girls are just missing. They could be runaways, anything. They don't have to have been killed by the same guy. Don't complicate things. Marlene Crandall is a huge gossip—she's been that way back to even when I was a kid." His eyes flickered a little but he did not acknowledge she had been his adoptive mother.

"Well, then," I'd backtracked, "maybe not the Stowe Strangler, just some random killer. Someone who gave her a ride, wanted some sort of payment, and things got out of hand when she resisted. It's happened before. She could have been hit by a car and left for dead."

"We haven't found her. And, anyway, you're calling the hospitals and morgues. If something like that happened, you're covering it."

"If her body's not rotting in a ditch somewhere," I'd said, just as Nate and Jossie walked back into the kitchen. Jossie had turned right around again and Nate had directed another frustrated look at me.

"I'm being realistic," I'd insisted.

"Maybe you could try to be a little less graphic," Murphy had suggested.

I'd been pissed off when he'd driven away in the Prelude. I hadn't hugged him goodbye, just said it to him from the rocker on the front porch where I'd been sulking when he, Nate and Vaughn had left. Jossie had been in the laundry room avoiding me—something she did all morning long.

Murphy had given me an exasperated look before he'd followed Vaughn down the front steps and gotten into the Prelude.

Nate hadn't even spared me a glance before taking off in the dusty black Explorer.

"You can all go to hell," I'd muttered, and rocked so hard hair flew into my eyes.

Two and a half hours later, I was fed up with calling hospitals and being ignored by Jossie. I'd volunteered to help hang out the laundry but she'd declined my offer and banged out the porch door as she'd trailed the scent of laundry detergent and wet cotton in her wake.

I couldn't get Bethany and the things I knew about her out of my head. Nate's observation that Bethany was the smart one of the duo. No driver's license. Bike left in the back shed. Shame at being pregnant and wanting to keep it a secret. Nate on his motorcycle off to check his grandmother's windows before the storm.

Everyone presumed that because Bethany was missing and the whole pack knew it and was looking for her, that she must not have confided in anyone who belonged to Maplefair. Everyone was looking fifty miles in every direction, but what if she was hidden in plain sight right here?

I got out of the rocker and pushed open the screen door. Jossie was around the corner of the farmhouse down on her hands and knees as she weeded a flowerbed. Heather cooed over the stuffed bunny clutched between her chubby fingers. That bunny made me think of the one with the worn fur and crooked ear among Bethany's belongings the day before. It made me doubly determined to do something that yielded results. My wolf might not be normal, but in human form I knew how to be logical and figure things out.

The somnolent drone of honeybees filled my ears as I leaped down the front porch steps onto the flagstone path leading to the dirt drive. I didn't even say goodbye or bother to tell Jossie where I was going.

My ponytail bounced against the back of my neck as I marched down the driveway toward the road.

Soaring pine trees and new-leafed maples lined the blacktop on either side broken only by the occasional field or apple orchard. Almost everyone in Maplefair lived along this road but they could hardly be called neighbors in the sense I was used to the term. Acres of trees separated most properties. All backed into the state park, which provided easy access when people wanted to shift.

Grandmother Emma, Nate's great-grandmother, lived two miles from the farmhouse. In a car it would have taken me less than five minutes to traverse the distance. On foot it took me over half an hour. It would have taken me less time, but I checked out the ditches on either side of the road to look for her crumpled body—victim of a possible hit and run. Part of me knew that was stupid because people of Maplefair lived up and down the road and traveled it daily. I would have presumed it had been searched at least once already. Sometimes the obvious was overlooked and it always paid to be thorough. I didn't find her. No splashes of blood or strips of clothing or even a discarded shoe. I hadn't really expected anything different.

The spring rain had brought on an energetic burst of growth and color. Wildflowers glowed in gem-like splendor against the luscious green of new-growth grass. Birch, oak and maple trees had filled out overnight—their leaves that specific shade of light green found only in spring. Birds sang intricate songs to attract potential mates and high above me the amazing blue sky was dotted with spun-sugar white clouds. My wolf stirred within me. These were her scents. This was her playground. I didn't want to, but I pushed her down inside me as far as she would go and continued looking in the ditches for Bethany's body—a gruesome counterpoint to the beauty of the day.

Grandmother Emma's mailbox was bright blue. I looked inside for mail I might bring to her, but the box was empty. I scolded myself—Grandmother Emma probably didn't get mail. She was Pack and old. No doubt everything would be covered by the Alphas and sent to them.

Fresh tire tracks imprinted the muddy expanse of the dirt driveway. I carefully avoided numerous mud puddles—my Skechers were new—and worked my way the quarter mile or so to the front yard. Bright green grass had been mowed to a uniform height in the recent past but the rain had encouraged a riot among the blades and they sprouted in uneven spurts for the sky. A white cinderblock house with a brick foundation squatted at the edge of the forest. Trees had been allowed to take over the back yard. Instead of flower beds, a series of lilac bushes not yet in bloom held pride of place along the edge of the front porch.

A small woodshed crouched to the right of the house separated by the dirt driveway.

No birds chirped in the trees that surrounded the house and woodshed. I didn't see them hopping among the blades of damp grass in the search for insects. It was nearly noon so perhaps they were avoiding the sun, but it was a mild April day, not high summer.

The house was closed up tightly—not an open window in sight. Old-fashioned curtains, fringed with pom-poms, were drawn, so they blocked out the light and prevented anyone from seeing in. It was a lonely place. Uneasy thoughts bubbled up in my head and sent tingles of apprehension down my spine. I didn't understand why. It was just a house. Sometimes old people gave up hope and barricaded themselves from the world. Maybe Grandmother Emma was like that. I would have thought she might have had a garden or even a clothesline, but apart from the grass and the woodshed, the yard was empty.

Concrete steps with damp patches from the rain led up to a screened porch door. I gave a tentative push and it squealed open. Usually the creak of a screen door was a comforting sound that made me think of dusky summer nights and cool mornings spent in a rocker, but this door made a discordant near shriek that set my teeth on edge.

The porch was empty except for a small white plastic garbage bag carefully tied shut. Even so, three flies buzzed around the edges—the only sign of life so far.

The front door was an uncompromising slate gray with a cloudy glass window inserted at eye level. A shade had been fastened to the frame from the inside and was pulled down so I couldn't see into what I presumed would be the living room or maybe the kitchen.

I knocked and listened intently. I heard nothing. It was noon on a Tuesday morning. Old people rarely slept late. She ought to be up and about but there were no shuffling sounds of someone behind the door. No television. No music.

Maybe she wasn't home, but that made no sense because according to Jossie, Emma never went out. Nate brought her groceries and all the things she needed. The garbage on the porch attested to the fact someone was there. It smelled, but not as if it had been spoiling there for days.

"Grandmother Emma, please answer the door." I knocked again, harder. "My name is Constance Newcastle. I want to talk to you about Bethany Dillon. I think maybe she might have come here to ask your help. I'm from the Great Council. I'm an Advisor. It's all right for you to answer the door, I'm Pack."

Nothing. I rattled the door but it was locked, so I went outside and circled the house to see if the back door might be open. On my way, I passed by the edge of the woodshed and gave it a quick glance.

Just beyond the building, parked so that no one could see it from the drive unless they made a determined effort to walk to the back of the house, was a dusty black Explorer. Nate and Jossie's car.

"You're not supposed to be here," I whispered aloud although there was no one to hear me. The tingles of apprehension intensified, making the backs of my ankles and the soles of my feet itch to run.

I should leave. But I didn't. *You're supposed to be halfway to New Hampshire, Nate.*

I moved toward the Explorer and talked aloud as if I tried to convince myself of something. "Maybe you stopped to check on Grandmother Emma. But if you're inside the house, why didn't you answer the door? Where are you?"

I prowled around the Explorer and when I got to the passenger side I saw the open door to the woodshed. It wasn't opened much more than a crack, but it was enough to attract my attention.

Alarm bells jangled in my head and along my spinal column, but I ignored them as I cautiously pushed open the door. It gave under the tentative pressure of my fingers and I stepped into the gloom of a small, cement-floored room. Sawdust was sprinkled across the floor and a sawhorse lurked in one corner while an old ladder was propped in another. A chainsaw hung on the wall opposite a stack of wood.

So Nate comes here to cut wood for his grandmother's wood stove. There was nothing wrong with that. But it felt wrong somehow. I remembered Nate's boots the night before had been streaked with mud and bits of sawdust. The mud was understandable—the driveway was nothing but mud. But why sawdust? Why would he have come into the woodshed? It was April and mild. There was no need for firewood in the weather we'd been experiencing this week.

A metal bookcase had been shoved against the wall near the chainsaw. There were tools on the shelves, not books. The dust on the floor near the bookcase was disturbed, as if the bookcase had been shoved a few inches to the left. I puzzled over this for a moment, then stepped to the bookcase and pushed. Tools rattled against the metal shelves. A wrench fell to the floor and narrowly missed my foot.

After I shifted the bookcase, I stepped back and my heart jackhammered so fast I felt lightheaded.

On the floor precisely where the bookcase had rested was a trap door. It had been deliberately hidden by the bookcase. Concealed like a dirty secret.

You should leave now, Constance. No one knows where you are. Go get Jossie at least. Call Murphy.

I realized I'd left my cellphone on the farmhouse porch a split second before the sunlight disappeared.

* * * *

Nate Carver stood four feet behind me. He was not smiling. The sunshine from the open door streamed around the outline of his body and created a strange sort of halo effect. Fear, bright and copper sour, flooded into my mouth and sizzled through my veins. But why should I be afraid of Nate? Was it his expression? His balled-up fists and coiled muscles as if he prepared to spring?

I crossed my arms over my chest and heard my heart slam against my ribcage so hard I knew he could hear it too.

"What are you doing here, Stanzie?" The way he said my name sent a shiver of dread down my spine. His gaze slid to the trap door and his big fists clenched tighter. I had nowhere to go, no place to run. But why did I want to run away from Nate?

"Smart girls don't hitchhike to abortion clinics in the bad parts of town, Nate. They go to the grandmothers in the pack. She came here, didn't she? Looking for Grandmother Emma? And something happened to her. Is Bethany down there in the root cellar? Are you covering up for your grandmother?"

His laugh sent chills down my spine. More foul-tasting spit coated my mouth. Sweat trickled down my back even though it was not hot in the woodshed.

"Where's Bethany?"

"You really want to know? You want to see her?" Nate advanced one step closer to me and I had nowhere to go so I held my ground even though I desperately wanted to run.

"I want to go call Murphy." I tried to stall him, but he kept coming, one slow step at a time.

"He'd never get here in time. He's halfway to the Canadian border by now. Goddamn Advisors, nosing into people's private business. You should have gone with him, Stanzie."

"Someone had to call the hospitals and the morgues."

"Yeah? Then why are you here? You're here because you're nosy." Nate was now three feet away from me and nearly close enough to reach out for me.

"Are you helping Grandmother Emma cover up something bad, Nate?" I whispered and he lunged for me.

Instead of cringing backward or trying to dodge to the side, I ducked down. His fist plowed through the air where my head had been and threw him off balance. I scrabbled in the dust for the wrench that had fallen from the shelf when I'd moved the metal bookcase.

He staggered against me, half falling over me. As he hit the wall, I closed my fingers around the wrench handle. By the time he managed to right himself, I was back on my feet and waved the wrench around. I hoped like hell he'd keep away from me long enough so I could escape.

I had no coherent idea what I was going to do. All I wanted was to run even though I knew he could run faster. He was stronger too. A part of me was so shocked that an Alpha would act like this, I was nearly paralyzed.

You should probably hit him with the wrench, Constance. Only, I didn't want to hurt him. I didn't want to be violent. I didn't want to act against an Alpha. I just wanted to get away.

"Put the wrench down, Stanzie. I'm not going to hurt you." Nate's mouth moved into a dreadful caricature of a real smile and a freezing flush of cold dismay swept over me as I estimated the distance to the door.

"You just tried to hit me." Maybe reasoning with a psychopath was not the best use of my limited resources. The idea that he was trying to distract me also crossed my mind. I was so not about to be psyched out by a lunatic. Even if he was an Alpha. Fuck that.

"Put the wrench down and I'll explain everything," Nate promised.

Fat fucking chance.

"You can explain it to me right now and then maybe I'll put it down." There was no way in hell anything he could say would make me put the wrench down, but he didn't need to know that.

"Put the fucking wrench down!" he shouted at me, spittle flying from his lips. He was so close to me droplets spattered down on my wrist and forearm. "You fucking bitch! Put it down!"

The volume of his voice nearly deafened me and I cringed despite myself.

"You won't get away with any of this. If you do anything to me, Murphy will find out and he'll fucking kill you!"

Nate just laughed, sending more chills down my spine.

"I'll fix him and that goddamn Pelletier too. Who does Vaughn think he is coming back to this pack like nothing ever happened? Making people remember why he left. I don't need this shit right now, Stanzie. Jossie's such an idiot. She goes and gets together with him at the Regional Great Hunt two years ago. I can do my fucking math well enough to know that kid is not my daughter. But have I said anything? I'm prepared to bring her up as my kid. I'm a decent guy. I'll do that, but those idiots think they can hide it from me? From *me*? And then he shows up on my doorstep like he never fucked me over? I see the way he looks at my bond mate. I see the way she looks at him too. What do they think? I'm going to let him make a triad with us just because he's Heather's biological father? No fucking way, Stanzie.

"Bullshit comes in threes, doesn't it? First that stupid little bitch comes here at the worst possible time so I have to take care of her. Then that goddamn bastard, Vaughn, shows up and now I've got you here in my woodshed. This is my private place! *Mine!*" Nate's voice rose to a roar and he lunged at me again despite the wrench.

All qualms about hitting him with it had vanished when he threatened Murphy and Vaughn. I was not going to let him hurt either one.

I swung with all my might and aimed for Nate's contorted, rage-filled face, only he put up an arm and I hit that instead. I'm sure it hurt, but it didn't stop him from barreling into me.

I slammed against the woodpile, my feet went out from under me and the wrench flew into a corner. The back of my head smashed into the top layer of wood. Everything exploded into razor-sharp stars with teeth that bit and swallowed my consciousness whole.

* * * *

Wracking sobs roused me from the void. Utter darkness met my eyes and I blinked as I tried to orient myself. Was I blind? Had something bad been done to my eyes? After a panicked moment I decided I was not blind. There was no light in the room—wherever I was. I suspected I might be in the root cellar beneath the woodshed, but I had no way of verifying that.

It stank. Piss, shit and blood, and beneath it all pain and absolute terror. The combination turned my already queasy stomach.

The back of my skull was on fire with pain that radiated outward and made movement impossible. Not that I could move much. It wasn't long after I decided I wasn't blind that I came to the horrible conclusion that I was chained. Wrists and ankles were secured to some sort of metal gurney. No mattress—nothing soft beneath me—not even a pillow. I was cold because I was also naked. Why the hell was I naked? Why was I chained? What the fuck was going on?

It wasn't me sobbing. That took a while to penetrate. I was disoriented and my thought process was extremely slow. After the first moment of panic, I couldn't even muster fear because of the pain in my head. I was numb emotionally.

"Bethany? Is that you?" My voice was little more than a croak. A flash of pride floated through my mind because I was able to reason out that the sobs could be her. That I even *remembered* her seemed an epic achievement.

The sobs halted for a moment and chains rattled. If it was Bethany crying, she was chained too. Just like me.

"Yuh...yes. Who are you?" Bethany sounded so scared my mental fog began to dissipate and be replaced by growing outrage. I'm pretty sure it took me a long time to be able to formulate my answer. Because all at once even though I could remember Bethany, I could not remember me. It was the fucking scariest moment of my life. Thankfully it passed and a rush of memory brought me back to myself.

"My name is Stanzie. Constance Newcastle. I'm an Advisor to Councilor Jason Allerton of the Great Council. Are you hurt badly?"

"The Great Council's looking for me? They know I'm missing?" Hope made Bethany's voice crack.

"Everyone's looking for you, Bethany." *Right now I hope they're looking a little closer to home than Canada.* With my memory of myself, I also remembered Murphy and Vaughn and where they were, which was probably a long, long way from here. My stomach clenched and, for a moment, I thought I might piss myself.

"I've been here so long. I don't know how long because there's no sun. I can't tell when it's day or night anymore."

"Are you hurt?" *Dumb question, Constance.*

"Yeah. I don't know how bad. He burns me sometimes. Beats me. Sometimes it hurts when I breathe deep. Is that a broken rib maybe? I don't know." She started to cry again helplessly.

Jesus Christ. Helpless terror flooded through me. *Jesus fucking Christ.*

I'd thought the bastard had helped his great-grandmother cover up a botched abortion, but what the fuck was this shit?

"Why is he doing this? What happened? How did you get here?" The questions tumbled out of my mouth like a group of acrobats in a circus of horror.

"I came here because..." I could hear her shame. Incredible that she could still feel shame after everything she'd been put through. Goddamn that bastard, Nate.

I struggled to keep my voice gentle when I talked to her. She didn't need me to panic and scream at her. I needed to stay calm and focused. If only so I didn't make it worse for her than it already was.

"Because you're pregnant. You wanted Grandmother Emma to help you." I prompted.

"Cody told." Bethany's tears choked her and I cursed myself. "I know we were wrong but—"

"Bethany, you are not to worry about getting pregnant. It happens. It doesn't matter, and no one is angry at you. Tell me what happened and how you got here. I need to figure out where we are and how the hell to get out of here."

Incredulous laughter filled the darkness and I cringed against it. She'd given up hope and I felt my own confidence, which was not that fucking high, plummet in response.

"You can't get out of here. How? He chained you up the same way he chained me. I saw him do it. He said you're too old for his taste but he'll still use you like he uses me. So he's going to do the same things to you he does to me. And neither one of us are good as the Other girls!" Bethany's terror increased the more she talked until at the end she screamed the words.

My own fear ramped up and I shoved it back down the same way I'd thrust down my wolf on the walk here. I would deal with fear later. I had no time for it right now. At least that's what I had to convince myself of so I wouldn't lose my fucking mind.

"Other girls? What are you talking about?"

"The Others!" Bethany could barely talk through her strangled sobs. "When I came here on Thursday morning to talk to Grandmother Emma! I saw him! I saw him with the plastic garbage bag. He was carrying it from the woodshed. He didn't see the rip and her...her arm...it was dangling. And there was blood and I didn't know what to do. He was smiling at me like he was taking out Grandmother Emma's trash or something. Until he saw my face and then he looked and saw the arm. That's when he came after me. And he told me he was going to do me what he did to that Other girl. And the ones before her. He was mad about that girl they found strangled in Stowe. He didn't kill her but because there's been missing girls, the newspaper started saying there was a serial killer. And there is! Him! But he didn't kill that girl. Not the one they found." She giggled, but it was anything but a good sound. My blood ran cold. "Isn't that funny, Stanzie? That's your name, right?"

At first I couldn't process it. Nate? The Stowe Strangler? A serial killer? But he was Alpha! My mind reeled. I pictured the sawhorse and the chainsaw in the woodshed. Oh God. Did he dismember the bodies? Is that how he fit them into a trash bag? Did he just throw them out? How could they go undiscovered if he threw them out? He must bury them somewhere. This was his killing ground and he must bury his victims here. Would Bethany and I be among them? But I didn't want to die. I didn't want to be tortured and dismembered and buried in the backyard.

Why had no one ever found the burial ground during a hunt? Pack were all through the forest here. How could they not come across it?

Stanzie, get a fucking grip, I lectured myself before I completely lost it and started screaming. Once I started doing that, I doubted I would be able to stop until my goddamn throat burst.

I thought of other serial killers I'd read about. Some of them buried the bodies in cellars. Grandmother Emma's house had a cellar. Maybe they were down there. No one visited Grandmother Emma but him. The feud had taken care of that. Emma had shut herself off from the pack because of some stupid pack argument that had taken place years ago. Maybe she'd wanted to make amends, only her grandson, the only one in her family who still spoke to her, prevented her. Maybe he told her stories, kept the feud alive in her mind. But how could she not know about the bodies in her cellar? About how her great-grandson used her property to kill young runaways and teen prostitutes? Was she in on it? Could she be? Or was she a prisoner in her own home? Holy shit, this was bad. This was really, really fucking bad.

Panic clawed at my head much the same way my wolf clawed at her head to dislodge the anger when she couldn't find a word. What the hell was I going to do? What could I do?

I jerked my wrists against the chains but they were securely fastened to the gurney beneath me. I tugged at the restraints but they would not slide over my wrist bones. In fact they were too tight and beginning to really hurt. My ankles were similarly restrained only I could not reach them with my hands to try to pry them off. I couldn't sit up all the way because the chains weren't long enough.

"It's no use," croaked Bethany. "We're going to die, Stanzie. Me first because I'm weak and he's had me longer. He's bored with me. He hurts me. He'll hurt you."

"Does he rape you?" I asked. The thought of that lunatic bastard inside me made me want to puke. I wished I hadn't asked her the second after the words flew out of my mouth. I'm always saying shit before I think first. Apparently, I would go, dismembered, to my grave not able to keep my goddamn thoughts from tumbling out of my brain straight onto my tongue like gushing water out of a faucet.

"Nuh...not with...I mean he does it with *things*. Like a bottle, I think. Something hard that hurts. But he won't use his dick because he doesn't want me to be able to shift."

Her answer appalled me.

"Why not? What difference would that make? You can only stay shifted a few hours," I muttered, but a split-second later it hit me. The restraints. My wolf's legs and paws were smaller than my wrists and hands. Definitely smaller than my ankles and feet.

I stared into the darkness. Crazy hope soared through me. If I shifted, I would be free of the chains. Giddy, violent relief surged through me and I nearly laughed aloud. If I didn't rein myself in, I'd be hysterical in a moment. How the hell had this poor girl done it for five days? I hadn't been here longer than five hours and I was already fucking losing my shit.

Think, Stanzie, think. Had Nate heard me and Murphy last night? If he'd heard us making love, he'd stay away for at least forty-eight hours. I wanted to believe that Murphy would find me before then, but what if he didn't? If Nate did come back within forty-eight hours, I could shift and run free to get Murphy. If Nate got in my way, I could hurt him badly enough so he wouldn't be able to hurt me. Disable him long enough to get help. I would probably have to do that anyway so he wouldn't hurt Bethany—turn on her in a rage after I escaped.

I gulped. Pack did not attack Pack, especially not in wolf form. It was against everything we'd ever been taught. I would have to hope my wolf could circumvent years and years of indoctrination. I almost thought it was bred into us that we couldn't attack in wolf form. I couldn't remember hearing about a single instance of it in all my life.

But fuck that. Fuck it! I had to do *something*!

I couldn't even start to let myself think that my wolf might not run or attack, that she might sit there and try to find the word for chains or gurney or... I shut off my profitless thoughts and tried not to tremble. If Nate didn't come back within forty-eight hours this whole line of thought would be moot anyway.

"I wish I never came here! I wish I never snuck out to see Cody. I promise if I can go home, I'll never see him again. I'll never do anything bad again! I promise! I promise!" Bethany's words became nothing but shrieks of terror.

It was a cycle she would repeat over and over again as the hours wore on. Sometimes she would be able to talk to me and tell me all the horrible violations he'd perpetrated upon her helpless body. Then she would start to scream, usually in the middle of a sentence as the horror became too much. Every hour Nate didn't show up was one more hour of terrible anticipation, which was almost worse than the torture itself.

I listened to her stories and her screams, and bit my lip until I tasted blood. Keeping exact track of time was impossible, but I sensed the hours slipping by.

At random moments I would think—*Murphy is turning back now. He's on his way to the farmhouse. Murphy must almost be there. Murphy maybe called me on my cellphone. I didn't answer. By the time he gets home he'll be a little worried and then when he doesn't find me, he'll really be worried. He'll know right away something's wrong. He won't wait around for me to come home. He'll come out looking for me. He'll see Nate's face and suspect something. I hurt Nate's arm with the wrench. Maybe he'll notice that. He'll tear this town apart to find me. He won't let me rot here. He'll find me. He must be almost back to the farmhouse by now. He must be there by now. He's finding my cellphone on the porch right now. He's asking Jossie where I am. Jossie will say she doesn't know. They'll look in my room. I won't be there. They'll find my purse, all my things. Murphy, of all people, will know I walked wherever I went. He'll know I would never hitchhike, never get in a car with a stranger.*

I berated myself over and over again for not telling Jossie my plans. But what if I had? They wouldn't be able to tell I was here. If I was underground as I suspected, they wouldn't be able to smell me. Maybe they would catch traces of my scent in the woodshed, but would they think to move the bookcase? Would Nate even let them that far into the shed? Would he let them on the property? There were so many things he could do to thwart anyone finding me. But I still should have told someone where I was going.

You weren't expecting to be ambushed by a serial killer, Constance.

I thought of the several times my gut instinct had told me to leave and I'd ignored the message. If I'd just left then and come back with Murphy and Vaughn, then maybe—*Stop it, Constance. Stop it! Concentrate on your plan going forward, not the one you should have made.*

In the absolute darkness, I readied myself. My wrists and ankles chafed—all my muscles ached. I wasn't sure how that would translate to wolf form. I might find myself crippled, unable to run or attack. That was best not thought about. There was nothing I could do to prevent that except not struggle in futility against the chains.

Meanwhile I listened to Bethany's tales of torture and degradation and suffered simultaneous bursts of fear and fury.

Murphy's got to be home by now. They've got to be looking for me. Please let them find the cellphone on the porch. Find my purse on the dresser. Let them understand that I haven't gone far and they need to search. Vaughn said it last night—a smart girl would go to a grandmother,

*not an abortion clinic. Let them remember that and Grandmother Emma.
Please.*

Chapter 5

The sound of the trapdoor being pulled open was almost an anticlimax. Bethany had fallen mercifully silent. I think she slept. I had dropped into a light doze myself, as if my brain tried to shield me by making me shut everything out. Or maybe it was late and the hour combined with the darkness and my aching head did me in.

I snapped into instant, horrible alertness when lights flicked on. A series of fluorescent bulbs in the ceiling glowed dimly at first and grew into near blinding brightness.

All the better to see you with, my dear. At first I didn't remember where that line came from. Then I thought about Little Red Riding Hood and I smothered a laugh. How frigging appropriate.

A spring-loaded ladder squealed as it descended to the dirt floor. It reminded me of a scene from a science-fiction movie—the part where the alien spaceship opened up just before the monsters appeared.

My heart sank into the pit of my stomach. A ladder. A fucking ladder? Unfair! Completely and horribly unfair! How was my wolf going to get up a ladder? She'd never seen, never even contemplated one. Even if she could figure it out, it would take her a while and it would be easy for a giant man like Nate to knock her off it—get her down and kick her. My wolf was not immune to kicks. She was not immune to anything.

Stanzie, stop letting him psych you out before you've even begun. Stop.

Bethany woke when the lights got bright. Her moans assaulted my ears then I heard Nate laugh. That royally pissed me off. I welcomed the anger because it was much better than the fear. The anger allowed me to go very cold and calm deep within myself and my scrambled, clawing panic fell away as everything focused into a crisp, crystal clarity.

Here was the hard part. This was make or break time. I needed my split-second ability to shift because if it took too long, Nate could disable me before I'd even finished. I had not counted on the goddamn bright lights. I had not foreseen the fucking ladder.

Go, Stanzie! I shut my eyes tightly.

When I summoned my wolf, she responded without hesitation. My fear and anger demanded her obedience. I ripped apart and reformed as we traded places. Blink of an eye. Yet before I was buried too deeply within her, I counseled her to attack the bad man, don't kill, only hurt him. Then find Murphy. Find Mur...

* * * *

Bright bright light. Hurt my eyes. Me scared. Me sooo scared. I want to make noise. Growl. My paws caught in metal things. What are they called? What is name for... Bad man! Bad! Bad! Bad! *He bad! Bad! He want to hurt me and girl. No! No! Bad man No!*

* * * *

Blood in my mouth. Coppery foul. I gagged. Bits of something shredded on my tongue. Reflexively, I spat them out. For a moment I was dazed, not knowing what I looked at but then it came to me. Shredded skin. I was staring at shredded skin.

Vomit choked my throat then sprayed in liquid chunks against the dirt wall. It smelled of blood and bacon and I puked again. When I wiped my mouth with the back of my hand, it came away bloody but I wasn't hurt. It wasn't my blood.

Bethany was very quiet—I recalled she was there and after that I remembered where we were.

I could hear her hammering heart almost as loudly as I could hear my own.

The stink of blood and terror was overpowering, but underneath it all lurked something worse. Death.

I was in a corner behind the metal hospital gurney. I used it as a support so I could stand because my legs were weak and unresponsive.

A figure sprawled in the dirt by the ladder. A man's body dressed in jeans and a t-shirt that was now more red than white. Face up with throat torn away in ragged chunks. Sightless eyes stared up at absolutely nothing. A mouth contorted in a silent scream of both terror and rage. Nate was dead and my wolf had killed him.

I clapped a hand to my mouth not sure if I was going to puke, laugh or scream. If not for the gurney, I would have collapsed to the ground.

I told you not to kill him. Inside my head my voice was mournful. Wolf-on-human violence could have been excused in this situation, but there was no defense for deliberate murder. My wolf hadn't even hesitated. I remembered everything with a vivid suddenness that made me cry out, my voice muffled by my hand.

He deserved it. He fucking deserved it. My voice was loud in my ears even though I didn't speak aloud. Loud as if to drown out the very treachery of the thought itself. *He. Deserved. It.*

"Stuh—Stanzie?" Bethany sounded very young and scared, but also hopeful. If she could see Nate's ravaged body, it didn't freak her out the way it did me. "You shifted back. Can you get me free? Please?"

For the first time I could see her. When I did, I started to cry. Her body was a mass of bruises and burn marks. The wrist and ankle restraints had chafed so badly she'd bled and her wounds were infected. I could both smell that and see the swollen red streaks that oozed a pus-like liquid. Her hair might have been blond, but now it was a matted, greasy mop of indeterminate brown. Blue, feverish eyes locked to mine pleadingly.

"Hang on," I forced myself to say past tears that clogged my throat. There was no time for crying. I would have to look for the keys in Nate's pockets. That meant I would have to go near him and face what I'd done to him up close.

No, Stanzie, no. Don't make me do this. Don't make me touch him. The fucking bastard.

Somehow I moved away from the corner. My bare feet slipped in congealing blood. It squished between my toes and I gagged but didn't puke. Dear fucking Christ what had I done?

As I looked down on his dead body, a primal rage tore through my soul and before I could stop myself, I'd kicked him, hard. Blood spattered and from behind me I heard Bethany laugh.

"You go," she shouted. "Kick him for me too. Right in the balls, Stanzie!"

I did what she asked and it felt really fucking good.

After that it was easier to look at him and do what I needed to do.

Nate's body was still warm as I knelt beside it and grimly began to search through his pockets. The only keys I found were the ones for his Explorer and I presumed keys to his house and Grandmother Emma's. I tried them all on Bethany's restraints to no avail. I also found his cellphone and after I let the keys drop in a defeated jangle to the dirt floor, I stared at it for a moment, breathing raggedly. I felt stupid and slow, as if my thoughts and emotions could not quite express themselves because they were being blocked somewhere near the source. The primal rage was gone. My mind felt strangely detached, almost as if I were coming loose from my own body.

How could that be? I marveled as I seemed to hover at the top of my own skull.

Bethany sobbed softly on her gurney, frustrated because the keys had not freed her.

"I'm so tired of being chained down. I don't think I can even walk anymore, Stanzie." It took her words a full thirty seconds to penetrate my shock-numbed brain. "Aren't you going to call for help?"

Murphy. I slammed back down into my body.

With fumbling fingers, I pressed his cellphone number into the keypad on Nate's phone and held it to my ear. The goddamn phone stank of Nate Carver and I had to breathe through my mouth. At first the call didn't go through, I had no fucking signal, but one weak bar came back when I moved to stand by the ladder.

Please, please, I thought incoherently. But what came after *please* I did not know.

It rang only once and then I heard Murphy say, "Nate, tell me you found her, man. I'm going half crazy!" He sounded far away and scrambled, but I could still hear that he was scared and frantic.

"Murphy, it's me." I sounded terrible. I didn't even recognize my own voice, but Murphy did.

"Oh, Stanzie! Thank Christ. Oh, honey, Nate found you? Where are you?"

I didn't say anything because my tongue wouldn't work and for a moment I had no idea on earth what the hell I was doing.

Amy Lee Burgess

"Stanzie? What's wrong? Are you okay?" His words flew at me like darting bees and stung me into a response.

"Can you come get me?" I bit my lip and tasted Nate's blood, which made me shudder. The words began to pour from my mouth and I could only hope they made sense because I didn't get a sense of what I'd said until later. It was like my brain was on a five-second delay.

"Please come to the woodshed next to Grandmother Emma's house. It's two miles from the farmhouse. Take a left at the end of the drive. She has a blue mailbox. Bring some clothes. Two dresses or something. We need clothes. And bolt cutters because I can't find the key. There should be something in Nate's workshop. Please hurry. I'm scared."

"We? Did you find Bethany?"

"Please just come. There's so much blood and I'm scared."

"Blood? Oh God. Are you hurt? Stanzie, are you hurt?"

"*It's not my blood*!" I shrieked into the phone, as I finally lost it just like I knew I would. "*Please just come get us! Come get us out of here*!"

A moment of stunned silence sizzled through the phone and I pictured Murphy's face, pinched with shock. But when he talked to me, his voice was almost preternaturally calm.

"I'm on my way, Stanzie. I'm not going to hang up. I need you to keep talking to me, okay?"

"I just want you to come here." I groaned. "I don't want to talk. I don't want to do anything but get out of here." I stood beside Bethany and realized she was squeezing one of my hands with her bruised fingers. Her face was paper white and tears oozed out of the corners of her eyes and dripped to the metal gurney beneath her.

"Are you trapped?"

I struggled to make sense of his words and he waited for me to do it. One thing about Murphy, he knew when to push and when to wait. Unlike me. Finally, I formulated an answer.

"No. I can't leave Bethany. She's chained up and I can't find the key. I told you that already. I'm scared! I'm so scared! I did something bad and I'm scared!"

In the background I could hear the porch door slam as Murphy burst through it. I heard Vaughn's startled voice as he said, "You found her? Where is she? Is she at Grandmother Emma's?"

"Don't forget clothes," I said when Murphy prompted me to talk again. "He took our clothes. We don't have any."

Murphy swore under his breath. Sounds of fabric. I think he ripped clothes off the clothesline.

I heard him tell Vaughn to find a bolt cutter and Vaughn's horrified exclamation.

"Just *do* it!" Murphy yelled. His control slipped, but he got it back almost immediately and told me again he was on his way. Crunch of running feet on the dirt drive, then car doors slammed. An engine zoomed to life. Murphy told Vaughn to turn left so I knew Vaughn was behind the wheel.

Shivers shuddered up and down my spine. I glanced down to make sure Bethany still held my hand. I couldn't feel anything.

"Is it almost over?" she whispered when she saw me look at her.

"It's almost over, yes. Murphy, Bethany's going to need a doctor."

"Okay," Murphy answered me. My heart hurt I loved him so much. I *suffered* with love for him. "I'll find a pack doctor for her, no problem. Is she hurt badly, Stanzie? Can she wait for us to find a pack doctor or do we need to bring her to a hospital."

"They'll ask way too many questions at a hospital. She's pretty banged up but she's not bleeding or anything. She needs a real doctor from the Pack, not some grandmother, Murphy!"

"Are you all right?"

That question brought a bubble of hysterical laughter to my lips.

"I'm fine." I knew I sounded anything but.

"We're almost there, honey. We're turning in now. I see the woodshed. You're inside?"

"There's a trap door and a ladder. The root cellar. That's where we are."

Car doors slammed. Running feet. The squeak of the woodshed door as it opened.

Murphy was down the ladder first, so fast he skipped every other rung. When I saw him, my whole body sagged in relief that was so intense it seemed surreal.

I threw myself into his arms and he held onto me so tightly I couldn't breathe. He'd seen Nate's body the second he was down the ladder as well as the gurneys complete with chains and restraints. He'd also seen poor, frail Bethany. His heart pounded against mine as he struggled to take it in and understand.

"Mother of God." He groaned into my ear and buried his face in my hair. It had long since come loose from the ponytail and was snarled and caked with blood from where my head had hit the woodpile.

"You *are* hurt." Murphy's fingers found the blood-stiffened strands of hair and the wound. He focused on that because it was far less horrific than anything else in the room.

Vaughn clattered down the ladder, took one look at everything and froze.

"Oh, goddamn. Oh fucking hell. No way."

He moved closer to Nate's body, stared down hard at his savaged throat.

"Your wolf do this, Stanzie?" He guessed, clearly blown away.

"She had to do it!" Bethany burst out from the gurney. "He would have done to her what he did to me then he would have killed us both. Don't you dare yell at her for what she did! Can't you see she saved us?"

For the first time Vaughn saw her and recoiled. When he recovered, he moved quickly to her side and I saw he had a pair of bolt cutters in one hand.

"Who are you?" Bethany demanded tearfully, and her face crumpled as she stared up at him in belated fear.

"My name's Vaughn. You're Bethany, right?" Vaughn made his voice deliberately soft and almost cheerful.

"I'm Bethany. Can you get me out of here, Vaughn?"

"Yes, I can. See?" He showed her the bolt cutters and she shrank away from them, face convulsed with terror. He quickly lowered them, his expression for one moment furious—not at her, but at what had been done to her. "Bethany, I need to cut through the chains and I'll see if I can't get those restraints off. It's going to hurt a little I think because of how raw your wrists and ankles are, but I'll be as quick and gentle as I can."

"I want my mom," Bethany begged him.

"We'll get you to your mom," Vaughn promised.

"My wolf killed Nate." I lifted my face to Murphy's so I could confess.

"He did all this?" Murphy's jaw was so tight my own ached in sympathy. Even though he was absolutely furious, his fingers were gentle on my bare skin as he stroked my back. I nodded.

"You need to call Councilor Allerton, Murphy."

"I need to make sure you're okay. We're going to get you cleaned up for one thing. Here, honey, here's a dress. Let me help you put it on." He pulled a blue cotton dress over my head. It wasn't my dress. It smelled like spring.

He helped me button up the back, as if that mattered a damn, and made sure to keep in bodily contact with me every second. That did matter. He reeled as he tried to make sense of everything. He pretended I wasn't going to be in trouble for killing Nate but I knew better. So did he. Every second he put off calling Allerton wouldn't change a thing except delay acknowledging the dull certainty of it.

Vaughn swore as he struggled with the bolt clippers, but he managed to cut through first one chain then another. I took the pink-and-white dress Murphy had slung over his shoulder and brought it to Bethany then helped her on with it as Vaughn snapped the chains attached to her ankle restraints.

"Now for the tricky part." Vaughn looked at Bethany, pale as skim milk, as she leaned against me and sat up for the first time in days. "You ready, Bethany?"

She nodded and held out first one shaking arm then the other so Vaughn could undo the buckles that secured the restraints around her wrists. The chain had been passed through a metal loop fastened to the restraint on one end and fixed to the gurney with the other. The chains had been kept too tight to allow Bethany to reach across to undo the straps herself. Effective and very cruel. The restraints were made of leather and hers were encrusted with old blood and pus. Like the rest of her, they reeked.

If Vaughn was repelled by the stink that surrounded Bethany in a noxious cloud, he hid it well.

While we tended to Bethany, Murphy got on his cellphone. He had to stand by the ladder to get reception too. After he relayed some of the story he listened at first, but then began to argue with someone in a low, furious voice. I didn't have the energy to eavesdrop. All my focus was reserved for Bethany, who clung to me. Removing the restraints hurt—ripped open scabs and rubbed against raw skin—but she didn't cry out. She went three shades paler and, for a moment, I thought she might pass out but she didn't. She was so brave. I wished I could be like her. So damn brave.

My own wrists and ankles were raw and oozing too, but nowhere near the infected horror Bethany endured.

"He buries the Others in the cellar in the house," Bethany announced, and winced as Vaughn removed the restraint from her left ankle. "He told me that."

Vaughn froze in total shock. Even Murphy skipped a beat in his argument with the person on the other end of the phone.

He said, "Oh, shit. I think the problem just got bigger. Hang on. I'll call you back."

"He promises them money for sex and they get into the car with him and he brings them here. Sometimes he has to knock them out first because they don't want to drive this far and they get scared so he hits them in the head. But lots of times he said they came without getting scared. The runaways especially. They thought maybe he would let them stay with him. That's another thing he promises. And food. Only he brings them down here to this place and chains them up like he did me and Stanzie. And he hurts them. He can rape them because they can't shift. He likes that part best, he said. He likes keeping them alive for a few days until he gets bored and they get too smelly. Too weak to fight back. He likes it when they scream and struggle. I tried not to scream, but I couldn't help it. I'll bet Stanzie wouldn't have screamed. She's really brave. She didn't cry once. She didn't scream. And she saved me."

Her eyes glowed with devotion as she stared at me.

"Everyone was looking for you." I pressed my forehead to hers, careful of her bruises.

"But only *you* were smart enough to find me."

I didn't think I had been particularly smart, especially the part where I hadn't told anyone where I was going. I'd been angry that nobody listened to me. Everyone had seemed fixated on the idea that Bethany had gone to a shady clinic and died there. I'd been pissed off that Murphy had told me to not be graphic around Jossie. Embarrassed. Sometimes it seemed like everyone else knew what to say and how to behave and I didn't.

"Why would an Alpha do something like this?" Bethany asked and looked between Vaughn and Murphy because she instinctively knew they both had been one.

"He was sick, Bethany," explained Murphy, although I think a part of him wondered the same damn thing. I know I did.

The four of us crowded together, we all touched in some way. We couldn't bear not to touch each other in order to drive back the horror and the betrayal that we all experienced. Pack were not supposed to treat Pack the way Nate had treated me and Bethany. We were supposed to protect each other. Even if we didn't like each other, we were never, ever supposed to turn on each other with such sick perversion.

"I was always a little afraid of him." A wince of shame shadowed Bethany's features. "I remember when I was a little girl being scared of him because he was so tall, but even as I grew up there was just something...spooky about him. It's like the smile never really got all the way to his eyes. Like he was faking it. It all seems so plain now but it was never so plain before. Just now that I know the truth. Isn't that weird?"

"We should always trust our instincts," Murphy said, his mouth tight. "I didn't like him much either, Bethany. You're right, there was something off." She reached out her hand for his and he took it. Poor Murphy represented all the males of the entire Pack at that moment as he swore to her she would never be treated like this again.

Tears pricked my eyes and I buried my face in his shoulder for a moment because I couldn't bear it. His arm tightened around me, but he kept his gaze locked with Bethany's.

"Jesus," muttered Vaughn. He looked as if he might throw up. He had Bethany's other hand and his free hand gripped Murphy's shoulder tightly. His eyes met mine when I lifted my face. "He's always been fucking weird and I knew he hadn't changed just because he'd grown up and bonded."

"Stuff like this is always easy to see after the fact," I said. "Not so easy to see at the time. We need to get Bethany home. Can we take her now?"

"Stanzie." There was a plea in Vaughn's voice. Was he begging forgiveness? Why? He hadn't done anything wrong.

"It's all right, Vaughn," I whispered. But he shook his head. I thought he might say something else, but he didn't.

Murphy's cellphone rang and startled all of us. Bethany's face screwed up. I thought she might cry. I nearly jumped through my damn skin.

Murphy took the phone to the ladder and answered it, his back to us. The moment we all lost contact, I felt empty.

"Let's get the fuck out of here." Vaughn looked around the root cellar, his fists clenched in barely suppressed rage.

Bethany tried to walk, but couldn't, so Vaughn picked her up carefully and brought her to the ladder. I didn't know how he would be able to scale it with her in his arms, but he did it. He had her hang onto his neck and wrap her legs around his waist. I saw her grit her teeth against the pain as her raw ankles rubbed together but she managed.

With my eyes averted from Nate's dead body, I followed.

The air in the woodshed felt cool and fresh and I gulped it down gratefully as it erased the miasma of death from my lungs.

Vaughn took Bethany to the house and kicked open the front door with a booted foot. There was a light on in the living room. I could see it from the darkness where I stood. I didn't want to go near the house. Girls were buried beneath it. Grandmother Emma was in there and I wasn't sure of her role in all this. She couldn't possibly be ignorant of it—she had to know—at least on some level.

"Stanzie?" The wind brought my name from Bethany's lips to my ears. I forced my fears away and walked through the darkness toward the lighted window, then onto the front porch. The garbage bag was gone.

Inside, the house smelled of lavender potpourri and Earl Grey tea—such normal, comforting smells. I tried to discern the undertone of decay and death but couldn't. Bastard had probably used lime and other agents to cover the smell and speed along decomposition. My wolf would probably be able to smell it, though.

At the thought of her, my stomach rolled and I gagged a little. I could taste Nate's blood and flesh and I rubbed my mouth with the back of my hand as if that would get rid of the taste.

An old woman in a blue-flowered housecoat and fuzzy slippers, her gray hair in a braid down her back, shuffled into the room as Vaughn set Bethany down on a sofa upholstered in brown plaid. The old woman looked frightened but determined.

"What has he done this time, Vaughn?" she quavered, one hand to her throat where the pulse beat visibly.

"It's worse than you can imagine, Grandmother." Vaughn's voice shook.

"You tried to tell us, son, back when he was just a boy. Nobody wanted to believe you. I believed you, but I wanted to protect my grandson. It was just animals. Dogs, cats, squirrels. Nothing we all didn't kill in wolf form."

"But he didn't do it in wolf form, did he?" Vaughn spat, his back to her as if he couldn't stand the sight of her.

"Maplefair helped you set up Riverglow, gave you money to get started, negotiated territory with Nightclaw for you. I did that, Vaughn." Grandmother Emma's face was bleak. Even she didn't buy her own bullshit.

"Yeah, and in return I kept my mouth shut about Nate and now look what's happened. If I'd had any fucking idea it had gone past animals into Others and now even Pack—how could you have stood by and let it happen, Emma? How?" Vaughn whirled around to confront her, but his face was gray with guilt.

"I'm just as much of a monster as he is, I know." She made no move to defend or excuse herself. I tried to find some empathy inside myself for them both, but I was so goddamned empty. "You pretend you don't really understand the truth and it somehow gets easier."

"He's dead." Bethany's face glowed with grim satisfaction and she struggled to sit up, but Vaughn was right there to gently push her back down. "Stanzie's wolf ripped his fucking throat out and the only I regret I have is that I wasn't there in wolf form to tear off his balls. You knew about this? You horrible old woman. You need to die too!"

Vaughn reached out to touch her shoulder and she grabbed his hand with both of hers and pressed it to her bruised face. Vaughn's mouth contorted, but he held still for her.

I couldn't stay in the room any longer. If I did, I would hurt that old woman.

I darted into the small, cramped kitchen. Everything was spotless. An old-fashioned porcelain sink had been scrubbed until it gleamed. A table with four mismatched chairs took up most of the space. A vase of wildflowers sat in the precise center of the blue-and-white checked tablecloth. Everything seemed so ordinary and safe but it wasn't.

Vaughn entered the room. He lifted me up and sat me on the butcher block countertop next to the sink. He ran some cold water on a dishrag and wiped my face. It came away bloody. Nate's blood.

"Your hair's full of blood. Are you hurt?" Vaughn probed the back of my skull with his fingers and I winced when they encountered the tender spot. "You are hurt. Oh, Stanzie. I should have said something. I knew I should have. The first thing I thought when I heard Bethany was missing was that Nate was behind it but when I got here he seemed so normal, so concerned. I'm such a fucking idiot. I *knew* better! I knew!" He wrapped his arms around me and I hugged him back then buried my face in his shoulder. I was shaking and so cold I didn't think I would ever know what it felt like to be warm again.

The front door opened and a moment later I heard Murphy as he talked to Bethany and Grandmother Emma. I held onto Vaughn until Murphy came into the kitchen.

"Vaughn, I need you to take Bethany home. The keys to the Explorer are in the ignition. I found them on the floor in the woodshed. A Pack doctor will meet you there. There's a Regional Councilor on his way over here to take care of Grandmother Emma. After you drop Bethany off, you need to get back to Jossie. I don't want her hearing this from anybody but you."

"What about you?" Vaughn drew me down to the worn linoleum floor, and kept his arms around me.

"I'm bringing Stanzie to the safe house in Hartford."

I was afraid to look at him, afraid his expression would match the grim resignation in his voice.

"The fucking safe house in Hartford? What the hell..." Belatedly, Vaughn understood what was happening. His mouth became very small and all the blood drained from his face. "Oh, come on. Tell me this is just a formality. The man was a monster, Liam."

"You don't have to convince me." Murphy sounded like he was either going to cry or start to swear. "It's not up to me though, is it?"

"Shit." Vaughn was the one who swore—a steady, profane stream.

"Vaughn." He stopped cursing when I put a finger across his lips. His brown eyes were wide with terror. "It's okay. Bring Bethany home. She's waited a long time to go home."

"I want to go with you, Stanzie. I want to explain to the Council about what I knew." He took both my hands with his and held on so fiercely I could feel my bones grind together. I tried not to wince.

"What you knew? What the fuck did you know?" Murphy snarled.

Vaughn froze for a moment but turned to face him. "Twenty years ago I caught Nate in the woods torturing a rabbit. He swore it was the first time he'd ever hurt an animal, but from the look of what he'd done to the rabbit I knew he was fucking lying. I brought him to Emma and his whole family got involved in it and I ended up the frigging bad guy. I was told to forget what I saw and drop it, and when I wouldn't I got the shit beat out of me.

"Grandmother Emma believed me, but she said she'd take care of it. She'd watch Nate and if he did it again, she'd make sure the Alphas knew. She was a fucking liar, Liam. She knew I wouldn't keep my mouth shut, so she helped set me up in Connecticut. Helped me, Peter and Callie start Riverglow. I kept away from Maplefair all these years because..."

"You're a frigging coward and didn't want to know what was really going on because you might have to do something about it?" Murphy's fists clenched and I waited for him to hit Vaughn but he didn't.

"Yeah," admitted Vaughn, head bowed. "I'm a frigging coward, you're right. I left and said to hell with everyone. I was sick of it. It was just animals. I never thought the bastard would ever touch people."

"One of the early indicators of a serial killer is torturing and killing animals as a child." Murphy's eyes glittered with fury. "And when you heard Bethany was missing, what did you think, Vaughn? And don't give me any bullshit stories about how her mother initiated your wolf. You suspected him. Admit it."

Vaughn jerked his head in agreement. A huge shudder rippled down his spine and back up again.

"And you said nothing. This whole time we're here, you said nothing?" Murphy's voice was deadly calm but full of fury.

Vaughn shut his eyes and bowed his head. If he'd been in wolf form, he would have rolled to Murphy's wolf and exposed his throat and belly. He would have been lucky not to have been disemboweled.

"You're just damn lucky Stanzie's still alive and not hurt badly. Or I would kill you, Pelletier. You bastard."

Vaughn's chest heaved, but he didn't look up, not even when Murphy grabbed my hand and all but yanked me away from him.

Murphy took me out the back door so I didn't have to see Grandmother Emma again, for which I was very grateful.

The night air was chilly and stars sprinkled across the black sky like silver pinpricks in velvet. I shivered and Murphy wrapped his arm around my shoulder as we walked toward the Prelude without speaking.

My feet were bare and the dirt drive was muddy from the recent rain. Mud coated my soles and squeezed up through the cracks in my toes. It felt disgusting and I grimaced. I thought longingly of my Skechers.

Murphy opened the door for me and his face was scared beneath the dome light. He bent down to brush my lips with his. They were cold. His skin was cold too. Shadows moved behind the lighted curtains in the house beyond us. Vaughn and Bethany came out the front door. Bethany was bundled in a winter coat—Grandmother Emma's. She and Vaughn clung to each other as they navigated the porch steps. Murphy got behind the wheel of the Prelude and watched them stumble across the muddy drive to the Explorer. Bethany had on a pair of slippers—also Grandmother Emma's. I wished I had slippers and a coat. I was freezing.

Murphy noticed me shivering and shrugged off his brown suede jacket so I could put it on. It smelled like him and I felt absurdly comforted. I was afraid to ask him how much trouble I was in for killing Nate. I knew there would be Regional Councilors waiting for me at the safe house. Maybe even someone from the Great Council. If not tonight, tomorrow definitely. Councilor Allerton would come too. There would be a tribunal and I would stand accused of the worst crime someone Pack could commit. Wolf-on-human murder. There was no defense. I didn't really have to ask Murphy how much trouble I was in because I already knew. I figured I had four days at the most left before the Councils voted against me. The penalty was death.

Chapter 6

Murphy barely had a chance to lift the wolf's head knocker on the front door of the Hartford safe house before it was pulled open. A stream of light enveloped us both as we stood on the steps in the draining predawn darkness.

Kathy Manning, wide awake as if she always greeted the dawn fully dressed and made up, drew us inside. Murphy was much more alert than I was because while I had dozed uneasily in the car, he'd driven the three-and-a-half hours between Easton and Hartford. We'd only stopped twice—once in Boston for twenty minutes so we could pack some fresh clothes and once just over the border in Connecticut so he could stretch his legs. Somewhere along the drive beard stubble had shadowed his cheeks and jawline. He looked tired yet strung out on the thermos of coffee he'd brewed at the condo.

I'm sure I looked terrible. I had on a pair of black loafers that didn't go well with Jossie's blue floral dress. The print was very prim and almost girlish—not my personal style at all. The loafers had been on the mat just inside the front door and after I'd rinsed the mud and blood off my feet, I'd slipped them on because my mind was traveling in a hundred other dark places and for once in my life I hadn't been able to concentrate on shoes.

We'd barely talked on the drive because neither one of us wanted to acknowledge the reality of what had been set in motion the second my wolf had torn Nate's throat out.

As I'd faded in and out of a hazy sleep, I'd watched Murphy's profile washed out pale from the oncoming headlights on the highway. The smell of coffee and despair had mixed and made my throat tight. It seemed like it took forever to get to Connecticut, but it had only been four hours.

As we stepped inside, the first slender beam of sunlight cut through the chill spring darkness and highlighted the parquet flooring in the foyer. Kathy shut the door on it and harsh electric light made my eyes ache. They were gritty and dry and all I wanted was to sleep in a real bed. Maybe forever.

Kathy Manning was calm as ever, but she did not smile. Instead, she was grave and withdrawn, as if she had a special place inside to store her smile when the situation was bad enough. I'd never seen it bad enough— except during my first tribunal when Grey and Elena had been killed. I didn't remember her smiling much then either. This must be her official business Council expression. I started to shake again. Murphy had gotten me a blanket from the condo. That, his suede jacket and the heater in the car had made me stop trembling, but had not completely erased the bone-crushing cold that seemed to isolate me from the rest of the world. Now the shaking was back.

"Take her upstairs and get her cleaned up. I'll make her some tea." Kathy and Murphy exchanged potent glances and, bone tired as I was, I knew something was being kept from me.

Murphy led me for the staircase as Kathy disappeared down the hallway to the kitchen.

Grateful for his support, I stumbled up the stairs and into the blue-tiled bathroom I remembered from when we'd last stayed in the safe house.

With a groan of relief, I sank down onto the toilet, the only place I could sit beside the floor.

"I'm so tired. When I get all this damn blood out of my hair, can we go to sleep, Murphy?"

For some reason that idea made him look wistful. "Stanzie, the Councils are going to charge you with murder. There's no easy way to say it, so I'm sorry if I just blurted it out."

"I know." I'd known that the moment he'd told me he was bringing me to the safe house. "Why else would we be here?"

"It's bullshit. That man was sick and twisted. Just for what he did to you and Bethany the Councils would have put him to death, let alone what he did to those Other girls. They've been digging in Grandmother

Emma's cellar. They've found...evidence." He avoided being graphic but I knew at least one of the Other girls had to have been only slightly decomposed—the one Bethany had seen him carrying in a plastic bag like she was garbage. He'd gloated about other victims to Bethany and she'd told me. I hadn't doubted for a second that it was all true.

"Wolf-on-human murder, Murphy. It's against the law. Only the Great Council has the right to pronounce death on someone Pack. I don't have that authority." I bowed my head. "I told my wolf to run, only hurt him a little so he couldn't hurt Bethany. But I panicked when I saw the only way out was a ladder. She'd never seen a ladder. Christ, stairs would have been a foreign concept as far as that goes, but at least she could have navigated them."

"Stanzie, the situation you were in, what you'd endured for hours as you waited for him to show up, come on. It's bullshit to think your wolf would have done anything differently."

"*My* wolf," I agreed. "Murphy, I have no defense. The Councils are going to vote against me."

"That's not true." All the blood drained from his face only to slam back into his cheeks a second later as he struggled with the magnitude of what that vote would mean. "They've already said if a precedent can be found, if something like this has happened before and that person was cleared, they'd do the same for you. We have to find the precedent is all."

"I've never heard of anybody's wolf murdering someone in human form before, let alone about someone who got away with it. Have you?"

Murphy scrubbed at his bloodshot eyes with a rough fist. "Not personally, but that's what the archives are for. Pack history, past Council decisions. If the case is there, Stanzie, I'll find it."

"*You'll* find it?" My heart raced so fast a flush of uncomfortable warmth engulfed my body and for a moment I was burning up. "You personally, Murphy?"

He took a deep breath. "I have to do this personally. I don't trust anyone else, Stanzie."

"The archives are huge. You, personally, are going to comb through every record?" I sounded like a lawyer cross-examining him as if he were on the stand in a court of the Others.

He let out the breath he'd been holding. "No, of course not. There will be lots of other Advisors helping. They're searching right now."

Murphy's gaze slid down to the watch on his wrist. "My plane's leaving in a couple of hours. I've got to get to the airport, Stanzie."

For a horrible moment I could not breathe, see or speak. Murphy was leaving me. I would be alone. The idea was monstrous.

When I got my ability to speak back, I pounced. "Where? Which archives are you talking about?"

The Pack had several archives located around the world. For centuries they'd been localized to the regions around them, but with the new, digital age, it was becoming possible to share and exchange. Many Advisors spent their entire careers updating the archives from paper to computer. It was slow because our knowledge base was miniscule. Another thing the people in the conspiracy detested—computerizing our records. They felt that was unsafe and dangerous, but then so was fire.

"The closest one is in Virginia."

There had been one in Boston, but it had burned down years ago. What had been salvageable had been moved and recopied.

Archive Advisors were circulated around different archives and many times they brought copies of records with them, so not everything had been lost in the Boston fire.

"Virginia?" My mouth trembled and I bit my lower lip to keep it still. "That's so far away, Murphy. I want you here." I stretched out to touch him but he was just out of reach. He made no move to come closer. If anything, he shrank away.

"Stanzie, please don't do this to me. Don't make this harder."

"Harder? I don't want you to go." My voice grew louder and shriller with each word. Murphy's jaw swelled with the first signs of anger. I didn't care. "I don't want you to go on some wild goose chase in Virginia. I want you here with me. We may only have a few days left and I don't want to spend them apart!"

"I am not going to lose you!" he shouted at me. I recoiled and hit my head against the shelf above the toilet. A hot lick of pain made it impossible to think for a moment.

When I could focus again, Murphy was huddled against the door, and his shoulders shook as he struggled to regain control.

His fear and mad grief filled the air with a sharp, acrid odor. "I can't lose you." His voice was a shaking whisper as he turned to look at me, his face twisted with anguish. "Please let me go do this, Stanzie. I have to do something. I can't just let this happen without doing anything to prevent it. Don't ask me to stand by and watch. Please."

My anger collapsed. It wasn't fair to think just of me when it was obvious this tore him apart. He'd be the one left behind. Again. I tried to imagine what it would feel like if our situations were reversed and a smothering pain closed down my throat so I couldn't breathe.

"But I'm guilty, Murphy." I bowed my head in shame.

He crossed the room, knelt before me and buried his face in my lap, as he sought comfort.

His hair was soft beneath my fingers and I shut my eyes to keep from crying. If I cried, I would make it ten times worse for Murphy. I also didn't think I would be able to stop.

"I was so scared. My wolf was so scared. I'm always so scared."

"You're one of the bravest people I know." His voice was muffled by the fabric of the dress I wore . Despite everything, I had to smile a little. He had a skewed vision of me sometimes. I wished I could be the woman he thought I was. I'd been working toward that, but I would never get there now. The least I could do is let him handle his side of this situation the way he wanted. He would have done no less for me.

"You'll miss your plane." I let my hands fall away from his hair. He lifted his face to mine and his fingers were warm against the side of my cheek.

"I am going to find it. I'm not going to let them rule against you. You have to believe in me, okay?"

"I believe in you," I told him. I did. I doubted he'd find what he would desperately look for, but that didn't change the fact I believed in him.

He kissed me very gently and got to his feet.

"You want to go downstairs with me?" He offered to be with me when I was formally charged. Perversely, now that I knew he was leaving, I wanted him gone. The sooner our separation started, the easier it would be for me to accept that I was going to be alone in this. I was appalled at myself on some level. Selfishly I wanted him to stay with me and watch passively as I was condemned. Of course he wanted to do something to prevent it. I knew he wouldn't be able to even if he would never admit it, but I needed to be strong enough to let him try at least.

Meanwhile I reeked of old sweat and blood. My hair was a rat's nest of tangles.

"I'm damned if I'm going to be charged looking like this." I tried to sound as if I really cared. "You go and I'll take a shower and wash my disgusting hair. I want all this blood off me. It's not all mine. I want to be clean."

Instead of leaving, he turned on the shower for me and helped me off with the dress. I flashed back to hours ago in that awful root cellar when he'd helped me put it on.

Just before I got into the shower stall, he hugged me and I couldn't help but think the next time I saw him I might only have a few hours at most left to live. Right at that moment I was still free, I still had the slimmest flicker of hope, but what if the next time we were together that hope was extinguished and we were forced to say goodbye for the final time?

If he thought of that too, he didn't say it or show it. I tried not to cling to him, but I don't think I did a very good job. He had to take my hands within his to get me to let go of him.

"Call me anytime you want to talk to me," he whispered into my ear just before he released my hands. "You won't be alone, Stanzie. I'm only a phone call away."

From somewhere I mustered a smile for him, but I couldn't watch him leave me. I heard the door close behind him, but I had my face tilted up into the warm gush of water and my eyes squeezed tightly shut. I told myself I had to understand the fact that I might never see him again. If he couldn't stand it now, it would be fifty times worse once he understood they'd voted against me. If they did that, he'd never come back and admit he hadn't been able to save me.

I wanted to scream his name, beg him to come back, but somehow I didn't. Somehow I didn't.

* * * *

Roger Samuels from the Great Council looked tired and grim, but also managed to be gentle. His light brown hair was thinning a little on the top so he kept it short. He had big ears and a small nose, which gave him an incongruous look as if he didn't quite match. Deep-set eyes were dark, his mouth wide and generous. The minute he spoke I knew he was from Chicago.

He took one look at me and rushed me into a chair. There was a pitcher of water on the conference table and two glasses. He filled one for me and watched me drink some of it, eyes concerned as I swallowed it all. I hadn't realized how thirsty I was. I thought of the mug of tea Kathy had gone to make me. It had been pretense, I suppose, to give Murphy the opportunity to tell me he was leaving. No wonder Kathy had not been smiling.

I'd managed a shower and gotten all the encrusted blood out of my hair but it had been surprisingly hard work. Not because the water and soap irritated the wound in the back of my skull, which it had, but because I was so tired. Every last bit of strength I'd had left seemed to wash down the drain along with the blood and soap.

All I'd wanted to do was crawl into a bed and sleep, but instead I'd forced myself to put on a pair of jeans and a clean shirt. I'd tried to focus on the six pairs of shoes I'd brought with me but they'd blurred and wavered in my vision and when I'd found myself on the brink of exhausted tears—a choice was just too much to ask of myself—I'd stuffed my feet back into the black loafers and called it a day.

The blood and most of the tangles were gone from my hair, but it was still very damp and I hadn't bothered with makeup. I was aware I must look almost as awful as I had before the shower and wondered why I'd even bothered.

I wanted Murphy in the worst way. I'd think about him and my whole body would seize into a huge ball of pain and longing. He was on a plane and I had to accept that. The fatigue made it easier to bear. I couldn't seem to focus on much of anything.

Councilor Samuels stared at me. He poured me another glass of water and took a seat beside me, not across from me. That was a nice gesture. He put no distance between us or attempted to erect barriers or a sense of authority.

"I'm very sorry to have to put you through this right now, Constance." His voice was as kind as his face, deep and distinct—a voice I instinctively trusted. "Unfortunately, the Great Council must formally charge you with the murder of Nathaniel Carver, Alpha of Maplefair in the state of

Vermont of the country of the United States. It's my duty to inform you of the events that will be set in motion with my words."

I clutched the water glass tightly and tried to concentrate on his words rather than burst into tears. There had been no easy way to say this and part of me was glad he hadn't bothered with small talk, but another part of me reeled from the shock, even though I'd thought I'd been prepared to hear what he had to say.

"There will be an investigation conducted to gather the facts surrounding the murder and when these facts have been ascertained and witnesses selected to offer these facts before the Great and Regional Council representatives who have been assigned this case, we shall proceed with a tribunal.

"In addition to the factual witnesses, there may also be character witnesses, representing both Nathaniel Carver and you. If you wish to name any character witnesses, you may do so." He paused as if to give me a chance to name people, but I was so tired I could barely focus on the movement of his mouth.

He waited for my response patiently but when I didn't say anything, he continued. "During this period of time, you will be asked to remain here in the Hartford safe house where you shall be provided with care and comfort. You are a guest of the Great Council and, as such, will not be permitted to leave the premises without one of us in attendance and at our sole discretion.

"When the fact-finding and witness selection has been concluded, the tribunal will be declared open and you will be brought before the Councils. Your testimony will be heard, along with any witnesses' and the Councils will consider the case.

"When resolution has been decided, sentence will be pronounced or all charges will be dropped and the tribunal will be closed. Your panel will include the entire Regional Council of New England because the murder took place in their jurisdiction and three Great Councilors. Since you are an Advisor to Councilor Jason Allerton, he has been asked not to sit on the panel. In this particular case because you were acting on behalf of a Regional Councilor, Kathleen Manning will also not sit on the panel.

"In the event charges are dismissed, you will be free to go and your character will be cleared. You will be allowed to remain an Advisor at the discretion of Councilor Allerton. Should you be found guilty of the charges, you will be stripped of your title of Advisor and put to death by the Hand of the Council. Nathaniel Carver's bond mate, Jocelyn Wilbanks, will be allowed to act as the Council's Hand if she so desires, however, if she declines, you may choose in her stead. The method will be poison. It should be painless. You will ingest it and become gradually paralyzed. In the end stages your respiratory system will shut down and you will suffocate. By that point you may well be unconscious. Your body will be cremated and your ashes scattered in a place selected by your bond mate.

"Do you understand the charges and the proceedings, Constance?"

"Yes, Councilor." I had to force my voice past the growing lump of panic in my throat. I already felt paralyzed as if I'd swallowed the coniine-laced drink that might be handed to me one day very soon. I had no defense and the man who had explained my rights knew it as well as I did. The compassion on his face illustrated that clearly.

I was grateful neither Allerton nor Kathy would have to vote against me. I thought of Murphy scattering my ashes somewhere and felt a cold clutch of despair.

The Devil's Hopyard, where we'd scattered Grandfather Tobias's ashes and Callie's and Peter's came to mind, and I shuddered. I didn't want to be where they were. I wondered if I'd walk, if I'd come back in a ghost or spirit form because I couldn't rest. That thought terrified me. I'd be able to see Murphy, but not touch him, at least not so he could feel it and to spend eternity doing that? No.

Grandfather Tobias's voice filled my head for a moment. I'd given him the coniine-infused hot chocolate and he'd begged me to forgive him for his role in killing Grey and Elena. I'd told him I would never forgive him.

"Then you condemn me to walk," he'd said, his face old and resigned.

I'd never seen him in ghost form, but sometimes I wondered if he were there. He'd told me he'd seen Grey and Elena with me after they died but I'd never been the slightest bit aware of them.

I shuddered again and Councilor Samuels reached out to pat my shoulder.

"I've been told some of the details," he said. "This is a very difficult case, and no matter what the outcome, you have my sympathy."

"Thank you, Councilor," I whispered, vaguely comforted by his touch, but mostly I wished I could close my eyes and push everything away for a while.

Chapter 7

My cellphone woke me. Disoriented, I sat straight up in bed and strained to see through the darkness. The mattress was wrong—not as firm as the one in my condo—and Murphy wasn't there.

My heart pounded with a frantic intensity and a leftover smear of bad dreams made it hard to separate reality from fantasy. Where was I?

Meanwhile my phone continued to ring and I reached out to find it on the bedside nightstand.

By the time I pressed talk and said hello, I remembered everything. The disorientation seemed preferable.

"Are you okay?" Vaughn sounded concerned and scared.

"Hey, Vaughn." I struggled to calm my frantic heartbeat. My head throbbed. I put exploratory fingers to the back of my skull and had to bite back a protesting yelp. Raw and very painful. Did I have another concussion? "Sorry. I just woke up."

"It's almost seven at night. Did you go to bed early?"

No wonder it was so damn dark.

"No, I went to sleep this morning around eight and I guess I've slept all day." I was dismayed. I had only a handful of days left most likely and now I'd just wasted one sleeping. I felt cheated. "Where are you?"

"Still in Easton. Shit, it's complicated, Stanzie. Advisors from the Regional and Great Councils have been digging all day in that goddamn cellar. They...do you want to hear this?" Belatedly he realized I might not want to know the details.

"Actually it helps to hear it." I propped myself up against the headboard and wished I had something to drink. I was almost unbearably thirsty. My tongue felt thick and my head fuzzy. "It's not that I doubted Bethany, but I want to know."

"Five so far," Vaughn said grimly. "They think that's it, but there might be more. The worst fear is that he's got another burial ground somewhere on pack property. It's not a good day here in Maplefair, that's for goddamn sure."

"Does everyone know?"

"It's a small pack. They know Bethany's back and we couldn't expect her to lie about what happened. Also..."

"Nate's dead." I finished his sentence because he didn't seem able. "Is Jossie very angry at me?"

"Are you crazy?" Vaughn demanded. "You're a hero to her, Stanz. To everyone here in Maplefair. Jossie...oh hell, this is part of the complications that have kept me here. You see, she told me something that blew my mind and I..."

"Heather." Once again I finished his thought because he couldn't.

"She told you?" Vaughn was incredulous.

"No, he did."

An awful silence fell between us.

"Oh, shit. Jossie was pretty sure the bastard suspected Heather wasn't his child. They weren't...well, they didn't have much sex apparently."

"No, he was too busy having it with Others chained up in his grandmother's root cellar," I sniped and, even though he wasn't there with me, I could imagine his expression.

"Well, she didn't know that. She only knew he wasn't very interested in her. She's a mess right now. Thinking about everything, looking back and blaming herself for not seeing how wrong things were with him."

"I guess everybody wanted to believe the best of the bastard." My tone was grudging and Vaughn sighed in my ear.

"Are you very angry at me?"

I didn't know what I was. "I'm trying not to be. I just—I don't understand, Vaughn. If you thought he might have done something to Bethany, why didn't you say? And when the subject of the Stowe Strangler came up? Why did you get angry at Marlene for bringing it up and make her sound like a liar when she had a good point?"

"He was Alpha." Vaughn swallowed audibly and, for a moment, I thought he might be in tears. "Alphas don't do things like that. I never thought he'd get to be Alpha if there was something really wrong with him."

"He was fourth generation. How could he not be Alpha?" I argued. "He'd have had to have paraded his kills under people's noses for them to not let him be Alpha. He was born for it."

"Why do they get a pass and not me then?"

"Because they didn't find him torturing rabbits in the forest."

"But his whole family knew about it!"

"Sure, the first, second and third generations of the founding family. You think they'd say anything? They needed him to be Alpha to provide the fifth generation."

"Well, I fixed that much at least," Vaughn whispered. "But it's not like I planned it. I know. There's no defense. I'm a fuck-up and I ignored this situation the same way I ignored the one with Callie and more people died because of me.

"Liam tried to get the Councils to put me on trial, you know that?"

I winced but didn't say anything.

"You know what the Councils said?" Vaughn's laughter was ragged and it was hard to understand him. "They said that while my silence was reprehensible, I hadn't done anything actionable. Basically, my name is mud but I'm safe. Meanwhile you saved everyone and you're on trial for your life."

He took a deep breath. "Stanzie, you have to know I'd trade places with you in a heartbeat. I've been begging the Councils to stop this bullshit tribunal. They've interviewed me and I've told them over and over that you're not the one who's in the wrong. I am. I know that! I know it!"

"Oh, Vaughn." I bit my lip so hard I tasted blood. It reminded me of Nate's and I shuddered. "You didn't know. It's not like you knew he had Bethany chained up in his grandmother's root cellar. You were looking hard at him and he held his shit together in public, and you didn't know for sure he was responsible for anything. There wasn't any moment where you knew for a fact what was going on and you kept deliberately silent.

"All I wish is that you'd told us about the rabbit. That's all. We're the Advisors. That's the kind of stuff we want to know, but I'm not Murphy, okay. I'm not blaming you for this."

"That's the trouble. You never blame me. You always forgive me and I don't deserve it."

"He killed a rabbit in the woods when he was thirteen or fourteen years old. No one will admit they saw him do it again. No one will admit they saw him do it before that. As far as you knew he never did it again. You had some vague suspicions of him when you heard Bethany was missing. You went with us to Vermont to check it out for yourself because you didn't want to blow things out of proportion. You didn't see anything that made you nervous.

"Everybody's real good a pointing the finger of blame after the fact, but while the shit's going down, it's not always that easy. Stop kicking yourself in the ass. Take care of Jossie and Heather. Help Maplefair."

"I'll be there as soon as I can. I don't care if Liam beats the shit out of me, I'm coming there."

I assured him Murphy wouldn't beat him. To do that he'd have to be here and he wasn't, but I couldn't bring myself to tell Vaughn that. He'd find out soon enough for himself.

* * * *

After a shower I wrapped myself in a fluffy blue bath towel. When I walked back into my bedroom, Kathy Manning sat in the chair by the fireplace. Her gray-blue gaze measured my progress across the floor to the closet where I found my suitcase had been unpacked and my clothes hung neatly. I knew she'd done it for me, and put things into the dresser drawers as well.

"I've made ravioli for dinner. Homemade pasta and sauce, of course," she told me as I threw on a pair of jeans and a navy blue t-shirt. I debated from among the shoes I'd brought and chose a pair of dark blue Chucks. "I also baked an angel food cake with lemon cream frosting."

The second she'd mentioned food, my stomach growled. I cast my mind back to my last meal—bacon and eggs in Jossie's farmhouse kitchen. It had been about thirty-six hours but it seemed like a lifetime.

"Can I have some water?" I was so thirsty my whole mouth felt dry as dust.

She smiled at me, the first time I'd seen her do it since I'd arrived, and tucked her arm in mine so she could lead me to the stairs and then to the kitchen in the back of the safe house.

I drank three glasses of water one after the other while she arranged the ravioli in a beautiful blue serving dish and the homemade sauce in another. She allowed me to bring the sauce bowl into the dining room.

The Colonial furniture gleamed with fresh polish. The table had been covered with a white cloth and blue willow china place settings. Cobalt blue wine goblets promised there would be wine with dinner.

Everything smelled so damn good I could hardly wait to dig in, but the number of place settings gave me pause. Five. I knew Councilor Samuels was here, but I wondered who the other two people were.

I didn't have long to wait. Before I could take the seat Kathy indicated, Councilor Samuels walked into the room followed by two other men. I recognized one of them from my tribunal after Grey and Elena were killed.

Councilor Adam Perkins was a member of the Regional Council and a past Alpha of Nightclaw, the premiere pack in Connecticut. He was tall and lean, with an aesthete's appreciation for clothes and adornments. The modern Brooks Brothers gray suit he wore was tailored to his tall frame perfectly. His nails were buffed and his haircut cost more than some of my nicer shoes. His own shoes were Gucci and they gleamed. Not a scuff or worn spot anywhere. They were classic loafers, the kind that never really went out of style and I estimated his were several years old but he might have just taken them out of the box. His pack jewelry was a gold signet ring, which also glowed with good care.

He looked down his long nose at me with fastidious dismay but didn't say anything.

The other man I didn't recognize. He was shorter and stocky with inky black hair and wide, expressive brown eyes. No matter what time of day it was and how many times he shaved, he would probably always have a five o'clock shadow. His face was floridly handsome and he carried himself with supreme self-confidence.

Councilor Samuels introduced him as Dante Armentano representing the Great Council. He was from Rome and spoke perfect English.

All three Councilors looked tired and hungry. Councilor Armentano saw the ravioli on the table and for a moment his expression became condescending as if he judged that Italian cuisine prepared by a non-Italian would automatically be awful. He was in for a huge surprise the second he tasted Kathy Manning's food. I didn't think anyone on the planet could taste something she made and pronounce it anything but exquisite.

"I'll get the wine. Sit down everyone," Kathy directed when the introductions were over.

Councilor Samuels attempted to gallantly pull out a chair for me, but froze when Councilor Armentano exclaimed, "But surely, Roger, she is not eating at the same table with us?"

She. He couldn't even bring himself to refer to me by name.

Hot shame burned my cheeks and I bowed my head to shield my face from their prying eyes.

Kathy, who was halfway through the doorway to the kitchen, turned back. Her face suffused with indignant rage on my behalf. She looked like a warrior elf princess for a moment—all fury and fire.

"Where would you suggest she ate, Councilor? Bread and water in the dungeon perhaps?"

"Oh, don't be melodramatic, Kathleen," Armentano answered with a patronizing smile. He used her first name too—a subtle reinforcement of his superior rank. "Surely, you can set her up in her room."

Kathy visibly struggled with a prodigious temper I had never suspected she'd possessed. She'd always seemed so placid and content. Always smiling. She was not smiling now.

"It's all right. I'm really not hungry," I said. My appetite had turned into a hard rock that sat at the bottom of my stomach. "I'll just go back to my room."

"No you will not!" Kathy was imperious. That was nothing new. "We'll eat in the kitchen, Constance. Surely, Councilor, that would be acceptable even to you?" The way she said *surely* sent shivers down my spine. Roger Samuels gripped the back of the chair so tightly his knuckles went white. Adam Perkins pretended an inordinate interest in his cuff links, and polished one with his coat sleeve as if he'd found a spot of dust. It was a thoroughly unconvincing performance.

I didn't think I could eat a damn bite, but there was no way in hell I would go against Kathy Manning when her face looked like that.

When I walked into the kitchen, I gave the three male Councilors a wide berth.

A small drop leaf table sat beneath a window. The leaves were down and two oak dining chairs with curved backs sat on either side. It was covered with a gold-and-white woven check fabric tablecloth that was fringed along the edges.

Kathy made a huge production as she dragged down plates and cups from the cupboard and banged them down on the table with such force I expected them to shatter on impact.

I got silverware out of a drawer and napkins and finished setting the table while she filled our plates. She gave me such a heaping pile of ravioli even I was daunted. Usually I could eat like a horse, but I was full just looking at the plate. It didn't help that the rock at the pit of my stomach expanded every minute. It would be a boulder soon.

"Eat," she ordered as she stabbed the serving spoon at my plate before she whirled back to the counter for the wine.

The blockage in my throat made me suspect I would have trouble, but I speared a perfectly shaped ravioli with my fork and watched her fill two cobalt-blue goblets with wine.

Councilor Samuels stuck his head through the archway which separated the dining room from the kitchen. He had the look of a man who'd drawn the short straw.

"Kathleen—Kathy," he said in a low voice that appealed to her to understand. "We need to stay objective here."

"Watching her chew will somehow rob you of your ability to be impartial, Roger?" Kathy glowered at him, fingers clenched around the stems of the wine goblets. He winced. "She's not going to eat from trays in her bedroom, that's final."

"No, I agree," Samuels said. "Perhaps she can eat before or after us. It's going to be crowded here for the next few days and we all need to cooperate."

Kathy's breath hissed between her lips like an angry cat's. "Don't you dare ask me to go home, Roger. I was told I could stay here and I'm staying."

"That's not what I said at all, is it?"

"You said it was crowded. The next logical step to take is to see if there are ways to make it not crowded. Tell Armentano to go to a hotel. I'm not budging."

I tried to make myself very small in my chair. There was no way I wanted to witness this.

"You're not doing yourself or Constance any good with this attitude, Kathleen," said Councilor Samuels with a sad shake of his head.

Kathy hurled one of the cobalt-blue glasses at the stainless steel refrigerator next to where Samuels stood. It smashed into shiny blue splinters. The wine made a dull red blotch on the front of the refrigerator. The earthy aroma of wine overrode the smell of pasta and sauce. The scent of Kathy's anger reeked above them all.

"Excuse me." Spots of color blazed high on each of her cheeks. She put the other goblet of wine down on the counter. She was out the back door in a flash, and slammed it behind her.

Samuels, to give him credit, had not even flinched. The shards of glass and splashes of wine missed him entirely, but he had to step carefully around them as he advanced farther into the room. Behind him two voices rose in consternation, but he ignored them.

"I'm sorry you had to witness that, Constance," he told me. I still had the speared ravioli halfway to my mouth but now I set it down on the edge of my plate and pushed back my chair.

"I appreciate everything you're doing for me, Councilor." I too avoided the glass and wine, and eye contact as I walked through the dining room on a retreat to my room.

* * * *

My own scream yanked me out of the nightmare. I sat straight up in bed, my nightgown stuck to my skin with cold sweat. I didn't know where I was and wherever it was, Murphy wasn't there with me.

Heart pounding, I put my palms flat against the sides of my skull and pressed hard as if I could crush the residue of the nightmare out of my head. I could still taste Nate's blood and flesh on my tongue and between my teeth and gagged.

A light in the hallway went on and my door opened. Kathy Manning stuck her head around the doorjamb. Her short, blond-streaked hair was tousled and she wore a white silk nightgown with a hastily thrown on aqua-blue silk robe that she still struggled to knot around her waist.

"Bad dream?" She gave me a sympathetic smile and finished tying the sash to her robe.

"I'm fine," I said, but my voice didn't match my words. I gulped back a sob and pushed some hair from my cold, sweaty face.

"I'll get you some water."

"I don't want anything. I'm fine," I repeated with the vain hope that the more times I said it, the more truthful it would become.

Had Nate screamed when I'd torn his throat out, or was the scream just me? Was it only in the nightmare that he'd choked to death on his own blood, or had that really happened?

And Callie really couldn't have been there with a gun. Could she? No. No. I shook my head wretchedly to dislodge all the damn senseless fragments but they clung as if dipped in some sort of psychic glue.

"Here." I became aware of someone small who sat on the bed beside me. A light flared on and I winced against the intruding brightness.

Faces at the doorway peered in. Male faces. Two of them. One had a blue-black stubbly beard.

"I'm fine," I said for the third time and pushed away the hand that held a cold glass of water.

The bedroom door closed and the male faces disappeared, but Kathy still sat beside me on the bed.

"Want to talk about it?" She smoothed the hair back from my sweaty forehead and I took a deep, shuddering breath but didn't speak.

"It was just a nightmare," Kathy whispered. "It wasn't real."

"For Christ's sake," I snapped. "You think this is the first goddamn nightmare I've ever had in my life? I've had plenty, especially since Grey and Elena died. Nobody was there when I woke up then, I don't need anybody now. So just go away, Kathy. I'm fine."

"You want to call Liam?" She waved a cellphone in front of my eyes and I turned my face away from it.

"I'll wake him."

"If he were here, you'd have woken him."

"But he's not here. Kathy, I am fine. Please go back to bed."

She bit her lip, her face full of concern. "I am so angry at him, Stanzie. He should be here."

"This is all I need." Tears clogged my sinuses but I was goddamned if I'd cry. No way.

The minute she moved away from me, I wished she'd come back, but I kept my head down until she was gone and the door closed behind her. The pillow next to mine was empty. The space next to my body was blank.

It's not like you were never alone before, Constance, I lectured myself as my face crumpled even though the tears did not come. They burned like acid in my sinus cavities but I could not let them out. At that moment I thought the only thing worse than being alone, was being alone when I didn't have to be.

Chapter 8

My tribunal began at ten o'clock on Thursday morning. Scrambled eggs and sausage sat like lead in the bottom of my stomach from a hastily consumed breakfast. I'd tried for a professional appearance with a gray skirt with light blue pinstripes and a lavender button-down blouse with French cuffs. My legs were bare and I wore my Christian Louboutin gray snakeskin peep-toe pumps. I'd coiled my hair into a loose knot atop my head, which effectively covered the healing gash where I'd hit the woodpile. Strategically placed pins ensured they would not irritate and give me a worse headache than the one I already had.

A choker of dull pink pearls and a matching bracelet and earrings were my only jewelry, apart from my peridot-and-pearl bonding pendant. I put that on a long silver chain that disappeared down the front of my blouse so only the pearl choker showed. I wished I'd brought nail polish with me, but I hadn't. I resolved to keep my hands in my lap as much as I could.

I'd been careful with my makeup. It was minimal but I hoped it hid the dark circles under my eyes and the sickly pallor. I was scared to fucking death. Beneath my J'adore perfume, I could clearly smell my own fear and I cursed myself. If I could smell it, everyone could.

Usually there were four Regional Councilors in New England, but today only two of them, Adam Perkins from Connecticut and Jack Hill from Maine, sat at the mahogany table in the large conference of the safe house. Kathy Manning was not allowed to be on the ruling panel and the other Regional Councilor, Rosemary Young, from Vermont, had recently been tapped for the Great Council.

Today she served in her new capacity for the Great Council, with Councilors Samuels and Armentano.

Three Great Councilors represented the gravity of the charge.

In contrast, when I'd been accused of drunk-driving and killing Grey and Elena, only one Great Councilor, Jason Allerton, had been present. The entire Regional Council had been there so the panel today was made up of nearly the same faces as three years previously.

Rosemary Young, a pretty brunette with serious hazel eyes and high cheekbones that hinted at Native American ancestry, pretended to be busy consulting her notebook when I walked past her to sit at the head of the mahogany table in the large conference room.

The Councilors sat at the foot of the table—ranged away from me. Armentano, as the senior representative of the Great Council, sat directly opposite me.

Three Advisors sat in chairs drawn away from the table. They each had a small end table for their notebooks. Two men, one woman. One of the men, a tall redhead with freckles that dusted his cheeks and forehead, had a laptop—high tech for the Pack. I wondered which Councilor he served.

The other man was Italian, which placed him with Armentano, but I wasn't sure of the redhead until Adam Perkins asked him for a refill of his coffee. Nightclaw was the high-tech Pack. Interesting.

The man brought me a cup too, unasked.

"I'm Josh," he introduced himself. "Remember me?"

When I looked into his face close up, I did recall him from Regional Gatherings. I'd never spoken to him though. Nightclaw members were notoriously snobbish. They'd never deign speak to, let alone befriend, anyone from Riverglow.

Josh searched my face eagerly. I don't know what he expected to see unless it was that he'd never looked a killer in the eyes before and this was his big chance. I wished he'd leave me alone. One of the Councilors cleared his throat and Josh moved back to his seat before I could do more than give a jerk of my head to indicate I did remember him.

Sugar bowls, creamers and spoons were in convenient trays on either end of the table. Since I had a cup of coffee in front of me, I gave my nervous hands something to do and doctored my coffee to my taste. It was hot and very good. Kathy had brewed it.

Although I'd expected to see him, Councilor Allerton was not yet in the room. It was selfish of me, but I couldn't help but think he might have put aside his personal issues for at least the small space of time it would take to condemn me.

Additional seating had been set up beyond the Advisors' row for my people. My pack. Murphy would have been sitting there if not for his obsession with finding a precedent in the archives. Councilor Allerton would have been there. Kathy Manning. Vaughn.

Instead the seats were accusingly empty and emphasized the fact I had no one. It had been like that the first time as well. All of Riverglow had sat at the mahogany table with the Regional Council and Allerton. They had not been there to support me, but rather convict me.

Look at the bright side, Constance at least you don't have that this time.

Kathy Manning came through the doorway and shut it behind her. She had a carafe of fresh coffee, which she placed closer to the Councilors. As usual, she was impeccably dressed in a dark gray linen sheath dress with a black bolero jacket. Her black pumps were low-heeled and classy. Her only jewelry was her bond pendant worn on a long silver chain that dangled between her small breasts and a pair of very small black pearl earrings. If she wore pack jewelry, I didn't see it.

She took one of the chairs beyond the Advisors. After all I did have one person there for me. I would have rather had her on the panel. I might have had a shot at clemency if she had been.

"I believe we are all here and we can bring this session to order." Adam Perkins, senior representative of the Regional Council, acted as chairman because the tribunal took place in New England—his territory.

Today he was dressed in a navy blue suit with a white linen shirt and an expensive but very conservative navy blue and black tie. Not a hair was out of place and his buffed nails gleamed under the soft light from the crystal chandelier hung above the table.

Everyone was dressed conservatively. It was not a time for individuality. The outfit I wore had been part of my work clothes wardrobe when I'd had an admin day job. Today it reminded me of the two years I'd spent alone in Boston. I didn't know if I could have felt more isolated and alone. My thoughts tried multiple times to skip to Murphy but I forced them to focus on the people at the table. Self-pity was not going to change a goddamn thing.

"Constance." Councilor Perkins became very serious and professional. "We've spent time compiling evidence and witnesses who will deliver this evidence before the panel. We realize this is a unique and special situation that will need more examination than simply the event in question itself. We need to understand why and how it came to be that your wolf would so forget our laws that she would kill a Pack member who was in human form. It goes deeper than simply that you were trapped against your will by Nathaniel Carver and were seeking release. So please be prepared to answer questions about your wolf and to hear other people give evidence about their experiences with your wolf.

"It is our hope that at the end of this tribunal, we will be able to come to the proper and just decision regarding your culpability.

"Generally, these cases are open and shut but we all agree that this one is not. No one at this table has ever served on a panel with such a grave accusation leveled before. Thankfully, wolf-on-human Pack violence is so rare as to almost be nonexistent. This will, without a doubt, be the most serious panel any of us here will ever serve upon and we want you to trust that we will do our utmost to be fair and objective—to judge with reason and not emotion." He paused for a moment to lock eyes with me so I would acknowledge his sincerity. I had the time to reflect that reason would most likely sink me, whereas emotion would have probably been my ally.

So cynical, Constance.

"We'd like to begin with you. We want to hear you tell us what happened, and more importantly, why you did the things you did. So, please take a moment to gather your thoughts and begin when you are ready. Don't start with the event itself, but rather the circumstances and moments leading up to it. Don't worry about how much time it takes you. We are not on a clock. This tribunal will take whatever time it takes. Do you understand? Do you want more coffee or a glass of water while you think?"

Unable to speak, I shook my head. I was pretty sure I would not have been able to swallow a thing. I had to wonder if I would even be able to speak, so I was grateful for the time to compose myself.

Sweat made my palms cold and slick, but thankfully my face did not perspire. Not that it made any difference. Everyone could smell my fear. All the J'adore in the world couldn't mask it.

Just as I was about to plunge into what I miserably suspected would be a disjointed and emotional recital, the conference room door opened.

Everyone swung around to stare at the interloper. After the door was shut during a tribunal, it was not supposed to be opened except by a member of the panel. Councilor Samuel's Advisor had been posted there to watch and make sure the door remained closed.

The man who nonchalantly strode in had different-colored eyes—one blue, the other brown. A shock of black hair curled in an unruly riot on his head and his clothes were casual and rumpled—a pair of jeans and a hand-knitted v-neck sweater with an intricate pattern.

Padraic O'Reilly—Alpha male of Mac Tire. My Alpha.

He looked jetlagged as hell, but he couldn't suppress a cheerful grin. "Sorry about barging in. My plane was late and I came here direct from the airport. Have I missed anything?"

I loved Alphas. They were so self-assured and cocky and Paddy was ten times that and more.

The Advisors shifted indignantly in their chairs, especially the redheaded one—Josh. The door shut behind Paddy and I wondered if Councilor Samuel's Advisor was young, female and due for some stern lecturing.

"It's customary to wait for the break if the door is closed, Mr. O'Reilly." Adam Perkins was flustered. He was a stickler for the rules.

"Nah, not when you've got one of my pack sitting in the hot seat. Alphas are always permitted to be present for all of a tribunal. Am I right, Councilor?" With an almost outrageous amount of self-confidence, Paddy swaggered to the chair next to mine and pulled it out.

"We've put some chairs in the back for..." Adam Perkins began but Paddy shook his head slightly and, incredibly, Perkins shut his mouth.

"Alphas have conference table privileges, don't they, Councilor? You know my name, but I'm not sure I know yours." His Irish accent was more pronounced than Murphy's, but when he talked I was still reminded of him.

"Regional Councilor Adam Perkins. Do you think we could proceed, Mr. O'Reilly?" I wondered if Perkins would transfer his pique to me but decided it was worth it to have someone sitting next to me. I was not alone after all.

In that moment I pledged my loyalty to Paddy O'Reilly. Although he'd been my Alpha for nearly six months, it was that moment it became real for me. I hadn't had an Alpha for nearly three years and I'd forgotten how it made me feel—as if I were a part of something greater than I was on my own, yet something that allowed me to be me at the same time. A sense of belonging, of rightness, of being Pack. I was no loner. Time and experience had taught me that.

"Ready when you are, Councilor Perkins." Paddy pulled his chair in and braced his elbows on the table as he looked from one end of the table and back to the other expectantly.

"Constance was just about to tell us what happened in her own words," Rosemary Young prompted me.

"Advisor Newcastle, please go on." Paddy emphasized my title, giving me a small wink that nobody saw but me. I wanted to kiss the man but restrained myself. I almost laughed but caught it back just before it burst from my mouth. If he was Mr. O'Reilly and the Councilors were all addressed by their title, Paddy was right—I should be addressed by mine. It hadn't been stripped from me. Yet.

"Advisor Newcastle, I'm sorry." Rosemary gave us both a sweet smile that was not a bit sarcastic. I think she was smitten with Paddy. By his satisfied grin, he thought so too.

"Bethany's panties had traces of urine on them and my wolf smelled something in the urine that she recognized on a gut level, but didn't know the word for." It was a blunt way to begin, but it had been the start of my suspicions that ultimately led to Grandmother Emma's root cellar. It got everyone's attention—that was for sure.

Beside me, Paddy O'Reilly became slightly less cocky and as my story went on, his expression altered more and more to one of serious concentration. He, at least, lived my tale. I'm not sure about the others. They struggled—some more than others—to remain objective.

"Ever since I started working on my wolf with Murphy, she's become increasingly obsessed with the names of the things in the world around her.

Before that she was obsessed with the experience of having everything rush past in a blur of scent and sound, vision and touch. She was mostly sensory and emotional, and now she's become focused on the intellectual, but she's still very emotional. Of course, so am I, so I guess that makes sense. I'm not sure." I frowned because I was tangled up in semantics rather than sticking to facts. I needed to concentrate more.

"I know what pregnant women smell like and I know the word, but she only knew what it meant, not the word for it. And so instead of hunting with the rest of Maplefair in the woods along the road where Bethany and most of the pack lived, my wolf sat in the clearing and tried to think of the word *pregnant*. Murphy's wolf and Vaughn's, they tried to get her to hunt with the others, but no way was she budging until she had the word. That's the way she is now. Stubborn and obsessed. Nate..." I stumbled over his name, blindsided by a rush of guilt and anger that choked me for a moment. Everyone noticed. The steady scratch of one of the Advisor's pens was the only sound for a couple of seconds.

He's writing my doom. God, so melodramatic, Constance.

"Nate's wolf tried to get mine to hunt too, but she didn't listen to him either." I managed to get the sentence out without my voice cracking, but knew immediately that I'd banged yet another nail into my own coffin. I saw Councilor Armentano's scowl and took a deep breath to steady myself.

Way to go, Constance. Thirty seconds into your narrative you tell the whole panel how little attention you pay to Alphas. Not. Good.

"From the start I thought Bethany might be pregnant. I mean it sounded like a classic case—shifting with her boyfriend at a Regional, being kept apart from him but probably still sneaking around behind everyone's backs. Being seventeen and somewhat irresponsible with things like birth control. It just seemed the most logical explanation and it was, but Jossie and Nate were adamant she wasn't pregnant. She'd taken the herbs after shifting at the Regional, she'd gotten her period so she couldn't be pregnant.

"Only that Regional was over three months ago. Plenty of time to get pregnant after. So when my wolf smelled her panties, she knew right away she smelled the urine of a pregnant woman. It all started to come out when I told everyone what I'd smelled after the hunt was over and everyone shifted back. Some of them, mostly men, were in denial about it, but her mother confirmed it. She hadn't known until the hunt. Until she smelled it too."

I looked at them and wished I knew what they thought. While Rosemary Young's expression was compassionate, the men on the panel were impassive.

With a sigh, I continued. "That's when it came out that the boyfriend, Cody, knew she was pregnant. He told us she'd been going to get an abortion. Even from the start of that story, I knew it was wrong. She didn't know how to drive and Cody did, but she wouldn't let him drive her to an abortion clinic. Her house is on this rural road that I doubt the town even plows in the winter. Nobody but Maplefair pack members live on it. It's at least four miles to any sort of main thoroughfare. Not a bad walk, I guess, but why would you do it when your boyfriend has a car? Who wants to have an abortion and be all alone when you've got a boyfriend who's beside himself with concern and wants to support you? She didn't even ride her bike.

"The nearest abortion clinic was thirteen and a half miles away. I looked it up. And that was a Planned Parenthood, which would have refused her because she didn't have any ID. I'm not even sure she had cash enough for a cheap abortion at one of the abortion mills that don't care about things like IDs if you have enough money. The nearest one of those—that I could find anyway—was seventeen miles away. No car. No bike. When I brought this up, everyone dismissed it and said she must have hitched. They were all convinced she'd had a botched abortion and was dead."

Rosemary Young flinched at the word *dead*. Or maybe the matter of fact way I said it. I couldn't tell. "I guess I leaned in that direction too, but not the same way they did. No matter how much I tried, I couldn't fit a scared seventeen-year-old Pack girl who'd never gone to a public school, who'd never made friends outside her own pack, hitchhiking seventeen miles in a strange Other's car to an abortion clinic where she'd be treated like a number. Not when she had been brought up with the idea that most grandmothers have herbal knowledge and they are the ones who handle things like unexpected pregnancies and most sicknesses.

"I knew she probably wouldn't go to one of the more prominent grandmothers in the pack because she wanted to keep it a secret. But there was one who never socialized with anyone but her great-grandson. Sure, he was Alpha but Alphas are...well, they're supposed to protect you and watch over you. And maybe Bethany hoped that even if Grandmother Emma said something to Nate, it might still be kept a secret. It was better than any of the alternatives and something had to be done."

A shaft of midmorning sunlight beamed through the partially drawn blinds in the windows and bathed the panel in a soft glow. Dust motes danced in the air exposed by the light and, for a moment, I wished I could float away and not have to continue my story.

"Anyway, that's what I thought, but when I tried to bring it up that morning at breakfast, nobody wanted to hear me. I suppose I was a bit harsh in the way I tried to explain. Everyone was so fixated on the hitchhiking theory that I told them if she'd done that, maybe she'd been murdered by whoever picked her up. That was my other scenario, the one I didn't put much stock in, but most of the puzzle pieces fit in a stretch if you ignored the part about her being a sheltered Pack girl.

"Jossie got upset, Nate got pissed because Jossie was upset, and Vaughn and Murphy just wanted to smooth things over and do something productive. I did too, my job was to call the funeral homes and hospitals around the area to ask if an unidentified teenage girl had shown up hurt, dying or dead. The more phone calls I made, the more I knew it was a complete waste of time. She'd gone to a grandmother, I just knew it. And maybe the abortion had gone wrong and she'd died and the grandmother was too freaked out to admit it or maybe she was just recovering there.

"Which is why I shouldn't have been so shocked to see Nate's SUV in Grandmother Emma's yard, but I was. Mainly because he didn't park out in the open, he'd pulled behind the woodshed as if he were trying to hide. Only nobody went to Grandmother Emma's, so why would he want to hide even if he was supposed to be at the New Hampshire border searching motels and abortion clinics?"

I stopped for a moment because I was getting ahead of myself. Paddy O'Reilly gave me an encouraging nod as if to say I was doing fine.

At least that's how I interpreted it and it buoyed me up a little. "I decided my job of calling around to hospitals and funeral homes was pure bullshit and that I wanted to do something productive too. Something that required more action than punching numbers into a keypad and talking to anonymous voices. So I walked down the road to Grandmother Emma's house."

For the first time one of the Councilors interrupted me. Rosemary Young.

"I'm sorry, Advisor Newcastle, but when you say you walked down the road, did you tell anyone where you were going?"

I suspected she knew the answer but was trying to get it onto the record in my words.

"I didn't. Jossie was there, doing laundry, and I could have told her, but she was avoiding me because of what I'd said at breakfast about Bethany being murdered by the person who picked her up hitchhiking. My cellphone was right there too, but I left that behind. I guess I was obsessed with the idea of proving myself right. It was important."

"Why?" The Regional Councilor from Maine, Jack Hill, leaned forward in his seat, his gray eyes stern.

Paddy gave me another slight nod. I was so glad he was there, but I wished it were Murphy who sat there instead. My heart wouldn't have beat half so hard and I wouldn't have felt half so sick if Murphy had been there.

I lowered my eyes away from Hill's penetrating gaze. He was a no-nonsense type of man—blunt and demanding. Probably narrow and puritanical in his outlook on things like Pack ethics. He would be merciless against self-doubt and weakness.

"Because of my wolf." The admission came hard, but it was honest. God, this was hell. I fucking *hated* this. "Because Gary Planchett laughed at me after the hunt. It was humiliating. It wasn't the first time someone's made fun of my wolf, but this time it really bothered me. Before I started working on her, I never cared what anybody thought. People are so hung up on what everyone else does or thinks, but I never was until I started working with her and realized how much she had to learn and figure out. I was ashamed of her and I hated that because she was the most pure and honest part of my life. And now she's not. Now she's..." I had begun to say *weak and flawed*, but realized that probably wasn't in my best interests considering my predicament. "...not.

"I wasn't really pulling my weight. I was dragging people down. So I thought if I could find out the truth, find Bethany, I could prove I could keep up. That's why I left without telling anyone anything. Anger and pride. Wounded vanity. But I never suspected the truth was as bad as it turned out to be. I never consciously thought Nate Carver had anything to do with it, especially not the way he did."

"Consciously?" Rosemary Young repeated my word as she leaned slightly forward in her seat. She sat on the side of the table, her body shifted toward me, her eyes alight as she empathized with me. Empathized and judged.

An ugly surge of resentment burned through my body. Every person at this table today, except me, was an Alpha or a former Alpha. Councilors. Leaders. They'd never had to struggle to keep up, they'd always set the pace.

The only place I'd ever set the pace was in wolf form—back when no one could outrace my wolf and it was all they could do to keep up.

That's how I felt almost all the time in human form now. Ever since bonding with Murphy and being propelled into the life of an Advisor. Only it was becoming more and more clear that I wasn't keeping up, I was seriously falling behind.

"He had sawdust stuck to the mud on his boots." I knew that sounded insane. Everyone in the room looked confused. "He could never sit still for longer than three minutes. I timed him. Three minutes and he'd be off doing something else, even if it was only to fiddle with an ornament on the mantel or check on the baby. He was constantly in motion, never satisfied or relaxed. It made me anxious. The kind of anxiety you can't put your finger on and you're not even really aware you're experiencing until you suddenly snap.

"There were weird undercurrents between him and Jossie. On the surface they were the perfect couple, but she almost always had some sort of physical barrier between them. Usually the baby, Heather. Sometimes just her arms crossed over her chest.

"When we arrived that first day, he was in wolf form, I guess pretending to search for Bethany on his own before the big pack hunt. My guess is that he went toward Grandmother Emma's house, so that he could lead the hunt away from her place the next day. Murphy was getting the luggage out of the trunk and I was near the porch when Nate came around the corner of the house in wolf form. He was growling."

That got their attention. My throat was dry so I took a sip of coffee. It was cold and I must have grimaced because Paddy got up from his chair, marched down to the other end of the conference table and retrieved the carafe. He refilled my mug and I stirred in sugar and cream.

After a few more sips of hot coffee, my jangled nerves were somewhat soothed. "Murphy was nervous even before Nate's wolf started growling. That set me off, I guess. Normally if someone Pack comes around the corner in wolf form, you don't immediately go on the defensive. But Murphy did and then I did too. And Nate's wolf kept growling. Murphy told me to get on the porch and shut the door between us. I think maybe he and Vaughn were going to try to get into the car. We were making escape plans, Councilors. Murphy slammed down the trunk to create a noisy diversion. That was my cue to run for the porch and I did, only Nate's wolf jumped me and knocked me down before I could make it."

The steady scratch of the Advisor's pen ceased. Councilor Young's face creased in shock while Councilor Armentano's dark eyes narrowed.

"I tried to cover my head with my arms, protect my face and neck, and then he licked me. It was all a joke."

They hadn't expected that ending although I don't know why not. I clearly had no bite marks and if Nate's wolf had mauled me, Murphy wouldn't have stayed silent about it even if I had.

"Rather in poor taste if you ask me," muttered Perkins, clearly indignant. "I hope you gave him a piece of your mind."

"I didn't know what to do. He treated it like it was no big deal." I said. "But that's the kind of guy Nate was. Always keeping you off balance in some way. Making it seem like if you said anything, you were the one with the problem, not him. I remember feeling sorry for Jossie having to live with him. I couldn't have done it. I would have gone crazy with his never being able to settle down, always having to keep in motion.

"So I think when I saw Nate's SUV behind the woodshed at Grandmother Emma's, that's why it made me feel so apprehensive. I was already freaked out by the sheer silence surrounding that place. No birds sang, no squirrels talked to each other from the woods. All the shades were down in all the windows and nobody answered the door. It was not a restful place. That low-level anxiety I'd been experiencing ever since Nate's wolf walked around the corner of the farmhouse two days earlier, amped up so hard that I wanted to run. It's like my body knew something my brain wouldn't acknowledge."

I shifted gears back to the story, but they were all with me. Councilor Young was a smoker—I could smell it clinging to her clothes. I knew by the way she shifted in her chair and cast longing looks at the door that she wanted a cigarette but there were no ashtrays in the room. Instead she reached for her coffee, gulped at it, and never took her gaze from my face.

"I tried to come up with reasons why he would be there, but all the reasons I could come up with—mostly having to do with checking up on Grandmother Emma—didn't explain why he hadn't come to the door when I knocked. I called out my name and everything, so they both had to know someone Pack was knocking."

I took another steadying sip of coffee. "When I was circling around to the back door, I saw Nate's SUV and, like I said, alarm bells started going off. I went closer to the car. I don't know what I was looking for and my legs kept telling me to run but my brain overrode the impulse. I felt so close to something, but I didn't know what. The woodshed door was open a little and I went inside. I saw the sawdust on the floor and the chainsaw hanging on the wall and I thought, 'aha, that's why Nate had sawdust on his boots last night.' It had been bothering me. I notice people's shoes. I have a thing for shoes."

I felt like an idiot blurting that but it was the truth and most of the reason why I'd noticed the damn sawdust in the first place. The first things I'd noticed about Paddy when he'd breezed into the room were his Doc Martens. They were well worn and comfortable-looking. He probably wore them almost every day. I'd noticed Kathy Manning's Jimmy Choos as well. It was just something I cataloged about people.

"Because there was sawdust all over the floor, I saw that this metal bookcase had been recently moved a few inches. I got curious. I also got scared. I didn't want to be a coward running away from some nebulous fear. I didn't understand why I was scared. It never dawned on me that Nate was a serial killer. Even saying it now sounds absurd."

Faces remained grim, but there were one or two nods of agreement.

"When I moved the bookcase, a wrench fell off the second shelf and nearly hit my foot. That distracted me for a second, but then I saw the trapdoor to the root cellar." I stopped talking because for an instant I was transported back to that wood shed. I could clearly see the wooden trap door and smell the sawdust.

I looked across the room at Councilor Samuels. He appeared caught up in my tale, his kind face full of trepidation.

"I'm not sure what I would have done then. Maybe I would have opened up the trap door. I think I knew Bethany was down there on some gut level. I couldn't hear her or smell her or anything, but I just knew. There was also this part of me screaming to leave, to run and get Murphy, get somebody because this was way too big for me. It was spinning out of control. That's when all the light disappeared." I shuddered, remembering that awful, panicky moment.

Paddy covered my hand with his and gave my fingers a gentle, reassuring squeeze. God, I was grateful for his presence. It was almost overwhelming that he was he was there. I had someone with me. I didn't know him well at all, but he'd become my Alpha without question. It had been so long since I'd had such respect and gratitude for my Alpha. I'd had it for Vaughn, Callie and Peter when I'd first joined Riverglow. Jonathan had not managed to inspire such loyalty and devotion in me, but he'd been my Alpha and I had submitted. But Paddy was more like the Alphas I remembered from Mayflower when I was growing up. Especially the last one before I'd left to bond with Grey.

A multitude of old, buried emotion spilled over me. I felt nineteen again in some ways and yet I was still firmly anchored to the present. I was a fraying rope being pulled in two different directions.

Nate had been an Alpha—that was one of the worst parts of the whole thing. An Alpha. From birth we're trained and expected to look at Alphas as leaders. People who will give us security and direction in exchange for loyalty. To betray an Alpha is very hard.

"It was Nate," I said, surprising myself that I was ready to continue the story. "And I knew when I looked at him that there was something very wrong with him. With everything. He didn't even try to pretend to be nice, to be rational. He had this look on his face that I recognized. I've only been an Advisor a few months, but when people have something to hide, they look at me the same way. I tried to imagine what he had to hide. I told him I thought it was bullshit that Bethany had gone to an abortion clinic. I asked him if Bethany was in the root cellar. I thought she was dead. Grandmother Emma had given her the wrong herbs or something. I accused him of covering up for her. That's the worst thing I could think of him doing.

"He said, 'You want to see her, Stanzie?' And his voice was so cold. I told him I wanted to go get Murphy. He laughed at me and said Murphy was halfway to Canada by now. He started ranting about Advisors, about everybody getting in his way and how he wanted to be left alone.

"He started screaming at me about how the woodshed was his private place. I kept talking about Grandmother Emma. I asked him if he were helping her cover up something bad. And then he went for me. He scared the *shit* out of me." My voice shook and Paddy gave my fingers another squeeze. His expression was a combination of horror and protective rage. I'd become his pack member just as deeply as he'd become my Alpha.

"The wrench was on the floor. I dropped down to grab it and his fist sailed through the air where my head had been. He went off balance and I got the wrench and managed to stand up. I didn't know what the hell to do. He told me to put the wrench down and I almost did because he's an Alpha."

My mouth trembled a little bit and I had to swallow something blocking my throat. "I was like, what are you doing, Stanzie, you idiot. He's not your Alpha! But still I didn't know if I could hit him. He kept screaming at me to put the wrench down and I screamed back at him that Murphy would kick his ass if he hurt me and then he said that that he'd fix him. And Vaughn too. Just the idea of Vaughn really pissed him off worse than he already was. He told me Jossie wasn't fooling him, he knew Heather wasn't his baby. He was so angry that Vaughn had shown up at their door. His eyes got all crazy and he went for me again, only this time I didn't duck. I was pissed too. He was not going to hurt Murphy or Vaughn.

"I swung at him with the wrench only I didn't hit his head like I was aiming for, I got his arm. I hurt him, but I didn't incapacitate him. He bashed into me and I slammed into the woodpile. The back of my head hit the edge of a piece of wood and then I guess I blacked out because that's all I remember until I woke up in the dark, chained to a metal hospital gurney."

I'd watched the panel's faces when I'd revealed that Vaughn was Heather's father. None of them were surprised. That part relieved me. I didn't want anyone to think Heather had that bastard Nate for a father. I'd confirmed something they already had been told and now it was going to be doubly believed and supported. Maybe something good could come of this whole fucking fiasco.

Now I was coming to the hard, horrible part of the story—the part where I had to tell them about Bethany's dark recital of Nate's atrocities and, of course, the ultimate horror—my wolf's fangs tearing his throat out.

Adept at reading the faces and emotions of those of us in the room with him, Councilor Perkins said, "Let's break for ten minutes."

Rosemary Young was the first on her feet and out the door—no doubt to answer the siren song of nicotine. The others weren't far behind her.

* * * *

Silent and dazed, I made no move to get up.

Paddy waited a moment then fished a small box out of his pocket. With a proud, almost reverent smile, he presented it to me. "It goes on the middle finger of your right hand."

Inside the box was a silver ring—obviously handmade. A series of interlocking lines that in the abstract could be taken for the claws. The claws of a wolf. Very distinctive and beautiful. The pack jewelry of Mac Tire—only worn by members.

"I had planned to give this you down the pack's pub in Dublin along with a glass of whiskey, but this'll have to do." He gave me a lopsided smile as he slid the ring on my finger and I smiled back although I felt more like crying.

"I would have liked that," I said wistfully as I pictured the scene. A small pub with lots of dark wood and strong Irish whiskey. "The pack has a pub?"

"We sure do." Paddy gave me another irresistible smile and, for a moment, sparks of attraction smoldered between us. It had been like this the first time we'd met at the chateau. He was a very sexy man, Padraic O'Reilly. In another life, in another time, I would have enjoyed being seduced by him. "I owe you a glass of whiskey the first time you see it, okay?"

I wanted to play along with the fantasy that I'd see this pub and drink this whiskey, but I couldn't.

"I would have been a good pack member," I said. "Probably more trouble than I would have been worth, but I would have tried to have been good."

Paddy's attractive face became very grave. "You know something I don't know? Who says you won't get the chance?"

"Come on." I examined the ring on my finger and wondered if they'd take it off before they cremated my body and, if they did, who they'd give it to—Murphy or Paddy. I'd wanted Grey and Elena's pack rings, but they had not been given to me. It had plagued me at first, wondering who had them or if they'd been melted down with their bones and flesh and scattered in the woods of the Devil's Hopyard.

With effort, I brought myself back to the present. "Let's be realistic. I'm never going to get to Dublin. I end here."

"You don't think there's any chance at all that you'll be cleared?" Paddy sounded honestly curious.

"My wolf killed someone Pack, Paddy. Someone Pack who was in human form. I have no chance. I don't want to get my hopes up thinking I have a shot when I don't." I didn't look up from the ring.

"You know," he told me. "There's a difference between unrealistic optimism and giving up completely. There's a happy medium in there somewhere. Is it going to be any worse if you have some hope of being cleared and you aren't than if you're convinced you don't have a prayer?"

"I don't want to die," I admitted. "Paddy, I can't think about it so I just make myself believe it's a done deal and then I don't have to. At least not right now."

"Horseshit," he said with an almost obscene cheerfulness. "Nobody wants to die, but we all do. Your death may be years in the future yet, woman. Don't give up."

His cavalier attitude grated.

"Easy for you to say."

His eyes narrowed. "I didn't fucking fly eleven goddamn hours to listen to this gloomy shite, Constance Newcastle. You're about five minutes away from telling the goddamn Councilors how and why you ripped that bastard fuck's throat out and you'd better make it good because if they think for one minute you wish you'd done differently, you're fucking doomed. Is that what you want? You don't want to die, but you're gonna go down without a fucking fight?"

"I told her to hurt him, not kill him!" I screamed into Paddy's face. He didn't draw back, he leaned forward so our foreheads touched. I lowered my voice because his mouth was two inches away from my own and it seemed ridiculous to yell. Paddy O'Reilly knew how to calm down hysterical females. That made me wonder about his bond mate. "Are you telling me to lie?"

"I'm telling you to tell it like it happened and not filter it through your human form guilt, goddamn you!"

"Tell it like it happened?" I drew away from him so I could raise my voice in disbelief. "I don't fucking remember! I saw the ladder and his boots coming down and that's all I remember until I was shifted back!"

"Then tell it that way! Tell it with some fucking passion and stop being such a goddamned baby!" He took me by the shoulders and shook me so hard I couldn't focus on his face and everything became a blur.

My head gave a sick lurch and the coffee and scrambled eggs in my stomach threatened projectile ejection.

My expression must have given me away because he stopped shaking me. Hot and cold flushes swept through my body head to toe and back again. It took everything I had not to puke on him, although a part of me thought he fucking deserved it.

"My head," I whispered, trying to explain, although by his contrite expression I thought he remembered the part of my story where I'd hit my head, although a bit goddamned late.

I wanted Murphy so fucking bad I thought I would strangle on the longing. In that moment I wanted him and also hated him for not being there. Paddy was a stranger. All that bullshit about feeling so grateful for an Alpha vanished beneath a disgusting wave of nausea. Alpha, hell. This man didn't know the first thing about me.

He knows you're a fucking coward, Constance.

Burning acid filled my throat. With a suddenness that startled Paddy, I dashed out of the room and up the staircase to the dubious sanctuary of the blue-tiled bathroom.

Vomit spewed into the toilet bowl and I was convinced for a moment I wouldn't have to face the rest of the tribunal and be condemned because I would choke to death on my own puke.

Eventually I stopped retching and clutched the sides of the toilet as I tried not to groan aloud. My head buzzed and spun sickeningly. I closed my eyes so I wouldn't have to watch the room lurch up and down. I wanted to be dead. Maybe everything would stop moving and hurting if I were dead.

When the world was stable enough for me to open my eyes again, I saw that Paddy hovered contritely in the doorway.

"Jaysus, I'm sorry," he whispered.

"I'm fine," I said as I calculated if I could stand up without hanging onto the side of the counter to keep my balance. The ten minutes of the break must surely have ticked away by now. "I'll be right down. I just need to rinse my mouth out." I looked down at my blouse and skirt to make sure I hadn't stained them, but I hadn't.

Paddy continued to hover and watched me gargle with mouthwash. I wet a washcloth and pressed it to my aching forehead. My face needed to be washed, but I didn't have time to redo my makeup.

I peered at myself in the mirror, horrified at how pale I looked. Like a fucking ghost. A zombie. A ghost zombie. All pretense of prettiness had fled from my face and left me to look gaunt and drawn. I had a sudden preview of how I might have appeared as a grandmother. It was too harsh to stare at very long, so I busied myself with a fresh coat of lipstick. After I fixed a few loose pins in my hair, I looked a little better—but not much.

Remorseful, Paddy dogged my steps down the staircase and back into the large conference room. We were the last ones there.

* * * *

News of my pukefest had apparently reached the panel because Adam Perkins gravely inquired whether I needed more time and that maybe we ought to break early for lunch.

The thought of food made me go hot and cold as a fresh burst of nausea swept over me.

"No, I can do this," I insisted, although part of me thought it was a distinct possibility that I might faint dead away at the damn conference table. Things were a little out of focus, but I thought if I could sit down it might get better.

Paddy took the chair next to mine again. The little box that had held the pack ring was still on the table next to a fresh mug of coffee and a plate of chocolate chip cookies. The smell of the sugar and chocolate made me almost gag so I pushed the plate toward the center of the table. Paddy got up and took it away to a side table.

I was nearly at sensory overload. Smells crowded in on me almost as distinct as they would have in wolf form. Three different types of cologne, six different brands of deodorant, Kathy's perfume and my own. Plus coffee, cookies, furniture polish, dry-cleaning fluid, tobacco, shampoo, mouthwash, someone's mint gum and the distinct Pack odors of eleven different people. Thankfully the windows were shut so I didn't have to directly deal with pollen, leaves, grass and exhaust.

A carafe of water and glasses were near enough for me to reach. I was thirsty. I gulped down half a glass of water that tasted mostly of mouthwash, but things evened out after that and I could concentrate.

"I'm ready to go on now," I told them, not sure what they wanted next.

"Tell us what happened after you hit your head, Constance," said Rosemary Young. She may not have been the chairman of the panel, but she was the only woman and, while they were all more or less sympathetic, she stood out as the most approachable and compassionate.

She tucked her bobbed brown hair behind her ears, lending her smooth face an openness and honesty that drew me. I focused on her because it was easier to imagine I was telling my story to one person versus than a roomful. If only that damn Advisor's pencil would stop its ceaseless scratch, I could really concentrate. What the hell could he be writing when no one was even talking for Christ's sake?

I chanced a look in his direction. It was the Italian Advisor, his dark head bent over a medium-sized pad of paper. He wasn't writing words but drawing pictures. Of me. Of the panel. His face was seized with concentration and when he looked up and saw that I stared at him, a slow, dazed smile spread across his face.

"*Scuzi*," he whispered.

"Can I see it?" I forgot for a moment where we were. He was a gorgeous man with wide, brown eyes and a perfect profile.

He held the pad up for my inspection. He was drawing me, as I suspected. Only he was being very generous. Under his pencil, my horrible pallor was rendered romantically pale. He drew me in profile and made me far more beautiful than I really was. In his drawing I looked haunted and surreal. I was probably haunted, but surreal was not a word that anyone could apply to my physical appearance.

Paddy took one look at it and rolled his eyes.

"Jaysus God, but Italians are terrible flirts," he remarked.

"Irishmen are full of...blarney." I hastily amended what I had been about to say which only made Paddy laugh. The Italian Advisor grinned and winked at me.

The redheaded Advisor, Josh, tried to appear disapproving but couldn't quite manage it. The way he looked at Paddy made me understand he had not made a ghoulish attempt to strike up an acquaintance with a murderess as I'd earlier suspected, but instead he was a typical Nightclaw snob. Paddy O'Reilly was Alpha male of the largest pack in the United Kingdom and I was a member of that pack. So it was my connections and not my deeds that had attracted him. That still didn't make me like him much.

The female Advisor, a short girl with bright gold hair and a rather unfortunate nose, was familiar to me. I'd seen her at Regionals. Her name was Kristen or Kristie. I couldn't remember which. She was from Wolfsong, a pack in Maine, so she had to be with Councilor Hill. She shifted indignantly in her seat and obviously thought the whole side exchange was scandalous.

The Italian Advisor whispered something into her ear, which seemed to mollify her a little. She adjusted her position so her foot touched his.

Councilor Perkins cleared his throat, which made him sound more than a little like a scalded duck.

The Advisors bent studiously toward their notepads while Paddy and I looked at the panel.

"Please continue, Advisor Newcastle." Perkins waved a hand to indicate I should proceed.

For a moment I marshaled my thoughts. Back to business. "I was disoriented at first. It was pitch-black and my head hurt. It took me a few minutes to clearly understand that I was lying on a metal gurney. It had grooves or channels in the side so it wasn't a hospital gurney like the kind they wheel you around on, it was like the ones in a morgue where the channels are so they can rinse away blood other body fluids."

Paddy winced then tried to make his face impassive. Most of the Councilors looked shocked as well.

"I was chained by wrists and ankles. Leather straps buckled tight with chains inserted through a metal ring sewn into the straps and then fastened to the sides of the gurney. The chains were brought up short so I couldn't sit up, bend my knees, or reach across my body. No way to undo the buckles and get free. I was naked and it was cold. I thought at first I was blind but I think that was more because I was disoriented than anything else. I could hear someone crying and it took me a long time to figure out it wasn't me.

"I smelled Bethany—I recognized her scent from the clothes and belongings we'd used for the pack hunt the day before. There were other smells too—piss, shit, puke, sweat, tears, blood and burned flesh." Each word made someone in the room flinch as if they smelled the scent as pungently and clearly as I had.

"When I said her name she stopped crying long enough to demand to know who I was. When I told her she got so excited to think that the Councils were looking for her. Like that would have even been in question. She thought everyone had given up on her. I told her we hadn't but she started crying again. She was convinced no one would find us and we were both going to die, her sooner than me because she was weak and he was bored with her.

"She told me all about what he did to those poor Other girls. He liked runaways best because they were more innocent, but he could work with prostitutes if he had to as long as they hadn't been on the street very long. He liked to make them cry. He liked to burn them and beat them and rape them. He liked them to lie in their own filth, chained and unable to move. He rarely had to kill them deliberately. Most of them died after a week or so. Infections mainly, although one girl had starved herself to death, refusing the food and water he offered. He'd thought about forcing her to eat but in the end let her do what she wanted so he could watch the process.

"He was big on watching. They were experiments to him. They weren't real people. They were Others to begin with, not even Pack. Sub human. Less than important. Their lives were worthless, which is why they were runaways and prostitutes. He was doing them a favor allowing them to achieve some meaning as their pain and degradation served him.

"He didn't like that Bethany was Pack because he couldn't rape her properly, not with his cock, because he didn't want her shifting. So he had to make do with objects. Bottles. The handle of a hammer, although he was pretty sure he was going to use the claw end at some point. It would probably kill her so he was saving that for last."

Although my voice was flat and emotionless, Councilor Hill's Advisor bolted to her feet and left the room without excusing herself. Her face was dreadfully pale and we all saw the tears in her eyes.

"Kathleen?" Rosemary Young looked at Kathy who was already halfway to her feet. She went out after the Advisor to make sure she was all right.

I hadn't been half as graphic as I could have been. I didn't want to sensationalize Bethany's trauma but I didn't want to sugarcoat it either.

"If he didn't like the fact she was Pack, why did he abduct her?" Councilor Armentano asked, although I was pretty sure knew the answer.

"He didn't do it on purpose. Bethany went to Grandmother Emma's house in search of an abortion. He was coming out of the woodshed with the remains of the latest Other girl in a plastic garbage bag. It had ripped open and one of the girl's arms was half falling out. Bethany saw it and so he had no choice but to take her."

I found it easier to say *he* rather than his name. In a way I objectified him almost as much as he had objectified his victims, but it was a coping strategy so I could finish the goddamn story without bolting out the door the same way as the Advisor.

I hadn't talked about it since it had happened. Murphy and I had not spoken much during the hellish drive from Vermont to Connecticut, and I'd spent most of the day yesterday asleep. No one had asked me what had happened until now, and the few times I'd used Nate's name had made me shudder so I tried to protect myself.

"Did you ask her to tell you all of this?" Rosemary Young's expression was empathetic.

"No, Councilor, she just started talking to me. I let her talk because I thought it might do her some good to get it out, although it made me want to start screaming. It was really hard for me to keep from going crazy trying to get free from the restraints. And then she started to cry again and I felt bad for not stopping her from telling me things. I think it made it worse, not better. She kept saying he was going to come back and do the things to me he'd done to her, and she kept begging me not to scream or cry because she couldn't bear it if I did."

My voice lost some of its dispassionate quality. "I was going to do my best not to scream or cry because I didn't want to give him the satisfaction, but I had this horrible feeling I wouldn't be able to keep my resolve. I'm not very good with pain."

I had very little doubt the first time he touched me I would have screamed like hell. Cried too, probably.

"I did ask her if he raped her." My face burned with guilt. "I didn't want him touching me like that and I guess I was thinking more of myself than I was of her, poor thing. I was naked on that gurney and I didn't know if he'd done anything to me while I was unconscious. It didn't feel like it, but still."

I shuddered and thought I must sound like a goddamn idiot galloping all over the conversational course instead of keeping on track. "That's when she told me about the bottle and the hammer. But that's when I got the idea. When she said he didn't want her shifting I didn't understand at first and didn't know what damn difference it would have made. It's not like you could stay shifted, you always have to come back. If he didn't want to deal with our wolves, he just had to stay away for a couple of days. I thought maybe he didn't want to do that, so that's why he used things instead.

"But then I actually saw it in my head. Me shifting into a wolf and the restraints falling away because my wolf s legs wouldn't be the same shape or thickness as my ankles and wrists. I could get free if I could shift. And I told myself I could run for help. That was my original plan."

The Councilors' eyes sharpened at the word *original*.

"Murphy and I had been quiet the night before, but he might have heard us. He should have been asleep in the downstairs wing of the farmhouse, but he never could keep still. For hours I agonized over whether or not he'd heard us making love. I had a little more than twenty-four hours left to shift and I needed to do it when he was there so the trap door would be open and I could escape.

"If he were smart, he'd stay away from the root cellar. I knew Murphy would tear the whole town apart looking for me. He'd know I couldn't have gotten far because I don't drive. But he didn't know about the root cellar and I was sure Grandmother Emma wouldn't tell him. Nate could keep Murphy away from the wood shed or at least keep an eye on him if Murphy insisted on looking inside. It would be a waiting game more than anything else and nobody suspected Nate of anything. So the smart thing would be to stay away for a couple of days. But I didn't think he could. I thought the draw of two woman chained in his root cellar would drive him crazy. He would be unable to resist."

I took a gulp of water and pressed my palm into the skin between my eyes. My head throbbed. "A part of me couldn't believe I was impatient for that madman to actually come back, but I was.

"Bethany hurt so bad. She'd been chained up for five days at that point. Five days, Councilors. Her body was giving out on her. I could smell that. I was in awe of her. She was so brave. She could still form coherent sentences and she still had a little hope left that she'd live. I'd only been chained there for six hours at the most and I was already starting to fray. My mind couldn't seem to really cope with the idea I was going to be tortured and die. I didn't want to end up buried in the back woods or in Grandmother Emma's basement. I didn't want to think about what he did with the chain saw besides cut cordwood for Grandmother Emma's wood stove.

"So I thought about shifting instead. I thought about Murphy and where he might be and what stage the hunt for me might be at. They'd find my cellphone on the porch. My purse upstairs in the bedroom. He'd know I couldn't be far. They'd go to all the neighbors and eventually they'd come to Grandmother Emma's. If Murphy really thought about it, Grandmother Emma's would be top of the list. He knows what I'm like when I'm determined to do something or find something. I don't stop. He'd figure out I didn't just go for a walk in the woods and fall down and sprain my ankle or something stupid like that. He'd know I went looking for Bethany. He'd know something was really wrong, not accident wrong. At least that's what I told myself."

Murphy, Murphy, Murphy. Each time I said his name, a hot stab of bitter longing pierced me. I was appalled at how much I'd come to rely on him in only six months. Had I been this way over Grey? I didn't think so. After two years in exile. I guess I grasped greedily at the first person who offered me a way back.

I hated myself at that moment. The person I had become was so weak and dependent.

You don't need him here, Constance, you just want him here.

Paddy sat beside me and offered support but I didn't want to take it from him either, for sudden fear I'd end up clinging to him too. Pretty soon if I didn't get a grip, I wouldn't be able to do a damn thing without somebody else helping or doing it for me.

If the panel noticed my break in concentration, they didn't say anything. Instead they waited for me to continue which I eventually did.

"I never meant to kill Nate Carver. I only meant to hurt him so that he couldn't turn on Bethany and then I was going to run to find help. That was my plan. I didn't even want to hurt Nate, but I thought he would be angry and irrational if my wolf escaped. Maybe instead of going after my wolf or getting the hell out of there in an attempt to escape from Pack vengeance, he might take out his rage and frustration on Bethany. I'd seen him flash into fury and I knew it only took an instant. Somehow he held it together when he was away from the woodshed, but when he was in that space, he gave himself permission to lose it."

"You don't know that," said Jack Hill. "I understand you are trying to explain your thought processes, Con— Advisor Newcastle, but I would appreciate it if you wouldn't speak for other people. It's okay to say you thought he was insane and psychotic, but not to state unequivocally that he was."

"Those decomposing bodies in the cellar and Bethany's abduction don't prove that?" I was outraged. My blood pressure spiked so that my cheeks felt hot and my hands curled into fists. "That's something a normal person does for a hobby?"

"Are you a trained psychologist?" Hill demanded. "Do you know how to clinically assess someone's mental health?"

Under his reproving, lecturing gaze and his condescending tone, I lost it. I already teetered at the edge of my control and now this bastard had started to nitpick and lectured me on what I could and couldn't say while I told my own goddamn story?

"No, but for Christ's sake, he chained me to a fucking morgue gurney! I suppose because I didn't personally see him rape Bethany with a beer bottle that I can't say that happened either?" At this point I screamed in frustrated rage.

When Paddy put a hand on my arm, I yanked it away from his touch.

"Leave me alone!" I glared at him and he met my eyes with his. He didn't attempt to touch me again, but he wouldn't drop his gaze.

Somehow, I'd ended up on my feet and now I backed away from the table and Paddy, as I tried to put physical distance between us.

I was hyperaware of every person in the room.

"I think we need to take a break," Rosemary Young suggested with a reproachful look at Adam Perkins for not saying it first. He stared at me, aghast, as if I were some sort of harmless lap dog that had suddenly gone berserk.

"If you want me to tell this fucking story, you let me do it my way. You know what happened! I ripped his fucking throat out and he's dead and nothing I can say about him with words will change that. He was a fucking psychopathic serial killer and I'm not going to walk on eggshells on how I say it! Fuck this! Fuck it!"

I continued to back up until I hit the wall. I turned on it in a rage and beat at it with my fists wishing like hell it was Hill's face instead. Or Murphy's. Or my own.

"Constance." Two people spoke my name at the same time, one on either side of me. My breathing was so loud I was amazed I'd heard them speak. The wall was cool against my hot forehead and my fists felt bruised.

"Leave me alone," I whispered, not sure what I would do if anybody other than Murphy touched me.

Somewhere in the background I heard Kathy Manning as she ranted at one of the Councilors. "You're pushing her too hard. This just happened a day and a half ago. She hasn't had any time to process this and you're pushing too hard. Jason warned you not to do that."

Jason Allerton. Another person who couldn't be here in person. Pressing personal issues. Murphy's frantic search through the archives was nothing more than a pressing personal issue too. Everyone was so selfish. They thought of themselves and how they needed to handle this. Nobody gave a damn how I felt.

I wanted to tell Kathy to shut the fuck up about Jason Allerton. Let him tell the Councilors that himself. We weren't supposed to speak for other people in this goddamn room. If I couldn't, she shouldn't be able to either.

"Constance, come sit down." Paddy was gently insistent and the Irish brogue in his voice was strangely soothing. Probably because it reminded me of Murphy. Damn him.

"I want..." I nearly strangled myself in my effort to not complete that pathetic sentence. I pounded the wall again with my fist, but weakly this time. It still hurt and I wondered if my fucking hand was broken. The cuffs of my blouse had slid up and the puffy, bruised skin around my wrists clearly showed the marks of the restraints Nate had used. I shuddered.

"What do you want? I'll get it for you. Just come sit down." Paddy bravely put his hands on my shoulders. I tensed but did not twist away. What was the point?

Paddy turned me around and led me back to my chair. Councilor Dante Armentano, the other person who had called my name, followed us.

"Now what was it you were wanting, Constance?" Paddy kept one hand on my shoulder and bent his head toward mine. I wished I could feel something for him but I only felt a tingling numbness that deadened everything it contacted within me.

"Water," I said because I couldn't tell him what I really wanted. He told me he'd get me whatever I wanted and it wasn't in his power to get Murphy to come here.

Councilor Armentano filled a glass for me and then pulled out the chair beside me. His dark, predatory face looked almost kind. "Constance, it's very important that we hear this story from you. We know what happened, that is true, but we need to hear your story."

"Then I should be able to tell it my way," I insisted. The water was tepid and flat, and I set it aside with a grimace. Paddy sat on my other side. He kept his hand on my shoulder and I wasn't sure if it was a gesture of comfort or possession. He kept his gaze locked on Councilor Armentano, his expression skeptical.

"Councilor Hill is being a little pedantic," said Armentano with a small, conciliatory smile. "He fails to appreciate the ordeal you've been through, possibly because you've been remarkably composed until just now. We are struggling to make sense of this. I hope you appreciate that."

"There is no sense to be made of something as cruel and stupid as this," I ranted, but I kept my voice low. Even so, Kathy Manning and the other Councilors who stood by the door stopped talking for a second before they resumed their heated conversation.

I looked down at my hands. My fingers were bruised, knuckles scraped raw. I'd been able to hold a glass of water so I hadn't broken any bones, but a small bubble of shame burst inside of me. What an idiot I must have looked. I hadn't done myself or my case any good—that much was clear. Now they would think I was an unstable hysteric and that I'd lost control and that was why Nate was dead. I yanked down the cuffs of my blouse.

Paddy made a small, protesting sound when he saw the bruises and abraded skin. His fingers tightened for a moment on my shoulder.

"We should break for lunch," decided Armentano, as he got to his feet and looked down the table to Councilor Perkins. "Adam, can we break for lunch?"

* * * *

The ham-and-cheese souffle in front of me was cold. I'd eaten maybe three bites then subsided into a morose silence. Paddy and Kathy kept up a stilted conversation around me. They made periodic attempts to draw me in, but I resisted.

We sat at the kitchen table. Cheery sunlight beamed through the window. Instead of a tablecloth there were woven wicker placemats. The leaves had been pulled up and two more chairs put out. Our napkins were red linen and had been placed beside our plates in gold napkin rings that gleamed in the sunshine.

From the dining room came the clink of silverware on china and muted conversation but I didn't bother to listen.

Paddy was angry because the Councilors wouldn't let me eat in the dining room with them and their Advisors. He hadn't said a word about how insulted he was, but I could tell by the scent of resentful anger that hovered around him and by the way his eyes flashed whenever someone in the dining room laughed or said something louder than usual. There had been a place set for him, but once he'd learned I would be eating in the kitchen, he'd simply picked up his setting, placemat and all, and sailed into the kitchen with it. Not a word spoken.

"I wish you'd eat something, Stanzie." Kathy sat across from me and her elfishly pretty face was puckered with concern. Her perfectly plucked eyebrows lowered as she narrowed her eyes. "If Liam were here, you'd eat. I'm so angry at that man. I asked him as Regional Councilor not to go to Virginia and all that man did was smile at me and proceed to walk out the door anyway."

My lips quirked a little bit even though I was depressed as all hell. I wished I'd seen that. Funny how people resent being treated the exact same way they would have behaved themselves.

Paddy smiled too. "I've yet to meet the person who could tell Liam Murphy what to do if he didn't want to do it."

"Stanzie could influence him, but she won't. Will you, Stanzie?" Kathy rolled her eyes and helped herself to a smidge more souffle.

"Not everybody can march up to their fears head on like you do and bash them into submission, Kathy." I stopped my listless contemplation of the cold souffle on my plate and lifted my gaze so I could see her. "Some of us have to sneak up behind them and stab when they least expect it. And even then it doesn't always work."

"What does he have to be afraid of?" Kathy's eyes sparked with impatience.

"Losing me, what else?" I answered.

Kathy's generous mouth tightened into a thin, displeased slash. "He isn't going to lose you. Unless you get so fed up with his ridiculous quest in the archives—which only twenty other people are undertaking at the same time—that you leave him. Which he would deserve."

"The tribunal is going to go against me. I'm going to be put to death for murdering Nate." I set my fork down and stared at her without blinking.

"Nonsense." Her voice was a soft explosion in the silence of the kitchen. She cast an anxious look over her shoulder toward the dining room but I didn't care if the bastards did hear me. I hadn't said anything they hadn't already decided to do.

"This tribunal is the nonsense. I wish it would just stop and they'd get it over with. And Murphy does too on some level. It's the anticipation that's the worst. And, anyway, he'll have to deal with the aftermath, not me. So please let him deal with this his own way, not yours. You always want people to do things your way and, newsflash, Kathy, most of the time we don't want to."

"It's my fault you're here. I was the one who wanted you and Liam to go to Maplefair. Jason didn't offer you so much as I commandeered you and he didn't stand in the way. I thought you needed something to do other than watch over Vaughn Pelletier. So it's my fault if they put you to death. I can't even be on the tribunal. They wouldn't let me. And now the one person you want with you isn't even here and I can't make him be here." Her face crumpled. Tears, big and hot, rolled down her cheeks and she made no move to prevent them.

Paddy looked like he wanted to be anywhere else in the entire universe. He stared at me as if I knew what the hell to do.

Kathy stuffed a knuckle in her mouth to keep from wailing. She got to her feet and blundered out the back door.

I stared at the smidgeon of ham-and-cheese souffle on her plate and felt about two inches tall. Kathy had wanted to eat that.

"This is a total, emotional shitpile, isn't it?" Paddy heaved a sigh that sounded like it had originated back in Dublin and followed him here to Hartford. "We're all of us floundering around like mourners at a funeral. Jaysus, Mary and Joseph."

"I'd go after her but I'm not allowed to leave the house," I told him. "Can you please make sure she's okay? It's nobody's fault what I did but mine. And if she hadn't sent us there, Bethany would be suffering still. She saved Bethany's life."

"You did that." Paddy pushed back from the table and went to the back door. "She's just standing out in the garden. There's a fence all around this house. You can surely go outside into the garden for some fresh air without someone raising a stink, can't you?"

"I could try," I said.

* * * *

A marble birdbath with a green-and-gold crystal ball set in the bowl sat on top of a slate paving stone. A circle of smaller paving stones created a space to stand within a glorious profusion of bright yellow daffodils and cool purple iris.

Kathy stood hunched over the birdbath as if she bowed in supplication to it. Her arms were crossed and pressed against her stomach and I thought maybe she felt sick.

But she was only crying really hard. I felt like such shit. With almost anybody else I would have known what to do, but Kathy was an enigma to me, an elf princess who wasn't quite the same as me and never let me forget it.

I had no idea how she'd react if I put my arms around her or if I even spoke to her. She intimidated me at the best of times, frustrated me most of the time and at this particular moment she scared me. My usual irritation with her was now flooded with the sort of pity I normally felt when I saw a dead dog on the side of the road or a small child bawling his eyes out after being smacked by a parent or sibling.

Pity was not an emotion I associated with Kathy Manning at all, especially feeling it for her.

"You really like me, don't you?" I heard myself say it and immediately cursed my inability to ever hold my tongue. "You're genuinely going to be upset if I'm put to death. You really are going to blame yourself and feel bad, aren't you?"

Kathy swung around. Her eyes were swollen with tears. "You didn't know that? You're like a daughter to me, Stanzie."

My mouth dropped open. Of all the things in the world she could have said, being like a daughter to her was the last thing I'd expected. I didn't know how to handle a confession of that magnitude.

"You're not old enough to be my mother," was my lame response.

"I'm fifty-three. I am so old enough to be your mother." Her voice took on a familiar, condescending edge, which riled me the way it always did.

"Who's an Alpha at twenty-one?" I countered.

"It happens, Stanzie. Sometimes in new packs. In small ones." Kathy drew herself up to her full height of just barely five feet and I stared down at her from my height of five foot seven and felt like a giraffe. She always made me feel like a giraffe.

"I have a mother," I said, but it was weak argument at best and we both knew it.

"People can have more than one mother. When you're a child, every woman in the pack is like a mother to you and every grown man a father."

"You're not my pack. You were never my pack." I continued to argue. I couldn't seem to stop. She wasn't my mother. I'd never asked her to be my mother. Why was I obligated to accept her in that role?

A flush of hurt indignation crimsoned her cheeks and one of the unshed tears trickled down her nose.

She wiped it away angrily. "So, all right, I'm not your mother and you don't want me to act like one to you. I'm sorry for that too. I'm sorry for everything."

"I didn't know you felt like that about me." My tone was accusatory, like she'd committed a crime in caring about me.

"Obviously, but if you think I make my butterscotch squares for just anyone and deliver them in person from a state away, think again." The crimson indignation faded into a pale reproach.

"You made Murphy snickerdoodles and Vaughn chocolate chip cookies." I still argued for some stupid reason. It really got to me that she thought of me as a daughter. My skin felt all prickly.

She waved Murphy and Vaughn aside with a sweep of her hand.

"I make cookies for everybody. Only special people get my butterscotch squares. Before you that meant Matthew, Tim and Jason. Sometimes my mother if she didn't get on my last nerve."

I tried to imagine someone irritating enough to get beneath Kathy Manning's thick skin and quailed at the thought.

"I didn't know."

"Well, now you do." She wiped her eyes with the back of her hand and frowned at the smudge of mascara.

A wave of resentment swept through me. I couldn't comprehend this. She made me feel like a dunce for not understanding her damn butterscotch squares meant she cared. How the hell was I supposed to have known that? Guilt fueled my resentment.

"How am I supposed to know that your constant poking at me and prying into my business meant you cared? And don't talk about butterscotch squares being a dead giveaway, that's not fair and you know it."

"What does a mother who cares do, Stanzie? You may call it poking and prying, but I call it affection. Apparently you got so little of it from your real mother, you don't understand and that just makes me even angrier."

"Don't talk about my mother. You don't know anything about my mother." I crossed my arms and pressed them into my body.

I hated the way she was able to thrust her knife between my ribs without even trying and then turn around and tell me I shouldn't be upset about it.

"My mother and I were very close when I was a little girl. She was very good to me!" I needed to make that clear because Kathy didn't understand. She hadn't been around when I was growing up and Lauren and I had been nearly inseparable.

"People don't just need their mothers when they're little girls." Kathy wiped more mascara from her cheeks, probably offended that I'd made her damn makeup run.

"I never asked you to be a mother to me."

"I always wanted a daughter," Kathy confessed in a low voice.

She laughed at herself and turned back toward the birdbath. "It was a little bit of a disappointment to me that Tim was a boy not the girl I'd always dreamed of since I was old enough to play with dolls. Not that I've stayed disappointed because I love him. But daughters are different somehow. For years I've secretly played mother to my favorite girls in my pack."

She shrugged as if bracing herself for a blow. "But you're the only one I ever made butterscotch squares."

"All we ever do is argue," I pointed out, baffled as to why she should feel close to me and how I could completely miss it. "You voted against me after Grey and Elena died."

"I didn't at first. The rest of the Regional Council persuaded me to change my vote. And then Jason undid it all and I was glad. You intrigued me back then, Stanzie, but I didn't feel you were a daughter until three months ago. That's when I started feeling close."

I massaged the back of my aching neck with my fingers. "I never knew. You treated me just the same as you did Murphy and Vaughn."

"Maybe you think so." She turned around and I saw more tears in her eyes. "I suppose it's a good thing I didn't have a daughter. Women never seem to understand me. Only men."

The more she talked, the more I felt like complete shit. I didn't know if I could ever look at her as a mother figure, but I didn't have to be so goddamn churlish and ungrateful. It was amazing and humbling to know that my situation affected her so deeply.

"Do you think you could make me some butterscotch squares tonight?" I asked.

"Maybe," she said frostily.

She unthawed a little to add, "Only if you go back inside and eat some lunch. I worked hard on that souffle and you pushed it around your plate like it was out of a package mix."

"Will you make Murphy snickerdoodles? After, I mean?" My voice stuck in my throat and for a horrible moment I thought I would cry. "Look after him a little maybe?"

"I'd rather kick him in the ass." Her voice wobbled too. "But maybe for you I might."

"He's going to need people," I said with a sigh.

"People will be there for him. If he lets us." Kathy looked doubtful that he would.

"See, that's where I count on you. You don't take no for an answer. He can't shut you out if you don't let him. Also, he cannot under any circumstances resist your snickerdoodles. It's a huge weakness of his." I pictured his face as it lit up in ecstasy when he bit into one of her magnificent cookies. I smiled even as I struggled so hard not to cry. I didn't want to give in to tears because once I started, I was afraid I would never be able to stop.

We didn't touch, but we walked very close and headed back to the door, our strange interlude in the garden over.

Chapter 9

The afternoon sun beat through the conference room windows with an almost malevolent vengeance. At least it seemed so to me thanks to my lingering headache.

The Italian Advisor, Marco, saw me wince when I walked into the room after lunch and hastily got up to draw the blinds. This produced an unsettling gloom that could not entirely be alleviated by the light cast from the hanging chandelier above the mahogany conference table.

I sat at the head of the table as Paddy hovered beside me. Kathy took the same seat behind the Advisor's chairs and the panel of Councilors filed in to take their previous places.

Kathy had managed to get me to eat a warmed-up plate of the souffle, which now sat in an apprehensive lump in my stomach.

Someone in the room wore the same cologne Murphy liked to wear only it didn't seem precisely the same because the body chemistry was different. It was enough alike to make me think Murphy was in the room for a moment, but he wasn't.

I'd probably smelled it all morning, which had added to my frustration that he wasn't with me. Odd how certain scents evoked emotional cravings.

Everyone took a few moments to settle. Water was poured, homemade chocolate chip cookies were passed around and chairs were adjusted.

Armentano and Hill had removed their jackets. Perkins kept his on, fastidious as ever, and probably conscious of his role as chairman of the panel.

Hill tried to catch my eye but I kept my gaze averted. The bruises on my hands were starting to ache and when I'd walked into the room I saw the marks of my fists on the wall.

At the moment I was drained and tired. I wished I hadn't eaten the souffle because it only dragged me down further. The scent of Murphy's cologne had sucked up the last bit of emotion inside me and now I felt hollow and insubstantial.

"Please tell us what happened when Nate Carver came back to the root cellar, Advisor Newcastle." Although Perkins was chairman, it was Armentano who spoke. He was the ranking member of the Great Council and he took control easily. He was the kind of man who would dominate any room.

My thoughts flashed to Jason Allerton. He had the same sort of effect, only not as brutal and invasive as Armentano's style. Councilor Armentano demanded attention. Jason Allerton simply was impossible to ignore.

"In your own words. There will be no more censoring," Armentano added with a look at Hill, who gave an emphatic nod that appeared more conciliatory than anything else. The very force of it made me think he did it under protest.

Rosemary Young's empathetic face was the one I focused on just as I had in the morning session.

"I don't know how long I'd been there in the root cellar plotting to shift and escape, but when the lights came on, they scared me because I was half asleep. I was disoriented and shocked that I had let myself doze off. So I was off balance. My eyes took a long time to focus. At first the light blinded me after so much darkness." I scrubbed at my mouth nervously and remembered I had not renewed my lipstick after eating lunch. Every other woman in the room was polished and perfect except me—the one in the unenviable limelight.

"The first thing I realized after my eyes adjusted was the ladder. I'd expected there to be a folding staircase attached to the trapdoor like you see in attics. But he had to lower a ladder. I remembered seeing a ladder propped up in a corner of the woodshed and cursed because my wolf had never seen one. I didn't think she'd know what to do with one. She'd never seen a staircase either, but somehow I guess I thought that would be easier for her to navigate. The whole plan started to unravel in my head when I saw that ladder." I scrubbed at my mouth again. My bruised fingers ached. I stared at each of the Councilors in turn defiantly. "You know about my wolf, how she's...different."

"That's what we want to hear about." Rosemary Young's smile was encouraging.

"Can you explain your wolf's reaction when you and Advisor Murphy began to work with her?" Councilor Perkins asked.

A dark smile quirked my lips before I pressed them tightly together to banish it.

"You know she bit him. You know that's why he was hurt and took the pain pills the Paris grandmother gave him and nearly died from them. You know that story."

The official story about Murphy's overdose in Houston was that the Paris grandmother who had given him the pain pills had made a mistake in the dosage.

"We would like to hear it in your words." Rosemary Young's voice was gentle but I now distrusted her. Maybe they were playing good cop, bad cop with me, and she was the good cop. I tried to remember how she'd been on the previous panel. She and Kathy Manning had sat together. I'd focused on their two faces as the most sympathetic.

"It was in wolf form. I bit Murphy's *wolf*, not *Murphy*!" Fear turned the spit in my mouth foul tasting. I reached out for the water glass Paddy had filled for me when we'd taken our seats.

"We understand that." Councilor Young's face had somehow turned sly and not sympathetic. Or maybe I was paranoid. Guilt swamped me as it always did when I thought about when my wolf bit Murphy's.

I cast my mind back to the moment when I'd realized what I'd done to him. I'd just shifted back and blood had been caked beneath my fingernails. Not mine, although I'd been bleeding too from a few shallow scratches. Murphy's wolf had defended himself, but far more gently than mine.

"It was the second time we shifted together. The first time after he'd offered to work with my wolf and I'd agreed to let him." My voice was stiff, saturated with guilt. I smelled of guilt too. Everyone in the room could smell it. I *hated* to think about when my wolf had bitten Murphy's.

"My wolf wanted to play and to run the way she always did. From the very start, she adored Murphy's wolf. She wanted to play almost as much as she wanted to run. But his wolf wouldn't play. He wanted her to show submission. My wolf never, ever showed submission to anybody's. She'd never once rolled to show her belly or throat if it wasn't in play and only after someone else's wolf did it first."

"She thinks she's an Alpha?" Adam Perkins blinked owlishly at me from across the table. He looked prim and disgusted because I'd never been an Alpha. My wolf's behavior was egregious.

"She wants what she wants." I knew that was not an answer, but I didn't have a real answer. "She doesn't think in terms of Alpha or hierarchy. Just that she wants what she wants. It used to be playing and running. Now it's words, but she has rolled to Murphy's wolf. She has." I pressed my lips together to avoid blurting how grudgingly it always was and how sulky she got after she did it.

"How is it that you know how to behave in human form but you don't in wolf?" Perkins seemed fascinated as well as repulsed. His eyes shone as he stared at me. Resentment burned a hole in my gut. I supposed it was fair to put my wolf on trial since she was the one who had ripped Nate's throat out, but why couldn't we stick to the event itself? Everything I could say about my wolf only damned me, while Nate's evil, psychotic behavior was put on a back burner. He should be on trial just as much as me only he wasn't. I had to remember this tribunal was set in motion on his behalf. He'd been murdered. It was the panel's job to decide whether what I had done was justified. What he'd done mattered only peripherally.

"I grew up in a pack." I knew I sounded churlish. "I know our laws."

"But they don't apply to your wolf?" Dante Armentano pounced. Beside me Paddy winced. I could smell a sudden whiff of anger from him, but he controlled it.

"I told her not to kill him," I whispered. "Only hurt him so he couldn't hurt Bethany while my wolf ran for help." My cheeks were on fire and I struggled to contain my turbulent emotions. I didn't want to lose control again the way I had before lunch. Each outburst like that only dug my grave a little deeper."

"It wasn't your idea to work on your wolf, was it, Advisor?" Dante Armentano leaned over the table and reached for his water glass. I stared at him, mesmerized and dismayed. "Perhaps your wolf has resisted changing too?"

"I didn't resist," I protested. "I wanted to change."

"We're talking about your wolf." His smile was more predatory than encouraging. Anyone would think my wolf had killed a fine, upstanding member of our Pack society, not a demented serial killer. The sheer brutality of this idea assaulted my sense of fairness. In a just world, wouldn't there be some allowance for the fact my wolf had killed a maniac whose objective that particular day had been torture and not murder? The murder would have been taken place eventually. We were allowed to defend ourselves after all.

"My wolf resisted only at first. That one time. She adores Murphy's wolf. She felt so bad when she hurt him. All she wants is to be safe again, so she won't feel scared and do bad things. She thinks the words will make her safe. So, okay, maybe she doesn't reason at the same level as most everyone else's wolves. That's my fault for keeping her the same and never making her change.

"Councilors, I wasn't even sure she would run for help when I shifted. I didn't know if she'd get sidetracked into figuring out a word for something she saw and didn't know. That root cellar was full of things she'd never seen before."

Shudders rippled up and down my spine at the thought of that putrid, filthy root cellar, but I wouldn't let it sidetrack me from story. I couldn't.

"I'd never shifted scared out of my mind before. My panic became hers and she wanted to run, she was going to run, but she saw Nate between her and the ladder and attacked. She just wanted to be safe. For six months she hasn't felt safe or happy or anything at all but this gnawing anxiety that she's not the same. She used to feel a part of everything and now she feels separate. She's aware of herself and she's desperate to belong again. She doesn't understand how to get there yet, but it's only been six months."

"Do you think she can get there?" Rosemary Young's eyes were very kind but I still didn't trust her. Now less than ever.

I didn't want to answer her question because the truth was I didn't believe my wolf could ever get there. She was too far behind, too stubborn, and every single time I shifted I hated it more.

I'd avoided shifting after Vaughn had come to live with us in Boston not only because I was focused on him and his grief, but also because I dreaded being in wolf form. And my wolf didn't like it much either.

I remembered when she used to strain to be free inside me. After sex and she woke within me, all she wanted was to break through and become real. The last few times, she'd remained very still inside me and I'd had to prod her out. I only shifted for Murphy. If it had been up to me, I don't know if I would have shifted.

"I don't know," I said only because I had to verbalize an answer and I didn't want to tell Rosemary Young that, no, I didn't think my wolf was capable of change. It was one thing to be on trial and wait for them to condemn me, quite another for me to denounce myself. I needed all the help I could get.

I was fighting for my life. I'd known this from the start, but it crystallized and became terrible and real to me at that moment. I could die. I would very probably die. It wasn't some abstract thought, it was concrete.

Fear galvanized me. Flames of fear licked up and down my spine. My heart pounded so hard I thought I would throw up. Paddy sat beside me, his hand on my arm as he offered me contact and connection. I hated Liam Murphy at that moment. Hated him so much it was hot and bright and so goddamn clear in my head I was amazed.

The next second I was ashamed. Why was I casting blame on him when I was the one who had deliberately kept my wolf childlike and simple? I'd had my chances to develop her and I'd turned them down, one after the other.

"We need to know what your wolf thought when she attacked Nate Carver." Councilor Armentano's dark eyes were very grave as he studied me from across the long length of conference table.

A bark of cynical laughter burst from my throat. I couldn't help it. What she thought?

"She didn't think *anything*. She was terrified and angry. The force of her emotions drove all thought out of her head."

At my words the Councilors exchanged glances. Paddy sighed and the long exhale of his breath underscored how much my answer had damned me.

Amy Lee Burgess

"No words at all? No coherent thought?" Councilor Samuels gave me one more chance.

"It's hard to think when you're ripping someone's throat out," I declared. Fuck it. My poor wolf. The truth was it had been almost a relief for her to be able to experience simple, yet powerful emotion again. The past six months had been grinding intellect poisoned by anxiety and frustration. When she experienced any emotion at all, it was always negative because she couldn't think of the word. She'd struggled to get rid of the emotions, even physically tried to dig them out of her head with her claws.

The rush of pure, unadulterated anger she'd let herself feel in the root cellar had been a return to the primal. My God, had she enjoyed it?

That thought froze my blood. Wrong. That was wrong and evil. A shock of rage infected me then. I'd become ashamed of my wolf and that shame had leaked through to her. I was the one who'd turned her into the anxious, frustrated, bottled-up wreck she'd become. All her so-called self-awareness had been me, as I looked over her shoulder and criticized everything she did.

And the one time in six months I'd let her be what she wanted, she'd been so angry and confused and terrified, it's no wonder she attacked with lethal force. She hadn't enjoyed killing Nate. She'd reveled in being herself again, that's all. But how could I explain something like that to the Councilors? Would they even begin to understand? I could barely wrap my brain around it, let alone explain it properly. I was fucked. I was so fucked.

"She thought, 'Bad man. Bad. No.'" The words burned like acid on my tongue. The Councilors looked at me and I wondered how long it had been since their wolves had reacted to the world like two-year-old children. By their expressions, it had been a long time.

* * * *

Councilor Perkins adjourned the session a little after four in the afternoon. Paddy had to tell me twice that he was going to check into his hotel before I acknowledged him.

On his way out, he stopped to talk to Kathy Manning, who was in the conference room doorway. They both glanced at me then whispered together. I paid them very little attention.

When Paddy was gone, I got out of my chair and walked to the doorway.

"Stanzie," began Kathy, but I ignored her and continued to the staircase. Once in my room I shut the door and tore apart my purse for my cellphone.

Murphy answered on the second ring and the sound of his voice released a flood of desperate longing that nearly drowned me with its intensity.

"Please come back here, Liam. I need you!" The words burst from my mouth before I could censor myself.

"Stanzie, I can't." He groaned. "I haven't found anything in the archives yet."

"There are twenty other Advisors doing the same thing as you are," I argued as his refusal smashed into the raging flood of my need.

"Not the same way as I'm doing it!" Murphy snarled, his temper ignited by my tone. "I can't sit around in Hartford doing nothing."

"You wouldn't be doing nothing. You'd be with me." But I knew it was a lost cause. I slumped against the bathroom door and slowly slid down to the floor.

"You've got people with you," he told me, half placating, half angry.

"You sent Paddy here, didn't you?" My voice was as flat as my future.

"No," he denied. "I told him what was going on and he was on the first plane to get to you. He's like me. We don't sit around on our asses waiting for other people to do things that need to be done. He's Alpha of Mac Tire and you're his pack mate. He needs to be there to protect you and make sure things are done right."

"So if you were Alpha, you'd be here?" I wondered and he sighed so loudly in my ear I winced.

"Will you please try to get over fact I'm not there? I'm not coming there, Constance, and I don't need you trying to make me feel guilty."

I fixed my gaze on the wall he'd once shoved me against another time I'd tried to reach out to him and had been repulsed.

"Well, I really hope that the idea you were off doing something other people were already doing gives you peace when I'm in an urn and you're scattering my ashes in the woods somewhere. I suppose it won't matter to me by then where the hell you were the last few days of my life."

"I told you stop trying to make me feel guilty!" His voice was so dark and awful a freezing chill shivered down my spine. I was glad I was sitting because my legs felt like empty, boneless sacks somehow attached to the rest of my body.

He'd yelled at me before, but never like this.

Terrible silence crackled in the dead air between us.

"I guess I'd better go now," I said in a voice I didn't recognize as mine. "Kathy's making supper and I should probably help her." A fucking lie. Kathy Manning never let anyone help her cook.

"Damn it, Stanzie. I'm sorry I yelled. I'm so goddamn tired I can't think straight." Murphy sounded stretched to the breaking point. I could hear the tears in his voice.

"Maybe you should lie down. Aren't you sleeping?" I pictured his bloodshot eyes and scruffy beard and got worried.

"I can sleep when this is fucking over," he said. "Sleeping is a stupid waste of time."

"If you're too tired to focus, you might miss something," I said.

He snarled. "Just let me do what I need to do, all right? I told you I'd sleep when this is over and, goddamn it, stop telling me what to do!"

Someone walked past my bedroom door. People spoke in muted tones at the head of the staircase.

"I think supper's ready." It wasn't a lie, but I didn't give a shit. I had no intention of eating anything. "I've got to go."

"I have to keep busy, don't you understand?" His voice broke and I listened to him cry but all I could think was, *You're not here with me. You're not here.*

* * * *

The sketch the Italian Advisor had worked on all day was propped up against an empty water glass at the kitchen table.

Kathy stirred something on the high-tech stove while outside the kitchen windows the afternoon shadows gathered into dusk.

My face in the sketch was impossibly beautiful. He'd fixed all my imperfections. My nose was slightly smaller, my eyes a little farther apart and I only wished my hair looked so wildly well mannered when I put it up. The face I looked at wasn't mine. It was my mother's without all the Benedict distortions.

I felt stripped and exposed. Exploited. I moved the sketch to the top of the microwave on the counter—facedown—and returned to the table. I knew better than to ask Kathy if I could help.

"I'm sorry I was rude earlier, Kathy. I walked right past you and ignored you when you tried to talk to me."

Kathy abandoned the gravy she stirred so she could look at me. "I just wanted to make sure you were all right, Stanzie." Her gaze measured my mood and, by her expression, she'd concluded I was in an emotional dead zone. Her face hardened for a moment, but soon softened. She wasn't mad at me.

A bottle of red wine breathed on the counter. She picked it up and brought it to the table where she filled two glasses for us.

"Roast beef tonight." She took a sip. "Everyone loves my roast beef. Do you want to know the secret ingredient, Stanzie?"

"I don't really cook things like roast beef," I admitted. Did Murphy like roast beef? The last time we'd had it had been here, three months ago, and it had been a bad night between us. He'd spent more time drinking wine than eating and I'd just pushed my food around on my plate.

Murphy. A stab of pain pierced the dead envelope of my emotions and I took a swallow of wine to chase it away. I had no time for pain. I had no time at all, really.

Paddy entered the kitchen then. He'd showered at his hotel and exchanged his jeans and sweater for a pair of putty-gray chinos and a black shirt. Black Oxford lace-ups and a well-worn but expensive black leather jacket completed his outfit. His hair was loose and very curly around his face. I'm pretty certain he couldn't get a comb through that mop, although it didn't look messy. He looked very Irish somehow. His eyes were bloodshot and tired. He was exhausted, but he still managed to grin when he saw the wine in my hand.

"Any chance of a beer?" He looked appealingly at Kathy, who pointed to the refrigerator. She was back with her gravy, wine glass in one hand, spoon in the other.

Paddy didn't bother with a glass. He found a Guinness in the ordered depths of the refrigerator and drank half of it in one gulp before he spoke.

I marveled at Kathy. Of course she'd known Paddy was coming, so she'd just performed her customary magic. Somehow everyone's favorites always seemed to appear.

I took another sip of the red wine. It tasted like dark sunshine—if it was possible to taste something like that. My wolf had—back in the days she'd played instead of obsessed.

Kathy gave a final stir to the gravy and removed it from the burner. She reached up to a shelf near the stove for a white ceramic gravy boat.

Paddy opened his second Guinness. Kathy took the gravy boat into the dining room.

While I drank wine, Paddy prowled around the kitchen with his beer. He saw the sketch on the microwave and turned it over so he could look at it.

"Damned good drawing of you," he declared as he glanced between it and me.

"Yeah, right," I scoffed. "Why do artists always make people look better than they actually do? It's insulting."

"You look just like this." Paddy looked between the sketch and me again, his brow furrowed.

"I do not," I argued, exasperated.

"Maybe you're the one who looks in the mirror and can't see herself for who she really is." He put the sketch back and pulled out the chair next to mine so he could sit.

"Fiona wants to know all about you." He poured me more wine as he spoke, even though I didn't want more.

Fiona was his bond mate, the Alpha female of Mac Tire. Also, incidentally, Murphy's twin sister. It had taken me a while to piece together that the sister Murphy talked to in Dublin weekly was Paddy's bond mate.

I'd spoken to her a few times, but I hated talking to strangers on the phone. I liked to look people in the eye and smell their scent during our first conversation.

"I've talked to Fiona," I said.

Paddy curled his lip. "The phone sucks sometimes. Murphy kept telling her how beautiful you are but he thought Sorcha was gorgeous so she doesn't think he's a good judge of women's looks. Or characters for that matter. Sorcha was a raving bitch, Stanzie."

"She was mysterious. Men went mad trying to figure out her mystery," I argued. Sorcha? Who the fuck wanted to talk about Sorcha?

"People do tend to repeat their relationship mistakes. She's been worried as hell about him ever since she found out he'd bonded with you. And you have to admit the circumstances were pretty fucked up." Paddy sipped his beer as if this conversation were not in the least bit eviscerating.

I looked at the ring on my finger. I wanted to fling it back in his damned face but I didn't.

"You're every bit as mysterious as Sorcha ever was," Paddy remarked.

"I am not!" I cried, incensed somehow even though a few days ago if someone had called me as mysterious as Sorcha I would have been extremely pleased. Now it seemed like an insult. I supposed the raving bitch insinuation was the reason why. "I'm an open book, Padraic O'Reilly!"

His lips quirked at the use of his full name. I think I even had an Irish lilt to my voice when I said it. Six months with Murphy and some of his ways had apparently rubbed off.

"You're a damsel in distress is what you are. And he gets off on that, always did. Lots of men do, but him more than most."

"What the fuck was damsel in distress about Sorcha?" I fumed. He grinned again. Unbelievable. The bastard was enjoying this conversation. Where the hell was Kathy? I cast my gaze around the room as if I could conjure her up from thin air but she was still in the dining room. I heard the faint murmur of people as they talked. She was obviously in conversation with one or more of the Councilors, which meant I was on my own.

"There she was, teetering on the edge of twenty-six, this close to being booted out of her pack for lack of a bond mate. And there was Liam, twenty-one and more naive than he'd ever fucking admit. She bonded with him because she knew he'd get to be Alpha of Mac Tire one day and that's exactly where she wanted to be. No small-town, tiny little pack for her, no. She wanted to lord it over a lot of people. And she did, bless her." Paddy raised his beer as if to honor her sacred memory, only his eyes were full of sardonic humor.

"You can't blame Fee for wondering if maybe her brother got himself into another tangled web of bitchy deceit with another small-town, tiny-pack woman with social climbing aspirations, can you now?"

"I don't give a shit if I am ever an Alpha, and I'm not likely to be now anyway. But even if I were, it would be one of the last things on earth I'd want. I just wanted to be with him."

"From the very start of it all?" Paddy gave me a skeptical grin. "I was there in Paris, remember? You were not in love with the man then. He was smitten with you, sure, but you were hung up on that poor German bastard."

"Murphy was not smitten with me." I looked at him incredulously. "Are you crazy, Paddy? He didn't want to bond with me. He only did it because..." I trailed off in horror and snapped my mouth shut.

"You were a damsel in distress?" Paddy finished for me.

"Well, so what!" I flared. "So what if I was."

"I'm just telling you some of the things Fee's afraid of," Paddy said.

"So if I'd been just a normal, average woman looking for a bond mate, I'd have had no appeal for him?" I'd always known that under normal circumstances Murphy wouldn't have looked twice at me, but somehow tonight, as I talked about it with Paddy, it became horribly humiliating.

"You'd have had to work hard, but I'm not saying it would have been out of the question." Seemingly oblivious to my mortification, Paddy finished his beer and set the bottle down with a contented sigh.

"Well, I won't need his help much longer and Fee can relax." I pushed my chair back and got to my feet. The smell of the roast beef in the warming oven nauseated me to the point I thought I would be sick.

I hated them all in that moment. Paddy, Fiona, Murphy. The absent Jason Allerton, who set me up in the first goddamn place. Even Kathy Manning.

God, I was alone. I was so alone.

* * * *

Vaughn, Jossie and Paddy were all in the kitchen when I came down for breakfast the next morning, drawn by the irresistible lure of the scent of fresh coffee.

In almost less time than it took me to process the fact they were there, I'd hurled myself across the room and into Vaughn's arms. He crushed me to him and buried his face in my hair. Shudders traveled up and down his spine that matched the ones that contorted mine.

When I inhaled his unique and beloved scent, some of the knots that constricted my soul loosened.

"Where's Liam? Still sleeping?" Vaughn held me close, his forehead pressed to mine as he smiled at me. The smile slowly died as he read the truth in my eyes. "Isn't he here? Where is he?"

"He's in Virginia looking through the archives to find a precedent. If he finds one, the Councils will rule in my favor."

Vaughn continued to frown. "He's got to do that? Aren't there Advisors who work exclusively in the archives? Couldn't they—they are looking too, aren't they? Jesus."

I pulled away from him and moved toward the coffee machine.

Kathy was there before me and poured me a steaming mug, which she handed to me.

"Bacon or sausage?" A red-and-white checked apron protected her yellow silk blouse and cream-colored pencil skirt. A pair of shiny nude pumps elevated her height by three inches but she still had to look up to meet my eyes.

"Bacon," I decided as I found the creamer and poured some into my coffee. It turned the color of caramel, light and dark swirls and I watched it mix so I wouldn't have to see the sympathy in everyone's eyes.

Jossie had Heather on her hip. She'd bound her long chestnut hair in a messy bun and wore one of her cotton floral dresses with a pair of very dated chunky-heeled navy blue pumps. Except for shoes, I'm not exactly a fashion plate, but Jossie's clothes were cheap, flimsy and worn. The dress she had on looked ready to fall apart in the next washing cycle.

Heather's clothes were cheap too, but scrupulously washed and maintained. I assumed they were hand-me-downs from other Maplefair babies. My heart ached for them both. I'd never been rich until I'd bonded with Murphy, but I'd never been so close to the razor edge of poverty as Jossie.

She saw me assessing her clothes and a slow flush suffused her face. Great. I didn't want her to think I pitied her. I'd ripped her bond mate's throat out and now I was judging her wardrobe? I couldn't believe myself sometimes.

Jossie handed a surprised-looking Heather to Vaughn who was just as taken aback and walked across the kitchen toward me.

When she held out her arms, I put down my coffee mug and hugged her.

Her perfume was light and airy, something feminine and floral but elusive, it rode just beneath her own personal scent and meshed well with it.

"I thought you'd be mad at me. I thought you'd hate me," I whispered as she held tightly to me.

"No!" She was distraught and appalled. "Stanzie, no. You...you *saved* me! I'm so ashamed I didn't know what he was. I knew something was wrong with him, but I thought it was me. I thought I was the one who was paranoid. He certainly made me feel like I was the one with the problem. I wish I'd never set eyes on him. Never bonded with him. They're saying some of the bones in Grandmother Emma's cellar are old enough to have been there for a decade and that's how long I've been with him so it's been happening from the start, maybe even from before I met him. How could I *be* so blind?"

Tears poured down her face and I hugged her again. I had no answer for that. We were Pack, we could smell emotions and the sour stench of *wrong*, but sometimes we ignored our senses and instincts. Was it an attempt at self-preservation? Pride? Ambition? With Jossie I was tempted to think it was self-preservation. Sometimes wrong became so insidious it seemed right.

In Vaughn's arms, Heather began to cry, no doubt alarmed by her mother's tears. Jossie rushed to her and took her. The baby wrapped her chubby arms around Jossie's neck, pressed her flushed face into Jossie's shoulder and wept with fear. Jossie rocked her, the need to soothe her child evident in her fiercely protective expression.

I added sugar to my coffee and stirred it as I struggled to contain my own emotions. Crying was not an option for me. I needed to keep strong and in control.

The sizzle of fresh bacon drowned out the sound of Heather's gradually decreasing sobs. Vaughn put his arm around Jossie's shoulders and as I saw them together, I thought—*family. They are a family.*

There was a rightness to them I'd never felt when I'd seen Jossie and Heather with Nate. Just his name sent a shudder of revulsion down my spine.

Kathy whisked a bowlful of eggs to a golden yellow and continued to make our breakfast.

The sounds and scents were normal, comforting, but I didn't feel comforted. I felt like an outsider watching everyone else. They belonged to the scene. I was beyond it.

As I sipped my coffee and tried to blend in, Paddy sidled over to me, his face alive with remorse. This morning he looked even more haggard and worn out than he had the day before.

"I could hardly sleep at all last night," he confided in a low voice as he stood close enough to me that our bodies touched. I wanted to step away but everyone was watching us, so I couldn't. I was trapped. "I felt like shit about what I said to you yesterday. Forgive me? If you don't, I think I might drop dead of exhaustion and guilt. Maybe you'd enjoy that?" He watched my face, looking for a smile, but I just shrugged. I didn't feel like smiling.

"It's okay, Paddy. I know you were looking out for Murphy. You're his Alpha."

"I'm yours too." He angled his body so his face was averted from the rest of the room and they couldn't read his lips. I had to strain to hear him and I stood right beside him.

"Only because I'm bonded to Murphy."

"Is that what you're thinking?" His tone turned ominously dark. "It's not good for my temper to listen to shite like that come out of your mouth, Constance Newcastle. You won't like my temper if it gets the better of me."

My mouth grew small. I had a temper of my own. To keep from blurting something inflammatory, I gulped at my coffee. It was hot and scorched my tongue.

"I'm not Sorcha. You tell Fee that I resent being compared to that fucking bitch." The pain in my tongue burned away my resolve not to say anything.

"Tell her yourself. Better yet, prove it. Prove you're not like her," Paddy challenged.

"It's a little late for that. I won't be proving anything except how adept Kathy is at judging poison doses of coniine when I drink it."

The whisk stopped beating against the side of the mixing bowl for a second but then resumed twice as briskly.

"Why should I have to prove anything?" I moved away from Paddy and retreated in a fury toward the kitchen table. Vaughn and Jossie watched me, openmouthed, while Kathy continued to prepare breakfast as if nothing was happening.

Paddy fumed by the coffee machine. "When you join a new pack, woman, you need to prove your worthiness. It's not just given to you. It's a privilege to belong to Mac Tire, not a right simply because you're bonded to Liam Murphy. The sooner you get over that bullshit notion the better!"

"The sooner you get over the bullshit notion that I will have the time to prove anything to you, the better. I'm already dead, don't you understand? I don't even know why you came. I don't need you. I don't need *any* of you!" I included all of them in my wrathful glare, but saved most of it for Paddy. I wrenched the Mac Tire ring off my finger so hard I nearly dislocated the joint.

"Don't you dare throw that at me, goddamn you!" shouted Paddy. "Nobody throws the pack ring at me and gets away with it!"

Just as I drew back my arm to fling the damn ring at Paddy's face, Councilor Armentano rushed into the room, followed closely by Councilor Hill. Councilor Samuels brought up the rear, his pudgy face aghast.

"What is going on here?" Councilor Armentano's appearance sucked up all the fury in the room leaving only unbearable tension behind.

Paddy recovered himself first and moved between me and the Councilors as he tried to shield me from them.

"Nothing at all, Councilors. Just a wee little argument. Nothing serious. You know the Irish. We'd rather brawl before breakfast than comb our hair and wash our faces. I was poking at her, trying to get a rise."

Armentano's expression turned skeptical. "Is that so, Advisor Newcastle?" He made a mockery of my title.

I couldn't see Paddy's face, but I could tell by the set of his shoulders he was pissed off at Armentano's tone.

I floundered. Paddy was my Alpha, I couldn't exactly contradict him, but neither could I lie to a member of the Great Council.

"I might have been pushing his buttons a little too," I squeaked.

Councilor Samuels bit his lip as if to ward back a smile.

Hill looked shocked. "Are you in the habit of pushing your Alpha's buttons, Advisor?"

"I'd expect nothing less from a true daughter of Mac Tire," said Paddy. "She's fitting in nicely. I can't wait to get her to Dublin and integrated with the rest of the pack. In Ireland we like to scrap, Councilors. She'll need to set her New England priggishness aside if she wants to hold her own with my pack."

"I beg your pardon!" Perkins, the consummate New England prig, shouldered his way past the others to stand by Armentano's side. "It's all well and good to talk about Irish shortcomings since you are Irish, but I do not think that gives you the right to cast aspersions on New Englanders. Priggish is an insult, in case you didn't realize."

Councilor Samuels lost the fight against his smile, so hid his mouth with one hand. Hill, who was as New England as could be, snorted. He was more amused than offended.

"Adam, I think we should leave this between Mr. O'Reilly and Advisor Newcastle." Armentano put a hand on Perkins's sleeve and adroitly led him back into the dining room. The others made way and followed.

As they filed out, I slipped the ring back on my finger. Paddy turned around and saw me do it.

He grinned. "I haven't been that bloody mad since Fee gave my best whiskey to that idiot Declan Byrne just because he told her he'd never seen eyes so green as the ones gracing her fair face. And him having Alannah Doyle for a bond mate. Doesn't she have the greenest eyes that ever were? Fee's eyes are hazel for one thing, not green and since she looks at herself at least two hours a day in the mirror, you'd think she'd be above falling for such a crock-of-shit line as that, wouldn't you?"

"Hazel eyes are green," I said and was rewarded with a huge bark of laughter that came straight from Paddy's gut.

"Aren't you and Fee going to be the greatest of friends and soul mates?" he said. I didn't give much for the so-called sense of premonition. I would never meet Fiona Carmichael, let alone become her greatest friend and soul mate.

Paddy saw the doubt on my face and gave me a stern look.

"Do not give up." He made it sound like I had a chance and I wanted to believe him. I wanted to see Heather grow up into the beautiful woman she promised to be. I wanted to try to be closer to Kathy Manning, perhaps be the surrogate daughter she'd always dreamed of. I wanted the chance to be a good pack member and come to trust my Alphas. Most of all I wanted Murphy. But it was hard to believe in anything anymore.

* * * *

"Please state your name, age and pack affiliation for the record." Councilor Perkins took his seat at the conference table. Vaughn remained standing. I'd moved over one chair to give Vaughn the one at the foot of the table, since he was the first tribunal witness.

Paddy sat opposite me, his face grave. I was fascinated with his different-colored eyes. One blue, one brown. He was not strictly a handsome man, but he was powerfully attractive and those eyes enhanced everything.

Vaughn had tried to subdue his teen-idol good looks with pulled-back hair and a dress shirt and tie, but he could only do so much. Time might etch a few lines around his eyes and across his forehead, but he would always make women's hearts flutter. He couldn't help it.

Jossie sat next to Kathy, behind the Advisors. Heather was sprawled asleep in her lap, her little rosebud mouth slightly open. I could see her eyes moving beneath her lavender-tinged lids and wondered what she dreamed.

Marco had fetched one of the armchairs from the front room so Jossie could be more comfortable with the baby. He treated her with the respectful deference all Pack men treated a lactating Pack woman.

Jossie was Alpha of Maplefair and had three months to find a new bond mate before she'd be forced to step aside, not only as Alpha, but also as an official pack member.

From the way her gaze followed Vaughn everywhere he went, I knew she'd found her next bond mate. What I didn't know was whether he'd found his. I suspected he might have, from the casual protectiveness he showed around her. But that could be as much for Heather, his newfound daughter, as it could be for Jossie herself. With their history, it was hard to tell.

"My name is Vaughn Pelletier. I'm forty years old and I'm currently without a pack affiliation." Vaughn's eyes flickered slightly as he confessed he was outside a pack's protection. People in the room subtly angled their bodies away from him. It was an unconscious snubbing. Vaughn had no status in their eyes. Since it had been more than three months since his bond mates died, he was no longer a member of Riverglow, and was what was known as a *loner* in Pack society.

"But until recently you were Alpha of Riverglow, isn't that correct?" Rosemary Young asked. She was not blind to Vaughn's good looks and sought to bolster his image a little, although by her slight grimace it was clear she didn't think much of Riverglow.

No one in New England did.

"That's correct, Councilor," said Vaughn and he sat after she gave him a nod. His hand crept toward his despised tie but then he seemed to remember himself and let it fall back to his side.

Councilor Hill's Advisor, Kristie, scribbled furiously into her notebook. Marco bent to his sketch book, his eyes alight with inspiration. Josh, the Advisor from Nightclaw, didn't bother to type anything into his laptop. The look he gave Vaughn was just short of contemptuous. I glared at him and he lowered his eyes as an unbecoming flush stained his freckled face.

"Mr. Pelletier, we've asked you here to this tribunal to tell us about your impressions of Advisor Newcastle's wolf." Perkins didn't bother to ease into anything.

A sick look flashed across Vaughn's face, but he quickly banished it. A sheen of sweat popped out on his forehead and I knew he didn't want to testify.

Beneath the table, I reached out and put a hand on his thigh. I wanted him to know he should continue and tell the truth, and that I'd never hold anything he said against him. He had to remember the tribunal after Grey and Elena had died, and all the awful things he'd said to spite me.

Today he clearly didn't want to be spiteful, but the truth would damn me no matter how gently he stated it.

"I thought I was going to talk about Nate, about what I saw in the woods when he was a teenager."

Adam Perkins shook his head. "That's not the area we wanted to concentrate on today, Mr. Pelletier. Please answer the question put to you."

Vaughn cast me an agonized look but quickly faced forward again and straightened his shoulders. "I met Stanzie...Advisor Newcastle at a Regional Gathering in New York state when she was seventeen. There was talk at the time that I might...that she might ask me to initiate her first shift, but it didn't end up happening. I was Alpha of Riverglow then but her pack decided she wasn't old enough."

I almost snorted aloud at that. My pack. My father, to be precise. He'd looked down his nose at Riverglow when I'd broached the subject of shifting with Vaughn. At seventeen, I'd been snagged by his teen idol looks, but I'd also sensed a gentle soul beneath them. My father had absolutely forbidden the idea of Vaughn initiating my wolf.

"You're a member of Mayflower, Constance," he'd lectured me, and ignored my pleading eyes. "You have a reputation to uphold. Riverglow is a tiny, insignificant pack with no pedigree, no history. That man is too young to be an effective Alpha. The pack has existed less than two years. How can that compare to Mayflower, which was here before the Revolution? You are growing up and you need to start thinking with your head and not your heart. I know the man is good-looking, but that is not important. Status, continuity, reputation, honor, those are the important things."

He hadn't exactly come out and told me that Riverglow had a bad reputation, but I'd read between the lines. After less than five years in existence, I hadn't seen how they could possibly have any kind of a reputation, but I hadn't pushed it. I did remember it, though, and it had definitely influenced my decision to join Riverglow three years later. By then I'd wanted to spite my father. The funny thing is, if he'd let me be initiated by Vaughn, I would probably be Alpha of Mayflower by now. My wolf might have been normal and his grand plans for my life could have been realized. Now that would have been ironic.

At the time, though, I'd been secretly relieved. At seventeen I had still been firmly my father's daughter and a dutiful member of Mayflower. Vaughn had been drop-dead gorgeous but I'd been a little scared of shifting and a lot scared of sex. It was only because my friend, Jocelyn

Wilbanks, had broached the subject of shifting with Vaughn that I'd mustered the courage to bring it up with my father. I hadn't been immune to peer pressure after all.

Jossie had been a stunning and joyful teenager, so different from the haunted and subdued woman of today. I cast my mind back to that Regional.

* * * *

Jossie clutches my arm. Her nails are painted bright, zooming red that hurts my eyes if I look too closely. Her skin is dusky olive compared to my very pale white. She is so exotic and different. Her long chestnut hair hangs down to her butt and she constantly whips it around. It is as frenetic and joyful as she is.

"Look!" she whispers, her brown eyes going wide with excitement. The faintest tint of rose blushes her cheeks and I can both feel and smell the animal heat emanating from her. Jossie at eighteen is a crucial year older than me—pumped full of hormones that are raging for release. Her wolf still slumbers, but she is waking. All she needs is sex. One encounter with a Pack male and her wolf will be part of her for the rest of her life instead of an abstract thought for the not-as-yet-arrived future. "It's him!" She invests the pronoun with all the longing, innocent yet obsessive lust that a teenager girl can muster. The force of it nearly blows me over and it definitely attracts the object of her desire.

He slouches against the trunk of a slender-trunked tree outside the small motel where we have all gathered. The motel is owned by a member of the Hudson, New York pack, Aspenmoon. Two small conference rooms have been opened into each other, but it's always crowded in there and many of the teens and some of the older people like to escape outside.

Jossie's crush, Vaughn Pelletier, is smoking. That makes him a definite rebel in my eyes. No one in my pack smokes. We are told it is disgusting, dulls the senses, and can cause cancer. Why would an adult choose to pollute his body with something evil like cigarettes? I do think he looks kinda sexy against the trunk of the aspen. He's wearing tight jeans and a navy-blue t-shirt. Nothing special or expensive. But he makes them look good. I especially like his boots. Doc Martens. I wish I had a pair but Paul says they are ugly and masculine and prefers me to wear sandals and low-heeled pumps. Sneakers if I absolutely must.

"He's an Alpha, Jossie!" I whisper back, appalled and yet attracted by the way he is looking us both over and smiling a little to himself.

"That means he knows what he's doing. In bed!" Jossie flings the last two words at my face, expecting the reaction she gets. I blush like hell and try to rush back to the sanctuary of the motel. Her crimson-tipped talons pinch as she holds me back.

"I'm going to talk to him. And so are you." She tosses that long hair of hers. I envy that hair. Mine hangs just above my shoulders in a neat bob with bangs. Until I saw Jossie's long, wild hair, I thought I looked sophisticated and grown-up. Compared to her I am a child.

Jossie's eyes dance with joy and desire. She's having fun. She always has such fun. Ever since I met her at the Regional in Maine when I was fifteen and she was sixteen, we always have fun together at Regionals. If Paul knew half the things Jossie says and a quarter of the things she convinces me to do with her, he'd never allow me to spend so much time with her. My one act of rebellion is to keep that knowledge away from him. I like Jossie. I wish we could see each other more than once a year. I consider her my best friend outside my pack. I suspect she has lots of best friends and I am not her only one, but I can pretend.

"What are you two girls giggling about?" Vaughn straightens up from the tree trunk and I am amazed and attracted at how tall and lean he is. My heart does this strange little jerk and I am flooded with feelings I don't know how to handle. I picture his mouth on mine and my stomach swoops. I bite my lip and watch him saunter closer, flinging the cigarette away. It hits the sidewalk and rolls off onto the parking lot asphalt. It's still smoking a little and I worry about fire even though I know asphalt doesn't burn.

"You!" Jossie is bold and tilts her head up so she can grin at him. She's almost a head shorter than he is and she is not a short girl. She's tiny in other places. Waist, wrists, ankles, shoulders, chest. I am more solidly built, and I wish I were more petite. Baby fat still clings to my curves and although Jossie says I look sexy, I don't think so. Sexy is tiny like her.

Vaughn thinks so too because he focuses most of his attention on her and stands so close her chest nearly brushes his. If he stood that close to me, my chest would brush his.

"I want you to initiate me," Jossie declares, fearlessly reaching out to trace the tip of her bright red nail along the edge of Vaughn's sexy face.

"Jossie!" I gasp in total horror even as my stomach does sensual flips, and I wish I had her courage.

A grin lights up Vaughn's Hollywood-handsome face and, without warning, he takes Jossie's wrists in his hands and captures her mouth with his, holding her so she cannot move away.

My face burns and I want to run away but I am mesmerized at the heat generated between them both. How can they kiss so long? How can they breathe? Are they really using tongues? It's broad daylight. There are so many people around. Why can't I move? What are these alien, engulfing feelings inflaming me? I'm going to ignite and burst into fire if they don't stop kissing.

* * * *

Vaughn's voice brought me back to the present. His hand found mine beneath the table, his fingers twined with mine. He sought comfort from me and I tried to give it to him.

"The next time I met Stanzie it was three years later at a Regional in Vermont. She'd met Grey Owens the year before. They'd been seeing each other since then and were bonding at this particular Gathering. Stanzie was fifteenth generation Mayflower and so I was really surprised when she came to me the night before the bonding ceremony and asked if she and Grey could join with Riverglow. I mean, well, let's be honest here, Riverglow was not a very prestigious pack. Mayflower was the oldest continuous pack in New England. Not the oldest in America, but the oldest here in this region. They are pretty proud of that lineage and Stanzie was the next generation. It didn't make much sense to me."

"Had you seen her wolf yet?" Councilor Hill probed. He seemed bored with this back-story, as if he suspected Vaughn were simply drawing out the time in order to avoid the real question.

Vaughn flushed and his fingers tightened convulsively around mine. "Yeah. Briefly. There was a Great Hunt and I saw her shift and take off like a shot. Ignoring..."

"Ignoring the Alpha leaders of the hunt?" Councilor Hill finished for him.

"She was young, barely twenty." Vaughn tried to cover for me and failed miserably.

Marco's pencil scratched the surface of his drawing pad as he raced to capture the tortured expression on Vaughn's face.

"So when she asked you if she could join Riverglow, did her wolf give you any pause at all?" Hill was relentless and Vaughn shifted in his seat. Beside me, Paddy sat very still, glaring down the table at the Councilors.

"No," burst Vaughn. "No. It was the fact she was Mayflower that gave me pause. I wasn't actually going to agree because I thought she should stay with her birth pack. She'd never have any status in my pack and I couldn't understand why somebody would want to throw away status." He took a deep, agitated breath. I squeezed his hand encouragingly and we looked at each other for a moment.

I hoped the whole table could understand how deep our friendship went. Vaughn had been my Alpha, my lover, my friend.

"She'd run away with Grey. Her birth pack had no idea she was in Vermont. I tried to get her to at least call them, but she wouldn't. She said if I didn't let them join Riverglow, they'd find another pack. She was never going back. I didn't ask her what happened to her to make her want to leave her birth pack behind, but I knew what it was like to start over.

"We'd asked people to join Riverglow, but nobody wanted to. They laughed at us. Here were two people who asked *us*."

Remembered humiliation sucked the color from his cheeks and he sighed. "I don't know if I did the right thing. Riverglow must have been such a comedown from Mayflower. She always seemed so happy, but I don't know if I let my pride ruin her chances."

"I loved being a member of Riverglow." I couldn't help but speak up. I wasn't supposed to, but damn it, Vaughn should not castigate himself. He'd given me a home. "I was proud to be in your pack, Vaughn."

He smiled at me and leaned his forehead against mine. We breathed in each other's scents and somehow that calmed us. My heart stopped trip hammering in my chest and the tightness in my throat loosened.

"After Advisor Newcastle joined Riverglow, did you find anything about her wolf troublesome?" At the sound of Hill's voice, Vaughn reluctantly pulled apart from me and gave his attention to the Councilors.

"Of course I did," he said unhappily. "Her wolf was like a child. Running and playing and listening only to her own desires. She wouldn't cooperate with the rest of us and it was clear from the start that when we hunted together, Grey would run with Stanzie and the rest of us would hunt. Sometimes I went with Grey and Stanzie. We all did. It became normal for us."

"And at Regionals?" Councilor Armentano asked.

Vaughn took a miserable breath. "We didn't go to many and the ones we did, well, mostly Stanzie didn't go on the Great Hunt. If she did, our whole pack went with her, not the rest of the hunt. We headed her away from them, actually. It was no big deal really."

Armentano's expression said otherwise.

"You never tried to work with her? Mentor her?"

Vaughn hung his head and didn't answer until I gave his knee a nudge with mine.

"I tried," he whispered. There was dead silence in the room except for frantic buzzing of a fly tapping against the window seeking escape. I knew precisely how that fly felt. The glass was a barrier that he could never hope to penetrate without assistance and more than likely he'd be swatted to death rather than shown mercy. Just because he'd been drawn inside by scents and circumstances that had seemed a good idea at the time.

"Stanzie didn't like talking about her wolf," Vaughn admitted. "We all tried at some point. Grey, Elena, me, Callie, Peter." His voice broke a little on Peter's name and he reached out for a glass of water.

"She said she was happy with the way her wolf was and she didn't want to be like everybody else and nobody could make her change." The ghost of a smile drifted across Vaughn's face. He sounded proud of my defiance or maybe he simply remembered better times when Callie and Peter had been alive.

"She said this to her Alphas?" Councilor Perkins was aghast.

Vaughn's mouth tightened—smile gone. "We were a small pack, Councilor. We were all friends and lovers. How do you force someone to evolve her wolf? How do you make her do it and not destroy your relationship?"

"For her own good perhaps?" Perkins snapped. "See where it got her? As her former Alpha, you should feel guilty. Once again you might have prevented this travesty if you'd done your duty."

Low blow. Vaughn made no move to defend himself.

"I would have left Riverglow before I evolved my wolf," I cried, incensed at the idea that Vaughn should bear more guilt. He was very good at piling guilt onto himself. He did not need Perkins's sanctimonious help.

"I don't understand why you so easily capitulated to Liam Murphy but not to your Alphas in Riverglow!"

"I told you why. Two years in exile. If I'd left Riverglow, Grey would have come with me. I wouldn't have been alone, don't you see? I wasn't sure of Murphy. I didn't want to be alone."

"You've been an extremely selfish young woman," Perkins lectured, and Paddy cleared his throat loudly.

"Are we ever going to stick to the subject?" he wondered. "I didn't think all the evidence had been gathered yet. You're going to be judging her before it's all been compiled, are you?"

Perkins and Paddy glared at each other for a long, tense moment until Councilor Armentano said, "If this continues, we'll be forced to clear the room of all nonwitnesses."

"She has a right to her Alpha's support!" Paddy objected, but he stopped glaring at Perkins.

Perhaps sensing the tension in the air, Heather's eyes flew open and she let out a protesting wail. Jossie tried to shush her, but she squirmed in Jossie's arms, her gaze fixed on Vaughn.

"Va!" She cried imploringly, and reached out her chubby arms to him as if she sensed his agitation. "Va!"

"She's saying your name." I bit my lip at the flood of guilty torment that stained Vaughn's cheeks. He wouldn't look in his daughter's direction.

She began to sob inconsolably and Vaughn muttered a curse beneath his breath.

A fifteen-minute recess was called and Jossie brought Heather to Vaughn. At first I didn't think he would take her, but he finally held out his arms. The moment she was safely tucked against him, her crying ceased.

"Va," she said again and touched her tiny fingers to his face. The stricken look of love and pain that contorted his features was hard to watch so I turned my face away. I escaped as quickly as I could to my room upstairs where I spent the recess trying to breathe. It had become so damn hard to breathe.

* * * *

I managed a bathroom break at the end of our fifteen-minute recess and assessed myself in the mirror. My hair, pulled back to my nape with a silver barrette, seemed very gold in the sunlight that sneaked through the blinds. My eyes were extremely blue, but I think that was because I wore a slate blue linen blazer and skirt that brought them out.

I touched my bond pendant, Murphy's pearl and my peridot, and a measure of strength and warmth coursed through me. I wanted to believe I had a chance. I wanted to be optimistic and positive.

Head high, I went back to the conference room and, in less than fifteen seconds, all my confidence drained away to be replaced by total numbness.

My parents—Paul Benedict and Lauren Newcastle—were seated at the table. Witnesses. In my worst nightmarish anxiety about the tribunal, never once had I entertained the hideous thought that my parents—anyone from Mayflower—would be called as witnesses. They'd had nothing to do with Nate Carver's death. Even less with my wolf.

My wolf. The tribunal wanted to know about her and they thought my parents could tell them? The only things my parents could tell them would damn me even more than I already was.

Heart pounding, I forced myself to walk to my chair. Paul sat in the one to my right, Lauren beyond him. Neither looked at me. Paul maintained a rigid, disapproving posture, his gaze fixed stubbornly on the door while Lauren kept her head down, glorious gold hair sliding across her perfect cheeks concealing her from me.

Lauren was so beautiful. The most beautiful woman I'd ever seen. Even now with most of her face hidden, she affected every male in the room.

Marco scrambled for his sketch pad, his dark, handsome face alight with admiration. Josh, laptop forgotten, had his eyes fixed greedily upon her.

The male Councilors cast quick glances down the table while Paddy all but drooled.

Only Vaughn seemed immune and that was because he was pissed off. He sat in the back of the room with Jossie and Heather and glared at the back of my father's head.

Lauren managed one agonized look in my direction, as if to beg me for something, but Paul put his hand on her shoulder and she turned away, face flushed.

When we were little, we alternated between calling our parents Mom and Dad, and by their first names. As we grew older, we were encouraged to drop Mom and Dad and, by the time we reached our teens and early twenties, we used their first names almost exclusively. We had to do this because of the way we aged. Lauren and I looked like sisters even though she was fifty-seven years old to my thirty-two. I could pass for anywhere in my twenties and she could pass for anywhere in her thirties. If we were in public together and I called her Mom, it would attract confusion and attention. So we went with first names.

The same thing with Paul. He was sixty, but he looked thirty-five tops.

Paul had reddish-blond hair and arrogant blue eyes. They were the exact same shade of uncompromising blue as mine, only I hoped mine lacked his arrogance. He was a superciliously handsome man. He had a sense of humor, only it was mostly sarcastic and directed at other people. Paul loved pointing out other people's flaws but did not much appreciate being made aware of his as he steadfastly refused to believe he had any.

Age had not mellowed him. If anything it had made him even harder and more abrasive. I remembered him being much more approachable and kind when I was a little girl.

I supposed he loved my mother, but secretly I always believed it was more possessiveness than anything else. He, like most men, was in awe of her beauty. It threw him off, made him uncertain, and so he clutched all the more tightly.

Lauren was breathtaking. If my hair was gold, her hair was spun sunshine. If my mouth was seductive, hers was ravishing. If my body was shapely, hers was like a goddess's. When she smiled, it was as if the whole world lit up with hope and beauty. Everything tawdry and sullen turned magical with revealed potential.

Her voice was sweet and clear, but halting, as if she were never sure of herself. And she wasn't. For all her devastating beauty, Lauren never believed she mattered much outside of Paul's protective influence. He had her wrapped around his little finger and twisted up in secret, horrible knots inside herself. Everything she did, she did for him. One cold look from him and her day was ruined.

Her normal expression was always just short of tears. Her incredible light blue eyes, the color of hyacinths, were perpetually filmed over with tears unless she worked hard to be cheerful.

People tripped over themselves to do things for her and she let them do it. I'd always taken care of her—once I'd gotten past the age of needing everything done for me. If Paul had been angry with her over some petty transgression, I would be the one who made her a cup of tea and brushed her hair.

I had never been able to have a heart-to-heart mother-daughter conversation with her, unless I played the role of the mother. All my hopes and dreams for the future had remained locked inside of me because I never wanted to burden her once I figured out they were in direct contrast to the life Paul had decided upon for me.

Unbidden, my very first memory washed me. I was maybe two years old.

* * * *

I am scared. Wren hugs me tight. I am small in the circle of her arms. She smells like flowers. I bury my face in her neck and feel her shaking. Wren-Mom cries. I pat her smooth, pretty face with my chubby little hand. I want Wren-Mom to smile. We can play together with the little dolls and the little house. If Wren-Mom will stop crying.

Then he is there too. Pa. His face is all mad when he sees Wren-Mom crying. He speaks too fast for me to understand but I hear some words I know. Wren, stop, no. And my name. Constance.

Wren-Mom lets go of me so Pa can lift me up into his arms. At first I don't want to go—Pa scares me sometimes. His face is all mad still but then he smiles at me. I am not scared anymore.

* * * *

It has been almost three years since I last saw my parents. They'd come to Grey and Elena's funeral grudgingly. The minute Paul had realized my pack blamed me for their deaths, he'd made a point to stand away from me. Lauren had brushed my shoulder with hers when she'd moved to stand with him. We hadn't spoken, but our eyes had met and the sorrow and compassion in hers made me shake. I'd tried to hug her, wanted to feel my mother's arms around me, but her embrace was quick and furtive as Paul's judgmental gaze burned into us both.

Awkward. It had been so damned awkward. I hadn't let any of them see me cry but I'd been howling inside.

"Hello, Paul. Hello, Lauren." My voice was way more confident than I truly felt.

Lauren gave a start and turned her face to me. Paul's shoulders became more rigid as he struggled with his temper. I knew from experience he wanted to acknowledge me, to let his anger show, but in the end he remained facing away from me.

"Hello, Stanzie." Lauren's voice was a shredded whisper. Paul's breathing became furiously audible and all the color leached out of Lauren's face. She bowed her head again to shut me out.

A small glow of satisfaction ignited within me, which was almost immediately doused by guilt. Lauren would pay for her acknowledgment of me. Paul would see to that. What had I really gotten from the exchange? Petty revenge? Using my mother as a pawn against Paul was an old game I should have outgrown.

My sense of smell was not as acute as it was in wolf form, but there was no mistaking the miasma of anger that steadily emanated from Paul's pores. His scent all but drowned out Lauren's. She wasn't angry—she never was—her scent was pure grief as if she were in mourning.

For me. If she'd only once had the courage to pick up the goddamned phone when I'd called, but she hadn't. I'd always come to second to him. Everyone did.

The Councilors were extremely aware of the tension between me and my parents. Rosemary Young was compassionate enough to be surprised by this, but the men merely seemed to tuck this bit of information into the growing file of condemnation that piled up against me.

Beneath the table Paddy reached out to put his hand on my thigh. It was oddly comforting even as it was intimate. For a moment I wondered what it might be like to go to bed with him then dismissed the thought. I didn't want to fuck him so much as I craved the intimacy. There was a difference. And however good he was between the sheets, I would never get the closeness I achieved with Murphy. That only came with love.

After my parents had stated their names, ages and pack affiliation for the record, Councilor Perkins leaned across the gleaming conference table. "Do you understand why we've brought you before this tribunal, Mr. Benedict?"

"Yes," said my father grimly.

"Tell us about your daughter, specifically with regard to the initiation and training of her wolf."

My father, a master at pregnant pauses, waited the precise number of beats guaranteed to rivet the attention of the entire room. "Constance was the fifteenth generation of Mayflower, which is the oldest-continuous pack in New England as you know, Councilor. We may not have the fancy connections to the Regional and Great Councils that Nightclaw does, nor the resources, but we've got status and history. Constance was told this as she grew up. She knew what was expected of her and she knew I'd be there to help her if she needed it.

"I hadn't intended for her to initiate her wolf until she was twenty, so it came as something of a shock to me when she asked if she could be initiated by Vaughn Pelletier at the Hudson, New York Regional Gathering when she was seventeen. I could hardly agree to it. In body she might have been developed, but not socially. The man was good-looking—he had all the young girls swooning—but Constance ought to have realized there's more to initiating one's wolf than an attractive partner."

Vaughn sat with Jossie, Heather and Kathy, his face stoic. A slow burn of resentment ignited inside me. It reminded me of how I'd perpetually felt around my father after that summer regional. All the old arguments we'd had hammered at my head and gibbered shrilly. He'd always accused me of being shallow and distracted by shiny, pretty things.

"I had a perfect candidate in mind for her initiation. Wes Hanover. Good man. Constance refused to work with him. Petty revenge because I'd blocked her liaison at the Regional." Paul's voice was smooth, lending him credence he didn't deserve, in my opinion. More resentment churned in my gut at the way he avoided saying Vaughn's name. It was also a blatant lie. Of course, Paul didn't see it that way so his scent remained virtuous, but I knew it. A part of me had been grateful he hadn't allowed me to be initiated by Vaughn. I hadn't been ready then, but soon after that had changed. It was then my resentment had begun to fester, not before.

"Lauren and I were very patient. We allowed her to come with us to the Great Gathering in New Orleans when she was eighteen." Even though I couldn't see Paul's face, I knew the expression of disgusted anger that must be spread across his face. I'd seen it often enough after the debacle of my wolf's first appearance in the cane fields behind the plantation.

"She gave me her vow, Councilors, that she would not sneak behind my back and shift for the first time with some young, idiotic teenager. But that's exactly what she did and the boy in question didn't even come from one of the influential European packs. No, he came from some tiny, insignificant pack with no pedigree behind them. There were several young men there from packs that mattered, but the boy she chose was good looking. Always with Constance it was the surface that mattered, never the substance.

"To further humiliate her pack, her wolf made a spectacle of herself— screaming and tearing around the field like a maniac. Our Alpha had to calm her down and that was incredibly mortifying for him—exposed in front of the whole Gathering like that. Mayflower was the laughing stock of the Gathering after that and we have not attended another Great Gathering since. It's doubtful we ever will."

I smoldered. Doubtful they ever would while Paul lived. He had a way of making everyone do what he wanted them to do because suffering the consequences of his temper and I-told-you-sos were not worth it.

"After we returned to Connecticut, I assumed Constance would be sufficiently ashamed enough to work with Wes at controlling her wolf, but then again she rebelled and refused. At first I thought she was simply scared and humiliated, but it became clear she was doing it to defy me." His voice grated at the remembered insult. Nobody defied Paul Benedict.

My expression, I hoped, was blank, as if I politely listened to someone I didn't know talk. But I'm sure my scent gave me away. Grateful for Paddy's hand on my thigh, I wished I could touch him back but I didn't want to give away the fact my father's testimony had the power to hurt me.

* * * *

I cower against the wall of my bedroom. Paul looms over me. His face contorts with rage. His fists are clenched and not for the first time I wonder if he will hit me. He's never hit me in my life but I've also never pushed back like this before.

"Are you going to hit me?" I squeak. Will I defend myself or crumple into a beaten, submissive heap on my bedroom floor?

For a moment the rage is so clear and pure across his face I freeze. Lauren's voice floats, coated with fear and uncertainty, from the bedroom across from mine.

"Paul?" Just one word, but full of fright and meaning.

"Lauren, be quiet!" Paul turns his rage to her, grateful, it seems, for a chance to bleed some of it off. She shuts up. She always shuts up.

"I wouldn't stoop so low as to lose control and hit you, much as you deserve it," Paul snarls as he turns back to me. "That you would even think I might hit you proves how much you need to work with your wolf. Anger, Constance, rage, fury. Those are emotions we, as Pack, will struggle with all our lives. But our wolves will help us if we let them. Why won't you listen to me?"

I don't say anything because I've said it all before, begged him before, and he is the one who won't listen.

After a moment, he shakes his head and slams out of my room. I hear them, then, Lauren and Paul, having violent sex so he can shift and run out his fury at me in wolf form. I try to block my ears but I can't help hearing their bed slam into the wall over and again and the creaking protest of the mattress springs. Nor can I block out Lauren's cries. He's hurting her, but she must like it on some level because she allows it. Or so I tell myself and have told myself ever since I was a little girl.

* * * *

"After that Gathering, Constance lost all respect for me, for Mayflower, for herself. Nothing proved it more than when she started consorting with Grey Owens." Again, I couldn't see his face, but I knew the exact way his lip would curl disparagingly.

Started consorting with Grey Owens—I tried not to laugh at how that sounded. As if I did it on purpose, conjured him by magic so I could further humiliate Paul Benedict. But that's not how it happened.

* * * *

I'm in line at the movies waiting to buy a tub of buttery popcorn and a soda. The conversation of Others around me makes a buzzing in my ears that I try to ignore. Usually I stay home but home is a difficult place now so I escape to the movies or the coffee shop in town. I take the bus, which I hate because it is loud and smelly and the Others crammed into it make me uncomfortable, especially when one of the young men tries to hit on me. Even when I keep my eyes down and my posture stiff, enough to let everyone know that I do not wish to be touched or talked to, they still persist. I try to like them, even a little, but it has been ground into me for years that I cannot trust Others. Also, they smell funny. Not like Pack. They douse themselves with colognes and aftershaves, and it still can't mask their weird Other scent.

At first it was overwhelming when I would go out in public, but the more I forced myself to do it, the easier it became to dial down my senses. Their smell would never be appealing, but at least now it was bearable.

"Hey there," says a man behind me in line. I stiffen. Not again. I ignore it.

"I'm talking to you." He is persistent and I hate that. I hate it more when he reaches out a casual hand to touch my shoulder. I whirl around to confront him, tell him to leave me alone, and when I do, I see him. A tall, lanky man with dark hair that he has loose around his face. It is long enough to pull back into a ponytail and thick. He has high cheekbones and friendly blue eyes. Attractive as hell. My body reacts despite itself and as I inhale his scent, I realize he is Pack. I have never met anyone Pack in public before. This is Mayflower's territory and he is not of Mayflower.

"You're not Mayflower. This town is ours," I blurt before I can stop myself. Because I don't care. Paul would care. Why am I being Paul?

His wide, generous mouth quirks into a beguiling smile.

"Isn't it big enough to share? Just for one night? I'm spending the summer riding my bike around the country. I could give you a ride after the movie if you like?"

Bike? My mind doubtfully conjures up a Schwinn with curled handlebars and pedals. Where would I...then my stupid brain clears and I realize he's talking about a motorcycle.

"I don't even know your name." I sound haughty but I don't want to. I'm so standoffish because I'm shy.

With gentle hands he maneuvers me ahead in the line. It has moved up while we talk. I like the feel of his fingers on my arms. Goose bumps rise on my flesh. I look more closely at him. He's my age maybe or a bit older. It's hard to tell with Pack but he doesn't seem very old. He's got confidence to spare—way more than me.

"Grey," he tells me with another wonderful smile. "My name is Grey. What's yours?"

"Stanzie," I say. "Short for Constance. I can't stand Constance."

"Stanzie," he repeats. "How about that ride?"

Something clicks into place between us and after that night we are never far apart. He takes day trips on his bike. Sometimes I go with him but not often because Paul doesn't like me to be far away. After a while what Paul likes ceases to be of such paramount concern.

* * * *

"The man completely beguiled Constance, spinning her tales of a summer road trip when really he'd been kicked out of his birth pack because he wouldn't submit to the new Alpha male. Do you think Constance would listen to me when I told her the truth?" Paul's voice was aggrieved. "She took Grey's side of it. Said Grey left of his own accord but if he hadn't, he would have been thrown out and she missed the entire point which was that the man would not submit to his Alpha."

I kept silent, but it was hard. Grey's new Alpha had been a mean, petty man who resented the fact that his bond mate had initiated Grey and they were attracted to each other. It had been a tense and awful situation that the Alphas had not handled well, leaving Grey little choice but to leave.

All that long summer Grey and I had sex, but it had been nearly October before I'd consented to shift with him. I still remembered how I'd shaken with trepidation and wondered what my wolf would do.

From the start my wolf had trusted Grey's wolf. Her own heartbeat had not frightened her anymore, but she'd refused to do anything but run and play. Grey's wolf, besotted with her as he was with me, had followed. I'd waited after we'd shifted back for him say something—anything—but he'd prudently left the subject alone.

It wasn't until we'd bonded and joined Riverglow that Callie said something to me about my wolf. I'd blown up at her and there had been miserable tension within the pack for a few weeks before the Alphas had given up. My wolf was, for the most part, left alone after that. Now and then someone would suggest I might want to work on her and I'd flare up and there'd be drama, but as the years passed, those confrontations became fewer. Everyone in Riverglow compensated and covered for my wolf and I pretended I was doing them a huge favor by benefiting them with my wolf's purity and innocence.

"After she joined Riverglow, the only contact we had with her was at Regionals," continued Paul, which was another lie because Lauren and I had had furtive phone calls every couple of months when she could ditch Paul and find a pay phone. Cellphones hadn't worked because Paul checked Lauren's incoming and outgoing numbers as a matter of course, and she hadn't wanted him to know we'd been in steady contact. I'd suggested prepaid cellphones, but the thought of keeping something like that a secret from him had proved too much for Lauren's conscience. The phone calls themselves had been nearly enough to break her.

"Tales of her wolf's lack of control and development were legion."

I pressed my lips together tightly in the attempt to hold back a caustic comment. As if people hadn't had anything better to talk about than my wolf at Regionals. I had barely been a blip on the radar, especially after I stopped participating in the Great Hunts and left them to Grey and Elena.

"Councilors," said my father, leaning closer to them over the expanse of the polished mahogany table. "It is my opinion that Constance's wolf is utterly defective and it isn't just her willfulness that has prevented any sort of development, it's the fact that her wolf is incapable. Wolves like that, while extremely uncommon, are not unheard of."

Beside me Paddy sucked in his breath at the coldblooded pronouncement. The idea that my wolf was damaged was certainly not a new one, but to hear it said with such remorseless certainty from the man who had sired me was like a physical blow.

Rosemary Young's face puckered with what I suspected was disgust. A father protects his offspring, especially if they were weak.

"Bastard," someone whispered. It might have been one of the male Advisors, but it also could have been Vaughn.

Paul's spine stiffened and he turned to survey that part of the room with his judgmental gaze.

"I'm a bastard for stating the truth?" he inquired as if the thought made no sense.

"You're a bastard for gloating about it. She's your daughter for Christ's sake." Vaughn's face was deadly white as he struggled with his temper. Jossie had a hand on his arm but she was angry too. And scared.

"I may have contributed to her conception," allowed Paul, "but I've ceased thinking of myself as her father and all that word implies. In fact, Pelletier, this is the perfect moment to make it official. I renounce her. I have no further interest in her well being or continued existence. After this latest transgression I hardly think the Councils will fail in their responsibility to cut her permanently from the Pack by putting her to death as she well deserves. I want no further stain on my honor. What she does no longer reflects on me or Mayflower. Two years ago you would have been the first to support me, but you've always been weak so it's no surprise to me that you've changed your tune. You never sustain anything. You simply exist and let everyone else propel you forward or push you back. Without your former bond mates to tell you what to think, you have no idea what to do. No backbone, Pelletier. You've always lived through women, letting them tell you what to do."

Paul's gaze traveled coldly over Jossie. "I see your self-preservation instincts have kicked in and you've found Constance's replacement before she's even been condemned to death. Well done."

With a snarl, Vaughn launched himself out of his chair. Paul was on his feet in a heartbeat and so were the Advisors and Paddy.

The Advisors formed a barrier wall between Paul and Vaughn, while Paddy went around it and grabbed Vaughn with both arms and pressed his forehead against the side of Vaughn's head so he could talk directly into his ear.

Paddy was a definite Alpha and, even though Vaughn was not in his pack, he listened. He shook with rage, but he listened.

"I think we can dismiss these witnesses," declared Councilor Armentano, aware of the potential of real violence. His tone was mild, but something flickered in his eyes and betrayed the fact he was angry.

Perkins and Hill escorted my parents out of the conference room. Neither looked back.

* * * *

"I think we should take a break," Rosemary Young suggested. She stared at me and I wondered what she saw because I felt almost nothing. So I had no father anymore. Big deal. I hadn't had one in years.

"I don't need a break if that's what you're thinking," I said and she winced.

"Stanzie, I think..." Paddy began in a placating voice, but stopped when I turned my head to look at him.

"I don't need a break. Let's just get this over with, okay?"

I renounce her. The words echoed in my head. *Her.* Not *you.* I didn't exist to my own father anymore. But, again, I hadn't in years. He'd just made a big production out of it in front of the entire Regional Council and three members of the Great Council. So what, it's not like any of them thought I was a pillar of Pack society.

"He's an asshole, Stanzie. He can't do that. You can't just speak words and undo blood." Vaughn's face was still ashen. Paddy stood close beside him, but no longer held him back.

I scrubbed at my face with my hands as if my fingers were erasers and I might be able to wipe away my own existence. *I renounce her.*

"Your wolf is not defective!" Vaughn pleaded with me, as if I argued with him. That statement pulled me back to reality, the gross ridiculousness of it. Vaughn was now going to lie to me to make me feel better?

"Oh yeah?" I widened my eyes a little as I stared at him, aware that Perkins and Hill had reentered the room and the door was closed against the outside world. "What changed your mind about that, Vaughn? Just because Paul had the guts to say it aloud doesn't mean you don't think the same damn thing yourself and always have."

Vaughn's face contorted under my attack. "Stanzie!"

I looked behind him at Jossie who was standing with Heather in her arms. Heather, sleeping and sweet, head tucked beneath Jossie's chin. Jealousy flared inside of me. I'd never experience that. No child of mine would ever tuck her head beneath my chin trustingly.

Kathy Manning stood beside Jossie, her gaze focused on me. The entire room seemed riveted on me, so why not give them a show?

"You want to know why I'm afraid to have a baby, Kathy?" I stared back at her and she refused to look away. "Well, I'll tell you why. What the fuck. Because my baby's wolf might be like mine, that's why. Defective.

Damaged. You think I didn't know why Grey turned down being Alpha when you asked him to take over, Vaughn?" I switched my gaze back to Vaughn, who winced.

Paddy gave me a warning look. He wanted me to shut the fuck up, I'm sure, but once I'd started talking, the vile poison that had festered inside for years bubbled up and frothed over my lips in a caustic cascade.

"You think I didn't know why suddenly everyone in Riverglow thought it might be a good idea if Grey and I formed a triad? You think we found Elena by mistake? A parade of women just happened to catch Grey's eye that particular Regional and you think I didn't understand why he was onboard with the idea of a triad? You think it didn't hurt me even though Grey swore she'd be the spare to the pair? Do you think I bought the idea that a triad would strengthen Riverglow? Yeah, right. A duo would have done that just as well. It was so Grey could be Alpha and he never would be if he was bonded to just me. He turned the opportunity down once before and told me it was because he thought Jonathan needed the experience more, but really it was because of my wolf."

I drew in a deep breath and held it for an excruciating moment. *I renounce her.*

"I *pretended* not to want a baby. I pretended! I've *always* wanted a baby. Most Pack women do, goddamn it. I'm no different, at least not in this fucking form." I gestured at my body and didn't know whether I would cry or scream.

"Liam told me your wolf is evolving." Vaughn's whisper was pitiful, but we all heard him because no one was making a sound.

"Liam Murphy is biased," I spat. "He's already been an Alpha. He can afford to be magnanimous."

"Constance." Paddy's face was firm and uncompromising. "I want to talk to you in the hall." He looked at the Councilors who were motionless. "Can we please take a frigging break? This all better be off the goddamn record."

"I want it on the record," I argued.

Paddy's gaze sizzled like laser beams into my skull. I could smell his anger now, even above my own. "In the hall, Constance. Now."

Glaring, I shoved back my chair. Paddy marched me out into the hall and the minute the door was shut behind us, he shoved me into the smaller conference room and slammed that door.

I waited for him to turn around—waited to be yelled and sworn at. My whole body vibrated like a tuning fork.

In my head I saw Lauren, head down, submissive, never even looking back. I knew damn well when Paul had renounced me he'd spoken for the both of them.

Paddy braced himself against the door with his palms flat against the wood. His shoulders hunched tight with angry tension. I wouldn't cry when he yelled at me. I wouldn't yell back either. I would take it.

"Come here." He turned around and his voice was indescribably gentle. And soft. "Come on, Stanzie. Come here."

With halting steps, I went to him, unsure of what he meant to do. Would he hit me maybe? Get me within striking distance so he could slap some sense into me?

When I was three steps away, he got impatient and pulled me into his arms. He rocked me until I unfroze and tentatively hugged him back.

"Aren't you going to yell at me?" It felt good to be held, but awful too because I had the distinct feeling I was going to cry and I didn't want to.

"Yell at you? No way." His hands were rough in my hair as he put his forehead against mine and we blinked at each other so close our eyelashes brushed. "Stanzie, to hell with that bastard. Mac Tire is your family. Liam is. You have family, understand?"

My throat squeezed shut.

"A person can be thrown out of a pack, Paddy. Bond mates can disappear in the space between one second and the next. This has happened to me before. I've been cut loose before."

"Stanzie, you belong to us. To me. Okay?" Paddy's different-colored eyes were fascinating up close.

I wished Murphy and I had gone to Dublin. Paddy had been patient, but maybe he'd been too patient. If he'd insisted, we wouldn't be standing in this damn safe house, eyelashes brushing, as my life wound down to the final moment when the poison kicked in and I could no longer manage to suck oxygen down into my lungs.

"You're a good Alpha, Paddy." When I touched his cheek, he turned his face into my palm. His eyes slid closed for a moment as a wistful smile drifted across his face. The muscles of his face moved beneath my hand.

"And you're a rotten witness." He opened his eyes and we smiled at each other before he wrapped a long arm around my shoulders and walked me back to the large conference room.

* * * *

During our absence, the Councilors had decided to break for an early lunch. We found Kathy in the kitchen warming up homemade buttermilk biscuits to go with cold pieces of chicken she'd fried the night before.

Jossie tossed a salad on a nearby counter while Vaughn bounced Heather on his knee at the kitchen table.

Paddy went outside into the garden and I busied myself setting the table. Aside from a pursed mouth, Kathy didn't offer any objections. Generally she hated having helpers in her kitchen, but we were on a timed recess and she couldn't afford to turn away assistance.

Marco and Kristie set the dining room table and we exchanged polite smiles as we inevitably reached into the same cupboards for dishes. The Councilors gathered in the front room. Josh frowned over his laptop at the dining room table.

Vaughn avoided my eyes as I set the table around him and the baby. Heather squealed with babyish glee as she bounced.

"I wonder what witnesses from hell they've got planned for the afternoon session." I deliberately sat down beside Vaughn, who angled his body away from mine. "It keeps getting worse, so I'm thinking maybe they'll resurrect Grey and Elena's ghosts for a glorious trip down memory lane to even further underscore how fucked my wolf is. That would be fun, huh? Or maybe a cross-section representative from every pack in the region who could go on at length about how everyone knows what a joke my wolf is and finally someone's going to do something about it. Oh, here's one—Nate's ghost and he can graphically describe what it felt like to have his throat torn out while he stood there defenseless and vulnerable with nothing for protect..."

"Stop it!" Vaughn grabbed my shoulder with his free hand and shook me hard. Heather goggled at us both as she watched my head flop around.

My hair clip flew off into a corner. "Goddamn it, Stanzie, will you shut up! I don't know what you're trying to prove, but none of us want to hear your bullshit, so shut up!"

I shut up. Heather looked at my face and, I guess, didn't like what she saw because she began to whimper. I got out of the chair to look for my hair clip. I found it under the radiator by the back door. As I was pulling back my hair, Paddy came inside. Right off the bat he noticed the thick tension, but aside from a glance at me, he did nothing but stand beside me.

I fixed my hair and sat again. Vaughn's cheeks were stained bright crimson and he wouldn't look at me, which was fine because I didn't particularly want him to look at me.

Kathy brought a platter of chicken to the table and set it down before she took a seat beside Jossie who was across from Vaughn. Paddy helpfully retrieved the basket of biscuits and took the chair placed at the end of the table. He began to fill water glasses from a pitcher while the rest of us filled our plates.

I wasn't the least bit hungry, but I knew I'd better try to eat something or Kathy would force feed me. I chose the smallest breast of chicken and a minuscule helping of salad. Paddy picked out the biggest biscuit and put it on my plate with a flourish.

As I stared at it in dismay, Kathy said, "Tell me, Stanzie, is Lauren's wolf normal?"

Vaughn choked on a sip of water. I put down the piece of chicken, which had been halfway to my mouth.

"Yes, Kathy."

"And Paul's?" Kathy speared a forkful of salad and smiled at me.

"His too."

Paddy pushed the butter toward me but I ignored it. I had no intention of eating the biscuit.

"What about your grandparents? And their parents?" Kathy took another forkful of salad and contemplated it for a moment before she popped it into her mouth.

"I really only know the ones on my fa— Paul's side," I answered. Mayflower was very reclusive. I had vague recollections of Lauren's parents, but they hadn't visited often and we weren't close. "They're all normal."

"Any stories about defective wolves on Lauren's side maybe?" Kathy nibbled on chicken, her teeth small, even and incredibly white.

"Not any I've heard. Paul wouldn't exactly broadcast that around, though."

"No," Kathy agreed. "But he might use it against her if he and Lauren got into an argument. They do that a lot, don't they?"

My fingers itched to crumble the biscuit into fifty million pieces but I managed to keep my hands in my lap. "Lauren doesn't exactly argue. She frequently pisses Paul off and he lectures her and then gives her the silent treatment for a day or so, but I never heard him throw any defective wolves in her face. Even...even after the Great Gathering when I shifted for the first time and embarrassed the hell out of him."

"So what makes you think your child's wolf would be anything like yours? Presuming, of course, which I am emphatically not, there's something wrong with your wolf in the first place?" Kathy tilted her head at me and gave me one of her brightest, most irritating smiles.

Vaughn sat in frozen horror beside me and didn't even notice that Heather had grabbed up a fistful of lettuce from his plate. Salad dressing dripped all over her dress as she crammed it into her mouth. She made the most comical face at the tart taste of the vinaigrette but continued to gum the lettuce. Paddy divided his attention between her and me. He grinned at both of us and hugely enjoyed himself.

Jossie kept a watchful eye on her daughter and tried to eat, but mostly moved food around her plate.

"I don't know," I said. Paddy picked the biscuit off my plate and slathered butter on it. I thought he would eat it himself, but he put it back on my plate and waggled his eyebrows at me.

"She must have heard you talking about it, Vaughn," said Kathy in such a saccharine sweet voice Vaughn blanched.

"I didn't hear Vaughn." Despite my resolve to stop my participation in this damn conversation, I leaped to Vaughn's defense as Kathy had known I would. Even though he didn't deserve it. "I heard Callie and Grey."

Heather reached out for the chicken breast on Vaughn's plate and Paddy adroitly pulled the plate out of her reach. Outraged frustration darkened her face until Paddy stuck his tongue out and she giggled. A smile flitted across Jossie's mouth and she reached across the table to give Heather a tiny piece of chicken, which the baby promptly stuffed into her mouth.

Kathy and I stared at each other across the table. "Callie," she said meaningfully. "A person who pretty much stopped at nothing in her quest to be Alpha so she could have a baby of her own. How strange is it that she'd try to sabotage someone else's chances?"

The only reason Vaughn didn't leave the table was because he was boxed in by me and my chair. The rising panic, grief and anxiety on his face matched the distressed scent he gave off.

"I never believed Stanzie's baby would have a wolf like hers," he blurted. Shame warred with pain across his face. He still wouldn't look at me.

"But you never told Stanzie this?" Kathy fixed him with her penetrating gaze. She didn't smile.

"I didn't know Stanzie knew what half the pack believed. If I had, I would have said something, sure, but why bring it up if I thought she didn't know? I really thought she didn't want a baby. She always said she didn't want a baby."

"You couldn't smell the lie?" Paddy looked mildly incredulous as he bit off a chunk of chicken and shook his head.

"We never really talked about it. Sometimes Stanzie would say it in passing, like if we saw a baby or something. I didn't smell any lie. I don't remember that I smelled a lie. Why would I even suspect she was lying in the first damn place? And why is this my fault?"

"You were Alpha at least some of the time, weren't you?" Paddy took another bite of chicken and Vaughn's mouth got very small.

"I was a shitty Alpha and a worse friend, so what? Fucking sue me." He passed an astonished Heather over the table to Jossie and forced me to move so he could get out. The back door slammed so hard the windowpanes rattled, which caused a startled moment of silence from the dining room.

"Happy now?" I asked. "You two are the tag team from hell, aren't you?"

Neither one looked a bit remorseful. Paddy reached out for a second chicken breast while Kathy continued to smile serenely.

"Va!" shouted Heather as she saw him stalk by the kitchen window on his way to the street. His expression was thunderous.

Chapter 10

Jossie sat with Heather in her lap in the back of the room with Kathy. Vaughn had not returned and the afternoon session resumed without him.

Heather was sleepy after eating, but she sat on Jossie's lap and stared at me as if she understood what was going on. Her brown eyes were watchful and wide and I could see the stain the salad dressing had made on the front of her dress even though Jossie had scrubbed at it with a wet paper towel.

I had to make an effort to dial down my senses. The person who wore the same cologne as Murphy had put more on during the lunch break and I finally pinpointed who it was. Marco, the Italian Advisor.

Councilor Perkins called the afternoon session to order. He wore a black suit today, which made him look rather like an undertaker and he'd obstinately retained his jacket although the other male Councilors had discarded theirs.

There was no one at my end of the table but me and Paddy so I presumed instead of more witnesses from hell, I would provide my own humiliation on the hot seat and Councilor Perkins's opening statement proved me right.

"Advisor Newcastle, we heard Paul Benedict's testimony this morning concerning the initiation of your wolf. We'd like you to elaborate on it. Tell us your side of it."

My side. Great. Memories and emotions collided within me and I was a teenager again, trapped beneath Paul Benedict's iron will. All the old the impossible-to-live-up-to expectations weighed down on me. Everything I thought was stupid, every action needed to be vetted and justified, every desire was wrong or misguided and nothing, absolutely nothing I did, was good enough.

Sometimes it's only when people got away and looked back that they could appreciate the terrible things they'd unthinkingly endured.

"Wes Hanover, the man my father chose to initiate my wolf, is four inches shorter than me, has sweaty palms and a nervous habit of clearing his throat every five minutes. I know Paul thought me amazingly shallow to want to be attracted to the man I was supposed to have sex with before I shifted, but I always thought he was remarkably two-faced considering he got to wake up every morning beside the most beautiful woman I'd ever seen. I suppose I was too shallow to see the substance beneath the surface of Wes's watery blue eyes and big nose, but the thought of that man's sweaty hands all over my naked body was enough to make me want to be sick. I used to cry myself to sleep at night thinking about it. I thought about running away to live in Boston and surrounding myself with Others so I'd never, ever have to shift. Deny the fact that I was Pack. But when I told that to Paul Benedict, he accused me of being melodramatic as well as shallow and distracted by the shiny, pretty things of life.

"If I'd had any idea how he'd react to the thought of Vaughn Pelletier initiating my wolf, I never would have brought it up. Paul had my whole life mapped out for me before I could even walk. It didn't include being sidetracked by pretty people but everything to do with honor, status and making him look good.

"Wes Hanover was Paul's best friend. I guess I should amend that. Paul doesn't have friends. He doesn't allow anyone that close. He has admirers. Followers. Sycophants. Wes's little girl, Cami, died when she was little. Paul told him that if he initiated me, it was the first step toward making a triad and bonding with me. Then he'd get his chance to be Alpha again and have a baby with me. Paul told me that Wes was a good man and I should be happy to have him.

"I'd known my whole life I wouldn't get any say in who I bonded with and up until it was time to initiate my wolf, I was resigned to that. Mostly. I always did what Paul wanted me to do. I don't think any child could have satisfied him. I tried. I wore the clothes he wanted me to wear. I cut my hair the way he wanted it. I studied the subjects he wanted me to know. I practiced playing my harp instead of playing with the other kids in the pack because that's what he wanted me to do.

"Saying no to being initiated by Wes was my first real act of rebellion and I didn't want to be bad, but I just...I couldn't..." I stopped for a moment and blindly reached out for the water glass. Paddy pushed it closer and everyone watched me swallow.

I could smell my bitterness, and it stank.

"I couldn't let my first time be with someone like Wes, let alone bond with him. I just couldn't. I know it was wrong, but..."

"How is it wrong to want to be attracted to the person you're going to bond with?" Paddy spoke out of turn, but none of the Councilors admonished him. "A parent guides a child, but doesn't make all their decisions. Wasn't there anyone you wanted to initiate your wolf? Besides Vaughn?"

"I was scared of Vaughn," I admitted. "Scared of what he made me feel, scared because I didn't know him. But we came back from the Regional and my fa— Paul decided it was time for me to be initiated. He told me to go with Wes. When I said no, he was disappointed and disapproving at first but he didn't exactly push it. I was seventeen, after all.

"Then we went to the Great Gathering in New Orleans and he made me swear not to sleep with one of the other teenagers there. He told me he knew some of them would do it, but I'd better not be one of them, I was Mayflower, and I should have more respect for myself and my pack than to do something like that.

"And I didn't mean to do it. But Rudi was—everything Wes wasn't. Tall and gorgeous and he didn't make my skin crawl when he touched me. I wanted him to touch me. He talked about bonding with me even though I knew Paul wouldn't allow it. I never meant to shift with him. I never meant to sleep with him. We weren't going to do it. We went with the others to the sugar cane field but we said we'd just make out, we wouldn't go all the way, but we were eighteen and everyone around us was naked and it was—it was too much, too tempting and so we slept together. It was perfect. And I thought *Here's the way it's supposed to be*. But we weren't going to shift, only when everyone else around us started to shift, we couldn't help it. It just happened. We lost all control."

"Of course you did," said Paddy with an understanding smile. "All those scents, all those teenage hormones. Jaysus, you two had no chance.

"My Alpha had to calm me down," I said with real shame. "Rudi couldn't. All the others ran away, but Rudi stayed with me only he couldn't make my wolf stop screaming because she was scared of her own heartbeat. My Alpha did, though."

I laughed a little under my breath. "Tony. There's someone I would have worked with on my wolf. I had a little crush on him. He was so nice and he had the best smile in the world. I always felt safe around him. After we came back from the Gathering, he offered to work with me, offered to initiate my wolf and I wanted him to but Paul said no. I begged him, but he said I'd showed such terrible judgment and lack of restraint in New Orleans that I'd lost my chance at having a say in the matter. As if I'd ever had one in the first place."

Paddy shifted indignantly in his chair and Marco muttered something in Italian under his breath that probably did not flatter Paul whatsoever.

"Paul Benedict told his Alpha no?" Councilor Samuels was clearly shocked. "I find that difficult to understand, Advisor Newcastle."

The New England area Councilors exchanged knowing looks. They weren't surprised because they knew him.

"Your Alpha let him get away with it?" Samuels saw their expressions but still didn't seem able to believe it.

"It's easier to let Paul have his way," I said, which was probably the understatement of our entire Pack history. "He was so angry at me. He wouldn't even consider me bonding with Rudi. Rudi's pack was willing to consider it until Paul made a point of insulting them and implying they weren't worthy of an alliance with Mayflower. You heard him, Rudi's pack had no pedigree and so it didn't matter what I wanted or Rudi wanted, it only mattered what Paul Benedict wanted. I was fifteenth generation and he drilled that into my skull until I wanted to scream at the unfairness of it all.

"Then I met Grey and Paul hated him from the start. He told me Grey would never be accepted into Mayflower and I should send him away. I knew the Alphas would back Paul, they wouldn't back me. It wouldn't have been worth the drama that would ensue. So I ran away with him. I loved Grey Owens. I loved him more than my birth pack. I didn't care about being fifteenth generation, I just wanted to be with him. And everyone talks shit about Riverglow, but up until Grey and Elena died in that car crash, I was the happiest I'd been in my whole life. Leaving Mayflower was the best thing I ever did."

Several of the Councilors nodded, but that didn't mean they agreed with me, only that they heard me. I was under no illusion that anything I'd said made me look good.

"Why didn't you work with Grey? Or Vaughn?" Councilor Perkins asked in, for him, a gentle voice.

Because he sounded truly empathetic, I gave him the unvarnished truth. "I was tired of people telling me what to do. Showing me how things went as if I were too stupid to figure them out for myself. When I shifted and let my wolf free, I was free too. I wasn't fifteenth generation Mayflower. I wasn't *me*. I didn't have any responsibilities or obligations and I could do what I wanted for the first time in my whole life. I didn't want to give that up, not even for Grey.

"Riverglow was so small and disorganized compared to Mayflower. There weren't any real authority figures there, not like Paul anyway. It was easy to defy them and every time I did, I felt freer. And just when I started to feel safe and maybe I would have worked with my wolf, I heard Callie and Grey talking about her. How she wasn't normal, she was defective, and if I had a baby, it might have a wolf like mine. For the first time I understood that it wasn't just because I didn't get initiated and refused to work on my wolf that she was like the way she was. I really thought everyone's wolves started out like her. I realized then there was something wrong with her. Something bad.

"So I got protective of her. If no one else would look out for her, I would. She would never find out there was something wrong with her because I would never let her know. I was angry too. Grey talked about everything with me, but not his suspicions about my wolf. So after that nobody got to talk about my wolf. She was what she was. And she stayed that way until I bonded with Liam Murphy and I thought I didn't have a choice anymore. There was no more Grey, no more Riverglow. Just exile in a condo in Boston. So I sacrificed my wolf to my fears and hoped for the best.

"For a while I thought maybe she could learn, she could evolve, but instead she got obsessed with learning the names of things so she could be safe again. She thought once she learned the names, she'd be able to run and play again. But the more names she learned, the more she understood she'd never know them all and so she'd never be safe again. I taught her that. After all the years of protecting her, I betrayed her and here we are today."

Something fragile inside of me broke. I felt it give way with a mental pop that was almost physically painful. I wanted to destroy everything. I wanted a target I could aim for and obliterate. I wanted it all to end in a frantic scream of rage and despair. When I swallowed I tasted Nate's blood and my tears.

So I aimed to destroy the only thing I had left—myself.

"Can we please stop this farce, Councilors? I'm not the one on trial here, my wolf is and she's broken! How many more witnesses are you going to call to prove that? My own bond mate isn't even here because he knows what he'd have to say about her. It's not like we could take her apart and put her together again so she'll be normal. She's a freak! A fucking freak! Put her out of her misery please! Take her out behind the woodshed and put a bullet in her brain. Nothing I can do or say will take back what she did to Nate or make her suddenly normal so what is the fucking point to go on?"

Uproar then. Paddy snarled at me to be quiet. Jossie burst into tears and Heather wailed with her. Marco threw his sketch pad on the floor, jumped to his feet and yelled something in impassioned Italian no one but Councilor Armentano understood.

Kathy cried, "Jason told you not to push her! Why do you have to push her?"

Paddy leaped to his feet and his chair flew over backward. He swore at the Councilors and told them they'd better not keep any of this on the record or they'd have Mac Tire to deal with and they sure as hell didn't want that he could assure them.

Councilor Young came around the table and attempted to calm him down. Perkins and Hill argued together about whether or not they'd pushed me too hard while Samuels wrung his hands and repeated "Oh dear, oh we can't have this" over and over again.

Armentano stared me down across the table and I sat there motionless and didn't blink or look away as we matched wills and battled it out in silence.

"You're right, Advisor Newcastle." When Armentano finally spoke, everyone in the room went deathly quiet. I couldn't even hear anybody breathe, although I did hear several hearts thud hard. One of them was mine.

"No," objected Paddy, but softly, desperately. "She's upset. You can't listen to her now. Let her calm down. Let me calm her down. I can do it, I swear, Councilor."

Armentano flicked his gaze in Paddy's direction and he felt silent.

"I didn't mean she was right that this proceeding is a farce or that we ought to condemn her. I meant that she's right her wolf is the one on trial, not her. And while we've listened to everyone speak about her wolf, including Constance herself, the one thing we have not done is listened to her wolf directly. And I think we should."

Paddy's face wrinkled in bewilderment. Marco said something in Italian, which probably translated best as *What the fuck?* Even the other Councilors looked confused except for Samuels whose face lit up.

"Yes!" he cried. "Yes, I think we really must hear from Stanzie's wolf."

A fifteen-minute recess was called and the Councilors asked me to leave the room while they discussed matters privately.

On his way out the door, Paddy eyed them suspiciously. His hand hovered at the small of my back. I let him herd me down the hall into the back yard where he prowled around the flowers while I sat on the back steps and stared at my shoes. Nude patent leather platform pumps. Nine West.

Kathy Manning lowered herself to a seat beside me and handed over a glass of orange juice. It smelled freshly squeezed.

Jossie sidestepped us both, Heather under one arm, her cellphone pressed to her ear. By her pinched face I knew Vaughn had not answered and she listened only to endless ringing.

"What day is it?" I asked because I had lost all sense of time.

"Friday." Kathy sipped her own glass of juice and watched Paddy prowl. "There's something very attractive about that man, isn't there?"

I shrugged because the last thing I wanted to contemplate was attractive males. My head hurt and I massaged my temples with my thumb and fingers but that didn't ease the tension or the pain.

Kathy got up and disappeared inside. She returned half a moment later with three ibuprofen pills in her palm. I swallowed them greedily.

* * * *

When the recess was over and we'd retaken our seats, Councilor Armentano stared across the expanse of gleaming table at me.

"We think it is imperative that we meet your wolf, Advisor Newcastle, and judge for ourselves whether she's damaged or whether she's capable of sustained, positive change. Tomorrow morning we'll gather at the Devil's Hopyard in East Haddam and shift. We'll need to find Mr. Pelletier. He's the only one here that knew your wolf before you began working on her with Advisor Murphy. We need his participation. Does anyone know where he is?"

"I'm sure he'll come back." Jossie's face was not as hopeful as her voice.

"What if I say no?" I spoke in a normal tone but from the way they looked at me it was as if I'd shouted.

"Stanzie!" Jossie's reproach was soft but I heard her and hated her for it. What did she know about anything?

"We can't force you to cooperate," said Armentano. "But this may be your last chance to protect your wolf. You won't take the opportunity?"

"I don't see any reason why she's got to be put under a microscope and dissected. You say I'd protect her. I'd say it would be torture."

"You have until tomorrow morning to make up your mind. Don't rush into a decision right now." Armentano was deliberately obtuse and wouldn't take my definitive no for an answer.

"I'm not going to change my mind," I warned him, but he only shrugged and declared the proceedings over for the day.

* * * *

Paddy, Jossie, Kathy and Marco badgered and pleaded with me to listen to reason. To escape them I retreated to my bedroom and locked the door. I put a chair under the knob to prevent Kathy from unlocking it and did the same to the bathroom door as well.

Then I sat on the bed and waited for morning.

Amy Lee Burgess

Three hours later someone knocked on my door.

"Constance?" The man on the other side of the door was last person I'd expected to be there. Well, the last person beside Murphy.

I surprised myself when I leaped for the door and threw it open.

"Councilor Allerton," I said to the man who waited in the hall. His jet-black hair was slightly disheveled. A shadow of a beard lurked across his cheeks and chin. His expensive black-and-white checked Ralph Lauren dress shirt was wrinkled. The first two buttons were undone and the fine link gold chain that supported his bond pendant winked in the subdued lighting.

His blue eyes were bloodshot and I could smell his exhaustion beneath the scent of his cologne and the lingering traces of stale air and jet fuel.

He'd never been anything but handsome and immaculate before this moment. For the first time he seemed less than perfect and that scared the hell out of me. In a week crammed with full-blown horror, Jason Allerton's lack of control was terrifying.

He flinched when I called him by his title and I gripped the edge of the door so hard my fingers ached.

"Jason," I amended. My voice shook.

"May I come in?" He was so tired he could barely stand. I forced myself to step aside and he walked into the room slowly. His black Gucci loafers needed a good shining.

He sank into the chair by the window and I switched on the hurricane lamp on the dresser. The shrouding darkness that had enveloped the room retreated but the light was merciless on his face. Lines of weariness radiated out from the corners of his eyes and for the first time I saw the grief there too.

For a wild, awful moment I thought the hunt had been canceled and he was there to make me drink the poison, and even though that's what I said I wanted, my heart still gave a startling leap.

Before I could say anything, Kathy burst through the door with a tray of hot food and steaming coffee. Two plates with silver warming covers. Two cups rattled on two saucers.

"If the both of you don't clean your plates, you're going to hear about it from me." She deposited the tray on the petit-point embroidered bench at the foot of the bed.

Two huge butterscotch squares wrapped in plastic wrap sat beside a creamer and sugar bowl.

Kathy's eyes brimmed with tears but she didn't cry.

Allerton waited until the door had shut behind her before he gestured at the tray. "Please eat, Constance."

When I didn't take anything, he sighed and got to his feet. I watched him take one of the plates and uncover it. Roast pork smothered with homemade gravy. Mashed potatoes. Peas. My mouth watered.

He set the plate on the end table by the chair and then poured himself a cup of hot coffee. No sugar or cream. He gulped at it gratefully as he walked back to the chair. By the time he sat, the cup was nearly empty.

I poured him more before I filled a cup for myself.

Allerton wolfed down his food without a trace of his usual perfect manners. I wondered how long it had been between meals for him.

I scraped the peas and potatoes from my plate to his, but ate the pork. He ate what I gave him and drained his coffee cup again.

We piled the empty plates and cups on the tray and each took a butterscotch square. I retreated with mine to the bed where I sat cross-legged and watched him take a first bite before I sank my teeth into the sugary, crumbly goodness.

"I apologize it took me so long to get here." Allerton brushed crumbs from his black dress pants. Some of the exhaustion had lifted from his face, driven away by the food and coffee.

I didn't say anything and continued to eat my butterscotch square. I concentrated on it, not him.

"Please understand, Constance, how much I wanted to be here."

"I hope your personal issues have been resolved," I said stiffly.

He blinked at me. "Resolved?" He repeated as if he didn't quite grasp the meaning of what I'd said. "Constance, what did they tell you about why I wasn't here?"

"They said you had a personal situation you needed to attend to."

He drew a deep, audible breath. "Didn't you ask what that situation might be? No, of course you didn't. I told them to tell you if you asked, but you never asked."

"It was none of my business." I swallowed the last of my butterscotch square and suffered a brief moment of mourning.

"My bond mate is dying."

Allerton was so blunt I forgot to breathe for a moment and only when I saw dark spots before my eyes did I remember to start again.

"Dying?" I stared at him in horror. "Why are you here? You need to go back to her."

His smile was sad and affectionate. "She's past the point where she knows if I'm there or not. You, on the other, know very well. I need to be here."

"But she's your bond mate!"

"And you're my Advisor."

"I'm not going to shift, Jason."

Exhaustion swept over his face and body again. His shoulders sagged and my own body ached to see the effort he expended to keep himself upright.

"I fucked everything up," I said.

"How? How precisely did you fuck everything up?" When Allerton said *fuck* I winced. I'd never heard him say that word before. "As usual, you're the one who figured everything out."

"And ripped a man's throat out in the process."

"The circumstances were extreme."

"But there's no excuse for the crime. Even if my wolf was normal and she did this, there'd be no excuse. The law says..."

"I know what the law says!" He didn't precisely shout, but I snapped my mouth shut and my face felt icy cold. For an awful moment I teetered on the edge of tears.

"I apologize. Please forgive me." He got to his feet and I knew if he touched me I would break down, so I scooted backward on the mattress until I butted up against the headboard and could go no farther.

He understood my dilemma and sank back into the chair.

"I don't want to shift. My wolf's been through enough. I don't want to make her do this too. It's not going to prove anything except what everybody already knows," I said as my heart beat at a sickening pace.

Allerton buried his face in his hands and, for an awful moment, I thought he was about to cry. When he lifted his bloodshot eyes, I saw they were dry but he was far from composed.

"Please," he whispered hoarsely. "Please do this. I can't make you, nobody can make you, but I can beg."

My eyes filled with tears. I blinked them away before they could start. "Don't." I was the one who begged now.

"Don't?" His voice twisted with anger. "Don't try to help you? Don't try to use my influence over you to help you save your life? You might as well tell me don't breathe. Don't care. Because I do care what happens to you, Stanzie."

"I know you do, but..."

"You don't. You can't. If you did, you'd shift. You'd understand that we're all trying to help you, not humiliate you. No one is trying to torture your wolf or hurt her in any way. We're giving you the only chance you have, don't you see? There's no precedent, Constance. Nothing in the archives. We have to set the precedent here in this tribunal. But in order to set it, we've got to interact with your wolf and see her for ourselves. We cannot rely on other people's perceptions and human judgment. Wolf to wolf is the only way this can be accomplished and again I beg you to meet us halfway on this. Please, Stanzie. Don't make me go to another funeral. Don't make me stand in a circle and watch Liam scatter your ashes. Don't destroy my faith in the Pack and the Great Council. Please."

I got off the bed and stalked to window. I beat my fist against the glass hard enough to make it rattle. The darkness outside was violated by the lights of the city. It never got dark in the city. There was no place to hide, no place to escape. Everything was out in the open.

It was a chance, not a certainty that if my wolf interacted with theirs, they'd absolve her of blame. Slim chance at that. Why should I force her to submit to them? One last humiliation on top of month after month of joyless dread.

"You're ashamed of her." Allerton's voice was scornful.

"Low blow, Councilor. You think I'll rush to her defense and tell you I'm not? She can't help the way she is."

"But you can. You've always been a fighter, Constance, never a coward. Why now, at the moment you most need to be strong, do you turn weak? Was my assessment of your character that flawed?"

I didn't say anything. Let him think what he wanted.

"Do you want her last time on earth to be the moment she ripped out Nathaniel Carver's throat? Is that how you want her to go out then?"

"Fuck!" I punched the window again and this time it hurt. The glass didn't break but it sure felt like my hand had. "That's not fair! That's so not fair!"

"You don't have the time left for me to be fair!" Allerton shouted at me and he got off his chair, rushed to stand beside me and punched the window. This time it broke and glass shards ripped gouges in his hand. Blood spattered everywhere and somewhere in the safe house an alarm began to whoop with a shrill intensity that set my teeth on edge and battered at my brain.

I put my hands to my ears and stared at the blood that gushed from Allerton's fingers. He made no attempt to staunch the flow and let it drip all over the carpet and his shoes.

His skin was gray. He swayed on his feet and would have fallen if I hadn't grabbed him.

The door burst open and three Councilors and two Advisors rushed in, eyes wide, not sure what to expect. Kathy was one of them. She saw the blood and turned so pale I thought she would faint.

"What the hell is going on here?" Councilor Hill demanded.

"Councilor Allerton is trying to convince me to change my mind and shift tomorrow," I said as I led him to the chair. He collapsed into it and clutched his injured hand to his chest. Blood smeared all over his shirt and jacket. Droplets dotted his chin and I tasted some on my lips.

"Did it work?" barked Hill.

Everyone stared at me, including Jason Allerton.

"Yeah," I answered, sick to my stomach.

"Well, not a total loss then. Will somebody please shut that damn alarm off? And who here knows first aid? Is there some sort of kit around here anywhere?" Hill stalked across the room to Allerton and bent to scrutinize his bloody hand.

"This how you usually handle stubborn Advisors, Jason?" he asked.

Allerton's lips twitched even though his face was taut with pain. "Stanzie's in a class of stubborn all her own. I have to get...creative, Jack."

"Well, I draw the line at bloodshed myself, especially mine, but to each his own." Jack Hill hunkered down so his eyes were level with Allerton's hand. Kathy rushed back into the room with a first-aid kit. The alarm cut off midwhoop.

"Thank Christ. Now I can hear myself think," muttered Hill and opened the first aid box.

* * * *

Outside my bedroom window a glorious spring day dawned. I watched the sunrise with a sinking heart because perversely I'd wanted it to rain. But that would have only postponed my wolf's trial, not canceled it.

I dressed in jeans and a black t-shirt with my hair pulled back into a high ponytail. My black ballerina flats made no noise as I descended the staircase. I wore no jewelry because I was going to shift and jewelry got lost easily in the forest. I felt naked without my bond pendant. Naked and perversely free. Halfway down the staircase I froze for a moment. Who the hell would I shift with? Paddy? Vaughn? If I had a choice, I'd choose my Alpha. He'd looked after me during the whole tribunal and if anyone could make me feel safe, it was him. I tried not to think of Murphy. There was no point to that and I was already fucked up enough as it was.

The Councilors and their Advisors had made decent inroads on their breakfast plates, and acknowledged my passage through the dining room with nods and waves of their hands. Marco called out an optimistically cheerful greeting and I gave him a distracted smile because I could not speak. My heart beat too hard and heavy for speech.

In the kitchen Paddy stood by the sink with a mug of coffee. He wore brown corduroy trousers and a tightly fitted black t-shirt. Jossie nursed Heather at the table and Vaughn sat in subdued silence beside them with a piece of buttered toast in his hand.

Kathy tended to a pan of scrambled eggs on the gas stove. She wore jeans and a chic red linen jacket that belted around her trim waist.

The back door was open, but the screen door was shut. It allowed the air to circulate. Murphy stood in front of the screen door, his face white with tension.

Time crashed to a halt then moved forward again. I was caught in the flux and struggled against the disorientation. Blood beat so loud in my ears I couldn't hear anything else.

"Murphy." I didn't know whether I whispered aloud or merely mouthed the words. "You came."

His whole face lit up when I spoke to him, but when I simply stood there and didn't go to him, his eyes lost most of their glow.

"You didn't think I'd come?" The tension between us was thick and made it impossible for either one to move toward the other.

Aware that everyone in the room either tried to give us space and ignore us—like Jossie and Vaughn—or avidly stared like Kathy and Paddy, I had to fight the urge to turn around and walk out of the kitchen.

I didn't answer and he flinched. I wished he weren't so damned gorgeous. His hair needed to be combed and he definitely needed to shave, but unlike Allerton, these little imperfections only enhanced his looks and made him edgy. His mouth was a thin slash across the bottom half of his face and he crossed his arms over his chest. Two examples of defensive body language. He knew he was wrong and he waited for me to forgive him like I always had before.

Only this time I didn't know if I could. So much had happened to me over the past two days and he hadn't been there for any of it because he'd been too busy in the role of knight in shining armor. Now he was back just in time to shift with me and save the day wolf to wolf?

Last night instead of sleeping, I'd tossed and turned, terrified and angry about my wolf. Who'd wanted her to change? Who'd suggested it in the first goddamn place? I'd thought he was worried about belonging to his pack again, but maybe he'd been more intrigued about saving my wolf. One more thing he could fix and be the hero over.

Had everything we'd shared been a lie? Had I fallen in love with a knight in shining armor or a real man?

Panic and fury scratched away at my love and all I could think was Murphy had betrayed me just like everyone in the whole world had betrayed me. My father, Grey and Elena, Vaughn, my pack. Jason Allerton. Everyone.

The added terror of being put to death by the Councils probably didn't help my reasoning or my wildly seesawing emotions.

"Aren't you going to talk to me?" Murphy's dark eyes were a combination of defiance and vulnerability.

Paddy cursed beneath his breath and Murphy's gaze flicked to him for a startled second but came right back to me again an instant later.

"I know my life's been kind of upside down and sideways the past few years, but I don't need anyone to save me. You didn't need to rush back today to play my savior."

Murphy took a deep breath. "I came back because I wanted to be with you. I wanted to shift with you."

"Maybe I don't want to shift with you."

His face paled.

We stood there in a standoff for a long time as the tension ratcheted up so high the sounds of breakfast and conversation in the next room ceased.

"Stanzie, your wolf adores Liam's. Doesn't she?" Kathy had long since abandoned the eggs on the stove, but she'd kept her back discreetly turned. Now she faced me, her eyes serious as she tried to reach me.

"What does that have to do with anything?" I took a step backward in some strange attempt to avoid the truth.

"There will be several Councilors shifted today. A lot of Alpha energy. Under normal circumstances your wolf would be terrified, but after what she's done it will be even worse. I think Liam's wolf needs to be there for her."

My lip curled. No wonder he was here. They'd ordered him to be here. "So he can be there. He can shift. I never said he couldn't be there, just that maybe I didn't want to shift with him."

"I...I can be with you, Liam." Jossie's voice was soft and unsure. Vaughn remained silent, his face expressionless.

Murphy looked trapped.

"Jossie." His expression was grateful as he looked at her. "Thank you. But I—I can't take you up on that. I only sleep with my bond mate."

Bond mate. Not *Stanzie.* *Bond mate.*

"You are so selfish, Liam Murphy!" I accused. My face felt on fire my blood was so hot.

"I can't," he whispered. His eyes appealed to me like a beaten dog's just before a brutal kick. "I can't."

"You're the selfish one, Constance Newcastle." Paddy moved away from the counter and took a step in my direction. "As your goddamned Alpha, I'm this close to telling you what to do. Is that what you want?"

"You can't tell me to sleep with him," I shouted then winced when I remembered the Councilors and Advisors in the dining room. "You know what? Forget it. Fine. I will sleep with him and shift with him and then this will be over and pretty soon I won't have to think about anything anymore. What the hell. What difference does it make?"

Paddy gave me an Alpha's dangerous smile and glanced through the archway into the dining.

"You can finish your breakfasts, Councilors. Everything's under control."

"Thank you for your permission, Mr. O'Reilly. You might want to think about eating yours. I'd like to get started as quickly as possible," Councilor Armentano called back.

Paddy stifled a laugh, but the amusement on his face died when he looked at me.

Which was fine because I couldn't find anything remotely funny about the situation at all.

Chapter 11

Deep in the woods, we could still hear the waterfall half a mile in the distance. We'd brought blankets and water in backpacks and, as we walked across the forest floor, our feet sank into soft drifts of decaying pine needles.

Above us, the fir trees soared into the brilliant blue sky. Because it was near the beginning of the hiking and camping season, we hadn't run into any hikers or rangers along the trail we'd chosen.

Once past the falls, we'd left the trail and made our silent way single file through the trees and underbrush.

Most of us had scratches on our arms and faces from forcing our way through. I could smell Vaughn's blood and heard him swear as he slapped a mosquito drawn by the scent of both his blood and his breath.

He had not offered an explanation of where he'd gone or an apology either. He was in a foul temper and muttered curses under his breath as he slogged his way through the thick underbrush.

Jossie followed him, her face set with determination. Each time he swore, her shoulders hunched as if she braced for a blow. Heather had been left behind at the safe house with Councilor Perkins's bond mate who had driven from Litchfield for that purpose.

Vaughn did not want the tribunal to meet my wolf. He hadn't said as much in words, but his body language and mood said it for him. Murphy and Paddy, both behind me, were pissed off at him. He wasn't doing my case any good, but didn't seem to realize that. I understood him, though. He couldn't make a worse case against me than my own wolf would do on her own.

Jossie's fear bothered me. Buried as it was under an avalanche of male anger, no one but me seemed aware of it. It dug beneath my skin and lodged there—a constant irritation worse than the slap of sharp branches or the whine of mosquitoes.

When she stumbled and went down on one knee and Vaughn didn't even turn around, I'd had it.

She cringed when I touched her shoulder and whirled around, her dark eyes wide. When she saw me, she sagged a little. I had an ominous, angry feeling she'd expected to see Nate.

"Vaughn isn't mad at you." The people behind me—Murphy, Paddy and Jason Allerton—were forced to stop. Vaughn took a few steps forward then turned around. A streak of blood made a red dash against one high cheekbone—souvenir of an ill-judged swerve around an obstacle course of branches. It was a testament to his anger. It made him vulnerable. So did Jossie's fear.

Jossie swallowed with an audible click. "I know."

I kept my hand on her shoulder and she looked at it and then my face. "I-I don't even know him. Since I was eighteen I've had this stupid fantasy about him. At first it was how we were meant for each other and then later, it was how he would rescue me and now he has and I don't have the slightest clue who he really is."

"You don't have to rush into anything, Joss."

"Heather needs a pack. Oh, Stanzie, you know how when you're in something so deep you can't remember the way things should be? You get convinced that you're the problem—that there's something wrong with you that you can't seem to fix?" Jossie's eyes, huge and hurt, scanned my face anxiously.

"I'm no good to anyone. Nate told me that all the time. I could give Heather to you and Liam, you could take her for me, couldn't you? So I won't screw her up the way I've let myself be twisted?" Her fingers plucked at my sleeve.

Where was the proud and self-assured girl I'd known since I was fifteen? Brash and beautiful, she'd been reduced to this insubstantial wraith, full of doubt and fear.

Rage bubbled inside of me. Goddamn Nate Carver. Goddamn him. If he'd been there I would have ripped his fucking throat out all over again—this time with my human fingernails.

"Nobody is going to take your baby away from you, Jossie."

"I know Vaughn's not mad at me, but he is mad and I keep thinking it's my fault and my mind goes around in this trapped circle and I don't know what to do."

Her mouth trembled into a ghastly attempt at a smile. "You know why I bonded with Nate? You were right all those years ago when you said what you said when I told you I was doing it. We got into a fight about it, didn't we? Our friendship was never the same, was it?"

I squeezed her shoulder again.

"Because Maplefair was Vaughn's birth pack. I thought I'd be closer to him somehow if I joined his birth pack. You tried to tell me he was estranged from everyone there but I didn't listen. I never listened to anyone. That was my problem, wasn't it? I didn't listen to Vaughn when he kept telling me he didn't want to leave Callie and Peter to bond with me and I didn't listen to you when you said it was stupid to bond with somebody just because of the pack they belonged to. I never did love Nate. But he never loved me either. You know what it was? I looked like I was eighteen all the way up until my late twenties. He liked teenaged girls, didn't he?"

At that moment she looked eighteen still—young, hurt and completely vulnerable.

"All those years Vaughn avoided me and I pretended I was so happy with Nate when I wasn't. And then at that Regional. It happened not too long after you'd been exiled and he was different. He didn't avoid me. He was the one who talked to me first. He talked to me. I was so jealous of you when you joined Riverglow. I was jealous of the way Grey looked at you. And you had Vaughn. So funny, Stanzie, wasn't it? We both wanted him when we were teenagers and I got him first, but you ended up his pack mate and saw him all the time. Fate's crazy, isn't it?"

"Jossie, Nate is dead and he can't hurt you or twist you up anymore. And Vaughn isn't perfect. He's not the fantasy figure you've made him into all these years, but he is a good man. You could be happy together, but you don't need to do anything right this minute. It doesn't all have to be decided in a blink of an eye."

Jossie's face screwed up and she burst into loud, painful tears. I pulled her into my arms and as I held her, I wished I could reach inside her head and sweep out all the crap Nate Carver had left in his devastating wake.

"I'm so ashamed. How could I not know what he was doing? I was terrified of him, but it wasn't the kind of terror that made you run, it was the kind that made you stupid. Dumb. Paralyzed. Why am I not on trial too? He was my bond mate and I stayed with him. I should have known what an evil man he was but I kept thinking I was the problem, not him. Never him. Vaughn only stays close because of Heather. He doesn't want me. He's never wanted me. I'd go away, only Heather needs a pack."

"I liked being the fantasy figure, don't you get it?" Vaughn's voice was harsh and self-derogatory. "Nobody ever made me into something larger than life like you did. I was the spare to the pair and I was afraid to be anything else. Jossie, I wasn't good enough for you. I never was. I don't know if I am now, but I wish you'd give me a chance. And not just because of Heather. We can take things slow, just like Stanzie said. You don't need to bond with me to keep me around. I'll stay until you're ready or until you want me to go."

"Everybody's talking about Stanzie's wolf, about Stanzie's wolf being broken, but if anyone's fucked up, it's me. You don't want to deal with me, Vaughn Pelletier, you've got your own shit to deal with!" Jossie wrenched away from me and glared at him.

I faded back until I came up against Murphy's chest. His arms went around my waist and I realized I could barely stand up because of the tremors that traveled up and down my spine and legs.

The emotions twisted and swirled around us all, tight as a net. I choked on them—we all did.

"Look, you're not some charity case I'm taking pity on, goddamn it." Vaughn visibly bit back on his anger and closed his eyes for a moment.

"No, I'm the mother of your child. That's all I am to you." Jossie's shriek roused a flock of sparrows from the pine trees and they flew off in an indignant, startled cloud of wings and frantic calls.

"Oh, for Christ's sake." Vaughn swept an agitated hand through his hair. "Jossie, that is so not all you are to me. You make me feel things I've only felt for one other person in my whole goddamn life, okay?"

Jossie, momentarily robbed of speech, stared at him. "Who's the other person? Stanzie?" Her jealousy blazed around her like a perverted halo.

Vaughn's face crinkled in amused confusion. "No. Stanzie and I have always made much better friends. I'd be the perfect spare to her pair. I couldn't be your spare, Jossie, it would drive me fucking nuts."

"Who then?" Jossie persisted, although her face softened a little.

"Elena." The admission was dragged from him under protest, but he told her.

"Oh!" Her voice became very tentative.

"Look, I was an idiot all those years ago. I liked being the spare to the pair because then I didn't have to feel much or take a lot of responsibility. Why do you think I let the Carvers set me up with Riverglow? Because I knew Peter and Callie would be the real Alphas and I didn't have to stick around Maplefair and make sure Nate didn't torture any more animals. Why do you think I initiated your wolf at a Regional? Because I knew I would only have to do it the first time and someone else from your birth pack would take over and do the real work.

"I got to be the first one to touch you and you looked at me with such admiration like I was special, I was scared that if you really knew me, you'd end up thinking I was a perpetual fuck-up the way everyone else did. A jolly, good-natured, beer-swigging fuckup, but a fuckup nonetheless. For Elena I thought I would try, but she shot me down and that just further cemented my inertia. But, damn it, I want to make something of myself finally. We've both got our shit to deal with, why can't we deal with it together?" Vaughn's smile was hesitant and unsure, but it brightened when Jossie held out her hand.

He took it and gave it a squeeze. "Now, come on, we're holding up the whole thing here. This fucking bullshit hunt or whatever the hell it is we're supposed to be doing."

"Stanzie's life depends on this fucking bullshit hunt, you asshole. Why don't you try to get with the program? Maybe just a little?" Paddy's tone sucked all the blood from Vaughn's face.

"But it is bullshit!" Jossie rose to Vaughn's defense and her face glowed into poignant beauty. "Stanzie's life shouldn't even be in question. The Pack owes her! She rescued Bethany. She rescued me. She rescued Heather." Her voice broke a little on her daughter's name. "Her wolf did what ours would have done in the same position."

"Did she?" Councilor Armentano called back from the front of the line. "I'm not certain my wolf would have taken the responsibility upon himself without benefit of the Pack's approval and judgment. Killing force is only to be used as a last resort if your own life is imminently threatened, which it wasn't at that particular time, Ms. Wilbanks."

"So she was supposed to have waited until Nate decided to slit her throat or strangle her or until she was too weak to move and it was too late to do anything? She had a finite amount of time to shift. Stanzie did the right thing," Jossie declared.

Councilor Armentano was unmoved. "We need to see Advisor Newcastle's wolf. We need to understand her and pinpoint where she is on her path of evolution and if she's capable of sustained, positive change. We have no way to judge her by listening to words of Pack in their human form. This crime, if it was one, was not committed in human form. It can't be wholly understood unless we shift."

"But her wolf isn't like ours." The admission was wrung hard from Vaughn and he looked absolutely miserable. "How can you judge a wolf that won't ever be—normal."

Murphy's whole body turned into a frozen block and the scent of his rage nearly drowned me. "You don't know your ass from your elbow, Vaughn."

Vaughn dragged his anguished gaze to meet Murphy's. "I know her wolf, Liam. I spent years with her wolf. You've had six months. Barely."

Murphy's teeth ground together in audible frustration.

"Her own father came out and said it too," Vaughn said.

Paddy stepped as close beside us as he could and his shoulder brushed Murphy's. Mac Tire stood fast together.

"Her own father saw her wolf exactly one goddamn time. The first time she ever shifted. Didn't you listen, man, to Stanzie's story that she herself told you these last few days? Paul Benedict would be the last man on earth to know what Stanzie's wolf was or wasn't."

"You're from Ireland," said Vaughan disparagingly. "Everyone in New England knows about Stanzie's wolf. Christ, half the Councilors on this damn tribunal know the rumors. Some of them have been on hunts with her and have seen us take her the opposite direction so she didn't screw up everything."

"Vaughn," Jossie protested, her face sick. "You're her friend. I don't understand why you're saying all this. It's as if you want her to be condemned."

"That's not true!" Vaughn raged. Tears of grief stood out in his brown eyes. "I want them to leave her alone and stop trying to judge her by the standards they'd use on everyone else. Her wolf's not like everyone else's! Her wolf's special. Stanzie's the one who used the words *broken* and *defective*. I have *never* seen her wolf like that. She's different in a wonderful, beautiful way. I loved running with her wolf. She showed mine how to feel real joy, you know that? But today, this here, is a travesty. We'll shift and Stanzie's wolf won't be able to keep up with anybody else's and what do wolves do to the weak ones in the pack? To the different ones? They drive them out. They cull them. Why can't we just leave her alone? Nate Carver was a sick fuck who deserved his fate. It's not as if Stanzie's wolf tore the throat out of some innocent bastard, is it?"

"But what's to prevent that from happening someday? If she's so different, so weak?" Armentano demanded.

Vaughn's ashen pallor became even more pronounced. "Now you're putting words in my mouth that I never fucking said. I never fucking said that. Stanzie's wolf wouldn't hurt anyone..." He snapped his mouth shut in horror.

"But she did hurt someone. She killed someone. And if she's as different as you insist she is and by working on her evolution, she's changed for the worse, we need to know that. We can't know that unless we shift." Armentano was unapologetic and almost cruel.

"I told you this was bullshit. You're setting a trap. You're setting her up to fail. I'm not going to help you do it. Fuck this." Vaughn floundered back down the trail, Jossie hard on his heels.

"Stanzie's wolf's biggest advocate is you, Pelletier. You leave now, you're a fucking coward." Paddy moved to block his path and Vaughn caught himself up short. Jossie almost bashed into his back but saved herself at the last moment.

"She needs you." Paddy was furious about that fact but stated it anyway.

Vaughn looked at me. "I don't know what to do, Stanzie."

I hadn't known how he'd really felt about my wolf. He reminded me of the way I used to look at her. He brought me back to a time when I hadn't been ashamed and desperate to keep up. We stared at each other and a hundred memories of running in the woods—these woods—together washed over us. Running, playing, full of joy and purity. I wished he'd told me how he'd felt, but maybe he'd thought he'd never had to because I already knew. Somehow, somewhere, I'd lost my way and my wolf paid for it. My special, different, wonderful wolf.

"You think I do?" I reached out and touched his cheek. His face was clammy.

His fingers curled around my wrist. "I don't want to be a part of your destruction."

"You are such an asshole," muttered Paddy.

Vaughn flushed. He flung my hand away. "Fine. I'll do this. But I still think it's bullshit." He turned around and forced his way back through the brush. Jossie shot me an anguished look and followed.

We continued on for another half mile until we came to a very small clearing with enough space to spread out six blankets. Murphy and I were flanked by Jossie and Vaughn and Paddy and Kristie. Above us were Dante Armentano and Maria, Councilor Samuel's Advisor, who had guarded the conference room door. At our feet were Roger Samuels and Rosemary Young. Beyond them Adam Perkins spread out blanket with Kathy Mannings's help.

Marco, Josh and Allerton would remain in human form in order to guard against possible intruders. I spared Allerton a brief moment of thought and wondered how he would feel as he watched his mistress make love with somebody else.

Pack were not precisely jealous—we couldn't afford to be—but we could sometimes be territorial.

Allerton looked marginally less exhausted this morning. He'd shaved, but the spring breeze and snatching branches had played hell with his hair. His jeans looked as if they'd been ironed, but pine needles clung to the cuffs. His right hand was bandaged and he clearly favored it. Again today he looked more approachable and vulnerable than I was comfortable dealing with.

Those of us who were shifting piled our clothes with the backpacks and empty water bottles at the base of a pine tree scarred and pitted with age.

We moved unselfconsciously because we were all used to being nude in large groups. Stripped of our clothes we became at once closer, both to each other and our wolves.

Everyone else moved to their blankets, but when I hesitated, Murphy drew himself up short and waited.

His eyes and body began to show signs of arousal as the others began to explore each other. I cursed my own traitorous body. When I looked at Murphy, my heart beat faster and there was a sudden rush of dampness between my legs.

It didn't mean anything. Pheromones flying through the air. It's a hunt. That's all it is.

Sometimes I wished I could believe my own bullshit.

"I want to be on top." I kept my voice low so no one would hear me, but I needn't have bothered. Everyone was focused on pleasure, not eavesdropping.

Allerton, Marco and Josh were too far away to overhear. Plus they had their backs turned.

We had to step over Paddy's legs to get to our blanket. His face was buried between Kristie's thighs and her face was contorted with lust—eyes shut tight.

That Irish bastard didn't need to perform oral sex to shift, he was just showing off. I gave his shin a little vindictive kick as I stepped over him and he hooked his foot around my ankle. All without missing a beat if Kristie's moans were any indication.

I would have fallen flat on my face if Murphy hadn't caught me. His fingers burned the skin on my arm and I jerked away so that he stumbled and barely avoided stomping on Jossie's face. His foot tangled in her long hair, but she didn't notice and neither did Vaughn.

Murphy watched them for a few seconds then looked back at me. His eyes glowed with a combination of passion and challenge. I was ensnared.

He waited for me to move into his arms then plunged his fingers through my hair. He took a handful of it and tightened his fist until I could not move my head. He rarely displayed such blatant possessiveness and never at the beginning of an encounter. I'd scared him.

His mouth claimed mine and his kiss was possessive too—demanding and deep. His tongue forced its way into my mouth and I bit it to show him he was going too fast and that I would be the one in control. It wasn't hard enough to draw blood, but he winced. His reaction was to give my hair a yank and redouble the intensity of the kiss until I was left gasping. I'd turned him on.

With a growl that vibrated against my lips, he lowered me to the blanket, his body moved over mine and he didn't let go of my hair.

"I want—to be—on top," I reminded him between breathless kisses. Rosemary Young let out a half scream, half groan and Murphy's body jerked in response. Mine did too and before I knew it, I was flat on my back and Murphy was inside of me.

I choked out his name, he whispered mine back and our tongues performed an erotic duel as we fought for dominance.

He let go of my hair so he could place both palms flat on the blanket on either side of my head. I grabbed his shoulders, wound one of my legs around his waist and used the other for leverage as I attempted to flip him so I could be on top.

He pretended to fight me, but in reality he helped me and when he was on his back, I sat up straight and set the pace where I wanted it. When he tried to touch my breasts, I pushed his hands away and he let them fall to his sides but he wasn't happy about it.

He moved one hand to my left hip and again I brushed it away.

"Stanzie?" My name on his lips was a plea but I turned my face away so I didn't have to see his face and moved faster.

All around us, people writhed and moaned. Paddy's hand cupped my ass for a moment and I turned my head to stare over my shoulder at him. He grinned cheerfully and we were close enough so I leaned forward and kissed him. He tasted of orange juice and lust.

When I turned back to Murphy, hurt flashed in his eyes and a fierce stab of gladness went through me. It was almost as strong as the flood of remorse that followed.

I buried my face in the space between his shoulder and throat and licked the sweat that glistened there. He sucked in his breath and this time when his arms came around me, I allowed them to stay.

To make up for hurting him, I moved my body in the way I knew he loved and he groaned. His hand tangled in my hair again and I heard him say something in Irish.

He felt so good and right inside of me. I wanted to believe in him.

"Liam," I whispered. "I missed you so much."

He kissed me and moved his hands to cup my face. I never wanted the moment to end.

We were suspended together between nowhere and ecstasy when a stifled moan of passion escaped Kathy Manning as her climax shook her. Murphy and I were swept along—helpless against the tidal wave of Pack lust that wound around us like a silken, invisible web.

Murphy drew in his breath when I collapsed against him. He held me so tightly I could barely breathe and I didn't want to move, but I had to. All around us the others were getting to their feet.

Kristie, Paddy's partner, had a dreamy, dazed expression on her face. She looked only at him, but his gaze traveled around the clearing. When Paddy saw that I was standing, he offered me a smile. Was my face as bewitched and faraway as his partner's?

Murphy stood close to me as we formed a small circle with the others. Everyone's eyes glittered amber or silver. Our wolves were ascending. We exchanged glances, and then broke apart to seek out the shadows to shift.

I went willingly enough with Murphy and when he dropped to his knees, his face contorted as the beginning pain of the shift hit him, I went down too, but I didn't feel any pain.

I didn't feel my wolf at all. Fur rippled up and down Murphy's arched back. First it advanced, then it retreated and finally it stayed. His body seemed to blink in and out of this plane of existence. Transparent then solid as bones shifted and rearranged. Pointed ears formed on the sides of his skull—a tail bushed out. Arms morphed into legs. Hands and feet became paws.

Transformation took less than one minute but I'd never watched the process before. I'd always been too busy with my own.

Murphy's wolf was sleek and light gray with white patches on his chest and one of his paws. His eyes were gold and when he saw me, he moved closer and panted wolf breath into my face. A faint whine pierced my eardrums. He nudged me as if to tell me to get on with it and I tried. I sought out my wolf within but couldn't find her. She hid from me and the more I pressed, the further away she went.

Snuffling sounds heralded the appearance of another wolf. This one was half again Murphy's size and dark to the point of near black. One eye was yellow, the other silver blue. They gleamed at me from a dark face flecked with white specks. Paddy.

He licked the space behind Murphy's left ear and Murphy submitted. They pressed noses together. Paddy was clearly the dominant wolf but Murphy did not roll.

More wolves began to appear—smaller females, larger males. One of the females was pure white with bright blue eyes. When I looked into her face a shock of recognition thrilled through me. It was Kathy. She was gorgeous. I'd never seen a white wolf before.

Vaughn's wolf was pure black, darker than Paddy's. His eyes were amber like Murphy's. He pressed through the other wolves to get to me and licked my chin, his golden gaze unwavering.

"Hi, Vaughn," I whispered and buried my face in the dark ruff of fur surrounding his neck. He whined in my ear. His nose was wet and cold.

Twigs and pine needles crunched beneath a pair of booted feet. When I looked up, I saw Jason Allerton. He towered over the eleven wolves gathered around him. He knelt down in front of me and rested his good hand on the back of Kathy's white wolf. She pushed close to his side and looked between him and me as if she tried to tell him something. Vaughn's wolf moved to his other side.

"Aren't you going to shift, Stanzie?" His face was so kind my throat squeezed shut and it took me a moment before I could respond. I knew he thought I was doing this on purpose, but he still chose to be nice.

The truth stuck in my throat for a moment before I could speak. "I can't seem to find my wolf. She doesn't want to come out."

For the first time I realized I was terrified, but it didn't seem much like my own terror. It was too free form, too unspecific and immediate. There was no threat. The most I should feel was dread because I did dread the shift. But I had complicated human reasons and this terror was not precisely human. She'd resisted me before, my wolf, but this was worse. It wasn't resistance so much as it was total disappearance. She was gone and all she'd left was her fear.

I looked down at the palms of my hands. Faint traces of silvery blue fur blurred and disappeared so that I wasn't sure I'd actually seen it. Fur in the palms of my hands was always one of the first indications the process of shifting had begun.

Allerton saw me look. Did he see the fur too or had I imagined it?

"Tell your wolf she has nothing to fear. No one will hurt her. It's a normal, natural response, Stanzie, but you need to reassure her." Allerton pitched his voice low. He emphasized the word *normal* and I groaned. There was nothing normal about my wolf and here was just one more thing to prove it.

I willed myself to shift. My palms itched but no fur appeared. When I reached out to that space within me where she'd always lived, ever since the first time I'd shifted with Rudi, I encountered blankness. Nothing. The looping, free form terror increased and I started to tremble.

"I can't *find* her!" My voice was full of anguish and loss. Allerton's face twisted in sympathy although I was pretty sure his wolf had never pulled a disappearing act on him like this.

Two wolves inserted themselves beneath my arms and pressed their bodies against mine. My fingers twined in their thick fur. Murphy and Paddy. Mac Tire against the world.

A reddish brown wolf with piercing green eyes prowled impatiently. Dante Armentano. I bit my lip.

"It'll be all right, Stanzie." Allerton reached out with his good hand to touch my cheek and drag my attention away from the red wolf. Paddy's wolf growled a warning and Allerton withdrew his hand slowly. His eyes never left my face but he was totally aware that Paddy had gone into protective Alpha mode.

"Paddy, that's Councilor Allerton." I pressed my face against the furry side of his face and he swiped my cheek with his tongue. Murphy's wolf's eyes were filled with adoration. When he pressed himself more firmly against me, he nearly knocked me over into Paddy.

My heart raced then slowed only to speed up again. The wolves stared at me and I didn't know what to do.

I hugged both Murphy and Paddy closer to me as if I might somehow merge with them.

"She's never been scared to come out. She hates to shift. I hate to shift!" My voice rose and one of the wolves near Allerton growled. Murphy's lips wrinkled and his sharp teeth were revealed. Paddy snarled and snapped at the wolf to his right—a small, dark gray female. She cringed away from him and hid behind a larger, lighter male.

"It's me blocking her, isn't it? Am I doing it?" Now the terror was mine too and I cursed myself.

"Stanzie, just relax." Allerton looked perfectly calm and at ease, but something in his eyes revealed his true emotions. He was unnerved. "I'll talk you through this if you let me. Close your eyes and breathe. Let the scent of the other wolves guide you. It should appeal to her, your wolf. She'll be drawn out if you let her. Stop thinking in words. Try simply to be."

Allerton spaced his words in a slow, even cadence and I relaxed into them as best I could. But I couldn't maintain it.

"I'm sorry," I whispered. My throat squeezed shut and I struggled to breathe. "I swore I would protect her. My wolf. From my father. From everyone who wanted her to change. She trusted me. That's why she worked so hard to be what I wanted her to be even though it sucked every last bit of joy out of her existence. But after what happened with Nate in that root cellar, I don't think she's trusts me anymore. So she won't come out."

I felt the first tears trickle down my cheeks. My eyes burned. I hadn't cried once since it had happened. Not once. The last of my strength and resolve was exhausted. I had nothing left.

A silvery gray wolf shivered beneath my arm. He felt so warm. His fur was rough on top, but I knew if I let my fingers sink in, it would become soft.

A wet tongue licked the tears from my face and I stared into the golden eyes of Murphy's wolf.

For the first time since I'd tried to shift, my wolf stirred inside me. She may not have trusted me anymore, but she still adored Murphy's wolf.

He whined as if he sensed her—maybe he did.

I flattened his ears to his skull with my hands and he licked my face again.

When I buried my face in the ruff of fur around his throat, I could smell him. It was a familiar, wonderful smell. I relived and remembered being in wolf form with him. How'd we'd played at first until I'd taken that away. Me. The human me who forced the wolf me to conform and not be different anymore. Murphy's wolf had never asked her to do that, only to learn how to submit to dominant wolves. Take direction. He'd reveled in the chase and the play as much as my wolf had. He always seemed sad when he couldn't entice my wolf away from her stubborn obsessive fixation on finding the words for things.

My wolf adored his wolf. All the human complications between us were erased when it was wolf to wolf.

Allerton moved away, the other wolves, except for Murphy's, followed him. I saw their shadowy shapes as they blended into the trees. Seen and unseen.

I let myself fall back onto the carpet of pine needles. They pricked my bare skin—itched and then my body convulsed as my wolf took control.

Fur sprouted in the palms of my hands. Bones cracked and reformed. Pain blossomed and withered as my body underwent the rapid, magical shift between human and wolf.

* * * *

Friend here with me, but strange Thems too. I can count Thems, only I too scared. Too many Thems. I smell Good Them. I know Good Them and Friend, but strange Thems are too many. Me scared so bad. Me did bad, bad thing. Me bad. I bad. I so bad. Friend lick my face, but me put tail between legs. I bad. My Alpha is here. He look at me. If I roll, if I show belly to my Alpha, what will he do? Will he let strange Thems hurt me? Will my Friend...maybe he mad too. I bad. Bad...

* * * *

Murphy's hand was warm on the small of my back. One of his legs hooked over one of mine. Vaughn sat beside me, a hand on my head. Paddy stood above us, his face solemn. He held my clothes out to me when he saw my eyes open. He was fully dressed. Vaughn and Murphy were naked like me.

I sat up and pulled my leg away from Murphy's. Vaughn watched me take my clothes from Paddy, then silently rolled to his feet and stalked to retrieve his. Paddy watched him go. Both of us smelled his anger.

I stepped into my panties. Murphy sat up so I could use his shoulder to brace against as I did an awkward one-legged dance to pull up my jeans. I didn't want to let him help me, but everyone else seemed to have nowhere else to look but straight at me, so I wanted to cover myself as soon as possible.

Nudity was not something to be ashamed of, but I wanted barriers between me and my judges. They'd taken enough pieces of me as it was.

Murphy's clothes were next to Vaughn's, but Vaughn didn't bother to bring them back. He barely waited until his jeans were on before he stomped back barefoot, his shirt over one arm, lips pulled into a snarl of fury.

"What the hell was that?" He reached down and grabbed a fistful of Murphy's hair so he could drag him to his feet.

Paddy tensed but didn't interfere. The Councilors and Advisors watched from the sidelines. Vaughn gave Murphy a shove. Murphy staggered backward, but managed not to fall. Barely. He made no attempt to fight back.

"You said you were teaching her wolf, helping her. What the fuck, Liam? Stanzie's wolf never rolls to anyone. Never gets scared. I fucking held my tongue when we shifted in Vermont for that goddamn hunt, but at least then she wasn't terrified out of her mind. But there was no joy, just blind determination to figure things out that never mattered a damn to her before. But today she was petrified. Who taught her fear? Who taught her the concept? She tries so hard for you, you know that? Stanzie and Stanzie's wolf. And for what? So you can take something beautiful and wild and twist it all up and ruin it just because you want her to fit into your fucking precious pack? Fuck you. Fuck you too, O'Reilly. Bet you think you're so great because Stanzie's wolf rolled to yours. She's never done that before to any of her Alphas. But did you smell her? She was scared shitless of your wolf. You get off on that maybe?" Vaughn's dark eyes moved to include Paddy in his fury.

"Stanzie's wolf isn't like ours, but that didn't make her inferior or worthless. I always thought Stanzie understood that. Stanzie used to laugh at anybody who suggested she try to change her wolf. She's not laughing anymore. You wanted me here to witness how much her wolf has changed?"

Vaughn swung around so he faced the Councilors. "Well, here's my opinion. She's not even close to what she used to be. Liam Murphy has poisoned her. Infected her with enough self-awareness to recognize she'll never be like everybody else and it's broken her heart and her spirit. If you want to judge somebody guilty, you want to cast blame, don't look any further than him." Vaughn's finger stabbed in Murphy's direction.

Tears of rage and grief glittered in his eyes, but he blinked them back with effort. With a snarled oath, he pulled his t-shirt over his head and stalked back for the path that led out of the forest. Jossie darted after him, but was careful to keep her distance.

Through the entire rant, Murphy had kept his head down, eyes fixed to the forest floor. Naked and vulnerable, he continued to stand there even after the sounds of Vaughn's retreat had faded.

I put on my bra and t-shirt and didn't say anything. I knew Murphy waited for me to say something in his defense but I didn't. Not one word. My shoes were still where I'd left them and I walked over to them. I used the trunk of a pine tree for balance as I slipped them on. I wanted to follow Vaughn back to the parking lot but I was still at the tribunal's mercy and couldn't leave of my own accord.

Paddy brought Murphy his clothes and boots and Murphy dressed. He never lifted his head, not even when Paddy gave his shoulder a brotherly squeeze. Paddy looked at me, his face grave and full of accusation. I still said nothing.

Chapter 12

After an excruciatingly silent drive back to the safe house where everyone took turns to shower and change, we gathered back in the large conference room.

Kathy, one of the first to clean up, had prepared coffee. She'd also set out several cold bottles of water.

I took one of the bottles and sat at the head of the table to await the verdict.

The Councilors had traveled together in one SUV so they could discuss their observations and come to a decision.

The grandfather clock in the hallway chimed four times and I took a swig of water. Would I ever hear a clock chime four again or had that been the last time?

Vaughn and Jossie sat in the back of the room. She tried to contain Heather, who wanted very much to go to Vaughn, but he ignored both of them, legs stretched out in front of him, slouched in his chair, face as grim and angry as I'd ever seen it.

"Va!" Heather cried forlornly as Jossie struggled with her wriggling body. Thwarted yet again, she burst into furious tears. Cheeks aflame, Jossie jumped to her feet and rushed for the door. Heather sobbed, "*Va! Va!*" but Vaughn refused to even look at her.

"Vaughn!" My first word since shifting back.

Vaughn's eyes jerked guiltily to my face. "I want to hear this. I want to hear what they have to say, Stanzie."

Only four out of the five Councilors sat at the table with me. Councilor Samuels was missing. They wore their traditional Council robes. Brown for the Great Councilors, dark blue for the Regional. It meant they'd reached a decision and were ready to announce it, but I'd figured as much anyway.

"We won't start without you." Rosemary Young poured cream into her coffee and gave Vaughn a look I couldn't decipher. Disgust maybe. Reluctant compassion? It was hard to tell.

Vaughn didn't look particularly convinced, but he got up and left the room.

"Liam." Paddy tried to get Murphy's attention when Murphy walked by the table. He gestured at the empty chair beside me but Murphy didn't stop until he got to one in the back. His hair was still damp from the shower and he wore a navy blue shirt I'd given him for Christmas with gray Dockers and a pair of Timberland boots I hadn't seen him wear since the road trip from Houston.

The boots were scuffed and worn, and should have been long since discarded, but he'd apparently hung onto them.

On the road trip I'd bought him a new pair of shoes every couple of weeks, the Timberland boots among them. Since our arrival in Boston and all the drama with Riverglow and Vaughn, I hadn't given him a single thing. I'd bought Vaughn lots of things, though. Anything to get his mind off Callie and Peter.

Paddy muttered something in Irish under his breath. He waited for me to do something, but I only drank more water.

Rosemary Young tracked Murphy's progress and shook her head. "Advisor Murphy, your place is with your bond mate."

I knew it then. They were going to put me to death and he would be their Hand. Even though I'd expected nothing else, something inside me gave a terrified leap and I had to work hard not to get up and run. I had nowhere to run, but if I'd been given the chance I would have started and not stopped until I dropped.

Beneath the table, Paddy's knee rested against the side of my leg. I was grateful for the contact because it kept me grounded. He was a good Alpha.

Murphy pulled out the chair beside me. He was careful not to touch or look at me. There was a faint scratch mark on his left cheek and his eyes were bloodshot. I understood suddenly that he'd cried in the shower and now he was drained and empty.

Who are you going to rescue now, Liam Murphy?

Paddy's foot brushed mine as he stretched his leg out so he could make contact with Murphy. If Murphy felt it, he gave no sign.

Kathy walked into the room with a large plate of butterscotch squares and one of brownies. After she placed the brownies at the Councilors' end of the table, she put the butterscotch squares directly in front of me.

"Now I know I'm doomed," I whispered. "Death row inmates always get their favorites for their last meal, right?"

Paddy sucked in his breath sharply. Murphy continued to stare at the floor and Kathy pursed her lips into a frown.

"Constance Newcastle, stop sniveling and eat."

"Yes, Mom," I said as I crossed my eyes at her. Tears sprang to her eyes and her mouth trembled.

"Now who's sniveling?" I asked her as I reached out to take one of the butterscotch squares.

"I hope you choke," she told me. Then we both smiled at each other. The urge to run passed away and I was myself again. I had to face this and I would be damned if I'd cry.

"Thank you, Kathy." I took a big bite of the butterscotch square. It was sheer fucking perfection on my tongue. I chewed and swallowed. "For everything."

"You're welcome, Stanzie." Her smile was serene and lofty, exactly the way that usually irritated me the most. And just what I needed. More of the cold despair evaporated inside of me.

This wasn't the first damn tribunal I'd endured and no matter what the decision was, I would face it head on. They could only kill me once, right?

Another blissful bite sent a sugary rush of false confidence through my veins. A lock of Murphy's blondish-brown hair fell across his forehead but he made no move to push it aside or look up.

My conscience and heart both hammered at me. I loved him and I resented him and it was tangled up in a huge, awful knot.

"Want a butterscotch square?" I pushed the delicate china plate in his direction. He threw me a startled look—hope flared in his eyes but it was soon quenched by his guilt.

He took the smallest piece and only because I'd spoken to him. I was under no illusion that he wanted it in the slightest except to please me.

His downcast gaze happened across the pack ring on my finger.

"Paddy gave it to me. He says he owes me a whiskey too. If I ever get my ass to Dublin."

"That was always the plan, wasn't it?" His voice was rough and so low I had to strain to hear it.

"I wanted my wolf to be perfect, so I have a feeling it would have been a long-range plan." I took another bite of butterscotch square and let it dissolve on my tongue. "It's not your fault, Murphy. My wolf. Vaughn's wrong. You didn't ruin her. I did that. All you ever did was try to help her."

Murphy looked like he wanted to say something, but in the end he only lowered his eyes and stared at the table.

I didn't want it, but I finished the last of the butterscotch square as Vaughn and Jossie walked back into the room. Vaughn held Heather, who was cuddled up against him, her head tucked under his chin. He had one hand on her back, beneath her little shirt. Pack children responded best to tactile sensation. They always wanted to be in contact with someone—usually their mothers or fathers, but almost anyone Pack would do.

I remembered how I'd played with my dolls and tea set beneath the table while my grandmother and mother drank coffee. I'd leaned against my mother's legs and put a casual hand on my grandmother's foot as I'd poured more pretend tea into my doll's cup.

My grandmother had always had the most interesting shoes. Buttons and bows. Straps and patent leather. Kitten heels and flats. The sudden insight of where I'd developed my fascination with shoes flashed within me. Duh.

Vaughn's whole face tightened when he saw Murphy at the table with me, but he didn't say anything. He sat in the back with Jossie and quietly fumed. Kathy moved to sit beside him and his face got even more pissed. I strained to eavesdrop but all she did was smile serenely, although her eyes were anxious.

Allerton entered the room, handsome and self-contained in one of his Brooks Brothers suits, but his hair badly needed a trim and it threw off his whole appearance. That and the ongoing grief that seemed to enshroud him wherever he went.

On his way past he put his good hand on Murphy's shoulder—a clear sign of support and solidarity. Comfort as well. Murphy didn't look comforted. He didn't look up at all.

When Councilor Samuels entered the room, he took a silent headcount then shut the door.

Councilor Perkins cleared his throat prissily to gain our attention. We were all riveted upon him anyway so the gesture was wasted.

He tugged at the collar of his robe and looked straight at me without blinking. Poker face. I braced myself and didn't blink either.

A week ago Murphy, Vaughn and I had driven down a dirt driveway in Vermont where a wolf had waited to confront us. I wished I could turn back time, reverse the settings to the moment before we made the turn and instead send us back to Boston and a different future—one where I continued to have one.

Coward, my mind whispered.

Perkins delivered the verdict in a measured voice for once not enamored with his own importance. "In view of your wolf's obvious ability to comprehend right from wrong, and her display of submission, this tribunal feels confident that your wolf is evolving and capable of sustained self-awareness.

"We've listened to witnesses' accounts of events and your own explanation of the thoughts and actions that led up to the moment when your wolf deliberately tore out the throat of Nathaniel Carver, Alpha male of Maplefair.

"We, the tribunal, are confident that you fully understand your actions and motivations and acted to save not only your life, but the life of another Pack member. The event in question occurred during the course of your investigation as an Advisor on behalf of the Regional Council of New England and the Great Council of our Pack. You were honor bound to find the truth and take proper measures to secure resolution. Normally this would have been to present your findings to a Regional Councilor or Councilor Allerton, but under the circumstances you had to act as their Hand and you did not shirk your duty." Perkins allowed himself a small smile.

"Therefore, Advisor Newcastle, it is with extreme gratitude and respect, that we, the tribunal, not only absolve you of the charges of murder in wolf form, but commend you for your quick thinking and courage. You are free to go."

Dante Armentano started clapping and the other Councilors joined in, followed by the Advisors. Everyone smiled. Rosemary Young had tears on her face.

"Yes." Paddy's voice was low, but filled with exultation and relief. He hugged me and planted a sloppy, heartfelt kiss on the side of my face. I could hear his heartbeat as it hammered fiercely.

Vaughn gave a war whoop that startled Heather, who goggled at him as if she'd never seen him before. He thrust her into Jossie's arms and leaped to the front of the room so he could drag me up into his arms.

He whirled me around in a giddy circle and his tears of relief were wet against my cheek.

"I knew they couldn't go against you," he said, although he hadn't known any such thing. His faith in the Council and the Great Pack had wavered, but it was now restored.

The Councilors and Advisors crowded in to pat my back and hug me. Rosemary Young called me a hero.

Marco kissed me ardently and told me I was beautiful.

Jossie gave me a one-armed hug. She sobbed against my neck as Heather reached out to touch both our cheeks.

"I can never, ever thank you enough," Jossie whispered.

Through it all I didn't say a word. I couldn't. I was numb and my head felt thick as if it were stuffed with some foreign substance that didn't quite allow me to experience emotion or coherent thought.

Their voices were loud in my ears, but very nearly incomprehensible. My arms and legs felt disjointed and unreal as I was passed from person to person. Everyone wanted to touch me, to kiss me, to look into my eyes, to tell me something, but I processed very little.

All at once they were gone and I was left alone in the conference room. Except for Murphy. He stood by the table and waited for me to notice him.

When I had been cleared of the charges, a huge shudder had passed through his body as if he'd thrown off some tremendously heavy burden, but he hadn't said anything.

Now he looked at me and his eyes shone. But they were still bloodshot and he had to hold onto the edge of the table to keep upright because he was so exhausted.

Fatigue oozed out of his pores, dragged down the corners of his eyes and mouth and shadowed his whole face with a shade of gray that made his skin nearly translucent.

If not for the table, he'd be on the ground.

"Murphy, you're exhausted. When's the last time you slept?"

"I guess I dozed a little on the plane," he admitted as if it were a crime.

"When's the last time you slept in a bed?" I pictured him poring through the archives as he frantically searched for a legal precedent. Saw him sprawled across library tables, binders and books for pillows as he snatched a few moments here and there, and never allowed himself to fall completely under.

His voice was raspy. "Tuesday night." We'd spent most of that night making love as the rain drummed down on the tin roof of the farmhouse. Today was Saturday.

"Paddy's got a hotel downtown. We can go there as soon as I get my stuff and you can sleep for two days straight if you want."

"I might need to make that three." He tried to laugh but it stuck in his throat. His eyes glittered as he looked at me. "Stanzie? Are we okay? We aren't, are we?"

"I don't know," I answered. It was the truth.

"It's because I didn't stay with you." He sighed.

"It's a lot of things," I said.

When his face contorted in confusion I said, "Things I can't talk about yet. I have to think about them."

"Fair enough." He didn't think anything was fair about this that much was clear by his expression. But he'd give me my time and space.

We walked to the door together and as he opened it, I cast one last look over my shoulder at the conference table. It was littered with empty water bottles, half-full cups of coffee and crumbs. The chairs were empty and behind the one where I'd sat, the wall was slightly dented and the paint flecked with tiny dots of maroon—my dried blood.

Heather's stuffed bunny sat in a lopsided heap against the leg of Jossie's chair. It looked forlorn and out of place as I felt.

"Wait a sec," I told Murphy and darted across the floor to retrieve the bunny. It smelled like Heather and Jossie—baby powder, breast milk and the scents unique to them that marked them Pack.

With my nose buried in the bunny's fur, I walked back to Murphy and out into the hall.

The ordeal was over, but the future—our future—was far from certain. I loved Liam Murphy like crazy but would that be enough? It was one of the many things I had to think about. Now that I had the time to do it.

Meet the Author

I am fascinated with the relationship between humans and animals. Stanzie's wolf's journey is my way of exploring the connections we have in common and discovering new ways of communication and understanding. I'm an ardent protector of wildlife and a huge fan of animals in general, wolves in particular. Hidden in Plain Sight gave me the opportunity to imagine what it might be like to access the feral and primal wolf within during a moment of terrifying danger. It also allowed me to create my first serial killer character and put all those true crime novels I've read to—hopefully—good use.

Amy's Website:
http://amyleeburgess.blogspot.com/
Reader eMail:
Amyleeburgess99@gmail.com

Turn the page for a special excerpt of Amy Lee Burgess's Inside Out

Inside Out

For Stanzie, being herself is more dangerous than ever.

There's no place like home...or is there? When Stanzie is asked to investigate her birth pack--Mayflower--she isn't prepared for what she finds. No one respects the Alphas and the newest adult member of the pack is being encouraged to leave. Why?

To make matters worse, the men are dangerously intent on mating and shifting with her. How far will the pack she thought she knew go to get what they want? Without her bond-mate, Liam, Stanzie must face this alone and, barely ahead of the threat of violence, solve the mysteries, and fast.

On sale now!

Chapter 1

When I woke, I was in bed with two men. One of them, my Alpha Paddy O'Reilly, had his hand on my ass. The steady, inhale exhale of his breath was warm against the back of my neck.

The other man, Liam Murphy was my bond mate. Deeply asleep, he lay curled in a ball at the extreme edge of the king-sized mattress, his back to me. Still I'd managed to hook one ankle over his in my sleep. Awake, I'm sure I never would have done it because I was angry with him.

He hadn't been there for my tribunal. Though I'd begged him to stay with me, he'd gone to Virginia to search the Pack's archives for a case precedent which would have spared me from being put to death on a murder charge. However, I saved myself—or rather, my wolf had. She'd shown the Councilors on the tribunal the way to absolve me. In the end, I'd been commended for my service to the Great Pack—a twist I'd never expected even in my wildest imaginings. I'd been convinced I was doomed.

Thoughts of the tribunal and Murphy's absence made sleep impossible. After I lifted Paddy's hand off my ass, I wriggled from beneath the comforter and sheets, and slid down to the end of the bed.

My reflection in the mirror over the dresser frightened me a little. Damn I needed to wash my hair. Or at least brush it. I pushed blond snarls away from my face and stared at my eyes. Darker blue than normal. Definitely troubled.

"Bullshit," I muttered and stalked across the bland beige carpeting. I made a pit stop at my suitcase, which inconveniently blocked access to the bathroom. I threw the first things that came to hand—jeans, a t-shirt, and underwear—over my shoulder. Then I snatched up my toiletries and makeup bag, and took a long, hot shower.

The scent of hotel body wash and shampoo clung to my skin when I emerged forty minutes later.

Paddy O'Reilly, leader of my pack, Mac Tire, hung up the phone on the nightstand and turned to give me a cheerful smile. His curly black hair never looked neat, but the extreme state of bed head he boasted this morning was truly phenomenal. Yet, he still managed to look appealing. How did men do things like that? It wasn't fair.

"Room service is on the way. Let them in if I'm still in the shower, okay?" The Irish lilt to his voice reminded me of Murphy's. By association, my gaze slid to the figure still huddled beneath the comforter. He hadn't shifted position and, while he wasn't exactly snoring, he breathed loudly.

Paddy followed my gaze and grinned. "Dead to the world, he is. Be that way for several hours by my estimation. Guess we won't be heading back to Boston today, will we?"

I scowled. "We could wake his ass up."

Paddy gave my wet hair a friendly tousle on his way past to the bathroom. "Nah. He needs his sleep, Stanzie. He hasn't done anything but grab cat naps here and there for the past four days. Boston will still be there tomorrow and the day after that too, I suspect."

But I wanted to leave Connecticut *now*. I'd wanted to leave yesterday when the tribunal cleared me.

The tribunal had really hung me out to dry emotionally. I'd had some awesomely terrible experiences over the past three years, but that had been one of the worst of my whole life. Since I'd turned thirty, my life had blown up and everything I'd thought I'd have until I grew old and died had been systematically yanked away from me until I clutched at what was left with increasing desperation.

I tried to live on the bright side, only it was getting harder and harder to find anything but darkness.

Liam Murphy was one of the brightest things that had happened since my first bond mates had died in a car crash the night of my thirtieth birthday. Six months ago, under strange and dramatic circumstances, we'd bonded. Somewhere along the line, I'd fallen in love with him. He had no clue whatsoever that I loved him.

I knew and accepted, sort of, that he'd never truly love me as he'd loved his dead bond mate, Sorcha, but I had thought we were great friends and even better bond mates. Now my faith had been seriously shaken. Something in me had broken when he'd left me to face the tribunal alone. Other Advisors had also searched the archives for a precedent to clear me. He could have let them do it and stayed with me, and I tried to understand his reasons, but it was so hard.

Murphy had plead exhaustion and fallen into a deep sleep the minute we'd walked into Paddy's downtown Hartford hotel room last night, but usually he did not curl into a fetal ball at the extreme edge of the mattress to avoid me. Normally he met my eyes when he talked to me.

My life was once again a shit mess. The first step to make it less shitty would be to leave Connecticut behind, but Murphy had to sleep.

I had very little sympathy. He could sleep when we got to Boston. With a rattling briskness, I whipped aside the floor length curtains across the hotel windows. Hideous late-morning sunlight jabbed my eyeballs and I muffled a curse. Fucking sun. What was I? A vampire?

Meanwhile Murphy hadn't moved a muscle. Oblivious.

I shaded my poor eyes with one hand and forced myself to stare out the window. The hotel overlooked the Connecticut River, but not from our room. We had a view of a glass-and-steel office building which accounted for the truly appalling glare, and three stories below, a sidewalk where several young saplings were trained against sticks and surrounded with wire fencing for protection.

The hotel boasted the largest ballroom in the city and I'd played my harp there several times for wedding receptions when I'd belonged to the Riverglow pack. If I closed my eyes, I could conjure up the peach-and-cream floral pattern of the carpeting and the phantom scent of baked stuffed shrimp and prime rib. I hadn't played a harp in nearly three years and it was more than that since I'd played professionally. Did I still remember how?

I let the apricot-colored curtains fall from my hand and turned to the king-sized bed. Murphy was still scrunched up beneath the covers. Just his blondish brown hair protruded. And one bare arm.

From the bathroom Paddy burst into an Irish folk song. I understood one word in five. Maybe. He had a pleasing baritone that shook the shower gel off the side of the tub by the sound of it. Or maybe the container slipped through his fingers. My enhanced hearing made it sound like he showered with the bathroom door wide open. No, wait, the bathroom door *was* wide open.

I almost tripped over the dark peach footstool that matched the armchair by the windows. Everything in the room was peach, apricot, cream, or pale blue. Except for the wallpaper. That had wide yellow stripes on a cream background. Or maybe vice versa, I couldn't decide.

On my way to shut the damn bathroom door, someone knocked on the front door. Room service.

Great. My hair still hung in wet strings around my face. I had no idea where the hair dryer was, though I suspected it was in the bathroom where Paddy currently shook the walls with his voice.

I cast a look at Murphy curled in the bed. Not a twitch of movement. With a sigh, I opened the door.

The bellboy wheeled in a cart. He was maybe eighteen. He looked at my wet hair and Murphy's bare arm against the king-sized mattress. Paddy's exuberant singing vibrated the shower curtain which was visible through the open bathroom door.

"Niiice." He gave me a lewd smile and made a production of removing the silver covers off the plates. Appetizing smells wafted into the air—eggs, bacon, butter, toast.

I fumbled a five dollar bill from my pocket and shoved it into his hand. He continued to gaze at me lasciviously. I could only imagine the tales he'd spin for the hotel staff when he left the room.

I herded him to the door and, after I locked it, I leaned my forehead against it and counted to ten, which didn't help matters.

Paddy stopped singing and shut off the water. When I heard him enter the bedroom, I turned around. "We're checking out."

Paddy elevated an eyebrow. Just one. I'd only ever seen Mister Spock on *Star Trek* pull that off. Paddy had one blue eye and one brown eye. The raised brow was above the blue eye.

Black curls were plastered down onto his skull and he wore nothing but a towel wrapped around his waist. The man's chest hair was marginally less curly than the stuff on his head. His bond pendant dangled from a gold link chain around his throat. I couldn't see which two birthstones made up the pendant because they were buried in the chest hair.

"In approximately fifty-five seconds, the entire staff of this hotel will think we spent last night in a torrid threesome."

"So?" He had another towel in his hands which he used to scrub at his hair. Curls sprang back into shape.

"So I don't care to be the object of all their lewd speculations. Plus, I hate it here." I stalked over to the room service cart and plucked up a crisp piece of bacon which I devoured in two bites.

Paddy looked around the room. "It's not the grandest hotel room in the world, but it's not hideous. For three hundred dollars a night, it better not be."

"Here as in Hartford, Connecticut, not this hotel in particular. Although now that you mention it, Paddy, this peach-and-cream color scheme gives me headache."

Perhaps in response to my rant, he nonchalantly dropped the towel around his waist and headed for the dresser.

I rolled my eyes. "Can you put on some pants, damn it? I'm trying to have a conversation about how indignant I am at the hotel staff's delusions and you're walking around without your pants. Or anything else."

He had a nice ass. Not as nice as Murphy's, but still nice.

"If you hold on for about twenty seconds I will have pants. I promise." Paddy cast me an amused look and opened one of the dresser drawers. "What do you care what Others think? They don't understand. You, Liam and I are pack mates. Pack mates frequently sleep in the same bed together. As many as the bed will hold sometimes. With or without sex involved."

I curled my lip at him. Yes, he had a point. When I'd been a member of Riverglow we'd go back to Callie, Peter and Vaughn's house after every hunt and pile in an exhausted heap on Callie's bed. No carnal thoughts in any of our heads, just exhausted sleep together.

We'd wake in an affectionate tangle half on top of each other. If I'd opened my eyes first and was on the bottom of the pile, it had sometimes taken me five minutes to extricate myself.

That seemed so long ago. Maybe I had forgotten some things about belonging to a pack.

I picked up the carafe of orange juice and took a slug. I couldn't be bothered with a glass.

"Hey, save some for me. That was supposed to be for all of us!" Paddy hastily withdrew a pair of black boxer briefs from the drawer and pulled them on.

"He who hath not pants, getteth not the orange juice," I declared and swallowed half the contents of the carafe in one long gulp.

Paddy balanced on one leg like a hairy stork and when he laughed, he had to grab the edge of the dresser so he wouldn't crash to the floor. The boxer briefs slipped down to his ankles. Truly a nice ass.

As Pack, we were not prudes and were used to group nudity. Group sex for that matter. But I still preferred to have most of my conversations with people who had their clothes on.

"I have pants, damn you, woman!" Paddy roared as I continued to suck down the orange juice.

Murphy unclosed one eye and peered blearily around the room until he found us.

"Liam, this woman is taking shocking advantage of her Alpha. My word should be law!"

Murphy struggled to focus. "Take care of Stanzie. Please, Paddy?" His fight to push aside the covers ceased as he fell back to the pillows and into sleep.

Offended, I set down the mostly empty juice carafe and stalked to the peach-colored chair by the window. I threw myself into it and drew my knees up to my chest as I stared out at the goddamn shiny glass building next door. I did not need to be taken care of. Who the hell was Murphy to delegate the assignment to Paddy as if I were some sort of weak little girl?

Paddy finished dressing—he put on a pair of dark brown corduroys over the boxer briefs, but nothing else, and fixed himself a plate of breakfast.

As he scooped eggs and bacon into his mouth, he watched me, but I refused to be drawn.

After he set down his empty plate, he got one for me and padded over on bare feet to hand it to me.

"Not hungry." My stomach gurgled. Paddy elevated an eyebrow again, this time the one above his brown eye, and put the plate on the little side table by the chair.

He went back to the cart and took the plate which would have been Murphy's if he'd bothered to get up and balanced against the edge of the dresser before he dug in.

Murphy abruptly began to snore.

I pressed an apricot-colored pillow to my chest and resisted the urge to throw it at his head.

Paddy's chewing didn't help me either. Resentment, seething and malevolent, swirled around me in an almost visible mist. Paddy smelled it—he couldn't help it with his enhanced senses—but continued to eat until his plate was once again empty.

He regarded the orange juice carafe for a moment and chose coffee instead. My stomach gurgled again. Murphy rolled over and stopped snoring.

"Are you pissed off because we haven't had the torrid threesome the hotel staff is supposedly gossiping about?"

I aimed the apricot-colored pillow at the coffee mug in his hand and scored a direct hit. Hot coffee splashed along the bottom of the dresser. The mug hit the brass handle of one of the drawers and cracked in two.

"A simple 'no, Paddy, that's not the friggin' problem, you idjit' would have sufficed." Paddy surveyed the damage with a rueful shake of his head. He found another mug and, before he poured more coffee, cast a wary look to make sure I had no more ammunition.

"Eating something might improve that temper of yours," he remarked and ducked to protect his coffee when I winged my fork at him.

"I don't want to spend the whole damn day in this cramped hotel room listening to him snore and you chew, Paddy." The smell of breakfast drove me crazy but I did not give in and grab up a handful with my fingers. Not even the bacon.

"So, who's stopping you?" He sounded impatient but not mad. Yet.

That response took me aback for a moment. He had a point. I was no longer a "guest" of the Councils, unable to leave the premises without an escort and permission. House arrest was over. I was a free woman.

Still suspicious, I said, "I can go out? Like leave the hotel?"

"The world's your oyster, woman. Well, within reason. I would like to take you out to dinner tonight so you'd need to be back here around six." He grabbed his watch from the dresser top. "That gives you nearly seven hours. That enough time for you?"

I didn't need another invitation. I leaped to my feet and dashed to the overnight case which held my shoes. All seven pairs. Before I'd even unzipped it, I started to fret. Did I have a pair with me I wanted to wear? I'd worn the ballerina flats yesterday and my Louboutin pumps didn't go with jeans, plus Murphy had given them to me and I didn't want to wear anything from him. That only left the nude pumps, knee-high brown boots, an impractical pair of red stilettos—what the hell had I been thinking when I'd packed? Sexy red stilettos at a tribunal?—my navy blue Chucks and the loafers I'd worn in the car on the way to the safe house from Vermont. Bleh. No fucking way. They still had mud on the insides from Grandmother Emma's dirt driveway.

I tossed them toward the trash can by the dresser. One of them actually made it in. Paddy ducked again until he realized I wasn't aiming for him.

Once the Chucks were tied, I stood and craned my neck around in search of a damn room card and my purse.

"I only have the one card." Paddy knew what I looked for which was somewhat amazing for a man. "Let me keep it in case I want to go out. You can knock on the door and Sir Sleeps-a-lot can let you in if you get back before me."

I opened my mouth to argue but he shook his head.

"Alpha," he reminded me and tensed, as if he expected me to throw something at him again.

I had the door half open when he called my name. I turned back and he tossed me something that jangled. I caught whatever it was automatically and stared down with dismay. A set of car keys rested in my palm. I didn't drive cars. Not since the night I'd crashed my birthday present Mustang and my bond mates, Grey and Elena, had been killed.

Paddy knew damn well I didn't drive. He had to. Murphy told him everything. I'd spent half the ride to the hotel yesterday white knuckled with fear because Murphy had been too tired to take the wheel and I hadn't known or trusted Paddy's driving. The bastard wasn't used to driving on the right side of the road, as he came from Ireland, and that had only added to my extreme anxiety. I had never been so glad to get anywhere in my life as when we'd arrived at the hotel.

Paddy had wanted me to help with the luggage and stay in the car as he parked, but the very idea of a parking lot, and an underground one at that, had proved too much. I'd shrilly demanded to be let out by the hotel entrance and I'd waited in the lobby. Murphy, exhausted as he'd been, had been forced to help with the luggage. He hadn't complained because he knew why I was scared.

In fact he'd looked absolutely guilt-stricken in the harsh lights of the elevator as we'd ridden to the third floor. He'd forgotten I would be scared to drive with Paddy. It was an indication of his level of fatigue, but at the time it had seemed yet another betrayal.

"You're fucking with me, aren't you?" I glared at Paddy and my fist closed over the keys so tightly I felt the edge of one of them dig into the flesh of my palm. It hurt.

"Maybe a little," he admitted and ducked when I threw the keys at his face. He knocked them away and they fell with a jangle to the carpet. When he looked at me, I knew I'd finally goaded him into anger.

"Throw one more thing at me, Constance Newcastle, and you'll be one sorry woman."

"Gonna beat me?" I mocked. He lunged at me and before I could escape out the door, he'd slammed it and had me pinned. I jutted my chin and braced myself for the blow, but it never came.

"I don't hit women." From his scowl, I guessed Paddy was highly insulted that I'd even entertained that notion. His mouth was approximately two inches from mine and the entire length of his body was pressed— none too gently—against mine. In fact, I found it a little hard to breathe. One of his hands was pressed flat against the door near my head, the other clamped firmly to my shoulder. A knee rested against my locked-together legs.

He elevated one of his brows again. "I do, however, kiss them. You are kinda turning me on here, woman." He dipped his mouth closer to mine and laughed uproariously when I turned my face and his lips landed on my cheek instead.

"Be a pity to make the entire staff of this fine hotel into liars, wouldn't it?"

"A threesome generally takes three people," I reminded him.

"So we'll wake Liam." Paddy moved his mouth to my ear and nibbled at my earlobe.

"Padraic O'Reilly, you let go of me," I demanded, but his breath in my ear did send a tingle down my spine. A small one, but a tingle nonetheless. Damn him.

"He did tell me to take care of you, Stanzie. I'd just be doing what he asked me. You want to make him happy now, don'tcha?" Paddy moved the hand on my shoulder south and I twisted away from his fingers.

"I don't..." I gasped when his knee nudged my legs apart. "...think this is quite what he had in mind, Paddy!"

"I've known him his whole life. You just met him six months ago. I think I might have a wee bit better understanding of how to interpret his words." Paddy nuzzled my exposed neck. "You smell fantastic, Stanzie. No perfume. Why do Pack women insist on wearing perfume and covering up their natural, gorgeous scents? Every Pack woman smells the same, yet different. You're nearly irresistible, you know that?"

"That's *why* we wear perfume. So big goons like you don't mack on us like we were catnip." I gave him a shove, but it didn't do any good.

"Every day for three days I sat next to you at that damned conference table smelling this scent and thinking what a good thing it was I was sitting down and the table was there." Paddy traced a circle on my neck with his tongue then sucked at the center of it.

"I'm going to tell Fiona on you!" Fiona Carmichael was his bond mate. And Murphy's twin sister.

"Fiona knows what Pack women's scents do to me." Paddy was supremely unconcerned. He moved his hand south again and this time found his target and gave it a gentle squeeze. "Oddly enough, she has the identical problem, only with the scents of male Pack members. Funny, isn't it?"

"Hilarious," I muttered.

"Wouldn't you rather sleep with me than have me drive you around the city?" He was back to my ear again and his tongue invaded with such skill my knees went weak.

"I'm never getting into a car with you behind the wheel again, Paddy."

"So is that a yes to sleeping with me? The bed's king-sized so Liam won't fall off. Probably." Paddy drew his nails up the side of my arm hard enough to leave red marks, but they didn't last.

"No. I'll walk or take the bus. But I seriously need you to let go of me so I can unlock the damn door."

He smiled at me before he relented and took a step backward. An entire foot of space now separated us. His playfully lustful expression was replaced by genuine affection. Paddy liked me. I had the sneaking suspicion I liked him too. I hadn't been close to my Alpha in a long time and for some reason the fact he liked me made me want to cry.

I don't know what he saw on my face, but he said, "Can't I come with you? Walking? I've never taken the bus in America yet, that could be fun."

I told myself he was just being kind and not protective. I could handle being alone. But it would be nice if I had some company.

"If you want to walk with me, you need a shirt. And shoes."

Paddy chuckled, but he did get dressed.

www.ingramcontent.com/pod-product-compliance
Lightning Source LLC
Chambersburg PA
CBHW020754250626
47155CB00003B/1066